M000209605

"Dana King's *Resurrection Mall* is a patchwork of desperation from a depressed river town written with genuine style and grit."
— Reed Farrel Coleman, *New York Times*
bestselling author of *What You Break*

"Another thoughtful, taut, suspense filled novel from one of America's best new writers, the great Dana King."
— Adrian McKinty, author of the Sean Duffy series

"*Resurrection Mall* is a brilliant crime novel that deserves to win every award in sight. One of the best of the year."
— Tim Hallinan, author of the Poke Rafferty,
Junior Bender, and Simeon Grist mystery series

"...draws you in from the beginning, like sipping a fine single malt that opens wonderfully in the glass and you have to keep sipping until the end. King has a skillful grasp on character and dialogue, and that, along with his rock-solid police procedure, makes for a gripping, authentic read. I am a big fan of the Penns River series, and I want more."
— David Swinson, author of *The Second Girl*.

"*Resurrection Mall* elevates Dana King's masterful Penns River crime series into the best hard-nosed police procedural since TV's *The Wire*. Fun, gripping and thought-provoking, this third entry firmly plants ace Detective Ben 'Doc' Dougherty in the ring with heavyweight crime-stoppers Elvis Cole, Alex Cross and Jack Reacher. Don't miss it!"
— Jack Getze, author and
Fiction Editor for *Spinetingler Magazine*

"Complex characters, smooth dialogue and a hell of a plot make this one a winner. Rest easy, Ross Macdonald. The torch has been passed."
— Terrence McCauley, author of *A Murder of Crows*

RESURRECTION MALL

DANA KING

RESURRECTION MALL

A PENNS RIVER NOVEL

Down & Out Books
3959 Van Dyke Rd, Ste. 265
Lutz, FL 33558
www.DownAndOutBooks.com

Cover design by Eric Beetner

ISBN: 1-943402-65-5
ISBN-13: 978-1-943402-65-6

To The Beloved Spouse and The Sole Heir,
the two primary reasons I get up in the morning.

PRONUNCIATION KEY

Western Pennsylvania has a rich ethnic heritage that is obvious from even a quick glance at the phone listings or any high school yearbook. Many of the names are hard to pronounce to outsiders who don't come across them often. Even for those who do, Western Pennsylvania natives have developed unique accents and pronunciations that bear little resemblance to how relatives in the old country would speak. This is not a Russian novel. Below is a key to pronouncing some of the more difficult or unusual names. Tolstoy never met his readers halfway like this.

Czárniak — ZAR-nee-ak
DeSimone — dih-SIGH-mun
DeFelice — dee-fuh-LEASE
Dolewicz — DOLE-uh-wits
Dougherty — DOCK-ur-dee
Grabek — GRAY-beck
Lucatorre — luke-a-TOR-ee
Mannarino — man-uh-REE-no
Napierkowski — napper-KOW-ski
Neuschwander — NOO-shwan-der
Wierzbicki — weerz-BICK-ee
Zywiciel — suh-WISS-ee-ul

*Because you know that the testing
of your faith develops perseverance.*
—James 1:3

*Now faith is the assurance of things
hoped for, the conviction of things not seen.*
—Hebrews 11:1

*You a bit much to have faith in, Rev. Hiring the kinds of
people you do, convicts and such, then expecting folk to
believe you surprised when things go wrong. I mean, I a
criminal and all, but I ain't no hypocrite.*
—Darcy Rosewood

CHAPTER 1

A lot colder at midnight than when Greg Twardzik pulled into the Allegheny Casino lot at a quarter to eight. Greg shoved his hands into his coat pockets and hoped his gloves were in the car. The breeze drilled a small hole dead center of his forehead, the hairs in his nose freezing together. It *smelled* cold, like when he restocked the ice cream freezer at Giant Eagle.

Tonight Greg's monthly run to the Allegheny. A true grind joint: slots and a bar, shitty restaurant. The unofficial slogan: Give us your money and get the fuck out. Greg saved his spare change each month the way geezers saved stale bread, except Greg fed the slots instead of pigeons. "Spare change" had an expansive definition in Greg's mind. Stop at Sooki's for a beer; beer cost two and a quarter; pay with a five. Tip Frankie a quarter, the other two-fifty is spare change. Next beer, another five. Take the kids to McDonald's on his weekend with them, pay for twelve bucks worth of food with a twenty: eight bucks spare change. Saved up ninety-two seventy-five in January, rounded to a hundred.

He'd come out the wrong door. Again. All the exits looked alike to Greg from inside. He'd get turned around looking for a promising slot, lose track of where he came in by the second scotch. He at least remembered parking his Pontiac looking straight across Leechburg Road at Wendy's. Came out on the Rabbit's Foot side, by the big fences with ivy or kudzu or whatever growing on them, a barrier between the casino and the residential neighborhood butting up against it. He should have taken the Horseshoe exit. Now he had to walk halfway around the building to get there.

The night started well. Hit for about fifty bucks half an hour in. The plan had been to put the fifty in his pocket and play until the hundred he came with was gone; go home with the winnings. A loser's mentality so early in the night. A jackpot that fast, there had to be more. There were two. Eight bucks within half an hour—big night brewing—then sixteen at eleven o'clock, about the time he started to wonder how much he had left. Hit the cash machine on his way to get the third drink and took out fifty—no, a hundred; still had twenty in his pocket. So he came with one hundred dollars, won seventy-four he should have stashed away. Lost the original hundred plus eighty from the ATM to go down one-eighty, not counting the seventy-four of house money he'd blown, which shouldn't count, it not being his money. At least he had a good time.

He found the aisle facing Wendy's, started walking. His car should be on the right, about three-quarters of the way back. Halfway there he still didn't see it. Probably blocked by the Ford Expedition he'd had to squeeze past, left wheels dead on the line. It wasn't.

Must be the wrong row, but how many of those big god-damn Expeditions could there be in this part of the lot? Greg turned his back on the Ford to face perpendicular to the line running from the casino to Wendy's to capture his bearings. Pointed at Wendy's and blinked his eyes. He'd nibbled the fourth drink, hearing rumors the local cops were cracking down on drunk driving. Coffee not a bad idea, once he found the car. He turned with great care and pointed at the Horseshoe entrance. It occurred to him the Expedition he'd parked next to might have left, and he was looking at a different one. He'd been careful to line himself up on Wendy's and the casino entrance, could be off a little after five drinks.

Tried a row to his left, then a row to his right. Freezing his ass off, he recalled something else he'd heard standing at the bar waiting for the sixth drink, one for the road. Paid attention to the barmaid who told him to be careful about the DUIs—paying attention to her tits more than what she said—a guy to his right bitching about cars stolen out of the casino lot. Greg almost asked, thought why would the guy still come if he thought cars were being stolen?

Focused now, expanding his search with each circuit. Trying the aisle he thought, then one on either side, then two on either side until he realized the guy at the bar wasn't some jagov blowing smoke. Cars *were* being stolen out of the Allegheny Casino lot, and Greg's was one of them.

CHAPTER 2

Ben Dougherty pushed back from the kitchen table. "Enough. Mom, that was great."

Ellen Dougherty smiled. "There's plenty to take home. I'll pack you a bum bag when I clean up in here."

Some things never changed. Doc—only his family called him Ben, or Benny—in his late thirties, still came home for Sunday dinner. Sat in the same place as when he'd lived there. Ellen sat closest to the sink and stove, ready to spring into action if anyone looked like they might be thinking about wanting anything. Tom sat across from her, turned his head one-eighty to see the television in the living room, like he'd done for almost forty years.

"Bum bags"—an echo of Ellen's mother, who never let her grandchildren go home without a poke containing at least a couple of apples and a Hershey bar. A phrase coined during the Depression, when she'd given bum bags to people worse off than her. At least she did until her husband lost his job at Scaife's and it became all they could do to keep from asking other families for handouts.

"What else can I get you?" Ellen still cleared the table like the waitress she'd been. Tom pulled a half-empty dish of cucumbers and sour cream closer to his plate. He'd miscalculated and not finished before Ellen started cleaning. The rest of his meal would be a competition.

"I haven't even started digesting what I just ate, Mom. I

4

have no idea what I want next. A nap, maybe."

"I heard Dickie Laverty had his house broke into this week." Tom stabbed the last two slices of cucumber, pushed the dish into Ellen's sphere of influence. Wrapped a finger along the edge of his dinner plate, where scraps of roast beef and mashed potatoes remained.

"His shed," Doc said. "Took his lawn mower, snow blower, leaf blower, chain saw. All the outdoor power tools." Doc knew, being a Penns River police detective.

"Anything you can do about it?"

"We took the report. Poked around." Tom looked up from his plate, piece of roast hanging from his fork. Doc said, "What would you like us to do? Someone takes his stuff out of town and sells it? Hell, someone sells it in town. Even if he recognizes it, can he prove it's his?"

"He knows what his riding mower looks like. He just bought it last spring."

"Did he write down the serial number? He can't take us up to some guy's house, point to a mower and say, 'That's mine,' and expect us to take it back and haul the other guy off to jail."

Tom chewed, unsatisfied. "You can do something. People shouldn't have to worry about having their things taken like that."

"I'm open to suggestions. I'm one of the guys who has to tell these people there's nothing we can do for them except write an insurance report. Town this size, half the people who've been robbed know a cop. We still can't help them. Doesn't mean we like it."

Ellen scraped and rinsed. Doc snatched a stray piece of Syrian bread from a plate destined for sterilization. Tom chewed and drank ice tea, said, "Seems to me there's a hell of a lot more of it than there used to be."

"I don't know if there's a *hell* of a lot more." Doc munched the bread without anything on it. "Be honest. You only care because Dickie lives practically across the street."

"There's a hell of a lot more around *here*," Tom said. "This used to be a quiet neighborhood. I can't remember the last time we had a break-in. Now we've had three in the past few months. I don't mean to pick on you. Someone has to do something, and you're the police."

"Three in three months after none in...what? ...five years? That's only three in the past five years," Doc said.

"I'm making a point," Tom said. "Don't cover it up with statistics."

"You're right," Doc said. "I shouldn't've done that. Still, three in three months? What you call a neighborhood runs down past the ball fields and up over the hill where the dairy farm used to be. That covers a lot of territory. They get that many in three weeks down the Flats. Twice that downtown."

"Yeah, but...I don't know...this has never been that kind of neighborhood."

"And it probably still isn't. Three in three months might be the law of averages catching up. Might be five more years till the next one."

"You think so?"

"No. Not unless we catch the guy."

"So what's the answer?" Tom said. "I got a lot of stuff in my shed. Most of it's old, which means I can't replace it with what insurance will pay."

"You really worried?"

"Shouldn't I be?"

The answer required diplomacy. "I can't say you should. Can't say you shouldn't, either." Tom's valuable equipment stored either in the garage attached to the house or in a shed thirty feet away. A motion-sensitive light on the house illuminated the shed's entrance. Neighbors knew Tom kept a .22 carbine handy to shoot coons and other varmints rifling his trash can. On the other hand, Doc did *not* want to face his father if he said not to worry and anything happened. "If you want, I know a guy can fix you up with a little siren, car alarm sort of thing. We can wire it into the shed door for you."

"No one should have to do all that." Ellen lingered on the periphery of all conversations, commented when she felt the need. "People aren't safe anymore."

"Don't get carried away," Doc said. "*Property* crime is up. Things get stolen. It's not like people aren't safe in their homes.

"We don't know that," Tom said. "Not with people's houses getting broken into."

"*You* know," Doc said. "I just told you. I'm kind of an authority on crime in Penns River. All the break-ins have either been outbuildings, or when no one's home."

"So what's Stush doing about it?"

"What he can." Stanley "Stush" Napierkowski the chief of police and a Dougherty family friend since before Doc's existence. The only person not a blood relative who could call him "Benny" and get away with it. Part of the reason Doc came back to The River after nine years as an MP was to work with his Uncle Stush. "Christ, Dad, you've lived here all your life. If we put every cop on the force on duty, we'd have about one per square mile. That spreads a zone defense pretty thin. What would you like us to do?"

Tom didn't have an answer. Doc knew he wouldn't and didn't like throwing down gauntlets. He also didn't like defending the indefensible when it wasn't his fault.

Tom said, "Well, then we need more cops."

Getting serious now. Complaining about the number and expense of government employees Tom's favorite topic, in a virtual tie with the Steelers' running game and the government in Washington. Doc couldn't help himself. "Cops are city employees, you know. It'll cost you."

"Why the hell should it cost me? We only have this crime because of the casino, and we only got the goddamn thing so it would cut our taxes."

"If it makes you feel any better, the casino's not crazy about us, either."

"Why not?"

"They got two or three cars a week going missing from their lot."

Tom brought his right hand into its "making a point" position, index finger extended. Pulled it back. "You're telling me the casino can't get good police service, either? Where's all the money going they're supposed to bring into town?"

"Ask the mayor next time you have a zoning meeting," Doc said. "Let me know what he says."

"Aw, hell. I did. Last time. About why we can't get this street plowed and salted like we used to."

"What'd he say?"

Tom took a beat. "I got the runaround. He talked for five minutes and it all made sense until I got in the car and couldn't remember what the hell he said."

"The mayor's good like that."

"He's up against it. Town's not set up for what's happened the last ten years. He's doing the best he can."

"He sure did the best he could to get Danny Hecker the green light to build the casino."

"You can't fault him. Everyone wanted it. Town needs the money."

"Last I heard we don't get much more in property tax than when we had a deserted building there, and most of the people who work there don't live here. It wasn't supposed to be that way, but Hecker drives a hard bargain and Chet Hensarling isn't exactly a master negotiator." The most charitable explanation Doc had, not wanting to discuss what else might have been involved to get the casino in Penns River and not some other town as bad off. "A lot of this always comes along with an operation like a casino. Gamblers aren't model citizens."

"It's regular people going in there, not gamblers. All they have are slot machines."

"You been in there?"

"Hell, no. You know I don't gamble."

Doc let that sit, not so long it would stink. "Sixty-something-year-old women in there grabbing two-four-six slot machines in a row, dropping quarters in them like Martians are in Natrona. I saw a guy didn't know his way around sit at one while some old biddy collected at the other end of the line. I almost had to drag the bitch off him. These people drink too much, they're more inclined to use recreational drugs, and there are always things like loan businesses and hookers around them."

"No one said anything about that."

"Some people did." The conversation sinking fast and Doc didn't want to go home with a bad taste in anyone's mouth. "It is what it is. We'll get a handle on it."

He turned to his mother without coming up for air. "Hey, Mom. I saw the other day Golden Dawn has chipped ham on sale, I think through Wednesday or Thursday. Isn't that where you like how they slice it best?"

"Oh, yeah. They cut it just right. It's out of the way to go there,"—three miles, not in the same direction as her other shopping, "—but it's worth a trip if it's on sale. You want some?"

"I got some. I would've got a couple pounds for you, but I didn't know how much you had and I know you don't like to let it sit too long in the freezer."

"If you see it again, call and I'll tell you if we need any."

"I did. You weren't home. Probably out cruising one of your doctors."

"You leave a message?" Tom always worried the message machine didn't work. His greeting sounded like someone held a gun to his head, told him to act natural.

"No. You never call me back, anyway. I knew I'd be over."

Tom breathed like he might say something, let it out. He didn't often call back. Not out of a lack of consideration. He'd forget to look at the machine. Part of Doc's Sunday routine included checking for calls since his last visit.

"Hey," Tom said, "you know anything about what's going into the old shopping center by the bridge downtown?" "Downtown" a relative and nostalgic term in Penns River, ninety percent of the businesses vacant. "What are they calling it? Resurrection Mall?"

"They asked what we can do to keep some of the vagrants and druggies away while they get renovated and open for business. They seem all right. Why do you ask?"

"No reason. Just wondering."

"I wish they'd put it someplace else," Ellen said.

"How come?" Doc said.

"I don't want all those holy rollers right here in town. I hear they're going to put one of those TV churches in. Make the whole town a big joke."

"That mall could put more locals to work than the casino."

"Let's hope you're right about doing some good," Tom said. "I wonder about the kind of people it will attract, is all."

Compared to what? Doc thought, held it. He'd dodged the first bullet, saw no need to double back into the line of fire. Let the conversation drift to less controversial topics. Tom noted snow in the forecast for Tuesday night or Wednesday morning. Ellen said they'd better get to Golden Dawn early on Tuesday. Tom expressed his belief—again—about how the Steelers needed to address their offensive line in the draft, over two months away. Doc went home with half a pound of roast beef and sufficient mashed potatoes and creamed peas for two meals. A typical Sunday at the Doughertys.

CHAPTER 3

Christian Love—birth name Alfonsus Tate—would have appreciated Doc's defense of him and his plans for Resurrection Mall. He'd broadcast services on cable access in Pittsburgh almost ten years, with outlets as far west as Wheeling and south to Morgantown. Time to grow, and Love's Resurrection Bible Church lacked the resources to expand in place. Enter Allegheny Casino.

Self-defined real estate tycoon Daniel Hecker finagled a casino license from the crumbs left over after the Commonwealth gave priority to people who knew what they were doing. He needed a location outside of Pittsburgh; Penns River was perfect. Less than twenty miles up the Allegheny, begging for someone to take over the shell of an abandoned shopping center. Hecker cut himself a better deal than casinos expected, even in depressed areas. Didn't recognize the smell of Russian mob on one of his partners. Hard to fault Hecker; the Gaming Commission missed it, too. The opening got more publicity than Hecker dreamed of when bodies started dropping: a drug dealer, a small-time crook and informant, four Russian mobsters, and almost the Dougherty family.

Christian Love would never wish such a tragedy; he wouldn't let one go to waste, either. In Penns River before the weekend, preaching to save this "Gomorrah on the Allegheny, with its sins of avarice and fornication, money changing, and preying on the addictions of the weak." Signed papers three months later to renovate a downtown strip mall no better off than the casino's antecedent. Called it Resurrection Mall. The banner over the main entrance read: "Not Razed, But Raised."

Almost a year later, as much bloom on that rose as in Ellen Dougherty's garden, second week of February.

"Rodney, close the door, please." Rodney Simpson pushed the door half shut, stood with his hand on the knob. Looked back at Love with the question on his face. "You can stay, son. I just don't want anyone to wander in and interrupt us."

Love not of those ostentatious television ministers. Sat behind an IKEA desk, in a pleather chair from the Salvation Army in Butler. His suit had cost and Love watched his weight so it would always fit, tailored never to go out of style. This one had spent its year in the public appearance rotation, now relegated to day-to-day work suit. Wore a plain gold wedding band, a quiet pinkie ring set with a small amethyst. Pewter crucifix around his neck.

"Brother Sylvester, how goes the work?"

Sylvester Lewis had been with Love from the beginning. A quiet man still somewhat in awe of the authority Love had granted him, overseeing all the work and contractors for Resurrection Mall. He cleared his throat, made a show of looking at the papers in his hand. "Dr. Love, we...uh...we had a setback this week. Work's moving along, no misunderstanding there, work is progressing, but we...uh...got a report from the plumbing inspector the fire sprinkler system on the north side of the building has to be replaced."

"Not repaired?"

Lewis took his time with an answer, in case a better one appeared. "No sir. Replace. What's there can't be salvaged."

"What about the food court?" The only revenue producing part of the mall.

"Repairs need to be made there, too, but...uh...but they told me the work can be done while it's open, or after hours. They haven't finished inspecting this side of the building yet."

An ache behind his left eye joined the stomach knot Love always felt when discussing business. His face remained placid. "Anything else?"

"The floors are going in maybe a little ahead of schedule, but the...uh...the glass contractor says he can't order no new pieces for storefronts till he sees some of what he's owed."

"How much are we behind?"

Lewis didn't bother pretending to look it up. "Eighteen thousand. A little more, actually."

Love turned to the man sitting next to Lewis. "Brother Cassius, can we pay him?"

Cassius Abernathy had been with Love almost as long as Lewis. Handled the money, in and out. More out on this project. "Not if we want to pay anyone else, including us in this room."

"Donations?"

"Down. We brought three investors in last week. They took a look around and said no thanks."

"Was Jacob Peete one of them?" Love asked. "You invite him down, like I asked?"

"Jacob Peete was one of them. He came the day you were taping downtown. Said he liked what you want to do, wished us good luck and all, then he passed."

"He passed?" Love paused, irritated for allowing his irritation to show. "I've seen Jacob Peete invest in areas made this look like the French Riviera. How could he pass?"

Lewis inspected his shoes. Abernathy didn't. "He saw them drug dealers hanging in the food court for what they were. Too polite to leave straight off, but that's all he was. Polite. I keep telling you to run them off."

A chair joint squeaked as Love sat back. He missed the comforting creak of the leather in his Homewood office. "They're not selling when they're here, are they?"

"No, but—"

"No offense, brother, but it's no crime to eat lunch out of the cold."

"We in the process of becoming one of the biggest employers in this town," Abernathy said. "The police can't do us a service? Run their black asses out?"

"I appreciate what you're saying, Cassius, I do. We're trying to create a haven here. A sanctuary beyond the church itself where people can feel safe to congregate. How can we do that when the police walk through hassling black folk minding their own business,"—Love held up a hand, "—at least while they're here."

"Amen to that," Abernathy said. "Thing to remember is, ain't be a sanctuary here at all, we don't get a handle on the cash flow."

Love unbuttoned his suit coat, leaned forward, elbows on the desk. "It's true, we have a dire situation here. If we can't turn this around, it's not only Resurrection Mall that's in jeopardy." Gave time for the implication to sink in. Gestured to the two younger men flanking Abernathy and Lewis. "Rodney, Jamal. Don't be bashful. You're younger and newer, and younger and newer ideas might be exactly what we need. Speak your minds."

Minds remained unspoken. Love waited until he couldn't bear the silence. "Nothing? Nobody has anything?"

Lewis cleared his throat, a tell he had something to say he'd rather not. "Dr. Love, I know how much Resurrection Mall means to you. To all of us. You know me. I spend as much time here as anyone."

"I hear you, brother," Love said. "More than anyone. I can't recall a time, dawn to dusk and beyond, that I've been here and not seen you."

Lewis ducked his head at the compliment. "That's why this so hard for me to say, but you know it's not just talking when...uh...when I say it might be time to think about... maybe...cutting our losses. Just think about it, mind you."

Abernathy made a guttural comment. Love glanced in his direction without moving his head. Said to Lewis, "You mean walk away, Brother Sylvester? Just leave?"

"No, not like that." Lewis dry washed his face, ran his hands through close-cropped graying hair. "We made commitments to people. It's just...it's just...it might be time to start looking for a...for a...I don't know..."

"Exit strategy?" Abernathy said. Then something softer that might have been, "bitch." Lewis shot him a glance, looked away.

Love gave Abernathy another look, turned his attention back to Lewis. "I don't disagree with you, Brother Syl. I've thought along those lines myself. The problem is, we can't. We used the church's good name to get the original loans. We'd have to take everything into bankruptcy."

"We could sell the mall, couldn't we?" Jamal Adams,

Lewis's assistant. Always eager to please, carried bad news like a hod of bricks. "Pay what we owe from that. At least be a way to keep the church."

Abernathy laughed in his face. "Who'd buy this piece of shit, boy? Why you think it was available for us? No one wants it. Been mostly empty near fifteen years." Rodney Simpson glared at Jamal as Abernathy spoke.

"Brother Cassius, please," Love said. "Let's don't discourage the young men from speaking. Jamal, I understand the thought. Under different circumstances, your idea has merit. Problem is, Brother Cassius is right. There's no one to sell to. Even if we could find someone, any money we'd get would go to the bank to pay the mortgage. We barely been paying the interest as it is. There's no equity to pay anyone else."

Jamal meant well and had no more knowledge of equity than he had of nuclear fission. He looked as if he might ask until the weight of Abernathy's and Rodney's eyes pushed him back into himself. Lewis patted the younger man on the thigh.

"Rodney," Love said. "Speak up, son. What do you say?"

Rodney Simpson didn't need to be asked twice to express an opinion. "I don't know 'bout y'all, Rodney going down with the ship. I'm here till the end, the very end. People wants to run,"—he made no effort to disguise the contempt in his look at Jamal, "—they can go. I'm staying. Don't make no difference to me."

"We all respect you willing to stand your ground, son," Lewis said. "You got to realize some of us have a lot more at stake than you do. You a young man. No offense, but the most you can lose is some time. A man your age got plenty of that. Dr. Love here, he got a whole church to worry about. People depend on him. There's only so much of a loss he can afford to take."

"Maybe he ain't weak as some people." Rodney stole a glance at Abernathy, who ignored him. "Rodney all in. I'll carry it for all y'all, it come to it."

"Son, you got no call to talk to me like that," Lewis said.

"He's right, Rodney," Love said. "Those are hurtful words. I know you don't feel that in your heart. It's your grief talking, your grandma gone only a few weeks. We all know how close you were. You might need a little more time."

"No, Rev—Dr. Love. I'm cool. I'm...I'm shouldn't a spoke to Mr. Lewis that way. It ain't right. I'm sorry, Deacon."

Love nodded, looked to Lewis. "Apology accepted, son," Lewis said. "I know she was all you had. I feel for you."

Love nodded with a half-smile. "Amen to both of you. Brother Sylvester worked harder than anyone on this, even me. If I was to be honest with myself—and I try to be—I have too many irons in the fire. Brother Cassius been doing his best to raise the money, but raising money is my job. It's his job to manage what I bring in. It's me not carrying my weight here.

"I owe people in this room. All of you. And I give you my word—today—things will change. Brother Sylvester, do what you can to keep work moving. Tell those we owe their time is coming, and we'll remember those who did us a service when we needed it. Brother Cassius, do what you can to spread what money we have a little thinner. Take half of my salary." Lewis and Jamal rose to protest. "No, it's what's right. My name in the papers, people talking about 'Christian Love's Resurrection Mall.' Well, the bad's on me, too. I'll tell Miss Eleanor to clear my schedule the rest of the week so I can get off my righteous ass and shake the tree. For everybody."

CHAPTER 4

Rodney Simpson had no interest in the Rev's position relative to his righteous ass; all Rodney cared about was making some money.

His grandma sent him for the job at Resurrection Mall. Raised him since his mother split one day while Rodney was at school. Never asked nothing from him till this. Saw it as more than a job. A chance to get him on the right track, work with people who knew the meaning of both work and God. Teach him to be a man while keeping him away from the friends she thought of as "aphids on a pea plant."

Rodney knew the road to improvement was paved with education; that didn't mean school. The best education—to Rodney *best* and *most practical* were the same—came from people who did what you wanted to do. What benefit to him who wrote some fucking book or fought a battle a hundred-fifty years ago? His friends knew how to make money. A scam here, shoplifting there, all cool so long as they were juveniles. Rodney older now, time to step up, and the drug business owned the only ladder in town.

Drugs were a sucker's game. The hoppers on the bottom took all the risks. Those that made real money never touched the drugs. That was the level Rodney wanted to occupy, but they had this whole working your way through the ranks thing, might as well make you join a fucking union. Plus, drug boys caught more beatings than Rodney cared for—

more than none—and the occasional bullet. Not part of Rodney's plan at all.

Hands stuffed way down inside his coat pocket when he stepped out. Gloves at home someplace; no idea where. Still living in the little house where Grandma's landlord let him crib as a courtesy, give the boy time to find something for himself. What she bought the insurance policy for: a start when she was gone. The few dollars she'd put aside with the church every week got her buried. The ten grand was Rodney's future.

Walked to Eazor's Deli, wind in his face, fingers freezing even in the coat pockets. Could have eaten in the Res Mall food court with everyone else. No good way there to avoid that little bitch Jamal, sure to be running his mouth about what the Rev said, the changes coming. Rodney didn't need to talk; he needed to think. No way a man could do both at once. Listen and think, sure. What could he learn listening to a Gump like Jamal?

Ate his meatloaf, mashed potatoes, and corn alone. Eazor's didn't serve okra, what he liked best with Grandma's meatloaf. Asked once and the white man behind the counter stared like he'd asked for sheep dick or some other exotic shit. Eazor's meatloaf was good for a restaurant. Fake mashed potatoes better than most, not as good as real; the gravy almost made up for it. Corn no substitute for okra. Never would be.

Picked out Cassius Abernathy as the man to hang with right away. Maneuvered around Jamal so Rodney got to work with Abernathy instead of Lewis, the Rev's original plan. Rodney recognized a man who knew what he wanted and how to get it without breaking any specific laws Rodney could see. Grandma sent him here for his own good, and to do good; no reason he couldn't do well at the same time.

Abernathy scared Rodney a little, not that he'd tell anyone. Why he kept his distance, watching, noticing anytime money changed hands it moved in Abernathy's direction. Contractors, tradesmen, roach coach vendors who came around before the food court opened. You did business with or at Res Mall, Cassius Abernathy got paid.

Rodney saw his niche there, laying in the cut. Not taking so much anyone would notice. Spread the sources around, a nickel here and a dime there and pretty soon you're talking folding money. Abernathy had it going on the way Rodney imagined it would work.

Rodney's problem, he got there late. Abernathy's operation already set up. Every day a lesson on how to maintain. Rodney still had to learn the start-up end. Opportunities would present when the needs of the mall changed as things progressed. The new sprinklers, for example. Different contractor needed for that work. Someone new for Abernathy to touch. Rodney would be ready, watching.

Piss Rodney off if Res Mall went tits up and left him with nothing except this minimum-wage-plus-a-quarter punk-ass job to put on his resume, like he'd ever need a resume, the things he wanted to do. Res Mall his ticket out of this shithole town, and that shithole little house he'd have to leave soon, anyway. The mall had to hold together for him to learn his craft. Learn it quicker if he could get Abernathy to bring him in as a partner—no matter how junior—if Rodney ever got up the balls to ask.

Rodney Simpson needed Resurrection Mall. Resurrection Mall needed money. Rodney Simpson had money. His ten thousand, thrown into the general fund, would disappear like sugar in ice tea. Might be he could use it some way to show Abernathy some skills; thinking outside the box and shit. Could be a man with the vision of Cassius Abernathy had use for a man with the skills of Rodney Simpson, once he'd seen those skills first hand.

CHAPTER 5

Days like this, Wilver Faison wondered why he didn't go to school. The slush from last week's snow refroze into a minefield on the curbs and sidewalks where residents hadn't cleaned up. Or where there were no residents. Step wrong and either slip and fall on a patch of flat ice or feel the sharp ridges dig into the sole of a sneaker.

Wilver not quite a dropout. Yet. Went to school once or twice a week to maintain a D average, or when the weather was worse than his financial situation. The rest of the time he worked as a runner for Cootie Highsmith's crew, selling heroin on the corner of Fourteenth Street and Third Avenue, watching for the signal and getting the drugs from the hiding place. Not much of a job, running back and forth across a block to get drugs. Not much else available for a kid with no car. No buses ran through Penns River. He either walked to work, or he didn't work.

Wilver started out as a lookout for Ivory Harris up on Fourth and Hileman, asked to move because he didn't want his mother and younger brother to see him. They never came the five extra blocks into this part of town, and he worked when David was in school. His moms never made him account for the extra money he brought home. Wilver knew Moms was using again. She kept it from him the same as he kept his source of income from her. He assumed she at least

24

suspected how he spent his days, both of them happier not knowing for sure.

"Wilver!" Eddie Simmonds showed two fingers across his chest. Wilver ran to the old tire, shot a look at Pookie Haynesworth, the lookout. Pookie signaled *all clear* and Wilver took two vials, ran them over to Eddie.

Wilver walking away, not wanting to stand too close to the actual transaction, heard his name again. Turned to Eddie, who gave confused. Wilver looked the other way and saw Cootie waving him toward his car.

Cootie let Wilver stand in the cold while he sat in the warm car with the window down. "Why Eddie calling you?"

"He had a buyer," Wilver said.

"I know he had a buyer, nigga, I seen the fiend walk up to him. Question I have is, why didn't you see him? Eddie shouldn't never have to call you for a customer, yo. You supposed to be watching for the signs. Ain't paying you to daydream while you working."

"Sorry," Wilver said. "I guess I'ze just cold. Thinking about getting warm."

"You don't feel the cold if you pay attention to business." Cootie looked both ways along the street. "Take a knee."

Wilver knelt, his face a few inches lower than Cootie's. "The time coming for some decisions to be made. By you, and about you. You feel me?"

Not really. Wilver kept that to himself.

"You smarter than any a these niggas working out here. Everyone know that. Shit, you probably smarter than me, but you smart enough not to let it show. You could be doing a lot more than running, *if* you acted like you got it in you. Missing at least one day a week, head not in it when you are here. You need to decide if you want in this, or not."

Wilver knew now he was supposed to say he wanted in, all the way, definitely, tell me what you want me to do. Saying so to Cootie—right now—would sound phony, playing up to the boss. He waited for Cootie to go on.

"Couple things going on the next few days. Donald be coming by for lunch later this week." Donald Woodson, the top of the Penns River drug pyramid. "He know who you are, and what you capable of. He know you got it here," — Cootie tapped his head— "but don't know do you have it here." Tapped his chest. "You need to show him."

"How?" Wilver said.

Cootie scoped the street again. Twenty degrees, wind blowing off the river, the no one out except the slingers and those who needed to score *right now.* "You know Slick Williams?" Wilver did. "Him and some other fool selling to them's working at Res Mall. Mostly reefer, maybe a little of our product. Everyone agreed Res Mall off limits. Niggas need some kind a place to hang and not get hassled. Slick breaking the rules."

"What's the plan?" Wilver said.

Cootie pushed out his lower lip. "Slick breaking our rules. We may have to break something on Slick. You in?" Wilver didn't say *no*; said *yes* too late to suit Cootie. "You in or you out. You ain't in tonight, don't come back tomorrow. You feel me?"

"Yeah," Wilver said. "I'm in."

"Okay. Corner of Ninth Street and Fourth Avenue at four o'clock. They gets off work about four-thirty, so Slick be there. You late, we go without you. You on time, do your job..." Paused for effect. "Donald said you carry it here, he wants a meeting. You know what that mean?"

Wilver knew. It meant more responsibility, more money. More risk. Less chance of turning back.

CHAPTER 6

Doc liked that Kate Shannon got herself out of the car. She'd lay back to let him open the door to get in, saw no need to wait for him to do something she could do herself. Doc liked a lot of things about Kate Shannon. The door thing came to mind as theirs closed as one in the parking lot of The Pines in Etna.

Kate worked as a barmaid at a lounge called The Den in Fox Chapel. Where Doc met her, showing pictures of Carol Cropcho and Marian Widmer, two women involved in a case he'd tried to close for almost two years. Carol was dead. Doc knew Marian had her done, he thought out of jealousy over a lesbian affair gone bad. He had Carol's diary with the detail to convict Marian and require all minors to leave the courtroom. Neshannock County prosecutor wouldn't touch it. Marian had already beaten Sally Gwynn on a related case. Sally wanted eyewitnesses to put Marian and Carol together, so once or twice a week Doc showed their pictures in places they might have gone, looking for someone who recognized them together.

Enter Kate. Not a cop groupie; the investigation made her wet. She'd go with Doc to show the photos. Kate spoke the lingo, knew the secret handshakes. People talked to her who wouldn't tell Doc he was bleeding. Then they went back to her place and screwed like meth-crazed minks.

Doc locked the car, looked at the lone tree in the parking

lot. "I think they're short at least one pine."

"They can't call it just 'The Pine,'" Kate said. "It sounds stupid."

"What about 'The Lone Pine Inn?' Or 'The Naughty Pine.' You know, not knotty—with the K—naughty. Without the K."

Kate put her hand in Doc's while they walked. Turned her head to look up at him. Not too far, Kate an easy five-ten in flats. "Why not 'Pining for the Fjords?'" Monty Python references always a risk with her.

"This is Etna. They might think it's a sexual reference."

"Why can't it be?" Kate shook her head. "You're so literal."

Not quite cave-dark inside, more like three a.m. in a bathroom with a strong night light. Candles on two-tops provided a glow designed for navigation, not recognition. "Too dark," Doc said. "No one will remember anyone here. They're not even going to be able to see the pictures."

"You do all your real drinking in bars, don't you?"

"Yeah. So?"

"You think a change in décor means a bigger flat screen. Places like this, where people rendezvous, these places go in and out of style sometimes. They have to mix it up. It wasn't always this dark here. Besides, how long has it been since these two went out together? Three years?"

"About that."

She looked up and opened her eyes wide as he held her chair. "Well, duh! There's probably no one here who worked then. We're looking for someone who worked somewhere else and saw them. These people move around, but they keep to the same level of lounge. That's who we're looking for."

The waitress came, dark features ghoulish in the light of the table's lone candle. Asked what she could get for them. Kate started with introducing herself, finding out the waitress's name was Melanie. Hi, Melanie, I work at The Den over in Fox Chapel and heard a lot of good things about this place from my girlfriend and they were off and running. Five minutes of social intercourse later, Kate ordered a Manhattan and Doc asked for a Bass he could have ordered without requiring Melanie to stop walking.

"Did your girlfriend really tell you about this place?" Doc said. Kate drank not much, had taken Doc to at least twenty different places since they started "dating."

"Sure. Remember Libby from when you came to my work to pick me up? You know, that time my car was in the shop? She heard about it from a friend and thought it was worth checking out."

"You have Libby canvassing for you?"

"I have *all* my friends canvassing for me. Girlfriends, guys I know, people at work. Most of them don't tell me much—I don't think they think I'm serious—but Libby's into it. She says she wants to be there when you make this broad do the perp walk."

"The perp walk?"

Kate shrugged and cocked her head, flicked a tendril of strawberry blonde hair away from an eye. "Libby watches a *lot* of television."

Melanie brought their drinks, setting off another five minute communion. Doc sipped, reminded himself to order two beers next time, one to drink while he waited for Kate to stop talking to the waitress. Gauche for Kate to hit Melanie with the reason for their visit too soon; they had to bond.

Used to drive Doc crazy until he realized how much he could learn about interrogation from Kate. She got genuine attention, waitresses taking the photos around to show the rest of the staff under better light where Doc had received a lot of *Sorry, don't know them, can I get you anything else?* Still, no one had recognized either Marian or Carol.

Melanie went off to do what The Pines paid her to do. Kate sipped her drink. "Ick. I hate Manhattans."

Doc swallowed. "Then why'd you get one?"

"They're the bartender's specialty. He's really proud of them."

"I heard. I *do* pay attention while you chat people up, you know."

"Then I suppose you noticed Melanie's hot for him. I think they're sleeping together, or will be soon. Anyway, if she's this into this guy and he's so proud of this drink, the quickest way to get her on our side without being too obvious is to flatter the drink."

"What makes you think she's hot for him?"

Kate sipped, made a face, shook her head. "You keep telling me what a hot shot cop you are. Don't you know anything about non-verbal communication?"

"I must. Sometimes I think it's the only kind we do, even when we're talking."

Kate stuck out her tongue. "You didn't notice how she went out of her way to mention him, or how the pitch of her voice changed when she started talking about him? She even shifted posture, moved her feet a couple of inches farther apart."

"So?"

"What happens when you move your feet apart?"

"Lower center of gravity? I don't know."

"It spreads your legs, dummy. I'll bet she didn't even know she did it. She'll probably get wet when I tell her how much I liked it." Kate pushed her cocktail glass across the table. "Here. Drink this before she comes back."

"I'm not drinking that."

"Oh, come on. It's nasty."

Doc let his face show an exaggerated version of what he thought of her comment. "I can't. First, it's a mixed drink, and I hate mixed drinks."

"That's not a can't. It's a won't."

He tapped his glass. "And I have this. *And* I'm driving."

"How much do you weigh?"

"How much do I—what for?"

"How much do you weigh?"

"Two-oh-five."

Kate waved her left hand in dismissal, pushed the drink with her right. "You can drink this *and* the extra one I'm going to order and still be only halfway to the limit. I'll risk it." Doc gave her a look. "Do you want me to get in tight with her?"

"I want you to show her a couple of pictures, not seduce her."

Kate reached across the table, pulled the glass to herself. "Here she comes."

"How is it?" Melanie said.

"You were right. Using Southern Comfort instead of bourbon makes all the difference."

Melanie glowed. "You want another one?"

Kate pointed to her glass. "I'm just sipping it for now. Letting it go down slow so I can enjoy it."

"Perfect. That's the way I drink them," Melanie left without a glance at Doc.

"She didn't even ask if I wanted another beer," he said to Kate.

"You don't need one." Pushed the Manhattan his direction. "Drink this so she'll think I did."

Doc looked at Kate, picked up the glass. Took a sip. Made a face. Checked Melanie's position. Poured the rest onto the carpet under the table. "Ahhh. *That's* the way to enjoy a Manhattan."

Kate snorted, took a quick inventory of the room. "You... are bad. What am I going to do with you?"

"We'll think of something."

And they did, though not Melanie nor anyone else at The Pines had ever seen either Carol Cropcho or Marian Widmer.

CHAPTER 7

Doc and "Eye Chart" Zywiciel, the patrol sergeant, stood outside Eye Chart's office discussing the merits of mixed drinks. Neither could find any. Doc a beer and ale man. Rotated between Bass and Foster's, with an occasional Molson Golden thrown in for variety. Sam Adams when it available and the mood struck. A boilermaker Eye Chart's idea of a mixed drink. "Not a shot with a beer chaser, either. I'm talking drop the shot glass in the beer."

"Only way to go. You're going to man up, man up."

"Fucking A."

"Detective Dougherty. A moment, please."

Jack Harriger, Deputy Chief. Insisted everyone call him Deputy—except for Stush Napierkowski, the chief—in a department where everybody, including the dispatcher, called the chief Stush to his face. Except Harriger, who referred to him as "Chief," or "Chief Napierkowski" to avoid confusing Stush with all the other Napierkowskis and chiefs on the force.

Doc and Eye Chart exchanged glances. Private conferences with the Deputy were treasured moments, to remain private until an appreciative audience could be found. "On my way, Jack," Doc said.

He found Harriger seated behind his desk and sat without waiting for an invitation. "What's up?"

Harriger kept his line of sight a foot to Doc's right, clenched his jaw. "Another car was stolen at the casino Thursday night."

"Old news. A Dodge Ram went missing last night. Waldstreicher took the report. I'm on my way to do the follow-up."

"Jesus Christ. How many is that now?"

Doc did a quick calculation. "Nine in...five weeks."

"What are we doing about it?"

"I told you. Wally took the report. I'll do the follow up. Their security guy—your buddy Rollison—will bitch at me because we're not doing enough. There and back in less than an hour."

"Well, what *are* we doing about it? About all of them?"

Doc's tone lost its flippancy. "What we can. We think they're going to chop shops."

"Where are they going to be chopped?"

"Don't know. Almost certainly out of town. We circulate flyers every time one walks away. Notify the staties. Not much else we can do."

"Bullshit. Allegheny Casino is the biggest employer in Penns River. I want something done, and I want it done now."

Doc's interest in the conversation ticked up. "Like what? We're working with the state police. We sent flyers to local jurisdictions. We don't have the resources to look out of town ourselves."

Harriger's face showed red. Choked back his first comment, said, "Have you searched Mannarino's dealership?"

"You have some probable cause I can use to get a warrant?"

"You know it's him. One of his crews."

"I have a pretty good idea it's him, sure. Last I checked, Judge Molchan didn't hand out search warrants with *we can't think of anyone else who might be doing it* as probable cause. If you have proof I haven't seen, I'll be happy to look at it."

"Even if it is a freelancer, you know he kicks up to Mannarino."

"If he wants to walk without a limp, he does. You want to cruise into Mannarino's office and accuse him of stealing those cars, be my guest. Let him laugh at someone else for a change."

"I'll talk to Chief Napierkowski. We can at least add some patrols to the parking lot."

"Where do you plan to find the bodies? There's a lot of other things going on. You know, people who live here having their homes broken into and their lawns pissed on. Maybe Danny Hecker can take some of the money he's carting out of there and hire a couple of minimum wage jagovs to walk around at night."

"The casino pays taxes. They're entitled to the same protection as any taxpayer."

Doc's increased engagement made it harder to enjoy Harriger's discomfort. "Do we patrol the private property of other taxpayers? No. They call us when they have a problem. We've had at least a break-in a week down the Flats. The best we can do is tell whoever's on patrol to drive by a couple extra times a night. A guy across the street from my dad had his shed emptied last week. Those people pay taxes, too. Fuck Danny Hecker."

Harriger's fists pressed into the desk. "I'm telling you I

want something done about this, goddamnit, and that's an order."

The heat in Doc's anger turned cold. "And I just told you we notified the surrounding jurisdictions and the state police and I'm waiting to hear back." A hand stifled Harriger's reply. "You want more, you're talking to the wrong guy. I don't make the patrol assignments, and I wouldn't add coverage to their parking lot if I did. Now, if you're finished, I have work to do. You want some help with the casino's problems?" Fished change from his pocket. Dropped two quarters on Harriger's desk. "Here's a half buck. Call someone who gives a shit."

Doc stood, turned to go. Harriger said, "Dougherty, I've had all the insubordination I'm going to take from you."

Doc spun to lean in on the shorter man. "You're not even close. You got into bed with people who almost killed me, my parents, and my cousin. I think about it every time I visit them and see the bullet holes in the brick. That buys me a lot of insubordination, and I plan to use every penny. Now is there anything else I can do for you? *Deputy?*"

Harriger quivered with rage. His phone rang before he thought of an answer. "Harriger. Yes. Sure. I'll be right in." Hung up. "The Chief wants to see me. We'll pick this up later, Detective."

"I always have time to chat with you. Deputy."

CHAPTER 8

Stanislaus Thaddeus Napierkowski had spent thirty-nine of his sixty-four years as a Penns River police officer. Twenty-three as chief. A nepotism appointment: his brother-in-law the mayor chose him over two senior men back when the mayor could do such things. It worked out. Stush grew into the job, after growing up in the area when what would become Penns River was three townships, each too small to enjoy the benefits of Class III cityhood. A quirk in the Commonwealth Code allowed the three to join together and create their own county in the bargain. Westmoreland County was not amused. The loophole closed six weeks after the articles of incorporation were filed in Harrisburg.

Stush knew everyone, almost literally. Everyone liked him, not quite as literally. His brother-in-law retired and moved to South Carolina about the time the burden of an economy that never recovered started to weigh on the city. Businesses faded away from the old downtown like patients dying in their sleep, escaping notice until something major closed and people realized it had been the last business on the block.

Empty storefronts and jobs on the hoof created a vacuum, which nature—true to its code—did not tolerate. Crime filled the void. The two trends developed a symbiotic relationship. Crime increased as businesses left; increasing crime drove businesses out. People preferred to shop at Pittsburgh Mills, and the bypass meant they didn't even have to drive through downtown to get there.

The crime went unremarked upon—the town's dirty little secret, like a spinster's youthful abortion—until a tipping point was reached and the Domino Effect took over. Downtown went first, taking the Allegheny Estates with it. The Estates had long been the town's poverty area—the closest thing Penns River had to a slum—so it didn't raise much of an alarm. Then the Flats—poor rednecks with cars in the yard—assumed to be stealing to support their meth habits. Now the residential and rural areas were no longer immune and the new mayor wanted something done. He saw Stush as a fat old man, unable to keep up.

Stush was a fat old man, and staying on top of things had become a bitch. He knew it better than anyone. Jack Harriger cozied up to the mayor and half the council, tried to push him out two years ago. Stush had been thinking about retirement, felt he'd earned the right for it to be his idea. Harriger got too close to the casino ownership, overplayed his hand when Stush had a heart attack. The situation resolved itself with four dead. Harriger not involved, still too close to keep the stink off. Stush became a hero when he got out of his sickbed and everyone saw how respected—and loved—he was among his force. Even the mayor admitted Stush could retire whenever he wanted, saving for select company, "So long as he doesn't take too long."

"Jack, have a seat." Stush waved toward an empty chair in front of his desk. Eye Chart Zywiciel sat in the other. "Let's talk about this casino situation."

"Thank you, Chief." Harriger kept talking to hold the floor as he sat. "I'm glad you're here, too, Sergeant. We need to find a way to increase patrols in the evening—"

"We're getting a lot of complaints about drunk drivers leaving the casino," Stush said. "Leechburg Road's an adventure after ten, especially on weekends. A guy got sideswiped last week on the bypass with his kids in the car, coming home from a movie in Freeport. We can't have that."

"Drunk drivers?" Harriger rebooted. "I thought you wanted to talk about the stolen cars."

"I'm sure the casino's not happy, but stolen cars aren't a danger to anyone. We don't get a handle on the drunks, someone's going to get hurt."

"I understand, Chief. Maybe we can kill two birds with one stone."

"How so?"

"Designate a car to cruise the parking lot. He'll not only act as a deterrent to the thieves, but should be able to recognize anyone coming out who's over the limit."

Stush rocked back in his chair. Nodded in Zywiciel's direction. "Eye Chart?"

Zywiciel pursed his lips, turned a hand over. "In theory, maybe. Word got out we were patrolling, thieves might think twice. Then again, good as these guys are, they might wait for the cruiser to pass by and do the job before he comes around again."

"It's worth a try," Harriger said. "At least show them we're taking their complaints seriously."

"I take everyone's complaints seriously," Stush said. "The casino, Pete Worthington—the guy who got sideswiped the other day—even Dickie Laverty, who I think is a pain in the ass but still shouldn't've had his shed cleaned out last week." Turned his attention to Zywiciel. "Three ways in and out of the casino, right? Two on Leechburg Road, one on Wildlife Lodge?"

"Yeah."

"Is there a place one car could see them all?"

Zywiciel thought as he spoke. "Possibly. Get the right space at Wendy's, or maybe even next door at the old tire store. I'll drive by and check, but yeah, I think he could see all three from there. Wouldn't be too noticeable, either."

"Good," Stush said. "Take a look and let me know."

"That's not going to help with the stolen cars," Harriger said. "Whoever's sitting across the street won't be able to see much in the lot, and he won't know if a car's stolen watching it drive out."

"Impaired drivers are the priority here," Stush said. "We catch a car thief, it's a bonus." Harriger opened his mouth. Stush cut him off. "We're shorthanded, Jack. I'll be damned if I'm going to tie up an officer to cover one parking lot."

"You're talking about tying one up to sit across the street."

"Where he can be on the move and up to speed ten seconds after getting a call. Find me a spot, Eye Chart. Looks like we have a plan."

"Ambushing DUIs is penny ante," Harriger said. "Whoever's stealing these cars leads back to Mike Mannarino one way or the other. They either work for him directly, or they kick up to him. Even Dougherty says so. We should push there. That's the way to kill two real birds with one stone."

"Deputy." Stush now avuncular as a statue. "Have you ever given a death notification for a drunk driving accident?"

"That's not the point, Chief."

"Have you ever given one?"

"What I'm saying is—" Harriger noticed the hardness in his boss's eyes. "No. I haven't."

"I've given eleven. Walk up to someone's house, usually at night, family watching TV, and I get to tell them Bill's not coming back from the basketball game, or Susie didn't get the milk. They come to the door distracted, maybe looking over their shoulder at a movie, thinking whoever was out forgot their keys or something and they see me standing there in uniform. They know something's wrong—why else would the chief of police come to your house, ten o'clock at night?—still, they look at me like they're reading the words come out of my mouth.

"The women get it. Open the door, look at me, and you see it in their eyes. Half of them start crying soon as I say their name. Husbands don't get it right away. Men assume things work out, but women, something way in the back of their mind always wonders when someone like me might come to the door and they know—they know *right now*— whoever's out isn't coming home. I'm sixty-four years old. I'll trade every car in that dump's parking lot, even jimmy the locks for the crook, to keep from ever having to give that talk again."

He faced Zywiciel. "Go find us a spot. I want someone there tonight."

Zywiciel nodded and went. Harriger did a slow burn, stood to leave.

"Hold on, Jack. I have something for you."

Harriger sat, said, "I think they might be okay if we did something to show the flag. You know, maybe take the unit you're going to stash across the street and let people see it driving through the lot every half hour or so."

"The senior citizen high-rise down on Constitution wants a dog-and-pony show. Give that PowerPoint Ginny Alcantara put together, make 'em feel safe. You can do it during the day—it's not like they have to go to work, or anything—but give them the whole nine yards. Dress uniform, hat, polish things up all nice and pretty. Make us look like we know what we're doing."

Harriger gave a face like the stick up his ass had turned sideways. "Again? I just did a presentation for the kids over at Belle View Elementary last week."

"I'm glad you reminded me. Went over so well, they want you at Campbell next week to do it again. Sorry to make you keep spit shining yourself, but you create a hell of an impression."

"Sherry Gibson should be doing school visits. She's the juvenile officer."

"She's been pretty busy lately, Jack."

"*I've* been busy lately."

"We've *all* been busy lately. It's just you make such a good impression in the Class A, you know? The fruit salad and scrambled eggs? Look like a real cop."

"Maybe you could do the senior center."

"Look at me. An old fart damn near as old as they are and twice as fat. I look like I slept in the bag soon as I put it on. No, Jack, you make an impression. You'll go."

"Chief—"

"You'll go, Jack."

Stush had enough left in the tank to leave on his own terms, not to get rid of Harriger. He knew Doc had gone from disliking the deputy to open insubordination and appreciated Doc never did it where anyone could see, force Stush to do something. Everyone else as close to an old-fashioned shunning as possible and still get the work done. No one blamed Harriger for what happened at the Doughertys' last year; still, that anvil broke the camel's back. Now anything Harriger didn't like became his new job. Did he want to be chief so much he'd put up with it until Stush retired? Would there still be too much stink on him to promote?

Stush loved being a cop. Always had. With luck, some day he could do it again. He was too old for this shit.

CHAPTER 9

Stretch Dolewicz handed an envelope to Mike Mannarino. "We can get more, you know. The way that Greek's chopping these cars up, we could ask for half again this much and he'd still make out."

Mike opened the envelope, riffled the bills. "It's worth the extra we let Pete keep just to bust their balls. How many we get now?"

"Nine."

Mannarino smiled. "In a little over a month. Retired spook runs security over there—what's his name, Rollison?—he must have Hecker's people crawling up his ass by now."

Mike Mannarino had learned to take his victories where he found them. Being boss of the Pittsburgh mob lacked the cachet it had in the days of John LaRocca and Kelly Mannarino—with whom Mike shared not a drop of blood, the rumor he spread at every opportunity be damned—it still provided a nice living.

"I hear someone put money on the street in Penns River," Mike said.

"I heard that, too, but I haven't been able to pin him down yet."

"Call Tommy Vig. He seems to know all about this guy."

"I guess he would. Tommy never liked anyone taking a nickel that could of been his."

"This douchebag isn't costing Tommy a cent," Mike said.

"This area was a big deal when my great-uncle ran things. Now Vig can't be bothered to come this far up the river. Someone saw an opportunity and took it."

"Tommy pays us protection, though, don't he?"

"To protect his operation. This was fallow ground." Mike lit a cigarette. "Find this asshole. Charge him a fine for not coming to me first and tell him I get my taste from now on. If he's good with it, I'll tell Vig to fuck off. He didn't want the territory. Someone else took it. That's capitalism."

Stretch arched his back, extended his arms over his head with locked fingers. "What if the new guy don't want the deal?"

"Bring him in for a bullpen session." Mike spent a year at Auburn on a baseball scholarship as a pitcher. Never threw hard, earned his way on a curve that broke both big and sharp and gave him the nickname "The Hook." Kept in shape and brought back old times by tying recalcitrants to a backboard in the barn behind his house and using them for a strike zone.

Stretch cracked something in his back. Nodded. "You said I should bring my nephew by. He's outside if you got time."

"Yeah, bring him in. I want to thank him for making those casino fucks miserable."

Stretch opened the door into the main room of the Aspin-wall Hunter's and Fishermen's Club. Half a dozen guys shooting pool, playing cards, arguing about something when they should have been working. Things would change when the books opened and guys got made again. The two jagovs taking turns missing combinations would cut each other's throats for the opportunity.

The kid with Stretch half his age and at least four inches

taller, and Stretch had no irony in his name. "This is my nephew, Ted Suskewicz. Ted, this is Mr. Mannarino."

Mike half stood, leaned across the desk to shake hands. "Jesus Christ, kid. How tall are you?"

"Six-eight."

"And *he's* been stealing the cars?" Stretch nodded. Mike said, "We got to find him a better line of work. No offense, kid, but you stick out like a railroad spike in a box of thumb tacks. This local cop—Dougherty—he has to know we're involved in this. He hears people saw someone your size anywhere near a stolen car and finds out you're working for me—and he will—we both got trouble." To Stretch: "Put someone else on this. What's that guy's name down Munhall, always looking for work?"

"Vasilopis."

"Another Greek." A beat. "Okay, him and Pete might get along. Tell him he does a good job, we might have more for him."

"Done." Stretch paused, another sentence ready to go. Held it back until Mike noticed.

"Something else?"

"Ted did okay with the cars, didn't he?"

"I just said so. You worried I don't think he stepped up? Nine cars out the same lot in five weeks? The kid's a machine. It's—you know, his size. He sticks out." The kid standing not six feet from him.

"The reason I ask, he did a good job on some other things before the cars. I'm wondering if you mind if he gets a little more responsibility."

Mike thought about the guys in the other room. All had years in. No one getting rich, except Mike. Disgruntled employees were trouble, so he took a smaller bite than most bosses to let everyone live in reasonable comfort. Comfort not always a good thing in their line of work. Mike knew if he tried to light a fire by taking more for himself—cut back their money—wives and girlfriends would bitch and he'd have a problem. Legitimate internal competition might be the thing to get some people off their asses. The new kid couldn't be made—not with a name like Suskewicz—still be useful when Mike had to tell a guy he wouldn't sponsor him, because he got out-earned by a scarecrow Polack.

"Take him with you to see the shy. Better yet, send him. Let him get his feet wet." Turned to Ted. "You got a nickname?"

The kid's eyes flicked to his uncle and back to Mike. "Uh…Ted, I guess."

"Ted's your name. What do your friends call you?"

An apologetic shrug. "Stretch."

"No good. We got one already and you're bigger than he is." Mike looked from the kid to Stretch and back. "Stretch. More of a stretch. Stretcher. Stretcher Suskewicz. There you go. Alliterative, too. That's good. People with alliterative names are doers," said Mike Mannarino.

Stretcher didn't look so sure. "Okay, Mr. Mannarino. If you say so."

"I do. Listen, do this thing with the shy, we'll put Vasilopis to work for you. Get your own little crew. We can always use some cars. Start there and branch out."

"That'd be great, Mike," Stretch said. "Thanks. Much appreciated."

"Yeah, really, that's great, Mr. Mannarino," Stretcher said with less enthusiasm.

"You two go see Vig. Stretch, tell that lazy prick Ryan to stop jacking off with that P90X piece of shit and get his ass in here. I got some real work for him."

CHAPTER 10

"So you're still dating Kate? This must be the longest relationship you've ever had with a woman."

"Not quite," Doc said. "You and I have been friends since high school. Now either screw this piece in or trade me places. It's gotta weigh eighty pounds and I've been holding it for like an hour."

"You volunteered, and it's only been about thirty seconds." Eve Stepler ran four screws into the façade fast as the licensed contractor she was, when not working as the set construction master for the Penns River Players. "There. Take a break, you big pussy."

Doc had stepped away when he felt the third screw take the weight. Working undercover as an MP, an instructor suggested acting classes. Doc found he liked it. Joined the Players when he came back to Penns River after his nine years, had a minor part in the spring show. Like all good team members in a small repertory company, he helped wherever when not on stage.

He stepped back to take in the scope of what they were building. "What the hell is this supposed to be?"

"Main street of Rumson." Eve pulled a nail from the half dozen between her teeth. The spring show was *Paint Your Wagon*.

"I saw the movie," Doc said. "I don't remember it being this much of a shit hole."

"Movie magic," Eve said. "Trick photography. Color balancing. Fast edits. Besides, the movie had Jean Seberg in it. I doubt you paid any attention to the sets."

Doc leaned on the next piece to be hoisted. "I'll bet you paid more attention to her than I did."

Eve stuck out her tongue. "That was around the time I started to wonder about myself, when I saw it on HBO. She was hot." Turned away to do some neatening.

"What did the board say when Gene told them he wanted to do a play with two husbands sharing a wife?"

Eve stopped working to give Doc her full attention. "You haven't read the script, have you?"

"I read it."

"I mean the whole thing, not just your part."

"Sure I have. Well, no."

Eve gave an exaggerated display of exasperation. "I knew it. He was afraid those Ten Commandments in school assholes would picket, so he went back to the original Broadway version."

"They're different?"

"Yes, they're different. The show opened in 1951. Weren't going to be no two husbands per wife in those days."

"What did they do?"

"It's a forbidden romance thing. Rumson's daughter gets involved with a Mexican."

"Wow," Doc said. "I had no idea."

"I can't believe you don't know more about Broadway shows than you do," Eve said.

"Well, for one thing, I'm not gay."

"You don't have to be gay to know about Broadway shows."

"True, but you have to care a lot about them to know that kind of history, and it helps to be gay if you're going to care that much."

Eve flashed him the finger, pointed to the piece of wood he leaned on. "Up." Waited until he showed effort holding it in position, said, "You going to marry Kate?"

"I thought you gave that yenta shit up after the Jillian fiasco." Doc grunted, shifted his grip. "Besides, shouldn't someone of your inclination set up gay marriages? I have my mother to handle this side of the street."

"No, really. All kidding aside. You're decent looking, have some size on you, a steady job, funny, and genuinely considerate when you feel like it. Why aren't you married?"

"Do you think we could have this discussion after I stop holding this heavy goddamn chunk of scenery for you?"

Eve stepped back, the second screw halfway in, Doc still supporting most of the weight. "It could, but I'm not as likely to get an answer."

Doc thought about letting go—teach her a lesson—knew the screws might not hold. Eve worked hard on these sets. The fact she knew he wouldn't let go didn't help matters. "You know how I am, my routine. Two nights a week here. Wednesdays at the Edgecliff for chicken wings or poor boys. Fridays I shoot pool at the Legion with my dad. Sunday dinner with the folks. The nights I'm home I read or watch a ball game. I've never met anyone I liked enough to make too much of a change for."

"Please. Those are things people do to fill time when they're between relationships. They're not reasons not to have one."

Doc ducked his head, repositioned his shoulder. "Based on past experience, I guess I don't feel like I'm missing all that much."

"You don't get lonely?"

"I get horny. I'm rarely lonely. Think about it. I'm with people all day. A lot of my job is talking to people."

"A lot of your job is arresting people. That's not a relationship."

"I get all I want of people on the clock. My time is *my* time. There's a group of regulars I like at the Edgecliff, and the people we work with here. A few guys at the Legion, and my parents. Hang out with my brother. That's a circle I'm comfortable with. Add the people I deal with on the job, and how many of them either got hosed or did the hosing, I don't need anything else in my life to keep track of."

Eve shuffled the screws in her hand. "Don't take this the wrong way, but, you know, your parents won't be here for you to shoot pool and eat Sunday dinner with forever."

"You going to screw this fucking thing in, or not?"

Eve drove the last screws. They assembled two more pieces in silence.

When they finished, Eve said, "I'm sorry. I shouldn't have said that about your parents."

"It's okay. I'm a little touchy about a few things. You hit two at once. You mind if I ask you a question? Not busting balls. I'm genuinely curious."

"Sure. What is it?"

Doc took a few seconds to work out the phrasing. "What about you?"

"What about me what?"

"You're all the things you said about me, with different

plumbing. Our tastes in women are even the same. Why aren't you married?"

"Don't tell me you don't know there's no gay marriage in Pennsylvania."

"I know. I also know you. You'd drive to Maryland in a heartbeat just to stick it in some people's faces, whether it meant anything here or not."

Now Eve took her time. "I guess I never met anyone I wanted to give that much of myself to."

Doc caught her eye, nodded. "There you go. I spend all day doing for people in one way or another. When I'm off, I do what *I* want."

"So you're saying you're selfish."

Some thought, then, "With my time I am. Think about it. You can always make more money. Time is the one truly finite resource, and no one knows how much they get. So, yeah, I want to decide how I spend my time as much as possible."

"So you can bullshit with drunks at the Edgecliff."

"It doesn't matter if I sleep it away, so long as I decide."

"Yet you spend two nights a week here with me most of the year. I guess I should be flattered."

"In your case I have an ulterior motive."

"What?"

"If I ever get a bug up my ass to have my house done over in rainbow décor, it might pay be to be tight with a lesbian contractor."

Eve had the hammer head in her fist when she popped him on the arm. It hurt all night.

CHAPTER 11

Stush had hated George Grayson as much as black ice and food poisoning. Not even Daniel Hecker—"As arrogant a prick as ever walked the earth," in Benny Dougherty's words—could ignore the disdain everyone in town felt for Hecker's Penns River liaison. Hecker promoted Grayson chief of staff, hired Rance Doocy to oversee this portion of the empire. Stush didn't detest Doocy close to as much as he had Grayson, now coming to the conclusion it was only a matter of time.

"Morning, Rance. Always good to see you. Have a seat." It was never good to see him, and who the hell named their kid Rance?

"Chief. You look well," Doocy said, sincere as a fat woman's husband when asked if her ass looked big. Wore a charcoal gray suit with a faint stripe. The shirt had vertical stripes; the tie's were diagonal. The current definition of stylish, the hold on a sixties' television run amuck. Even Stush said Doocy dressed like the best man at a Polish wedding.

"What brings you in today?" Stush said.

"A lot of cars have been stolen out of the casino's parking lot."

"Nine, last I heard."

"Nine is correct. We've done what we can to keep word

from getting around, but people talk. What can be done about it?"

"I'm no public relations guy, but I'd say the best way to keep them from talking is to stop all those cars from being stolen."

Doocy paused to let Stush know he didn't appreciate the attitude. "We agree on that. Now what can we do to stop the cars from being stolen?"

"Me, I'd hire some security. Patrol the grounds. Maybe issue claim checks like a valet service. You know, a car can only leave the lot if you prove it's yours."

Doocy looked at Stush like he'd suggested razor wire and machine gun towers. "Aside from creating unnecessary congestion, do you have any idea how much that would cost?"

"Probably less than the bad word of mouth if cars keep rolling out of there on their own."

Stush picked jelly beans from a bowl, braced for the *disgruntled taxpayer demanding services* rant. Doocy said, "You had no issues with increasing the police presence for this Resurrection Mall operation."

"Resurrection Mall is in an already high crime area. Patrols downtown had already been beefed up before they bought the property."

"I don't recall hearing about an increased police presence during the casino's construction."

"No crime there to speak of before the casino opened. Not that I'm suggesting any cause and effect."

"So you're telling me you're not going to do anything about the vehicle thefts."

"I'm surprised whatever little birdie keeps you up to speed hasn't told you we've already done something." Stush had no doubt the little birdie a brush-cut Harriger's canary. "We're positioning a car on Leechburg Road where it can see all three entrances."

"Rumor has it that car is tasked with preventing drunk driving. We applaud your concern in that area. No one wants an injury. An officer across the street won't do much to stop car thieves."

"If you had an eye in the lot, we'd have the unit moving in a heartbeat."

Doocy flicked lint from his knee. "To take the report. By the time our man called it in and your dispatcher alerted the unit, the car would be gone."

"Your man calls in the description, license, and which exit and direction the car took." Doocy looked as if he might speak. "Dispatcher hears it's a casino call, it has a priority placed on it. Like every call from the casino, by the way. It's standard procedure."

"That's clearly inadequate."

"We can only answer the calls we get. If you have a way to report things in a timelier manner, we'll be there. Right now we only know a car's missing when the owner calls. If someone tipped us while we had a chance to get to one with the thief inside? Different story."

Doocy stood, dissatisfaction oozing between every mismatched stripe. "I'll report back it's your opinion we aren't doing enough to protect our customers' vehicles."

"Not quite what I said. It'll do. Be sure to tell Mr. Hecker I said hello. I'm sure Ben Dougherty sends his best, too."

CHAPTER 12

Wilver Faison didn't like to be late. Not his fault today, little brother David out of school with a cold, their moms not worth a shit since she started using again. Wilver saw no irony, the son of a junkie working for a drug dealer. He'd outgrown her, in and out of rehab regular as the seasons. His father in a Tennessee prison for cutting up a Mexican over a woman. At least he'd been working at the Nissan plant in Smyrna, about ready to send for the family. Wilver could forgive a one-time fuck up, no matter how long-lasting the repercussions.

Wilver hurried because he had a special invitation to today's lunch. Cootie Highsmith asked—told—him to be at the Resurrection Mall food court at one o'clock so people could talk to him. The people Cootie might want to have talk to Wilver were the other slingers—cool enough—then Cootie let slip Donald Woodson would be there, the top of Penns River's small pyramid. Woodson on the scene implied a promotion. A lunch invitation could mean something beyond Cootie. And here he was, running late.

Running for real. Dodged LaDasha Thompson with her baby buggy. Almost ran over that shriveled old bitch Mrs. Harrison. Saw Glen Brown and Jerome Sheffield cutting school. Some dude he sort of recognized from around, Darnell or Deron or something, older guy—in his twenties—hanging with a hard-looking motherfucker. Rent-a-cop gave him a look for running. Wilver made an apologetic face, tapped his wrist where a watch would be.

Turned the corner into the food court and saw Cootie talking to a guy across the way. Checked his cell phone. 12:58. Two choices: pee, or be on time. Might as well not show if he didn't make the pit stop, or he'd be squirming like a shorty in a hot church.

Came out of the men's room at 1:01. His group stood away from traffic, pointing at restaurant signs. Three open so far; they ate at Lucille's Fried Chicken every day. Wilver started that direction. Saw Darnell/Deron pull a ski mask over his head. Other guy already had his on. Wilver slowed. No point being at Lucille's when they robbed the place.

He stopped altogether when the two men didn't go to Lucille's. Walked over to the dealers. Coats opened. Shotguns appeared. Wilver backed away two steps. Someone said, "What the fuck—" the rest covered by the sound of the first shotgun. Then the other, one firing while the other racked. Wilver transfixed, watching. None of the dealers even threw down. The shooters walked among the bodies with pistols, making sure. The one Wilver didn't know turned to the one he sort of knew. Said something. They both ran.

Wilver turned and ran back the way he came. People thought he was fast coming in should have seen him leave.

CHAPTER 13

"This place must be touched by God. Looks like at least ten shotgun rounds and not a scratch on anyone except these mopes. It's a fucking miracle."

Doc said, "Ever see anything like this when you worked Pittsburgh?"

Willie Grabek shook his head. He'd spent thirty years as a cop in Pittsburgh, most of it in Homicide. "I retired here for some quiet and a little extra cash. Never saw anything like this when I had a real job."

Doc knew he should be canvassing the handful of people who lacked the quickness or smarts to walk away before patrol arrived. Not ready yet. Not sick or upset. In awe. He'd been in Iraq and never seen anything like this, right here in Penns River.

Rick Neuschwander, Penns River's third detective, doubled as crime scene tech. Had a good reputation; Pittsburgh called when they had an opening. Contaminated his crime scene with whatever he'd had for lunch before he opened his kit. Doc looked away, let him recover his dignity.

"I start on the left, you start on the right, meet in the middle?" Doc said to Grabek, nodding toward the ragged line of potential witnesses.

"What the hell. We already know what they saw."

Two men. One was tall or short or average size. The other was short or tall or average. Both black. Probably. Masks.

Long coats. Shotguns. Doc had a headache. Paused to look back to Neuschwander, tagging and photographing shells. Not that it mattered. Shotguns and pistols in the river by now.

Doc spoke with the security guard last. Protocol said go to him first. Doc knew Elmer Ford had less than two months' experience and no training worth the name. Not quite an expert witness.

"You okay, Elmer?"

"Yeah." Elmer a little old and a little heavy and a little slow. Nice guy, careful not to look anywhere close to the bodies. Worked for years on Allegheny County road crews. Retired last fall and took the rent-a-cop gig for something to do and a little spending money. He hadn't signed up for anything like this.

Doc glad the old man hadn't had a heart attack. "What did you see?"

"Oh, Lord, Doc. I only seen when it was over. I heard. Never heard nothing like it. First thing I thought something exploded, maybe one of them propane heaters the work crews using. I come over this way to see could I help. Got about to there—" He turned to point, which brought the bodies into view. Looked away, his arm aiming almost one hundred eighty degrees from his line of sight. "To there and I heard them jacking the slides and thought, 'Oh, Lord, that's shooting.' I didn't know what to do. I...I waited. Till it stopped. Time I got here all's I seen was...that." Snuck a glance toward the dead men.

"Did you see the shooters?"

Elmer looked toward Lucille's, away from the victims. He cried without sound, tears and snot covering his face.

"Elmer. Did you see the shooters at all?"

"Two men running away. Halfway to the church over there before I noticed them. Just seen their backs. Couldn't even swear it was them did it, 'cept it looked like they had guns in their hands."

"What were you doing when you heard the shots?"

"Didn't know they was shots. Not right away."

"You thought it was an explosion. Propane, maybe."

"Yeah. Them workers using propane heaters for working in the cold like it is. Even inside here, get away from the food court, it cold as hell in places."

"Where were you when you heard it?"

"Never heard a shotgun fired indoors. Sounded like an explosion." A short glance at Doc, then away. "Scared me. I was just scared."

"It would've scared me, too, Elmer. What were you doing when you heard it?"

"There's five of them, ain't there? Five men dead. Just that quick." Elmer tried to snap his fingers, fanned.

"Yeah, there's five. Nothing you could've done, Elmer. If you'd got here any sooner there might be six laying there. You did fine."

"I was over by where the bookstore gonna be. Walking along, keeping an eye on things. I spend lunch time handy to the food court 'cause it's busy then, but after I like to stretch my legs a little, make a circuit, know what I mean?"

"Checking your perimeter. Focus on where trouble is most likely to be, catch up everywhere else when you have a minute. Did you see anything unusual while you made the rounds? Anything stick out?"

"It was pretty quiet. Too cold for people to be out, they

didn't have to. A few bums come in from the cold. The Rev lets them hang up handy to the work crews, closer to the heaters, long as they don't get in the way. We let them stay in the hallway by the main entrance at night now so's they can sleep inside. Even with no heaters it's better than being outside in the wind. We seal it off so nothing gets stole."

"You recognize any of them? Know any names?"

Elmer looked at Doc like he'd only then noticed him. "Recognize who? I said it was over when I got there."

"The bums, Elmer. Did you recognize any of the bums?"

Elmer took a second to shift gears. "I recognized them, sure. Not like I know them, not their names, anyway. I know them to see them. Couple a nicknames."

"What are their nicknames? The ones you know."

"T-Bone. Mouse."

"Would you recognize the others if you saw them again?"

"They in here every day. Might be back tonight. Supposed to be near zero."

Slim odds the bums would say anything, even if they knew. Doc would send a unit by when the mall closed for the night, another to check with Elmer in the morning. "So there were a few people around, and the bums. What about the workmen?"

"The usual guys. I stop in couple times a day to shoot the shit, see how things are coming along."

"Could any of them have seen the shooters on the way in?"

"Not unless they come out to take a piss. No, not even then. They got their own back there."

"Let me be sure I have this right. You hung around the food court until the crowd thinned out. Then you walked back this way to check on everything you couldn't keep an eye on while you were watching the food court." Doc trying to get Elmer to play the movie back in his head, describe it as it passed before him. Not pushing too hard. He wanted to break a memory loose, not shove it underground. "You hear noise from the workers, and see the bums hanging close as they can to the heaters. What else do you see?"

Elmer heaved a sigh, almost a sob. He'd stopped crying. "There was a boy. Running. I give him the stink eye and he pointed to his arm like telling me he was in a hurry."

"Pointed to his arm?"

"You know, like he had a watch."

Duh. "This kid, was he running toward the food court?"

"Yeah."

"How old?"

"Don't know exactly. All's I can say is he shoulda been in school."

"Elementary school? High school?"

"High school. Fifteen, sixteen, seventeen years old. Thereabouts."

"You see him leave?"

Elmer looked at Doc, at Grabek. At everyone he could see and not let the five dead come into his field of vision. "Since all this, you're the first person I could swear to seeing."

"You recognize him if you saw him again?"

"Hell, yes. I *know* the boy. You might know him, too. Wilver Faison? Hangs with Jeff West?"

Oh, yeah. Doc knew Wilver Faison.

CHAPTER 14

Christian Love reminded Doc of a gutted house, collapsing in on itself. "Please tell me what I can do to help."

"Answering a few questions is all we need for now, sir," Doc said. "It won't take long."

"Ask, son. I'll tell you what I can."

"Did you know the men who were shot?"

"I haven't heard their names."

Doc didn't need his notes. "Cootie Highsmith, Dyson Clary, Elijah Weatherspoon, Ivory Harris, Donald Woodson."

"No. I didn't know them."

"Never heard of them?" Grabek said.

Love shook his head. "Should I have?"

"They ate lunch in the food court every day the past three weeks," Grabek said. "Every drug dealer in town worth mentioning."

"Oh, that was them, then."

"You knew them?" Doc said.

"I'd been told drug dealers had been seen. I didn't know who they were."

"You let them hang around," Grabek said, not asking.

"There's no law against eating lunch where you want. They never caused any trouble. If they had, we'd've asked them to leave."

"No drug sales on the premises?"

"No. Wait. I can't say 'no,' not straight out. I can say, not as far as I know. I can't swear there were never any drugs sold on the property."

Doc spoke before Grabek could continue. "Dr. Love, we should probably get something straight right away. You're not a suspect, so we're not required to advise you of your right to an attorney. If you'd like to call one, we can come back."

Love showed no offense. "Why would I need a lawyer?"

"Let's say you're a person of interest," Grabek said.

"How so?"

"Someone gets shot in your house, we take an interest in you."

"But this isn't my—I see your point. No, I don't need a lawyer. I'll answer whatever you want to know." Love and Grabek maintained eye contact longer every time one of them spoke.

"You said they were no trouble," Doc said. "To you. Did anyone else have any issues with them?"

"Like I said, not to my knowledge. Far as we knew they were five young men looking for someplace to eat out of the cold."

"I told him to run them off." Cassius Abernathy not as charitable as Christian Love. "They cost us money every time they walked in the door. People not wanting to hang where they did. Investors knowing them for what they were. He don't see it. This is about to go under—take him with it—and he still turning the other cheek and shit."

"Are you blaming the mall's financial trouble on them?"
Doc said.

"All of it? No. There's plenty enough fucked up here to
drain money away. Still, this ain't Baltimore. It ain't Dee-
troit. People there sit next to a blinged-up drug dealer don't
think nothing of it. This town ain't that far gone yet."

Doc doubted Abernathy spoke like that around Love.
Dismissed most of it. Stress does things to people. "Does Dr.
Love know how bad things are financially?"

"The fuck you think? I don't tell him? Got-damn right he
know. He about to lose everything. This place, his church,
the whole motherfucker, something don't turn around quick.
I told him, 'Run them niggers out. They costing you money.'
He kept telling me they ain't done nothing. My ass. What
they done was bleed him dry, and all's they had to do was
show up to do it." Abernathy wiped a soaking forehead with
a wrinkled handkerchief. "I'm a deacon of this church. I
shouldn't talk like this. I'm just so—demoralized by it all.
When does it get better?"

Abernathy seemed more pissed than demoralized. Doc
chose not to pursue the semantic discussion. Still debating his
next question when Grabek spoke up. "You know any of
them?"

"Their names. Never spoke to any."

"How'd you know they were drug dealers?"

Abernathy stuffed the handkerchief into his breast pocket.
"You see some a the things I seen, you know when you're
looking at a drug dealer."

* * *

Sylvester Lewis appeared defeated.

"I don't know about the money coming in. You'd have to ask Cassius. What I know is, I have to talk to people every day we owe money to and can't pay. It's a difficult situation for a church to be in. If people can't trust a church to make good on their word..."

"Did you know any of the dead men?" Doc said.

"I seen a couple of them around. Not their names or anything. See them in the food court when I ate lunch sometimes."

"Sometimes?" Grabek said. "We have information they ate there every day."

"*I* don't eat there every day. I don't eat the same time when I do. I didn't go down there looking for them. They could've set next to me and I'd a missed them. God don't give any man more than he can handle. Sometimes I wish He'd reassess my capabilities."

"Were they selling drugs here?"

"I saw one or the other walking into the mall from the construction area a few times. It's possible they sold marijuana to men on the work crews. Could be something stronger. I don't know."

"You tell anyone?"

"I didn't think there was anything to tell, seeing a man walk through the mall."

"You said a minute go you thought they were selling drugs to the work crews. Why didn't you say something?"

Lewis took his time. Doc had never seen anyone look more tired. "No, sir. I believe what I said was it was possible. If I didn't, I apologize. It's been a day. I don't know if I'm coming or going."

Doc stepped in. "You're the liaison between Dr. Love and the contractors. Do you have a list of everyone who's been working here for...say the past three weeks?"

"No. I deal with the contractors. You'd have to check with them for who's working."

"Can we get a list of the contractors?"

"I don't know it'll do you much good." Doc raised an eyebrow. "I think quite a few of the workers are here off the books. Kind of day laborer sort of thing. I think that's why things are moving so slow and we've had some of the problems we've had. People have to be brought up to speed every day 'cause the man got the work to where it is now didn't come back."

"We'll still need to ask."

"I really don't see what good it will do."

Grabek's patience had left the building. "We want the list of contractors. It's not the kind of thing we need a subpoena for. Just give it to us and we'll be on our way for now. If not, I'll go to the office and write the affidavit and be back before you leave for the day. No judge is going to jerk me around on a request like this with five bodies down."

Doc relaxed when he saw Lewis deflate even more. "I don't have a list. Not like a single piece of paper. I can get one for you in an hour or so. It's the best I can do."

Doc spoke before Grabek could. "That will be fine, Mr. Lewis. Thanks for your time."

CHAPTER 15

Doc left Grabek to wait for the list and took the car to the Allegheny Estates. The Estates weren't built to be a project. The hope had been to provide affordable apartments for new families coming to town for work, the buildings easy walking distance from the James and Larimore mill. The first residents moved in July 17, 1969. J&L started closing sections of the plant in 1971; by 1975 the whole Penns River operation was history. Forty-five hundred jobs lost in a town of thirty-five thousand people in less than four years.

The smart ones got out. Others stayed, holding onto the hope the union would get their jobs back the way a teenager listens to a crush say, "I can't imagine any circumstances under which I'd go out with you," and thinks, *She didn't say there weren't any, just she can't think of one. There's still a chance.* No, there wasn't.

Evictions followed. Landlords walked away when the cost to throw people out became greater than the income from a new tenant. The buildings fell into disrepair. Squatters were rampant. Penns River condemned everything under eminent domain and converted the buildings worth saving into public housing. Tore down the rest. The Estates didn't meet the definition of slum accepted in Chicago or Detroit or Baltimore. In Penns River, the prevailing philosophy was white people found there after dark deserved what happened to them.

Imelda Faison—she pronounced it "Eye-melda"—lived on

the fourth floor of 1122 Fourth Avenue. Doc took the stairs. He needed the exercise and walking was quicker and more reliable than the elevator. Rapped on the door with his knuckles. Waited. Rapped again, called, "Mrs. Faison." Waited. Hit the door with the side of his fist, called louder. "Mrs. Faison, it's Ben Dougherty." Waited. Pounded the door, yelling, "Penns River Police, Mrs. Faison. I need you to open the door now." Waited.

The door opened three inches, all Doc needed to know Imelda had fallen off the wagon hard enough to leave a mark. Hooded eyes, runny nose. Emaciation where there had been a healthy thinness last time he saw her. "Uh-huh. What you want?"

"I want to talk to you without standing in the hall."

"'Bout what?"

"Wilver."

"He in trouble?"

"I don't know." Doc lowered his head and voice to Imelda's level. "But you will if you don't open this door right the fuck now."

"Fuck you. You got no right to talk to me like that. Fuck you." The door started to close.

Doc got a foot turned sideways in the crack. "I'll violate you with Family Services. David will be out of here by the end of the day." Doc already hip to where David would go. The kid would be much better off and everyone knew it, including David.

The pressure eased on his toe. The chain slid off and Doc stepped in before Imelda could change her mind.

He'd met her twice before. Once in County and once here. This more like the County version, except she had detoxed in lockup. Well-toxed today, the latest high still wearing off from her looks. Addicts disgusted Doc. Addicts with children infuriated him. This addict had children he knew and cared about.

"Thanks for letting me in. You mind if we sit?" Imelda flapped a hand in a gesture could have been an invitation to sit or leave or die. Doc took the closest kitchen chair. No point being obvious about looking around while he looked around.

The eat-in kitchen and adjacent living room had been shabby but clean when he'd been here a year ago. Things weren't dirty, or even unclean, today. More like unkempt, as if Imelda had hired entropy as a housekeeping service. Jeans and T-shirt in good condition, the shirt on at least its second day of wear. Espresso machine on the kitchen counter, flat-panel TV of at least forty inches on the wall in the living room, new recliner.

Imelda sat, poked a book of paper matches with a finger. Doc said, "Is Wilver around?"

"You see him?" Doc didn't answer. "You don't say, so I guess he ain't around. You can leave any time."

"When's he due back?"

"When he gets here. The boy come, the boy go. He don't tell his mother. I don't know when he coming back, or if. I stopped worrying about him."

"He eat his meals here?"

"Some."

"Which? Breakfast? Supper?"

"Whatever one's he's here for."

"How often is he home, Mrs. Faison?" No answer. "What's he do for money?"

"Nothing I know about."

"He must be doing something. Espresso maker, TV, recliner. Either Wilver's making money or you have a rich and generous lover." Doc let Imelda watch him look her over. "I'm guessing Wilver's making money."

"Fuck. You. Force your way into my house then insult me. Get your ass out 'fore I call the po-lice."

Doc slammed his shield holder onto the table in front of her. "I *am* the police, Imelda. Pull your head out of the clouds or your ass or wherever it is and pay attention. Wilver maybe saw something happen over at Res Mall a few hours ago. People saw him there. It's in his best interest to see me before the people he saw find out he saw them, or there won't be any more TVs or easy chairs or espresso, which you might want to think about drinking a quadruple before you say anything else stupid to me. Now where the fuck is he?"

Imelda sat back in her chair. Her chin dipped like she might go on the nod again. "I told you. I don't know."

Doc slid his badge holder back around his neck. Pulled three business cards from the case, dropped them on the table. "Give him one of these when…if…he comes home. Give one to David, in case he sees Wilver first. Keep one for yourself on the off chance you're overcome with lucidity. Just remember, I need to talk to him almost as bad as he needs to talk to me. Do *not* forget. This is the kind of mistake you might only get to make once."

CHAPTER 16

The uniforms had stumbled onto a bum for Doc to talk to. Stumbled in the literal sense, rooting through what appeared to be a pile of blankets and possessions abandoned when the shooting started. Grabek on the scene at the time. Took one look, shook his head, and went to the food court to supervise Neuschwander, who needed supervision like a duck needs galoshes.

Doc returned to Resurrection Mall to find Tony Ulizio holding a person of indeterminate age, race, and gender by the collar with an extended arm. "You still looking for bums?" Ulizio said. Doc let the man sit on his pile of stuff while he squatted next to it, careful not to touch anything, doing his best not to look like he was being careful not to touch anything.

"What's your name, buddy?" Up close it was a man, a light-skinned black who could have passed for white back in the day but for the broadness of his nose. Hard to guess his age, except to say younger than he looked. The recent bitter cold did not keep him from smelling like a Kennywood Dumpster in July.

"You po-lice?" Doc took the lanyard from inside his coat. Let him have a good look at the badge. "Do I have to say?"

No one had ever asked that before. "I don't guess you *have* to," Doc said. "I can't promise I won't have to ask later, but, you don't want to tell me now, you don't have to."

"What's your name?"

"Detective Dougherty."

"Detective's your first name?"

Doc let his lips smile. "Ben."

"Delonte Bickerstaff," the bum said. "Don't shake my hand. You don't know where it's been."

Doc smiled all the way. "Mr. Bickerstaff, you been here all day?"

"All day and night. You been outside lately? Freeze your dick off taking a piss out there."

"No kidding," Doc said. "I meant right here, this spot."

"Hard to say. No clock I can see, and it's not like I have any place to be in a timely manner. Since before the shooting started, I can say that for sure."

"You watch people come and go, or were you taking a nap?"

"I wasn't sleeping one off, if that's what you're asking."

"No, sir, I knew you weren't," Doc said. "I've seen my share of drunks and junkies. You're as sober as I am, and have been."

"Then why don't you go ahead and ask me did I see the two men with shotguns?"

"Because I'm interested in more than that."

"You're not going to tell me about how you're interested in me and how you can help me get off the street if I help you catch these men?"

"Do you want me to help you get off the street?"

"I'll be damned," Bickerstaff said. "An honest man. An honest cop, no less. What if I told you, yes, I want you to help me get off the street? What would your conditions be?"

"What conditions would you like?"

Bickerstaff took a few seconds to size Doc up. "Yeah, I like to watch the people come and go. Make up stories about where they've been, where they're going, why they're here. Passes the time."

"Anything or anyone stick in your mind today? Besides the men with the shotguns."

"Some children who better either start going to school or come see me to discuss their career options. Young woman looks like she's on something. Hard to guess what. I think she's blowing construction workers for money. You interested in any of that?"

"Interested? Yeah. Will we do anything about it? Maybe notify mall security. We're spread kind of thin and this business today won't lighten our workload any."

"You really ain't bullshitting, are you?"

"Would you like me to?"

Bickerstaff thought. "Maybe a little. You're depressing me. Supposed to be my job, being homeless and all."

"I'll try not to harsh your mellow," Doc said.

"This kid, he came running through here like his hair was on fire a few minutes before the shotgun men came by."

"Ever see him before?"

"I have, but he's not one of those skipping school on a regular basis. I've seen him maybe three times the last couple of weeks. One of those probably after school was out. Hard to tell without a clock."

"Would you recognize him if you saw him again?"

Bickerstaff spoke without rancor. "I just said I already recognized him from before. Why wouldn't I recognize him again? I know you're paying attention. Why not ask me what you really want to know, which is would I be willing to identify him if I had to?"

Doc gave up his squat, sat on the floor next to Bickerstaff's pile. Still not touching anything. "Would you?"

"If it came to it, yes. It won't. His name's Wilver something. Last name might be Faison. Lives over in the Alleghenies."

"You won't have to," Doc said. "You already confirmed something else I heard."

"The two with shotguns." Bickerstaff took time for the words to find him. "I saw them come in."

"Can you describe them?"

"I mean, I saw the shotguns under their coats. I didn't recognize them for shotties until I heard the shooting. At first it something just seemed a little off. I saw them and—god-*damn* me—I was more interested in making up their story than paying attention to what I saw in front of me. Where they were going. Where they'd been. I never gave them a good look."

"Did you see them come back out? After the shooting, I mean." If Doc had been in Bickerstaff's place and not been a cop, he would have burrowed into his pile of stuff and stayed there for hours. Didn't want to embarrass the man, still had to ask.

"They didn't come back this way," Bickerstaff said.

"You sure?"

"I'm sure. I didn't hide. I watched for them."

So no one got two looks at them. Slick. "Anything stick out about them? Body type, maybe? Either of them short or tall? Fat or skinny?"

"Is Elijah Weatherspoon one of those killed?"

"Yes, sir," Doc said. "You know him?"

"We used to be kin, in a way."

"How so?"

"Let me see. My ex-wife's sister's brother-in-law. Met him a few times at family functions when he was a kid."

"You know anything else about him? Anything lately?"

"He'd come through here most days around lunch time, usually with friends," Bickerstaff said. "He'd look at me like he knew me, almost like he'd say hello a couple of times, then keep walking."

"You ever speak to him?"

"Thought about it once." Bickerstaff shrugged. "He had his reasons, if he didn't want to talk to me. Hell of a thing, a drug dealer ranking higher in the social hierarchy than a law-abiding vagrant."

"You knew he was a drug dealer?"

"Everyone knew. Jeans hanging down, brank-new Timberlands. Wore a fur-lined hoodie he'd open as soon as he got inside, show off the bling."

"You know the names of any of the other guys you'd see him with?"

"I knew Elijah since he was a boy." Bickerstaff held his head to keep Doc in his peripheral vision. "We had a family picnic once. Might have been someone's anniversary, over Memorial Park. Somebody brought a football. Elijah was relentless. Asked everybody until he finally wore enough of us down to get a decent game of touch going. Boy had no talent whatsoever. His enthusiasm's what I remember. He had more fun that day than..." Bickerstaff cocked an eyebrow and gave up on the thought.

"When's the last time you ate?"

"Last night. The food court people give us a look at what's left before they throw it out. I expect they're already gone today." Fixed Doc with a look. "You one of those humanitarian cops? The kind what joined up to help people? If you are, this is where you offer to take me to Nader's Deli or someplace and get me some hot food."

"You're a man who appreciates honesty, so I'll be honest with you. I'm one of those cops who joined so I could run the siren and lock people up." Doc eased himself up into his squat. "I couldn't in good conscience take you into someone's business, where other customers might be. Not the way you smell."

Bickerstaff laughed like he hadn't done it for a while. "Good on you. I was setting you up to mention that myself."

"I will get you fed, though. One more question, if you don't mind."

"People aren't in the habit of asking me questions. It's a nice change."

"You're intelligent and well-spoken. I'm guessing you have some education in you. How'd you end up here?"

"Would you believe me if I told you I choose to live like this?"

"If that's what you're telling me, yeah."

"You're awfully gullible to be a cop," Bickerstaff said. "I guess they know what they're doing, hiring you." They shared a smile before he went on. "All decisions need to have context. A man can string together a series of what seem like good ideas at the time, taken by themselves, and end up— hell, I've seen some end up worse than this. Dead, even."

"What did you do before?"

"I don't ever think about before. There's today and there's tomorrow. Before doesn't matter."

Doc waited until he was sure Bickerstaff had finished. "You gonna be here a while?"

"Like I said, my appointment calendar is clear for the rest of the day."

A few food court employees lingered, telling each other lies about what they'd seen, getting over the shock. Doc scored most of a chicken, mashed potatoes, and a large Coke before Lucille threw away what was left. Delonte Bickerstaff thanked him, not so much Doc had the feeling the man had been worried about starving.

CHAPTER 17

Doc's hands and feet smarted as they warmed. Everything that could be done today had been done, except the obligatory press conference. Stush had let the media cool their heels—and everything else—in the parking lot since they started arriving half an hour after the last shot was fired. They were getting antsy, Stush needed a briefing before he spoke with them, and the detectives had to compare notes to give it to him. They ate Taco Bell take-out and recapped five death notifications on the same day, instead of enjoying warm showers and drinking hot tea with bourbon.

"Cootie Highsmith," Doc said to Grabek.

Grabek spoke as he bit into a taco. "The usual. Good boy, bad company." Paused to push escaping lettuce into his mouth. "Slipped the last few years. His friends dragged him down." Swallowed, chased it with a swig of Pepsi. "Black parent speech Number Forty-Two."

"Mrs. Highsmith?"

"Yes?"

"Detective Grabek, Penns River police. May I come in?"

"Is there a problem?"

"May I come in?"

"Yes, please. I'm sorry."

She backed off three steps. Grabek stepped in. "What can I do for you, Officer?"

"It's Detective, ma'am. Are you Darcella Highsmith?"

81

"*I already said who I am. You're disturbing me, Detective. What is this about?*"

A man came into the room from a hallway. "*What's this?*"

"*This man's from the police. I'm trying to find out what it's about.*"

"*Well? What's it about?*"

"*Are you Mrs. Darcella Highsmith?*"

"*I already told you I'm Mrs. Highsmith.*"

"*I need to know if you're Mrs. Darcella Highsmith.*"

"*Yes. Yes, I am Mrs. Darcella Highsmith.*"

"*Who are you, sir?*"

"*I'm her husband. Ronald Highsmith. What's wrong?*"

"*Is William—Cootie—your son?*"

The woman's face fell. The husband kept up a better front. Both knew before Grabek said the words. "*I'm afraid I have bad news. William has been killed. A couple of hours ago. In Resurrection Mall.*"

The woman froze. Mouth open, one hand holding the other near her chin. The man said, "*What happened?*"

"*He was shot with four other men in the food court.*"

"*What with?*"

"*Shotgun.*" No need to include the head shots today.

"*Hunh. I knew it only a matter of time. Didn't figure a shotgun, though. That's cold.*"

"Who had Dyson Clary?" Doc had a list of who'd gone to see each family. No idea where he'd put it. Find it in the morning when he didn't need it.

"He's mine, too." Grabek unwrapped another taco as he spoke. He had notes—stenographers marveled at his note-taking ability—never referred to them. Didn't need them for himself, used them as an outline for the report. "This one was a saint. Never in any trouble, mother has no idea why he was hanging with known drug dealers. He must've just been standing there when it happened. She knows he couldn't have nothing to do with that."

"*Can I see him?*"

"*Tomorrow morning. We'll send someone around to give you a ride to Pittsburgh.*" Whole basketball team on slabs down there. Need a jitney to take everyone for the identifications.

"*Why we got to go to Pittsburgh? You said it happened over to Res Mall.*"

"*Neshannock County uses the Allegheny County morgue. We'll take you down and give you a ride back.*"

"*You will?*"

"*Might not be me personally. We'll send an officer.*" She liked that idea better.

"*What was he doing there?*" both said to each other.

Grabek went first. "*It happened in the food court, around one. Did he say anything about what he was up to today?*"

"*He don't live here no more. Not for a couple years.*"

"*We know. He has a place over in Tarentum. I wondered—since he was in the neighborhood—maybe he stopped by.*"

"*He don't very often through the week. He has his own life now. Comes by Sundays to see do I need anything.*"

"*Do you know any of his friends who might be able to help out with what he'd been up to?*"

"*I know his old friends. He don't talk much about them no more. I don't know can they be any help.*"

"*Do any of these names ring a bell? Cootie Highsmith?*"

Elijah Weatherspoon? Ivory Harris? Donald Woodson?"
None did. "When's the last time Dyson was here?"

Vonetta Clary walked to a small mantel. Photographs of a
boy growing into a young man, some framed, other tucked
into corners of the frames. Ran her fingers across the glass
over the smiling face of a boy about eight years old. Left the
room through a short hallway into what appeared to be a
bedroom. Closed the door behind her.

Grabek put his card on the coffee table and let himself
out.

"So I guess you had Elijah Weatherspoon, Noosh." Doc
not so tired he didn't remember who he'd seen.

"Yeah. He...uh..." Flipped through his notes. "Well, the
best I could do was an aunt." Pronounced it *ant*. "Lives in
Vandergrift. His parents...uh...she's the closest family I
could find on short notice. They—I guess the mother moved
a while ago. They're not close. I couldn't get a lead on the
father or any grandparents."

Why Neuschwander had the one notification. Weatherspoon's people the hardest to find, Neuschwander the best
researcher. His first notification, to boot. Doc would have
gone with him, knew they didn't have time for him to do
three.

"You get anything from the aunt?" Doc said.

Neuschwander shook his head. "Uh-uh."

"I should feel worse, I suppose. Tell the truth, I hardly
knew the boy. Wouldn't recognize him if he walked in the
door with you. Don't know the last time I seen him. I guess
that's sad, now that I think about it. His mamma and daddy
God knows where. I'm the one you found for next of kin and
I don't even know the boy."

"Nothing at all comes to mind, ma'am? What he did for money, who his friends were?"

"No. Sorry. Would you like a glass of wine, Mr.—" looked at his business card, "—Noochunder? You look like you're taking this harder than me."

"Sounds about right for the day," Doc said. "I didn't get much from Ivory Harris's people. Father wasn't home. Mother told me Ivory was a good boy. Came by every week or so with a little money, sometimes a small gift. Had their car fixed for them. Apparently her idea of small gifts includes a washer and dryer and what appeared to be a brand new kitchen table and chairs. I asked what he did for a living and she told me he worked over at Carlton's, that big beer distributor across the river."

"He was a distributor, all right," Grabek said. Balled up taco wrappers, tossed them in the trash. "No way she doesn't know. No one's that stupid."

"There's no limit to how much people don't know when they don't want to. The place was clean and picked up. Everything showed age except for the washer-dryer and kitchen set. If I had to guess, a new couch would've been next. They don't have much. What they do have, he brought them. Nothing so extravagant it couldn't be denied. So..."

"What about Woodson?"

"Donald Woodson, Senior?"

"Donald Woodson, yeah. What you need?"

"Is Donald Woodson of 1360 Leishman Avenue your son?"

"Not for a long time." A pause. "What about him?"

"He's dead, sir. He was—"

Woodson held up a hand. "You can save this for someone

gives a shit. His mother be home in a half hour or so. You can wait in here where it's warm if you want."

"No," Doc said. "I got nothing on Woodson."

CHAPTER 18

Jack Harriger was as sure as always. "You know it's Mannarino. It has to be. No one else around here could pull something like this together. Not this ruthless, and not with this level of violence."

Not since we took care of your little Russian buddies, Doc thought.

No one beat Willie Grabek at being sure of himself. "Mannarino don't work with the coloreds, and everything we know says the two shooters were jigs. Besides, he's into this whole Vito Corleone thing. Likes to keep up the appearance there's no crime in his town. He wanted those spooks dead, he'd lure them out someplace and do them like he did those two at Hartwood Acres last year."

Doc caught Stush's eye. Stush nodded, posed his hands palms down. Grabek's racial tolerance borderline since he hired on. The last six months had seen a decline to where Stush might have to do something. Today not the day.

"Willie's right," Doc said. "Not to mention, he'd have no reason to kill these guys. We know Mannarino's not above brokering packages; he wants nothing to do with street sales. He can't get away with his white guys selling down there, and—Willie's right again—he won't work with blacks on a day-to-day basis. He might be as confused as we are. No one I talked to has heard anything about a crew looking to take over. Of course, we don't have NSA-caliber intelligence down there, either."

Stush spoke to Neuschwander. "You get anything worth knowing, Ricky?"

"Ten shotgun shells, five nine-millimeter casings. I didn't notice anything noteworthy in the strike marks on the shells or casings. Four of the bullets deformed too badly to get ballistics. The fifth might have possibilities if we find the gun to match it to."

"The gun's in the river," Doc said.

"Fucking defeatist attitude," Harriger said under his breath.

"Never made it across the bridge," Grabek said. "These guys are pros. The guns were cold and now they're gone."

"Speaking of pros, Willie," Stush said. "You ever come across anyone who did this kind of work when you were in Pittsburgh?"

"Not even close. The only time I worked more than a double was the time that nutjob aced three cops. You guys have one bloodthirsty fucking town here."

"I doubt someone local did it," Stush said. "Forget all that 'how professional they are' stuff. For as long as they'd have to be exposed, odds are someone would've recognized them."

"Someone could be stepping up," Doc said.

"Hell of a step," Grabek. "There hasn't been an unsolved shotgun hit in Pittsburgh for Christ knows how long. Shotgun murders, yeah, domestics and someone with a drunk on. Nothing professional. I can't say for sure they're not local; it's not my first guess."

"What is your first guess?" Stush said. "We're bullshitting here. A wild-ass guess is fine."

"If we were talking straight up white Italian OC, I'd figure Chicago or New York. It being blacks, I'm thinking Detroit or Baltimore. D.C., maybe. Unless…"

"Unless?"

"Unless it's a black gang thing. You know, Bloods or Crips or whatever they call themselves now."

"You sure those Russians aren't back?" Neuschwander said.

Grabek shook his head. "No, they wouldn't farm this out, especially not to coloreds. Russians take pride in doing their own heavy work. They want everybody to know they did it."

No one spoke for almost a minute. Stush said, "Willie, how are your contacts in Pittsburgh?"

"Rusty, but I can oil them up pretty quick."

"It's a reasonable assumption, even if a local reached out to Detroit or someplace, they needed somebody they knew from around here to vouch for them. Sound right?"

"It doesn't sound wrong."

"First thing in the morning, start calling in favors. Benny, what's the drug situation downtown?"

"The junkies all went underground when the word got out. They'll keep their heads low tonight in case there are aftershocks. They're going to start to hurt come morning. I already asked Eye Chart to add some patrols, have them pay special attention to the corners and general behavior."

Stush rocked back in his chair. Linked his fingers across his stomach, tapping his thumbs. His thinking posture. "What did we find out from the people at the mall? Do we know who was there?"

"We got statements from everyone we could round up," Doc said. "No one saw shit. One of Love's deacons gave Willie a list of all the contractors on site the past few weeks. We're going to try to get a list of everyone who worked there lately, but that's iffy."

"How come?"

"Lot of them are day laborers, working off the books. I doubt they even have names for some of those guys. Pay them in cash and see who shows up tomorrow."

"That's not a union site?"

"Not officially. I have a suspicion they pay what they can get away with and bill Love the prevailing wage."

"Lean on them. I'm willing to give the companies and the workers a pass if they can tell us who worked there, especially today. Or if anyone who has been working didn't show up. I don't care if we have to round up vagrants and have the contractors pick faces out of the line. I want to know who's been working there."

"What about Hear No Evil, See No Evil, and Speak No Evil?" Grabek said.

Stush looked to Doc. "Translate."

"We talked to Christian Love and his two deacons. Their stories were, uh, disappointing."

"Disappointing how?"

Doc glanced toward Grabek. Grabek gestured for him to go on. "The project—Resurrection Mall—is, maybe, going under. The renovations are more expensive than they expected, the businesses are picking up slower than they'd hoped, and investment and contributions aren't making up the slack. There's debate whether having drug dealers hanging around scares off customers. We heard they sure as hell scared off some investors."

Stush's mouth hung open. "You think the church did it?"

"No. But...right now, until we see who picks up the drug trade, the only people we know who stand to benefit are those with an interest in Resurrection Mall. We at least have to clear them."

"Fuck a duck," Stush said under his breath. "All right. Here's what we'll do. Willie, you go to Pittsburgh. Find out who might be able to pull something like this off, either on his own or by making a call. Ricky, don't give up on your evidence, but push these contractors. Get the names of everyone who worked on the project in the past...I don't know, three weeks, let's say. Who came, who went, and especially who might have come today, or didn't come today and had been. Then I want complete backgrounds on Love and those deacons. Get what you need from Willie and Ben. Questions?"

"What do I do?" Doc said.

"Just because we got five bodies doesn't mean there's no other crime in this town. Be ready to drop everything and turn on a dime, but for now, these two are the homicide squad. You're the rest of the detectives." Doc opened his mouth, caught a look from Stush, closed it.

Stush checked his watch. "Almost nine-thirty. Willie, you have a drive, hit the road. You want to work the phone, set up your meetings from home tomorrow, go ahead. Whatever you think will get you up and running quickest. Check in with me a couple of times a day. Ricky, you had the shit job today, go home. Take a long shower, have a couple of drinks, be back at eight. I'd give you the day off, but I need you."

Stush made eye contact with Harriger. "Jack, there's about fifty reporters and camera crews outside waiting for a statement. We can't put them off much longer. Benny and I will handle them. You, I want to take care of reconciling the overtime and court slips, and figuring out what the hell's going on with the maintenance records for all the cars. It's a goddamn mess and I half think Earl Stirnweiss is screwing us."

Harriger's face fell so hard it bounced. "That's what you want me to do *now?*"

"It doesn't have to be tonight," Stush said. "You can go home and do it in the morning if you want." Then, to Doc, "Let's go, Benny, so we can get out of here tonight, too."

CHAPTER 19

Willie Grabek slept in. Most days he had to be on the road at seven to get to Penns River by eight. Could have made an appearance at a Pittsburgh roll call, chose to set up visits with old acquaintances from home while drinking his second cup of coffee. Willie was dressed—his sloth had limits—lacking a tie, suit coat, and shoes to be official. His gun in the holster, hanging from a coat rack. He used to be more careful. No one else had access to it now.

Soft-boiled three eggs and made two pieces of toast. Took his breakfast and third cup of coffee into the living room. Turned on *Fox and Friends,* lowered the volume. He didn't care what they said. Fox as full of shit as the others. At least O'Reilly was entertaining. Grabek watched Fox in the vain hope Elisabeth Hasselbeck would pull a Sharon Stone. Give MSNBC and *The Daily Show* something serious to talk about.

Kept the sound down so it didn't interfere with his thoughts. Turned yesterday's massacre over in his head all the way home, drank two beers, a Seagram's and water, and slept like a brick until his gut woke him around three. Farting, Pepto-Bismol, and moving to the recliner didn't help. Dozed off near five-thirty, woke feeling as rested as he ever did. The Resurrection Mall shootings joined him in the shower the way most people took ear worms with them.

None of it made sense. The Penns River drug trade not

worth killing one person over, let alone five. Witness descriptions were all over the place; Willie sure the shooters were black. They killed each other for the goofiest reasons. The cops are all thinking drugs when it might have been a woman or a car repair or the shooters were Ravens fans. Grabek didn't screw with motives for black-on-black crime. Let the DA worry about it. He'd tried thinking like them when he was younger. His clearance rate went up when he focused on how, and stopped worrying about why.

So, think about the how. Two shooters. Shotguns and nines. Knew the targets would be there. No big secret; they ate there every day. Not too smart in a high-risk occupation like slinger, which meant these guys were dumb even by black standards, or dealing drugs in Penns River not considered a high-risk occupation. All prior drug-related violence had been user-on-user.

A few things the witnesses agreed on. Shooters stayed together. No one thought twice about the ski masks, single digits outside in the middle of the day. No hollering or yelling. Far as Grabek could tell, not even a word to get the victims' attention. Each body with at least two shotgun wounds. Neuschwander found ten shells, the victims so close some patterns hit more than one. The killers strolled through the mess they'd created—no one said they hurried—popped a nine in every head, not risking deathbed statements. Took their time getting clear, then ran for the exit. Not panicky. Quick. No one they passed got a good look.

Not locals. Grabek spent thirty years as a Pittsburgh cop, sixteen in Homicide. Never seen anything like this. It had to be someone brought in—Chicago, Detroit, Baltimore; St.

Louis coming on the past few years—or someone new in town.

Not amateur hour, either. Money had changed hands, quite a bit from the looks of things. Someone local must have paid it. Someone local may have collected it. If they had, it got spent. TV and movies loved to show professional hit men, living in luxury, having their fees wired to Swiss bank accounts. Grabek knew better. Contract hitters, killers who'd work for someone they didn't know and would never meet again, had drug habits or expensive tastes in cars or clothing. Or women, plural, with expensive tastes. Or he'd need to find a woman to work off the testosterone. Someone would flash a roll, or run his mouth hoping to wet his dick. Willie Grabek would hear about it when he did.

At ten he put the dirty dishes in the sink and went downtown to build the web one of these mopes would touch sooner or later. Being lazy had its benefits. Lazy people took their time. People who took their time didn't miss much.

Rick Neuschwander had never been in the Army, still did more before eight o'clock than Willie Grabek sometimes did all day. This morning he'd been up at six to shower and help Shirley get the bigger kids fed and off to school, then played with little Lothar while Shirley cleaned herself up for the day. An unfortunate name for a baby, but Uncle Lothar's will had been more generous to Rick than to the other nieces and nephews, Rick his godson. Increased his benevolence by dying three months before the birth, when the Family Neuschwander needed a new minivan, new baby equipment, and braces for Tina. After such a gift, Grandma Neuschwander had said, how could Rick and Shirley name the baby anything else? Grandma was ninety-three and owned a pile of SAP and Lufthansa stock little Lothar could sit on and see over the steering wheel of the new minivan. Still lived like a refugee, which she had been, seventy-five years ago. Rick and Shirley tried to sneak it in as a middle name. Not good enough. The doctors said to humor her, she had no more than a year left. You don't want her changing the will—again—then dying before the rest of the family could convince her to change it back. So Rick acquiesced, though his faith in medical science had weakened in the aftermath of being oversold on the wonders of vasectomies.

Signed into work at seven-fifty-five. Made a cup of coffee and took one of the doughnuts Stush brought in a few days a week *to uphold cherished police traditions.* Bavarian cream. Checked his mail and email to see if any lab results had come back. He'd sent the requests at eight last night. The lab opened at eight in the morning. Penns River and Neshannock County too small for their own facility, so everything went to a private company, backlogged from three weeks to a year-and-a-half, depending on the test. Nothing in his mail except an invitation to a forensics conference he already knew the city wouldn't pay for.

Called all the contractors on Grabek's list. Everyone he needed to talk to at a job site, go see him there. Most would be at Resurrection Mall, seeing what was up, gone by the time Rick could get there. Asked for call backs, knew he'd have to go to each contractor's office to. No one calls cops back.

Looked up the contractors' addresses and plotted a route for the afternoon. This had priority over the backgrounds checks on Christian Love and his two deacons; chasing from site to site would be a waste of time. Rick decided to fill the morning with background searches, eat the sandwich and potato salad Shirley packed for him, then make the rounds of the contractors in the afternoon.

He didn't like background checks. He'd pore over minute pieces of evidence and obscure report terms like a twelve-year-old with a Victoria's Secret catalog. The science and logic—the certainty—of it fascinated him. If the evidence said you were there, you were there. Period. It didn't matter if you said you'd never been there. It didn't matter if you swore an oath on your children's heads. If the evidence said a right-handed man six feet tall who weighed between one-seventy and one-eighty-five and had size eleven feet was there at the time in question and you were a right-handed man six feet tall who weighed between one-seventy and one-eighty-five and had size eleven feet *and* your fingerprints were found there—well, it didn't matter *when* you said you'd left the prints. You had some 'splaining to do.

Computer records didn't sing to him. Ben Dougherty could start a search, know where to look next, split the screen to look at two records side-by-side and tell in an instant which piece didn't belong. Even Grabek said Dougherty was a savant. Rick wished Doc had drawn this gig, knew Dougherty had people and interrogative skills Rick lacked. So Doc worked the field while Rick did the background checks.

Started with Christian Love. Not his real name; no big surprise. Clean, with a habit of hiring associates with law enforcement issues in their past. Rick understood how a preacher would be interested in second chances. He also knew how many ways that could come back to bite him.

Cassius Abernathy and Sylvester Lewis had much more interesting histories.

CHAPTER 20

Doc didn't argue with Stush about his assignment because he tried to avoid arguing with people who were right. Grabek knew people in Pittsburgh and elsewhere who also knew people who might be able to get a lead on the shooters. Doc knew a fed who told him things when he felt like it and could extort a favor, and damn little then.

Neuschwander needed to be doing what he was doing, too. Once the evidence had been collected and sent to the lab, Doc could run background checks and canvass the contractors at least as well. Better, in some ways. Doc more comfortable with computer searches, and knew how to lean on a contractor. Problem was, someone had to keep up with the other pending cases, and Neuschwander didn't multi-task well. Doc could keep more balls in the air than anyone else on the force. Between growing up in Penns River and working patrol before he became a detective, he knew—or was known by—as many people in town as all the other cops put together.

He entered Novotny Salvage at eight-thirty. Frank Novotny sat behind a gunmetal gray desk. Mid-sixties, thermal undershirt under a flannel with sleeves rolled halfway up the forearm. Strands of gray hair in need of a trim wandered from under a *Novotny Salvage and Recycling* baseball cap. Steam wafted from a Steelers mug. A short cigar burned in an ashtray.

"Cheese it, the cops," Frank said, looking at the opening door. Then the greeting he couldn't resist. "Ehhhh, what's up, Doc?"

"How long you known me, Frank?"

"I don't know. Since before you left for the army. Twenty years?"

"And that's the best you can come up with? Every fucking time you see me."

"You want comedy, go down the Benedum. I hear that guy you like's coming to town. What's his name? Gaffigan? I quit listening to comics when Dangerfield died."

"Too expensive. I'll rent the DVD when it comes out. What can you tell me about storm sewer grates?"

"This a trick question? They cover the storm sewer so people don't fall in."

"That's what they're supposed to do. Problem is, fifteen of them aren't."

"What the hell are they doing, then?"

"That's why I'm here. They're missing."

"Why are you telling me?"

Doc gave disappointed. "Scrap metal, Frankie. People steal them for scrap metal. And, since you are the premier scrap metal dealer in the valley, I have to think they at least stopped by."

Frank sipped coffee, rocked back. "I haven't seen anything like a grate."

"So you wouldn't mind if we had a uniform walk around the lot and look for them."

"No, but listen to one thing first. I wouldn't take a grate, but I don't personally check everything comes in here. Johnny McConnell does a lot of stuff. Johnny's a nice kid, hard worker, but he's dumb as a rusty flagpole."

"So if an officer walked the lot and found grates stamped *Penns River Public Works*, them being here would be an honest mistake." More like a miracle, since Penns River sewer grates had no such markings.

"What I'm saying is, I can't swear we don't have any. I don't think we do. You want to have a look around, go ahead. You find anything, we'll see if Johnny can remember who brought it in."

"Thanks, Frank. You're a prince."

"That all?"

"Now that you mention it, you haven't seen an increase in copper plumbing, have you? Seems half a dozen empty houses with *For Sale* signs have had the copper ripped out the past few weeks. Foreclosures, mostly. Now, I know you're a legitimate market for copper tubing, and it's impossible to tell where it came from. Still, has someone who's not usually a customer been in a lot lately?" No answer. "Or a regular seem to be doing a lot more demo work than usual?" No answer. "Probably not. If you think of anyone, though, it might help to negate an honest mistake or two on storm sewer grates. Just saying."

Patrol Officer Sean Sisler met Doc at a large split-level over the hill from Doc's parents. Sisler's holster strap hung open. Backing up routine patrol calls not part of Doc's portfolio. Sisler still new, so Stush had sent Doc by.

"What do we have?" Doc said.

"Might be a rabid coon."

"What makes you think so?"

"Woman lives here had her kids outside, saw it come in from the fields there. She thought it was weird, seeing one in the daytime, and kept an eye on it. Says when it got about fifty or sixty feet away it started snarling and barking at them."

"It barked at them?"

"I asked. She said she couldn't think of any other way to describe it."

"What'd she do?"

"Hustled the kids inside. Said it chased them right up to the deck."

"Anyone bit or scratched?"

"Uh-uh. They're all scared shitless, though."

"You call Animal Control?"

"It's his day off." Penns River Department of Animal Control consisted of Ron Webster and voice mail.

"Shit. I hate fucking with rabid animals. You see it?"

Sisler shook his head. "I was coming for the field glasses when you pulled up."

Doc drew his sidearm. "They have any pets?"

"No," Sisler said over the open trunk lid.

"Good. Shoot anything with four legs. This bastard won't be afraid of you." Doc afraid enough for everyone and everything involved.

Sisler popped up with the glasses. "Let's take a look."

They took their time getting around the house. Four stairs up to the deck and Sisler panned the rolling terrain while Doc kept an eye closer in case the animal had doubled back.

"There!" Sisler said. "I got him."

"Where?"

Sisler crouched on the same line of sight. "Look straight

over my head. There's a piece of deadfall leaning against another tree. Makes like an A without the crosspiece. About fifty yards in front of it. He'd walk right under the arch if he could walk a straight line."

It took Doc a few seconds, until the raccoon crested a small rise. "Jesus Christ. Look at that thing."

"Yeah. He's not long for this world. He'll bite anything he can catch, and he'll chase anything he sees."

"How far do you make him?" Doc said. "Two hundred yards?"

"At least two-fifty. Another fifty to the tree line."

"I don't think we can get there in time to shoot him."

"Unless he sees us and turns to fight," Sisler said.

"Yeah. Great."

Sisler handed Doc the field glasses. "Don't lose him. I'll be right back."

"Where are you going?"

Sisler said, "Don't lose him," and disappeared around the house.

Doc watched the coon stagger toward the trees, stopping to snap at imaginary threats. The head jerked hard enough to throw it off stride a couple of times before it disappeared into a depression.

"You got him?" Sisler had the AR-15 rifle from the patrol car.

"Pretty much the same line, in a little swale right now."

"Find him before he gets to the woods." Sisler locked and loaded, pulled the charging handle.

Doc kept panning. "You gonna shoot him from here?"

"If he shows himself. You don't find him in ten or fifteen seconds, though, we're going to have to hunt him. No telling where he'll come out, he stays in that little hollow."

Doc wanted to hunt a rabid animal not as much as he wanted to face a man with a gun, the man at least having some thought of self-preservation. Contemplated talking Sisler out of it, knew he couldn't. Both ways: the wrong thing to do, and Sisler looked like he'd go alone.

"There!" Doc said. Hunched down like Sisler had done for him. "Take my line. Ten, maybe fifteen yards from the tree line."

Sisler in no hurry. "I see him. Don't move. When I say, don't breathe."

"You can get him from here?"

"Shhh." Doc felt Sisler still as ice at his back. Sisler took a full breath, said, "Don't breathe." Exhaled, fired at the bottom of the breath. The coon hopped straight into the air. Landed on its back, twitching.

"Goddamn, Sisler. That's nice shooting."

"Shhhh. Stand perfectly still." Sisler shot again. The coon stopped twitching.

Doc stood. "Where'd you learn to shoot?"

"Sniper school."

"Army?"

Sisler gave a dismissive look. "The Crotch, man. *Hoo-rah.*"

CHAPTER 21

Doc and Sisler in Fat Jimmy's Tavern. Doc drank Miller Genuine Draft. Sisler a shot of Jack Daniels and a Rolling Rock. They'd been off shift twenty minutes. "Sniper school, huh?" Doc said. "No fucking way I could've shot something the size of a coon from over three hundred yards, and I qualified as expert. You must be hell in deer season."

Sisler threw back the shot. "Took me three years to get one. I could shoot, even when I was a kid. Couldn't hunt for shit. Got one every year since I was seventeen, except for the year I got deployed. You like venison? I dropped a nice ten-point last year."

"You keep it. It's a limited supply thing. Never know when you'll get more."

Sisler waved him away. "I'll get more the week after Thanksgiving. No, really. I'm an arrogant SOB. Shot one with a pistol a few years ago."

"You have one of those long barrels with a scope?"

"I'm not going to drink with you if you're going to insult me," Sisler said. "I've shot with those guys. Special sights, with radar and satellite target acquisition and shit. Practically have rifle barrels on the gun, building firing positions before they'll shoot. I shot mine with a six-inch Smith and Wesson .44 from a Weaver stance. Sixty-three yards." Sisler paused to drink the last of his Rolling Rock. "I like the challenge, pass up clear shots early in the week if the deer doesn't meet my standards." Smiled. "Wait till Thursday or Friday before I'll shoot just anything. I'll bring you in some jerky tomorrow. You hunt?"

"Never got into it," Doc said. "I used to track them when I was younger. Go out off-season and see how close I could get. Stopped one day when I was in those same woods we were by today and found a streaming pile of bear shit." Chuckled, sipped his beer. "The idea of killing a deer never appealed to me. No offense. My dad used to hunt, brought home a buck more often than not. I have no problem eating what someone kills. I think I got turned off watching cable shows of these assholes killing something just to kill it, hang the head off the wall."

"Well, I do keep the heads," Sisler said. "Eat everything I can, though. Know a guy in St. Mary's who butchers them for me, makes sausage and jerky. Cuts some steaks and makes ground meat of the rest. Probably more expensive than buying beef in the store, but it's good eating, and I accomplished something. I pace myself so I run out the week before Thanksgiving. Gives me incentive for the week after."

Doc pointed to Sisler's glasses, raised an eyebrow. Sisler passed a hand over the shot glass, tipped the Pilsner and nodded. Doc caught Jimmy's attention, gestured. Jimmy nodded and made no other motion to imply he'd got the message.

"You said sniper school in the Corps." Doc said. Sisler nodded. "You do any work in Iraq or Afghanistan?"

"Nope. First week in Afghanistan, still getting acclimated, we took a mortar attack. I was scrambling to a firing position with my spotter and fell. Broke my collarbone. It healed funny and I was never the same shot after."

Doc raised an eyebrow. "Really," Sisler said. Showed Doc a fist. "Used to be, on the range, fifteen hundred meters and in—" opened the fist, "—poof. After I got hurt it was barely four hundred. Lost the secondary MOS, became kind of the informal sniper for my team. You know, 'Hey, Sis, I think he's over there.' Why I always preferred the sixteen to the M-4. A little better range."

Jimmy waddled over with two fresh beers. Wore a Casey Hampton Steelers replica jersey. Hampton had been a Pro Bowl nose tackle. Jimmy had seventy-five pounds on him.

Sisler reached for his wallet. Doc touched his arm, shook his head. "On me. Thanks for the show today." Handed Jimmy a five. "How's Little Jimmy hanging?"

"Beats the fuck outta me," Jimmy said. "Ain't seen him for a while. I may have to get back on my exercise routine. Problem is, playing with Little Jimmy was my exercise routine. Could be the start of one a them vicious cycles."

"Whoa whoa whoa," Doc said when Jimmy moved to leave. "I have a question before you go."

"You don't want your change?"

"Yeah I want my change. The question's on my mind now and it could be a week or two before you make it back."

Jimmy took his time showing Doc the back of his right hand, then flicked the middle finger up and back. "Is this going to be a fucking snitch question?"

"No. It's an opportunity for you to allow the public-spirited citizen I know is in there to come out. Someone is stealing your tax dollars. You should be outraged."

"All the more I see you work, I have to figure it's you stealing my tax dollars. You never do shit," Jimmy said.

"I'm hurt," Doc said. "Here I am, off the clock, still working a case that's stymied local law enforcement for over a week. That's the dedicated public servant I am, not to mention I'm patronizing your business, allowing you to keep a roof over your—and Little Jimmy's—head. And all you do is give me shit."

"Aw, for fuck's sake. What?"

"We've had some storm sewer grates go missing, and a lot of copper is walking out of empty houses. You get the kind of trade here might be into something like that, no offense. You hear anyone run his mouth lately?"

"You shitting me?" Jimmy said. "People stealing grates outta the road? What kind of low-life motherfucker does a thing like that? Oh, and fuck you, by the way."

"Fuck me?" Doc said. "For what? This time, I mean."

"For saying my...uh...clientele would do something like that. Whyn't you ask them yourself?"

"You want me to?" Doc started to stand.

Jimmy grabbed Doc's shirt, dragged him down. "Jesus Christ, no. I'll keep an ear open. I'm still insulted."

Doc rolled his eyes. Jimmy said, "You only ever ask me to help with boring shit. Sewer grates and plumbing. How come you ain't asking about them five spooks got aced the other day?"

"Do you know anything about it?"

"Well, no, but—"

Doc gave him the hand. "We're like ninety-nine percent sure that's a black thing. Look around." Gestured to include the room full of white men. Standard attire of flannel shirts and blue jeans. Ball caps over hair either cut to the nub or unacquainted with a barber at least six months. Goatees surrounded by three days' worth of not shaving. "Not exactly a target rich environment for intelligence. On the black community, I mean."

Jimmy scanned the room. "I think Phil Herlinger worked on a black guy's roof last summer."

Doc swallowed beer, smiled in Sisler's direction. Had a thought and turned back to Jimmy. "You know if anyone who hangs here is working at Resurrection Mall?"

Jimmy snorted. "Don't you know they only hire niggers down there? Found a way around the unions, don't come looking if you're a white guy."

Doc made a mental note to ask Neuschwander to check into it. Looked at his watch, finished his beer. "I got a place I need to be. Sis, great work today." Sisler tipped his glass in acknowledgement. Doc said, "Jimmy, you get me something on these metal thefts, I might could get the Board of Health to look the other way."

Jimmy kept his middle finger extended until the door closed behind Doc.

CHAPTER 22

Jefferson West opened the door, said, "I thought you might be David. Come on in."

Doc wiped salt off his shoes on the mat, closed the door behind him. "I feel as though I owe you an apology, Mr. West. It's been a while since I've been around."

West nodded toward Doc's usual chair, walked into the kitchen. "You don't owe anybody a thing. I'm the one volunteered to be a foster parent."

Doc sat, spoke up to be heard in the other room. "I did kind of guilt you into it."

West came back to the living room with two Beck's and a pair of frosted glasses. Handed one of each to Doc. Sat in his recliner and poured for himself. "I would of done it sooner or later. Those boys had no one else. What you did for them, to get everything set up, your conscience should be clear. I mean it."

Doc filled his glass, took a sip. "That's nice of you to say. I mean to take more of an interest. It never seems to transfer into actually coming over here." Settled into the chair. "How have you been?"

"Retired more every day. I keep my hand in around the neighborhood, doing odd jobs. Nothing too strenuous."

Doc spent most football Mondays drinking beer and eating chicken wings with West and a few of his friends at Earl's Bar across the river in Creighton. Hadn't seen him since the end of December, six weeks ago. West looked grayer. Thinner in a way suggesting the weight loss had not been his idea. "Been over to Earl's lately?"

"Not so much since football's over. I don't go out at night hardly at all since it got so cold. Old bones don't like it. You'll see."

Doc guessed West to be early sixties. Last winter he'd worked outside every day for a solid week, fixing his and a neighbor's gutters after a freeze split them. Colder this year, true, and West a year older. He'd aged more than that. Doc said, "You see the boys much since their mom got out of county?"

"I see Davis most every day. Spends a couple-three nights a week, when his mother's on the nod. Says he don't like it when she gets like that. Scares him."

"I guess it would. What is he? Ten? Eleven? How long has Imelda been back on the junk?"

"Oh, my." West did a brief calculation. "Since before Thanksgiving, at least. Maybe even Halloween. Tell the truth, I had my doubts early as Labor Day. Maybe she was just chipping then."

"Jeez, Mr. West. I saw you almost every Monday last fall. You should've said something. I'd of gone over."

"That's why I didn't tell you." West sipped his beer. "You their friend, and I know you worry about them, but you'd have to go over there as a cop. It's not a cop situation. I been keeping an eye on them. I'll call you if I think the boys are in any kind of danger."

"You still have the OP in your spare bedroom?" West had set himself up an observation post a year ago. Binoculars and a notebook lay on a chair next to a window with a line-of-sight all the way to the railroad tracks. West copied his observations into a spreadsheet on his computer every day.

"Not so much since you picked up my notes last summer. Been busy, and it do get tedious waiting for people to do things you don't want to see them do.

Doc took a second to reconcile *retired more every day* with *been busy.* "Wilver been around?"

"I don't see so much of him lately." West took a substantial swig.

"You know what he's up to?"

"Can't say for sure."

Doc finished his beer. "Mr. West, I went over there the other day. Imelda looks like she's using regular again. Says she doesn't know when Wilver comes or goes, but she has a new chair, a new television, and a kick-ass espresso maker. I never left the kitchen and spotted at least twenty-five hundred dollars of new stuff, and her clothes weren't raggedy, either. If she's working it has to be minimum wage, and I doubt she has a sugar daddy. So we have a junkie with no obvious means of support who owns a big screen TV and other expensive accessories. She has a teenage son and is evasive when asked to account for his time and whereabouts. What conclusions can we not unreasonably draw from this?"

West finished his beer. "That's why I ain't said nothing to you about this, neither. You'd have to be a cop."

"Illegal activity, yeah. I have to be a cop."

"And this really not a cop situation either."

"How you figure?"

West started to speak, paused. Said, "Another beer?"

Doc did a quick calculation including body weight, time expired, and Fat Jimmy's. "Sure. Thank you." Waited while

West went to the kitchen for the beers and his argument.

"I almost told you a couple times," West handed Doc another ice cold bottle. "Thought about it a lot. Police isn't what's needed there right now."

He saw Doc phrasing a response and hurried on. "I know. I'm pretty sure Wilver's working with some dealer, so he's breaking the law. I know that. I see how things are going here the last year or two. My main worry is those boys. I tell you what I think about Wilver and you start looking around, he's liable to go away. You know him. He's not a bad boy. He goes down to Shuman, gets put in with some true hard cases, what happens to him? What happens to the mother, with no support? It'll all roll down on David, and he the only one blameless here." Neshannock County lacked the resources for its own juvenile detention facility, exported its miscreants to Allegheny County's Shuman Center.

"You know I get some discretion on how hard to land on someone." Doc pondered the available options. "Some."

"You gonna turn him out as a snitch? Cut him a deal? It's hard to put snakes back in the box. You give him a pass and something else turns up, you might have to answer for it. I know you'll man up. I didn't want to put you into a situation where you'd have to."

Both men sipped while Doc considered what to say next. Settled on, "You heard about what happened at Resurrection Mall, right?"

"Sure. Everyone know about that."

"Wilver was there."

"He can't be involved."

"He might've seen something. The security guard—you know Elmer Ford—saw him running hell bent for leather, like he was late for something. This is right before the shooting started. We know the victims were all drug dealers, and they ate lunch there together around one most days. What if Wilver was supposed to meet them? He gets there two minutes sooner, we might have six bodies today. Drug dealing's a risky business, especially for a kid who should've been in school."

"You think he saw something?"

"Don't know. I can't find him."

"You think something happened to him?"

Doc shook his head. "I think he's keeping his head down. As he should be. Here's the problem: if he did see anything, or if the shooters think he saw anything, then everyone involved on this end—me, you, especially Wilver—wants me to find him first."

West ran a hand over his short nap of hair. "Them boys always in the middle of something. Good boys, too. Not their fault. Unlucky as hell."

Doc and West met the boys two years earlier, their mother in county custody. Wilver and David walked away from their foster home to squat in a vacant townhouse next door to West and were there when a murder took place. Doc and West had hidden them as the sole viable witnesses. The plan turned to shit—such plans always do, Penns River was not Hollywood—until fences had been mended and strings pulled to make Jefferson West a legitimate foster parent.

"They are good boys," Doc said. "Even if Wilver is on the brink right now. You have any idea how I can get a handle on him?"

West shook his head. Swallowed. "David real careful not to say anything when I ask. I think he knows, though. Of course, if a trained interrogator was to talk to him..."

Doc chuckled. "It might make a difference. Can you get a hold of David when you need to? It'll go easier if it's you who's looking for him."

"Usually."

"The basketball team plays Gateway tomorrow. JV game starts at six or six-thirty. How about I swing by and pick you guys up around five? We'll get something to eat, watch the games, I'll bring you back, and we'll see what we can pick up. Make sure he knows Wilver is invited, too. I promise not to grill him while we're together, but I can open the door to talk to him later."

"He'll like that. I'll call you soon as I know he can come."

CHAPTER 23

Doc served as Neuschwander's wingman for a visit to Christian Love's office, nine o'clock in the morning. This should have been Neuschwander's party—he found the lead—he asked Doc to take it. Begged him, almost.

"We're taking down the crime scene tape on our way out this morning, Dr. Love," Doc said. "The officer who's been keeping an eye on it will leave then, too. Things will be pretty much back to normal for you."

"Thank you, Detective," Love said. "This is much appreciated. The food court's our primary source of income for the time being. It might as well have been closed since this happened. A few gawkers is all we get. Will we be able to clean up the blood and damage?"

"Once we take down the tape, it's all yours," Doc said. "Do whatever you want."

Love thanked him, then, "I appreciate the courtesy. I doubt it took two of you to tell me this. Is there something else?"

"Yes, sir," Doc said. "Before we get into this, please understand, we have to do background checks on anyone of interest."

"Detective...uh, Grabek? ...made that clear when you were here last. Should I assume you've found something?"

"There are a couple of things we wanted to bring to your attention. Things we weren't aware of, and you may not be.

Rather than waste our time, and possibly place unwarranted suspicion on someone, we're hoping you can address them."

"You say 'unwarranted suspicion.'" Love's eye contact direct, almost challenging. "So you suspect them already?"

"No, sir. We have no suspects at this time. As Detective Grabek said the other day, they're persons of interest. Nothing more."

Love glowered. Well short of the high-intensity glare Grabek got, nothing like what a potential contributor would receive. "I'm listening."

Doc glanced at Neuschwander, busy looking into a corner. Said, "Cassius Abernathy and Sylvester Lewis have both done hard time. Abernathy served nine-and-a-half years of a twenty-year sentence for aggravated assault in Jackson, Michigan—"

"I can save us all some time, Detective. I am well aware both my deacons have been incarcerated, as have almost half the black men in this country. I am proud to say this church is a haven for those who wish to put their lives straight again."

Doc waited until certain Love had finished. "We're not here to cast doubt on your efforts or results. We still need to go over their records in some detail, if only to be sure we're all working with the same information."

"Does this mean you're going to tell me what you know, and I'm expected to fill in any blanks?"

"No, sir. You're free to give us as much or as little information as you want. This is not a formal interview. We know Resurrection Mall is in a less than secure financial position and don't want to do anything to jeopardize the project itself. We also want to be sure you know what we know, in case a situation arises where you want to take proactive measures."

Love increased the intensity of his look fifty percent, made a dismissive hand gesture.

Doc began again. "Abernathy served nine-and-a-half of a twenty-year sentence for—"

"Agg assault," Love said. "You told me already. He did his time at the Cooper Street Correctional Facility in Jackson, Michigan. You told me that, too. He went there for beating a man into a coma over what I believe was a drug debt while he was employed by...Clifton Butler, who was, at the time, the biggest drug dealer in Detroit. Mr. Abernathy's prison record is clean. He was released—" eyes to the ceiling, "—eleven years ago and has had no arrests since then. Are we on the same page now?"

"A few arrests for lesser offenses and held overnight once as a material witness to a homicide, but, as you said, those were before the AA jolt. We're good here. Now, Sylvester Lewis—"

"Deacon Lewis served two years of a six-year sentence for possession with intent to distribute in Menard. That's in Illinois. He violated his parole by using someone else's urine to pass a drug test and served the rest of the six years. He then had the bad timing to shoot a man in the buttocks during one of Chicago's periodic gang crackdowns and was charged—and convicted—of attempted murder. He accepted Jesus as his personal Savior and was paroled about ten years into a twenty-five year sentence. I personally signed the papers to allow him to leave the state and get away from the influences that might bring him down again. His obligation to the State of Illinois expires the year after next. There is no way he would do anything to endanger that."

Doc bided his time, lest Lewis's history had an appendix. "Like Abernathy, a couple of piddly things before the first intent to distribute beef."

"Now you're going to ask me why I didn't tell you this before."

"No, sir," Doc said. "You were under no obligation to say any of this, and you aren't now. I understand why you'd be reluctant. These men are close to you. You trust them. I have enormous respect for your ability to do that, I really do. Please look at it from my side for a minute. These are two men with histories of violence." Doc raised two fingers on each hand to forestall Love's interruption. "Not long lists of violent acts, but serious violent acts all the same. Both of them are a little lucky they don't have murder charges in their files."

"That's unfair. The State of Illinois admitted in Sylvester's parole hearing the attempted murder charge was too much. Gangs were in the news and someone tried to make a career out of him. Neither man had murder on their minds."

"I didn't say they did," Doc said. "Still, Abernathy beat a man unconscious. A small error in judgment, a less robust victim, and someone dies. Same thing if Lewis's aim had been off. Murderous intent or not, someone dies, it's at least manslaughter."

Love's indignation dipped a notch. "That was a long time ago. For both of them."

"Yes, sir, it was. That's why we're here today, paying you a courtesy visit, and neither one of them is in the interview room at the City-County Building. Understand something. The level of violence here the other day, no one just does that. This wasn't some guy who snapped and shot up a mall. This was thought out, and planned, and well executed. That means when we come across two people who might see a way to profit from what happened, and have been known to use violence in the past, we have to look at them. Even if we know they didn't pull the trigger."

"Do you really think anyone associated with Resurrection Mall benefits from this?" Love said. "Whatever problems we had with business and investors before have doubled, at least. People think it's not safe here. I have no good argument for them."

"I agree with you," Doc said. "This was a loser for everyone. That doesn't mean similar mistakes haven't been made. You'll never go broke betting on the shortsightedness of criminals."

Love took a deep breath, held it a second, sighed. The escaping air seemed to take his energy with it. "When does it end? When are these men clear of their past? I've known them both for over ten years. This church wouldn't be where it is today—*I* wouldn't be where I am today—if not for those two men. I have four brothers. Two my mother gave birth to, plus Cassius Abernathy and Sylvester Lewis. Will they ever be more than criminals to you?"

Doc took time to give Love's question the thought it deserved. "Eventually. Probably. Ex-cons who stay clean reach an age where not even cops think of them as suspects."

"There's no forgiveness? You'll hound them until they're too old to be a threat?"

Doc had little time to debate the philosophy of forgiveness, and even less inclination. "Dr. Love, let's get something straight. Forgiveness is your job. I don't care what Abernathy and Lewis did, or didn't do, in their reckless youth. All I care about is how it might help me to find out who shot five people to pieces in your mall the other day. If something had been stolen, I'd look for thieves. Broken windows? I'll look for known vandals. Five shotgun murders? I'm looking—hard—at people not averse to violence. It may not seem fair to you. Maybe it's not. It's the best I have.

"I'm going to catch these guys. For your sake, and for the sake of what Resurrection Mall might mean to this town, I hope Lewis and Abernathy are far away from it. It doesn't matter, though. I take my clearances how they come."

CHAPTER 24

Rodney Simpson saw the detectives go into Love's office and come out. Watched as they walked through the mall like men with someplace else to be. No sooner had he relaxed when he heard his name on Christian Love's voice.

"Rodney, perfect timing, son. Are you busy right now?" Nothing that couldn't wait. "I need you to go to the food court and take down the crime scene tape. Get the floors and tables cleaned up the best you can. See Deacon Lewis for what you need. Oh, and ask him to detail some of the workman to repair the damage you can't clean. Get Jamal to help if you need it. Thank you, son."

Now Rodney was the fucking maid. Mopping floors, cleaning blood off tables. Hired for what he thought was a supervisory position, working at Cassius Abernathy's right hand, passing down orders. Handling the money. Hadn't taken him long to figure out that at Resurrection Mall money ran through the cracks like melting snow on a cheap porch, and Abernathy never let a drop hit the ground. Rodney knew Abernathy's deal within a few weeks, lacked the experience and chops to figure out how he did it.

The plan had been to make himself invaluable. Followed Abernathy everywhere, listened so hard he could quote the man's portions of conversations almost verbatim. Love sometimes called Rodney "Radar" for how well he anticipated the demands on his boss's time. Abernathy showed his appreciation by making Rodney a punk. *I need you to. Pick this up. Drop that off.* Treated like the house nigger while that pale Uncle Tom motherfucker Jamal acted like one, brought more into the high-level councils every day. Well, maybe not an Uncle Tom Uncle Tom, not like in the book, the people Jamal sucking up to being black and all. Whatever the word for niggers who shuffled around black folk like they's white, Jamal was it.

Rodney gathered and disposed of the crime scene tape. Found the mops and brushes and buckets and Pine-Sol on his own. Would not ask Jamal for help with anything unless both his hands cut off, and then only for things he couldn't reach. Let the boy wipe his ass, maybe. Took off his suit coat and tie, rolled up his sleeves. Spread a contractor's bag on the floor to kneel on, keep his suit pants from getting wet and bloody, scooting around like some cripple on a cart he'd seen in an old Eddie Murphy movie, the one his grandmother liked so much.

He missed his grandmother. Never let on like he loved her, always looked forward to knowing a meal would be waiting anytime he came home. She'd fix him something until supper time, after which a full plate of whatever she'd eaten would be in the refrigerator to be microwaved. And pie. Or ice cream, sometimes homemade. Pink mints in a dish on the end table closest to the television. Never seen those mints anyplace else. Grandma had them all the time.

Never stole so much from her she'd miss it. Knew she didn't mind, would have given him the money if she didn't think it would spoil him. Letting him take it her way of making him earn it. Grandma no saint, a grandma before she was forty, raising her second brood until Rodney the only one left. His mama bailed for good one day when he was at school. Why he'd quit going. Nothing good happened there, and bad shit happened at home while he was schooling.

Scrubbed the floor like he wanted to strip the finish. Stopped for a breather, leaning on the brush, felt for a second he might cry, not knowing where it came from. How quiet the house was now. Now the food smells were stale and decay from pizza boxes and take-out wrappers. The landlord said he could stay so long as he kept up the rent. Rodney had no such idea, a shotgun house in Sharpsburg not his idea of a proper place for a young single man with prospects.

Resurrection Mall was his future. Rodney knew it his first week on the job. Like college, where he'd learn the trade, with Abernathy as his mentor. Learn right here and he'd make good money for the rest of his life. Lots of niggers his age would spend his grandma's insurance on cars or bling. Rodney put it back into Resurrection Mall, an investment, like paying tuition. Never told a soul. His business. His chance to learn. If the mall went under, his moment would pass. Lucky to have found a role model like Abernathy, he'd not find another one, and he knew the mall was their connection. Love didn't need him for the church. Rodney had to do what he could to keep Res Mall afloat.

Two hours he scrubbed and cleaned. The floor looked as good as it ever had, the tables wiped down and reorganized. Did his best to hide the pellet marks in a couple grazed by shotgun blasts. Stood and dropped the brush into the bucket. Stretched his shoulders, cracked his neck. Almost ready to put everything away when Jamal came bopping up to him.

"Why didn't you tell me you were cleaning up?" Jamal

talked whiter than any white man Rodney ever met. "I would have helped you." And got credit for volunteering to get himself dirty. Fuck him.

"I got it." Rodney gathered the contractor's bag. Put on his suit coat, hung the tie over his shoulders. "Ain't no thing, getting a little dirty."

"There you boys are." Sylvester Lewis came from the other side, a set of car keys hanging from one finger. "This looks very nice. You boys got it standing tall. Good work."

"It was Rodney, Mr. Lewis," Jamal said. "He was finished by the time I got here."

Lewis looked around the court, then at Rodney. "Well done, sir. Well done. This an unholy mess last time I seen it. Dr. Love be proud of you when I tell him."

Lewis tossed the keys a foot in the air and caught them. "Dr. Love needs someone to take his car to the airport, pick up Woodrow Williams." Both young men's eyes lit up. Woody Williams made successful television shows and movies faster than people could watch them, about black families in everyday situations doing what they could to get by. Lewis looked at his watch. "Damn. Sorry, I owes the fine jar a quarter. Rodney, you been working hard, but..." Lewis scanned Rodney's tie across his shoulders, wet spots on his knees, wrinkled suit coat. "It's later than I thought. No time to get you cleaned up and to the airport before the plane." He flipped the keys to Jamal. "Car's in the usual place."

"The Town Car?"

Lewis nodded. "You got a little more than an hour to get there. Plenty a time, but none for fooling. Go on, now. He on American four-three-one-two. Look for him where they come out from the security area."

The heat spread from Rodney's face down his neck to his shoulders. Lewis said, "I'm sorry, son. Mr. Williams might be looking to make an investment. We got to make an impression and there's no time to get you presentable. I promise I'll make it up to you."

"Ain't no thing."

"We do have something else we need, though. I was going to send Jamal, but...you drive to work today?"

"Every day." Rodney never knew when opportunity would present. He wanted to be ready.

"Dr. Love need you to run down to the Greyhound station, pick up a couple folk on they way in from Cincinnati. Friends of his. Or friends of a friend. Or something. You know where it's at? Downtown off a Penn, by the train station?"

All Rodney could do to say, "Yeah. I know."

"Go ahead and get cleaned up. Stop by the office for some gas and parking money before you go."

Rodney already three steps gone, picking up speed. "That's cool. I'll carry it." These motherfuckers had no idea how much he was carrying. Woody Williams on his way because things had been cleaned up at Res Mall. The corner had been turned. And Rodney going to the Greyhound to pick up some bus-riding bamas.

CHAPTER 25

Daniel Rollison. Retired spook. Former private investigator. Director of Security at Allegheny Casino. A quiet man who enjoyed little, showed it less, and preferred fear to respect. Thought the casino gig would ease him into retirement, negotiated a small piece of the action if he stuck around a few years. Didn't realize he'd be running a daycare center. Still had the intel mindset of ruthless discipline, working now with subordinates who spent most of their day thinking of ways to let their buddies get away with shit while his bosses tried to spend as little money as possible.

One good thing about the Penns River police station this morning: Dougherty wasn't there. Dougherty was good—not as good as he thought, and not in the same league as Rollison—as stiff-backed as anyone Rollison had ever associated with. Not unlike Rollison in that regard, except Rollison himself was not inflexible; he was strong-willed.

At least Stan Napierkowski didn't screw with him. Offered much appreciated coffee—warmer today, almost twenty degrees—engaged in small talk while creaming and sugaring. Rollison enjoyed small talk as much as the Terminator. Like the good Terminator in *T2*, he'd learned to mimic it when necessary.

The Chief's chair creaked as he settled into it. "I got to admit, I wonder sometimes about getting you out for a few beers, listen to some of the stories you must have. I know you can't tell them, and I'll never put you on the spot. I do wonder sometimes."

"It's a lot like being a cop," Rollison said. "Hours and days of boredom, then a few minutes of terror."

"Must be some funny things happen, too, though they're probably not funny at the time."

"Sometimes." The hours and days of boredom like a roller coaster compared with the tedium of waiting for Napierkowski to ask why he'd come, Rollison determined not to bring it up.

Napierkowski sipped his coffee. Stirred it again. Took another taste. It occurred to Rollison the old man might be playing the same game, waiting for him to go first. Rollison had the will. He could sit and not say a word until Napierkowski went home to supper and still be here when the fat bastard came in the next morning. Much of that negated by Napierkowski's home field advantage. He could do what he wanted. Rollison could accomplish nothing else until this was done. Came because Dan Hecker thought he might get better results from the Penns River cops than had Rance Doocy. What Hecker didn't know—and Rollison knew all too well—the only person Penns River cops enjoyed sticking it to more than Hecker was Rollison. Napierkowski wouldn't give him what he asked for, and would delight in wasting as much of Rollison's time as possible not giving it to him. Rollison didn't get dealt losing hands often, recognized one when he drew it. "Chief, we have a problem at the casino I hope you can help us with. I'm here to work it out between two professionals."

"I'm glad you come down here today." Napierkowski in full rube mode. "Saved me a trip up there." Sipped coffee.

Set the mug on the desk. Leveled his eyes with Rollison's. "Your bartenders don't seem to know when someone's been over served. Single car accidents are up almost fifty percent the last few months. So are fender benders and sideswipes. Someone's going to get hurt. What can we do about it?"

"Observing whether a person has had too much to drink isn't a science," Rollison said. "People drink. Sometimes they drink too much. I doubt the percentage of casino customers who leave impaired is any greater than any other drinking establishment in town. We're bigger, so it's more evident."

"It's possible," Napierkowski said. "I don't have statistics on where the drunks come from. Let's say, for the sake of the discussion, it is true. Fact is, because the casino *is* far and away the biggest, uh, drinking establishment in town, you're still the biggest problem. Highest concentration of potential offenders. So you'll get the most attention."

Rollison took longer forming an answer than Napierkowski wanted to wait. "To be fair, Fat Jimmy's probably produces more drunks per capita on an average night than you do. He's down the Flats, though. His customers live there or even farther out. You turn your drunks loose on the main street through the residential and light business part of town. Or they take the bypass like a rabbit with flames coming out its ass. Your drunks are a much higher risk. I don't want you to think I'm busting balls here. I'm trying to do you a favor."

Rollison arched an eyebrow because he knew Napierkowski expected it. "Who has the deepest pockets around here? Some drunk hurts a kid—or, God forbid, kills one—what's he have to lose in a lawsuit? A house with a mortgage? Car with payments due? Maybe a 401(k). Insurance might go a hundred grand, a million if he's lucky. But some jagov blows a point one-eight on Allegheny Casino booze and lawyers will line up to sue your boss's balls off. Hang them on their wall right next to the law school diploma where everyone can see."

Hecker had no more chance of losing such a judgment than of catching AIDS from Hillary Clinton. Attention from the suit itself, the public perception of a rich man getting away with something, coupled with the car thefts, all things the casino could do without.

Publicity, the newest four-letter word in Rollison's vocabulary. Spent his whole life avoiding it the way a cobra does a mongoose. Now he depended on it. Poker is a game of skill, and blackjack can be beat if you bring a team of rocket scientists with you. Craps has an allure of its own: the table, the people, the movement, the *action*. Slots are solitary; the vibe antisocial. Put in a coin. Push the button. Wait. Repeat and repeat and repeat...Something has to get that person to believe watching lights flash is fun and exciting and worth a guaranteed loss over time. Marketing. Advertising. Publicity. People are not going to go somewhere for dubious reward if they're afraid their car will get stolen while they donate money to some rich bastard who let a kid get killed by a driver the fat cat helped liquor up. Rollison had done and sanctioned things in service of the government he wouldn't admit to someone who'd been with him when he did it. Wanted straight scotch and a shower after meetings with the marketing gurus.

"No argument, Chief. The casino wants to at least appear to be a good neighbor." Napierkowski shot him a look. "I level with you, you level with me." Napierkowski sat back, a satisfied look on his face.

"You mentioned to Doocy—who I think is as big a tool as you probably do—something about a valet ticketing system. We both know that won't fly. It's an inconvenience to the customers and too large an expense. I think you floated it as a starting point. Fair enough. I might be able to get them to go along with setting up Breathalyzer stations by the exits. One of our security guys sees someone he has doubts about on his way out, he politely takes him aside and has him blow in the straw. No legal ramifications, the test can be refused without prejudice, and any results can't be used against him. The guy blows point oh-eight or above, we call him a cab."

Napierkowski laced fingers across his gut, tapped his thumbs on it. "What if he's clearly over and refuses the test? Or flunks it and insists on driving?"

"Let's see if I can sell this much first. I get it past my bosses, maybe solutions to your questions will present themselves."

More gut tapping. "Maybe someone could give us a call. You know, under the radar."

"That's asking a lot. I doubt they'd go for it." Rollison pretended to think longer than he did. "Not saying it couldn't be done. Look, I don't like drunks on the road any more than you do. My problem is, what good does a call do? Our guy won't know what car the drunk is driving. How would you know who to stop?"

Tap-tap-tap. Pause. Tap-tap. "If you went that far, I think it would be in the interest of public safety to have some patrol activity in and around the lot. Get a heads up, watch a drunk get his car, follow him until some probable cause for a stop made itself available. That might well put a damper on people roaming the lot looking to drive away in cars didn't belong to them. You think?"

It wasn't much. But it wasn't nothing.

CHAPTER 26

Ted Suskewicz—now officially "Stretcher"—unfolded his eighty inches from under the wheel of his new Buick—paid for, with a receipt—and walked into Acme Used Video. Acme a one-stop shop for victimless crimes. Sports gambling, recreational non-narcotics, phone numbers of women who'd become an intimate associate for one hour or one squirt, whichever came first, no pun intended. Activity Mike Mannarino's "no crime in Penns River" edict allowed, so long as the profile stayed low and The Hook got his taste. Henry Miskinis had expanded into loan sharking, which gave Tommy Vig a case of the ass. Penns River his territory, though he hadn't been there for other than social business in years.

Uncle Stretch more than a little perturbed when Vig told him Miskinis was the offender. Stretch collected from Henry every week, never heard of a shylock operation. This made Stretch look bad. He would have taken care of Miskinis himself, remembered he'd been told to let Ted cut his teeth. They made the rounds once as a team. ("This is Stretcher Suskewicz. Talking to him's the same as talking to me, and you know who talking to me is the same as.") The standard response: Sure, Stretch, no problem, you want some coffee, a beer, a shot, a sandwich, couple a shirts, sneakers? You got a dog, I got fifty pound of Purina in the back. Ted asked his uncle to let him take his shot.

Miskinis sat on a stool behind a glass counter, watching

Maury Povich on a nineteen-inch television. VHS tapes and DVDs covered three walls in no apparent order. An open doorway at Henry's right led to a back room. A sign over the threshold read *18 and up only.*

Ted stood where a customer would to pay. Henry ignored him, engrossed in the travails of a woman whose husband had slept with her boyfriend's sister and daughter while the boyfriend had something going on with the woman's mother.

Ted tired of waiting, tapped on the glass counter. "Hey, uh, Henry, is it? You got something for me?"

Henry's eyes didn't even flicker from the screen. "Adult section's in back."

"I'm not a customer," Ted said. "I'm here for the envelope."

Henry looked up for a second, then back to Maury. "Where's Stretch?"

"He brought me around last week, remember? This is my route now."

"Commercial's almost on. Give me a minute." Ted gave him four, then Henry stood up. "Goofy goddamn bitches. Like dogs in heat." Opened a drawer under a counter set into the back wall. Took out a manila envelope, folded over and held tight with a rubber band. "Here you go."

Ted made a show of counting the money. "There's only five hundred here."

"Five hundred's my kick."

"Not anymore." Ted had his speech planned. Rehearsed it in the car half a dozen times. "Five hundred *was* the kick. When this—" looked with disdain at the racks of videos, "— was all you had. Now you're making loans. Puts you in a different tax bracket."

"I make book here," Miskinis said. "I always have some paper out."

"It's one thing to carry people who owe the book, charge a few points for your trouble. It's something else to put money on the street unrelated to what they call your core business."

"It's all the same," Miskinis said. "Loans is loans."

"That's your opinion."

"Your opinion's different?"

Something not right here. Miskinis had to know someone else would be in if Ted came back with a light envelope. Miskinis didn't seem to care. "You know it's not my opinion we're talking about."

"You think I give a fuck about your opinion, Junior? I've been running the same business twenty-six years, and the kick is five hundred. You want more, you can kiss my Lithuanian ass." Turned back to the television. "Tell your story walking. My show's coming back on."

Ted thought about busting the place up, get Miskinis's attention. It felt off. Maybe Miskinis was testing him. Or Mannarino. Maybe even his uncle. On the other hand, maybe Miskinis had someone behind him no one knew about. The police, maybe. Shit, feds, even. He thought about pushing it, didn't know what he'd do if Miskinis told him to fuck off. Knew better than to get into a situation before he had an exit strategy.

Stealing cars did have its benefits. They never talked back.

CHAPTER 27

Penns River won the JV game in overtime, fifty-one to forty-nine, when a Gateway three-pointer at the buzzer hit the back of the rim. Doc and David Faison at the concession stand for hot dogs and Cokes not ninety minutes after David put the hurt on an Arby's Super Roast Beef sandwich, large curly fries. Large Mountain Dew, a chocolate chip cookie, and a chocolate shake to drink in the car on the way to the gym. Kid eleven years old, five feet tall, weighed seventy-five pounds—at most—clothed and soaking wet. Doc didn't imagine too many junkie mothers had fat kids. David couldn't depend on a similar feed anytime soon, despite Jefferson West's best efforts.

West begged off when Doc came by. Said he'd slipped on a ladder; sitting in roll-out gymnasium bleachers no way to rest an old back. Hard to bullshit a cop, and West lacked the gift. Doc picked the basketball games because he knew David lived for them, and West enjoyed the atmosphere, feeding off the boy's enthusiasm. This kept up, he'd have to ask about the man's health, after all.

"This kid Cheatham had twenty-eight last week against East Allegheny." Once West told him about Doc's invitation, David ditched his homework to find everything he could about Penns River's opponent. "They don't rebound for shit, though." Doc looked at him through eye slits. "Sorry. They get outrebounded every game. We double-team Cheatham, we should win."

"Should be no problem, if our varsity team has as much size on them as the JVs did," Doc said. "He can't make every shot, and he can't beat us by himself if they can't get him the ball."

"They plays good D, though," David said. "No one scored fifty points off them the last five games."

The first half was a grind. Cheatham was held to eight points. Penns River couldn't throw the ball into the ocean if they stood on the beach, trailed nineteen-eighteen at the half.

David and Doc stayed in the bleachers for halftime. "Too bad Wilver couldn't come," Doc said. "He'd enjoy this."

He didn't have to look to sense David trying to shrink himself. "Yeah, he pretty busy now."

"School?"

"Yeah, school. School keeping him real busy lately."

Doc let it alone a few seconds, then, "He working anywhere?"

"Yeah, he...well, part-time and all. Nothing regular. Picking up a little here and there."

They sat amid the shifting crowd. Students waving and yelling to friends. People picking their way back to seats. Doc watched out of the corner of his eye while David stared at the mid-court circle as though playing a video game on it.

The second half a different game. Shots fell for both teams, negating some of Penns River's rebounding advantage, and the Pilots eked out a fifty-one to forty-seven win.

In the car, Doc waited until the heater warmed them both. "I need to talk to Wilver, David. The sooner the better." David looked out the window. "He's not in trouble, and I think I can keep him from being in trouble, but I really need to talk to him. He doesn't have to come to me. I can bump into him somewhere, away from who he runs with. No one will know he talked to a cop. I'm not going to ask him to snitch, but I really, really need to talk to him."

David's voice carried tears. "He didn't see nothing. He told me."

"So you know he was at Resurrection Mall that day. When the dealers got shot."

"Yeah, I know. He didn't see nothing. I swear. He talk to you and someone find out, they think he snitched."

"Calm down," Doc said. "I can take care of that. What's important is, people saw him. There's nothing to keep the guys who did the shooting from finding out someone recognized him. He's not really safe until they're put away where they can't hurt him."

David fussed under the seatbelt. Sniffed back a sob. "David," Doc said. "You won't be helping me. You'll be helping him."

"He don't stay with us at night no more. I really don't know where he go."

"How often do you see him?"

"Every day. He either see me on the way home from school or at home. Sometime Mr. West's."

"Next time you see him, tell him to get in touch with me. He can call, or you can, or Mr. West. Tell him I'll meet him wherever and whenever he wants. He can set it up so he's comfortable no one knows. Tell him what I told you: people know he was there, and we can't afford for the wrong people to hear about it. I can fix that."

"You sure? You promise?"

Doc took a beat. Whatever happened to Wilver, the trust he'd established with David over the past two years couldn't be jeopardized. "I promise I'll do everything I can." Hurried on before David could say anything. "What I'm sure of— what I *know*—is I can do more to help him than anyone else, and the sooner I can talk to him, the more I can help."

CHAPTER 28

Doc home not twenty minutes when the doorbell rang. Shook it twice, zipped, flushed. Washed his hands and opened the door to find Special Agent Ray Keaton. Keaton eased past and walked to the kitchen. Placed a bag with a small grease stain on the table and opened the refrigerator door.

"Come in." Doc closed the door.

Keaton spoke with his head in the refrigerator. "I know you're not out of beer, Dougherty. Do I have to bring the wings *and* the beer?"

Doc moved a couple of things, took a bottle of Sam Adams and a can of Budweiser. Opened the Sam, handed the Bud to Keaton. "I don't need any wings. I've already eaten."

"No one *needs* chicken wings." Keaton stared at the can in his hand. "Seriously?"

"My uncle came over last week. He doesn't like what I drink, so he brought his own six-pack. One was left."

Keaton gestured toward Doc's Sam Adams. "I bring you these allegedly legendary wings from that place across the way you love—what's it called, the Edgecliff?—and I get the Bud?"

"It's the King of Beers." Doc took a deep swig. "I settled for brewer, patriot. Besides, like I said, I'm not hungry."

Keaton stared at the less than full beer in Doc's hand. Opened the Bud. "You gonna offer me a seat?"

"I haven't so far, and I've had every opportunity."

Keaton snorted, shook his head. "You know you're supposed to call a doctor after it lasts four hours, right?" Pulled out a chair and sat. Opened the bag of wings, pulled one apart, took a bite. Looked around while chewing. Reached back to the kitchen counter to tear a paper towel from a roll. Swallowed, sipped his beer, made a disapproving face. "Don't you want to know why I'm here?"

Doc sat, took a wing. "Could I stop you telling me even if I wanted to?"

"How's your case going?"

"Which one?"

Keaton's expression showed what he thought of Doc's answer. "The dealers who got clipped at Resurrection Mall. You know, the case that has this—how'd they put it on *Dateline?*—'Forgotten little town on the banks of the Allegheny' in the news again this year."

Doc thought about giving the usual bullshit. Gnawed on the wing more for something to do than out of hunger. Not in the mood for bullshit, regardless of which direction it traveled. "We're nowhere. Talked to the families, talked to people at the scene, ran backgrounds on anyone we think might have something to gain. The only guy we know of who might be able to identify someone is in the wind. Scared shitless, I expect. We're pretty sure the shooters are from out of town, maybe even out of state, so our usual local sources aren't much help. Grabek's beating the bushes with Pittsburgh. So far, nothing. Which means we're nowhere."

"Thinking the shooters might be from out of state." A growing pile of bones showed Keaton's appreciation of Edgecliff wings. "Did you ask your uncle for help?"

"As a matter of fact, we did."

"And?"

"Our uncle told us to go pound salt. As usual. Said he'd be happy to look into specific individuals, maybe call the marshals if someone had a fugitive warrant out. Until we had suspects, he had no jurisdiction."

Keaton broke two bones apart, pulled off the meat with his teeth. "That might be the best part about working for Uncle. We get to decide when we have jurisdiction. Does wonders for the stats."

He finished the wing and picked up another, delaying what Doc hoped would be a more substantial response. Doc wanted to go to bed. Keaton appeared to want to eat eleven wings out of the dozen. Ate two more while Doc nursed his beer, neither man speaking. Keaton wiggled the empty can of Bud, raised his eyebrows. Doc pointed to the refrigerator. Keaton opened the door, rooted around. Came out with a Sam Adams, gave Doc a dirty look. Doc said, "I figured an investigator who couldn't find a good beer in a refrigerator full of it didn't deserve one."

"Two beers do not fill a refrigerator."

"You still missed them."

"They were behind that bag of—what is that a bag of?"

"Leftovers from my mother's Sunday dinner."

"Shit. What's in there?" Keaton turned toward the refrigerator.

"Sit your ass down. That's tomorrow's supper."

"What time?" Doc flipped him off.

"Fine." Keaton took another wing from the bag. "These wings will be plenty. You sure you don't want another one?"

"Not so much I'll risk losing a finger."

"Smart ass." Keaton tossed a wing Doc's direction. Talked as he chewed. "A couple of nights ago some small-time loser walked into a bar in Homewood and started throwing money around and running his mouth. People who know him said he's strictly nickels and dimes. Now he has cash, and he made sure every broad in the joint knew it."

"What do I care about some Pittsburgh knucklehead?"

"Someone asked how he's so flush all of a sudden. He said he had a score up the river someplace. The biggest thing I heard of the past week is this cluster fuck you got here."

Doc gave away nothing. "This guy have a name?"

"Sort of. Keep in mind, this is a crowded bar, my source is getting this secondhand from a guy who didn't know this yo personally. Thinks it's one of those Lee names."

"The guy's Asian?"

"No, not Asian. You know, LeRon or LeBron or LeJuan or something like that. Place is called The Stop, down on Frankstown. Pretty much of a shithole, from what I hear, but there's a lot of action there."

"Does your...source know if this LeRon or LeBron or LeJuan is a regular there?"

"From what I hear, he seemed to know a lot of people, so it didn't sound like the first time he'd been in."

"My partner's working downtown since it happened," Doc said. "I'll have him check it out. The Stop, you said?"

"Yeah. On Fransktown. LeRon or LeBron or LeJuan. You want to write any of this down?"

"No need. Big time federal agent comes to my house—"

"Special Agent."

"...and lets me watch him eat chicken wings while he drinks my beer, I'll remember everything he says."

Keaton rolled the bag with the bare bones into a ball, tossed it in the trash. "You ever wonder why I go out of my way to help you? I know I do." Took a final swig and set the dead soldier on the table. "You're out of beer. This time I'm sure."

CHAPTER 29

Doc didn't start the next day any earlier than usual. Call Grabek at eight, he'd still wake him. Any earlier and the lazy prick even money not to answer the phone. Almost dropped his coffee and doughnut when he saw Willie already in the office.

"I'm glad you're here." Doc said, swallowed a mouthful. "You'll never guess who came to see me last night."

"Sally Gwinn's engaged, so you missed your chance with her," Grabek said. "It couldn't have been the Widmer broad, or you'd be dead. I give up."

"Our normally estranged uncle."

Not even Grabek could remain blasé about that. "Your pet fed made an appearance? What's his name again?"

Only Doc and Stush knew Keaton's name. The more people knew, the better the chances it would slip out. It slipped out, Keaton's days of talking out of school to small town cops were over, unless he made new friends in Alaska.

"He says a mysterious source in Pittsburgh told him some small-timer named LeBron or LeJuan or LaRon or something was in a bar on Frankstown Road a couple of nights ago." Doc tasted his coffee. Too hot.

"It's DaRon," Grabek said. "DaRon Turner."

The doughnut didn't make it as far as Doc's mouth. "You knew?"

"Found out yesterday afternoon."

"Why didn't you call me?"

"It was getting late and I didn't want to interrupt you running down a hot sewer grate lead. Thought I'd come in and tell you in person before your day got revved up."

"So Penns River developed a lead without him. He'll be disappointed," Doc said, his own adequate for both of them. Rare to have a chance to get one over on Grabek. Getting shot down this way almost like having the hottest girl in college invite you up to her room for coffee and getting only coffee.

"I'd bet you twenty he knew, if I had a way to prove it," Grabek said. "Even give you five-to-one he heard the word out and saw a chance to look like a mensch without giving anything away."

"You have a chance to find out anything on Turner?"

"Not much," Grabek said. "Name, address, what he drives, criminal record, who he hangs with and where he hangs with them. It's a start."

Doc tested his coffee again. Still too hot, he drank some anyway to take his mind off how bad Grabek was punking him. "You planning to share? You know, before that smug grin wraps its way completely around your head and your brain falls into your neck."

Grabek smiled at last. "DaRon Turner is twenty-nine years old. Lives in the Hill District. I know, big surprise. Drives a Malibu that isn't as sweet a ride as he thinks it is, but still isn't bad. Half a dozen arrests, two convictions, one suspended sentence, one probation. All piddly-assed stuff. Two for possession of reefer, a D and D, reckless driving, assault, uttering—"

"Uttering?" Doc said.

"You know, knowingly using a forged document to deceive—"

"I *know* what it means. What did he do to get charged?"

"The way I hear it, he was on the fringe of a fight a couple of cops were breaking up. Refused to leave after several requests and one cop got the red ass and decided to take him in. Recognized his phony ID and hung an uttering on him. I don't know, maybe the cop was going to night school and just learned about it. However it went down, someone in Zone Two must've liked it, so the charge stuck."

"The two convictions?"

"Pled out on both controlled substance beefs. Nothing else went to court."

"Not even the assault?"

"Witness recanted and the victim dropped the charge." Grabek's photographic memory. Read the sheet once and would never have to look at it again. Described the scene of his first homicide in such detail, twenty-three years later, Doc had a dream about it as though it had happened to him.

"Doesn't sound like much of a record to graduate to five shotgun murders." Doc said.

"It doesn't, does it? What makes Turner interesting is, he recently started running with a hard case named Darcy Rosewood. This Rosewood has nothing like shotgun killing on his resume, either, but a couple guys I talked to said it wouldn't surprise them to hear he'd stepped up his game."

"Anything going on with Rosewood?"

"Don't know. I thought you might want to come downtown with me to see can we round up Turner and brace him. If Rosewood's name spills out, we'll look for him, too. I know it's not much, but we're nowhere on this. Shake the tree a little."

Grabek should have been a walnut farmer, he loved to shake trees so much. Doc had nothing better. "Sounds like a plan. You want to drive, or should I?"

Grabek swung his feet back to the floor. "Let's take two cars. I don't want to have to come all the way back here to turn around and drive home." Grabek lived in Ross Township, forty-five minutes in no traffic, a bitch when 28 was under construction, which was most of the time. Threatened to move at least once a week, which put him north of a hundred so far, with never a call to a real estate agent.

Doc stopped short of the door, turned to look at him. "Why didn't you call and ask me to meet you down there instead of coming all this way?"

"I wanted to see the look on your face when I told you," Grabek said. "Knowing you thought I been jacking off all week."

Doc's opinion unchanged. Grabek knew enough cops in Pittsburgh to fall into the Turner lead between strokes. "Where do you want me to meet you?"

"Zone Five. You know where it is?"

"Washington Boulevard, up by the tennis courts."

"My buddy will meet us there in about an hour."

"You taking 28?"

Grabek nodded. "No point slogging our way through Oakmont and Verona this time of day. I'll meet you in the lot. I want to see Stush for a minute."

Outside, Doc pulled the city car next to Grabek's cop style, driver's window-to-driver's window. "Tell me the truth. Why did you come out here today? I know you. No way watching my reaction was worth the drive."

"Stush said he wanted to see me in the station by the end of the week. *Proof of life* I think he called it," Grabek said. "That doesn't mean the look on your face wouldn't have been worth it all by itself."

CHAPTER 30

Donald Bieniemy looked more like a high school social studies teacher who doubled as the football coach than a cop, except for the knife scar that ran from outside his right eyebrow to below the ear. Average height, barrel chest, waist about to slip over his belt. Sleeves rolled halfway up his forearm, with short, nappy, receding hair.

"Donnie Bee." Grabek extended a hand.

"The Black Polack. In the flesh." Bieniemy took the hand and pulled Grabek close for a back slap hug.

"The Black Polack?" Doc said.

"Oh, yeah," Bieniemy said. "This pierogi grinder here could talk a brother into confessing to shit he didn't even know had happened, forget whether he done it or not. Talk shit to a black man like he in his head, living the same life. Give the boy credit, he never took anyone down for something he knew they didn't do—not so far as I know—but he sure got his share of cooperating statements from brothers who thought he would if they didn't. Ain't no one played at feeling a brother's pain—black or white—like the Black Polack."

"I'm not like that anymore," Grabek said. *Goddamn right*, Doc thought. "My conscience bothered me."

The day speeding by too fast for Doc. First Grabek knew about DaRon Turner. In quick succession, he learned Grabek not had a black friend and a conscience. Next he'd be expected to believe Grabek had some superhero power, like invisibility or the ability to turn himself into beer.

Grabek and Bieniemy bullshitted around for half an hour, talking about people Doc didn't know and cases he'd never heard of. Thirty seconds short of him screaming to get on with it, Grabek said, "Do you have anything on this Rosewood?"

"A bad actor all around," Bieniemy said. "Stick-up man and hired muscle. We think he pistol whipped a 7-Eleven clerk in October because he didn't like the guy's attitude. Dude was already getting robbed, and Rosewood hammered him for...not kissing enough ass, I guess. Fucked him up pretty good. We don't know of him doing any hits, but I wouldn't put it past him."

"Even something as dramatic as the Res Mall job?" Doc said.

Bieniemy rubbed his jaw, a finger lingering at the base of his scar. "That is a jump. Thing is, best information we have right now is DaRon Turner was either involved, or had something to do with your situation. I don't see any way Turner steps up from being a knucklehead to the big time without a mentor or something. Rosewood makes more sense."

"Maybe having a partner egged them on," Grabek said.

"Or he got a hold of some Columbian courage," Bieniemy said.

"Rosewood a user?" Doc said.

"We have suspicions. He's irrationally mean sometimes, like with that 7-Eleven clerk. He's also paranoid, which is good for him because we *are* after his ass."

"Any charges on him?" Doc said.

"No, or we'd have him. He don't make it a secret where he hangs. His name comes up all the damn time, like he some kind a Keyser Söze criminal mastermind. Nice to take a piece of shit like him down before he develop a following, know what I'm saying?"

"So Turner's our direct connection," Grabek said. "Rosewood maybe a step beyond. How do we get to Turner?"

"We know he hangs at The Spot over on Frankstown," Doc said. "We could look for him there."

"Uh-uh," Bieniemy said. "Both of you stick out. He'd hear two Penns River cops looking for him before you had the car locked coming in. If he's your man, you'd never see him again."

"You got a phone number?" Grabek said.

"Landline for the address."

"That's not where people who are looking for him call. What about a cell?"

Bieniemy smiled, showed a dead tooth on the right side. "The Mad Doctor making an appearance?" Grabek's schemes, infamous in Penns River, appeared to be more popular in Pittsburgh. Maybe he did used to be better than Doc had seen or gave him credit for.

"Hear me out," Grabek said. "We hit him up on his cell, which makes it more likely to be business and has the added advantage of us not having to wait until he's home to get him. We'll call him like there's follow-up work in Penns River. If he agrees, then he had to be involved in some way."

"Best be me who calls him," Bieniemy said. "Both of you sound as much like white cops as you look."

"Assuming we can get a cell number for him," Doc said.

"I been thinking about that," Bieniemy said. "Friend of

mine worked a GTA rip a few months ago. They pulled the DNRs on a suspect and ran the names through a reverse directory. Part of me wants to say Turner's name might have been one of those came up. Let me check with the detective, see what I can find."

"Vic Cresson still working Grand Theft?" Grabek said.

"Sure is. You know Vic?"

"Hell, yeah. We go way back. He coulda been the best car thief around if he wanted to." Turned to Doc. "This guy can open your car with a slim jim fast as you can do it with the remote entry fob. He's a fucking savant."

"Why he's working stolen cars. We ain't found a crook knows more about stealing cars than Vic. Could of made some real money, he weren't so goddamn honest and shit." Bieniemy looked at is watch. "You two get some lunch. See a movie, maybe. Come back around two. I should have something for you by then."

The two Penns River cops walked into the Zone Five bullpen at one-forty-eight. Bieniemy held up a slip of paper.

"DaRon Turner's cell number," he said. "Step into my office and we'll give him a call."

Bieniemy sat at his desk, directed Doc and Grabek to an adjacent cube. "Press whatever button comes on when I pick up."

"You're not worried he might recognize the station number?" Doc said.

Bieniemy shook his head. "We got a Google Voice thing rigged up to spoof a seven-two-four number." Penns River's area code.

Doc made a mental note to ask how they did that and lifted his phone's receiver. Bieniemy picked up, Doc pressed a button, and the tones of Turner's number came across the line.

Turner answered after the third ring. "What up?"

"DaRon Turner?" Bieniemy said.

"Yeah. Who this?"

"I'm not going to say over the phone. We did a little business last week up in Penns River. I'm sure you remember."

"I remember. Why ain't you call Darcy like before? He the one put everything together." The three cops made eye contact and smiled. "I don't even know how the fuck you got my number."

"How the fuck you think I got it, nigga? Got it from Darcy, case I ever needed y'all and he not around. I can't round him up and I need to talk with you."

"About what?"

"A little clean-up business left over from our gig last week. Nothing heavy, but it need to be done quick."

"How not heavy? And what kind of cheese we talking?"

Bieniemy rolled his eyes. "This is why we worked through your friend before. This the shit you don't talk about on the phone, you feel me? You wants to talk specifics and shit, we meet. I'll make it worth your while. Where you at?"

"Taking care a some business in Wilkinsburg."

"Meet me..." Bieniemy looked for guidance. Doc put his thumbs and forefingers together to make an O. Bieniemy smiled and nodded. "Meet me at The O in an hour. You know where it is?"

"Everyone know where The O at, motherfucker."

"Okay, then, where?"

A deep sigh came over the line. "On Forbes, behind them towers at Pitt. A hour kind of tight, you know? What about later?"

"An hour's when I can do it," Bieniemy said. "You in? Or should I wait for your friend to call me back and tell him you ain't interested?"

"Calm down, nigga, I'll be there. You paying for my dog, is all." Hung up.

The cops put down their phones. Smiles all around. Bieniemy said, "You boys ready for second lunch?"

CHAPTER 31

The Original Hot Dog Shop has serviced munchy-crazed Pitt students until three-thirty in the morning for over fifty years. Menus hand-painted on the walls not often read; people come to the O for dogs and fries.

"Why are we here?" Grabek sat with Doc at a table away from the door. Bieniemy's half-eaten at another table.

"Because I'm hungry," Doc said.

"We ate not two hours ago."

"*You* ate not two hours ago." Grabek gave Doc the *I know a place* speech when Bieniemy turned them loose for lunch. Took them to a sketchy Middle Eastern joint Doc told Bieniemy, "Specialized in falafel, hummus, and abdominal cramps." Doc ordered the most innocuous thing on the menu, didn't like it, then watched Grabek eat, calculating how long before he could order a fish sandwich and fries at the Edgecliff. "We have to look like customers. You don't want the hot dog, nibble off one end. I'll eat the rest. I'm starving."

Doc finished his dog, broke off and ate a quarter of Grabek's, scraping off most of the sweet relish. Dawdling over his fries when Bieniemy pointed to a skinny black guy in his late twenties wearing a hoodie and Steelers watch cap. Doc and Grabek each took an elbow and steered him to Bieniemy's table before Turner realized the person he was there to meet wasn't coming.

Grabek waited for the initial bluster to run down, said, "DaRon Turner?"

"The fuck you think I am, motherfucker?"

Three badges came out.

"Detective Grabek, Penns River police."

"Detective Dougherty, Penns River."

"Detective Bieniemy, Pittsburgh. I believe you know my close friend, Detective Kennedy. Oh, and Officer Dunphy sends his regards."

"Fuck me. That uttering motherfucker want to haunt me into my motherfucking grave. What y'all want with me? I a busy man."

"Who'd you think you were talking to when I called you?" Bieniemy said.

"When you called me, when?"

Bieniemy sighed. "Motherfucker, why are you here?"

"I'm hungry. Why the fuck you think?"

"You hauled ass from your important business in Wilkinsburg for a hot dog? D's Dogz right there on Braddock."

"How you know I in Wilkinsburg?" The cops stared. "Fuck all y'all. What you playing with me for?"

"Who did you think was on the phone?" Grabek didn't sound to Doc like anyone looking to build rapport with a brother.

"A guy. You know, someone I know."

"A name," Bieniemy said.

"Don't know no name. A guy I know, is all."

"You know a lot of guys, you don't know their names?" Grabek said. Doc let his weight back onto the seat. Grabek and Bieniemy had done this before.

"You know how it is. You meet people. You know him to see him."

"You knew this guy to talk to him," Bieniemy said.

"Yeah, well, see like, you know, a figure of speech. I knows this guy to talk to him."

"You know him to talk to him about some business went on in Penns River last week," Grabek said.

"I don't know nothing 'bout no business in Penns River."

"You didn't hear anything on the news? Or that night you were throwing money around The Spot?" Bieniemy said.

"You mean them five niggas got offed up there? Fuck, yeah. Everybody know about that. I don't know nothing about it myself, personally, what I mean. Like, I know those guys got aced, from what I heard on the news and shit."

"So what business did you do in Penns River last week?" Grabek said.

"Who says I did any business there last week? Or ever? I barely know where that shithole at."

"You did, nigger," Bieniemy said, his accent three shades blacker than at the station. "I axed you about following up on our business from last week and all you axed was how heavy and how much. Didn't spend no time wondering what the fuck I's talking about."

"You a lying motherfucker. All y'all. I never said nothing about nothing in Penns River. You said you had a job is all I heard. I always ready to talk about a job."

Doc leaned in, stared holes through Turner. "Listen to me. We can do this here, three cops busting your balls. We leave looking pissed off and you can act the big man, told three pigs to kiss your black ass. Or—" he raised a finger, "—we can take you back to Penns River and alert the media we got a lead. Let them see you get a ride home a few hours later. Then tomorrow we pick up your boy Rosewood. How's that going to look?"

"We're going to bring him in, anyway," Grabek said. "You already gave him up on the phone.

"And if you call to give him a heads up, he'll know it was you put him in," Bieniemy said.

"So you can talk and we'll all pretend you didn't, or you can shut up and we'll let on like you did," Grabek said. "Treat us right, we might even give you a chance to testify, buy some time off your jolt."

"Jolt this, motherfucker," Turner said.

Grabek grabbed Turner's left pinkie, pulled it away from the ring finger until Turner couldn't ignore the pain. "Pay attention, you little cocksucker, and I don't think I'm calling you names when I say it. They haven't executed anyone in Pennsylvania in something like fifteen years, but the death penalty is still on the books. Five at once, with shotguns, in a public place, for *hire*? They'll bump you to the front of the line and put the needle to you so fast you won't have time to get horny. It can be you *and* Rosewood, or it can be you *or* Rosewood. Think of it as a race: the first one to cooperate wins. If Rosewood sees the writing on the wall and cuts a deal—and we all know he's smarter than you—you'll take the needle for you both. Is that how you want it to go down?"

"Break that finger and it's your job, motherfucker," Turner said through the pain.

"Fuck you, boy. I'm retired." Grabek finished building bridges to span the racial divide for the day.

"All right all right all right," Turner said. Grabek let go.

159

"There's a guy up in Penns River. Got something to do with some church mall they got there. He called Darcy and said he had a job for him. Something heavy. Darcy and me been hanging, so he axed did I want in."

"And you did," Grabek said.

"Fuck no, I did. Darcy talking about some nice money and I'm all like, 'Tell me more,' till he start telling about killing niggers and I'm all, 'No, uh-uh, thank you, call me another time.'"

"Where were you last Wednesday, early afternoon?" Doc said.

"How the fuck I know? Where the fuck were you?"

"I was at Resurrection Mall, cleaning up your mess."

"Ain't no my mess about it. I have to think to remember where exactly I was. I know it weren't Penns River."

"Where?" Grabek said, reached for Turner's hand.

Turner snatched it away. "What day we talking? Wednesday, you said? Lunch time, or thereabouts? Could be the day I went to the zoo."

No one spoke for several seconds. "You went to the zoo," Doc said. "On Wednesday."

"What?" Turner said. "Now you gonna say the zoo closed on Wednesday, or some such shit?"

"The high temperature last Wednesday was thirteen degrees," Bieniemy said. "You went to the zoo in thirteen degrees." Not a question. More like trying it out on his ear.

Turner looked away, scratched his forehead. "I don't like it crowded." Doc might have laughed if he weren't a little sick to his stomach.

Grabek said, "What's the name of the guy in Penns River? The one who called Rosewood?"

"Darcy didn't tell me no name, not after I said I's out."

"What's he look like?"

"Motherfucker, I just told you I never met him. Darcy don't tell me the nigger's name, you think we gonna meet?"

Doc sat back in his chair, let his eyes roam. Grabek and Bieniemy exchanged glances. Grabek flapped his hands in an exasperated gesture and stood. Turner started to get up.

"Sit your ass down," Bieniemy said. Waited for compliance before he continued. "We done here. For now. I'm a tell you one thing. These two from out of town, but me you have to watch for all the goddamn time. And I'm telling you today—front a witnesses—I know you lying about that massacre up there. These two going to come to me when it time to pick you up. And I'm telling you now, you miserable little faggot motherfucker, when I come for you, you *will* resist arrest, even if you unconscious when you do it. We straight?"

Turner sat with hands folded on the table, all bluster gone. Nodded.

Bieniemy looked to Grabek. "You boys want to take him with you?"

Grabek look at Doc. Raised an eyebrow. Doc shook his head. Grabek said, "Keep him. Property values are low enough up there already."

CHAPTER 32

Stretch Dolewicz strode into Acme Used Video, bat in hand. Nephew Ted trailed, curious how far this would go. Came the same time as before, Henry Miskinis watching Maury Povich. This time Stretch didn't give Ted a chance to see which avenue of American depravity Maury traveled today. Raised the bat overhead, brought it down on the glass countertop six inches from Miskinis's hand. Shattered two sides, bent the frame. A shard nicked Miskinis's cheek. The second swing right-handed, rolled the wrists over like a good pull hitter, took the nineteen-inch TV dead center.

Miskinis jumped from his stool. "Hey, Stretch! What the fuck?"

Stretch pushed him back with the end of the bat. "Ted. Dump the bins."

Ted expected things not to go well for Miskinis, hadn't anticipated this much aggression. Obvious Stretch had no worries about being seen, or of consequences if he were. Ted put both hands under a three-by-six table with six-inch sides heaped with videos and flipped it. Took his time doing the other three.

"Now the walls," Stretch said.

"Hey, come on, Stretch," Miskinis said. "You made your point." Got speared with the bat for his trouble.

Racks of videos ran along two walls, floor to ceiling. Ted did a thorough job on each. Took his time stepping through

162

and on them walking to his uncle. Stretch tossed him the bat, nodded. Miskinis didn't say a word while the kid broke every piece of glass in the store except the windows.

Ted lobbed the bat to his uncle's open hand. Stretch pressed the end against Miskinis's chest again. "Tell me about how putting money on the street is the same as what you been doing for twenty-six years. I want to hear it."

"Hey, Stretch, Jesus Christ, I swear I got nothing new going on. A guy loses and can't pay, I carry him for points. I ain't soliciting nobody."

Tommy Vig's mistake; someone else was the new shy. "That's not the point anymore," Stretch said. "There's respect anyone who comes from a certain person is entitled to. You didn't show it."

"He was wrong, Stretch. I thought he was shaking me down."

"You known me how long?"

"Christ, I don't know. Twenty years, at least."

"At least. And I come in here, with him, and tell you talking to him is like talking to me, and you think the very next fucking time you see him he's shaking you down?"

"Stretch, what he told me was wrong."

"I vouched for him, cocksucker. You're telling me if I came to you and had something wrong, you'd tell me to fuck off?"

"No, no, hey, Stretch, I hope that ain't what he told you," Miskinis said. "I never said to fuck off."

"Does 'kiss my Lithuanian ass' ring a bell?"

Miskinis's face fell. "It ain't the same thing."

"Close enough." Stretch tapped the register with the bat. "Open the drawer."

"Jesus Christ, Stretch. Look around. You made your point." Stretch rocked back, ready to launch the register into the bleachers. "All right. All *right*! Goddamn it. Give me a second. Don't take it all, okay? I haven't been to the bank yet."

Miskinis opened the drawer. Stretch reached in, took every bill. Miskinis muttered something and Stretch pulled a ten from the stack, stuffed it into Miskinis's shirt pocket. "Here's lunch on me."

"Yeah, yeah," Miskinis said, more to himself than anyone else.

Stretch made a point to come down hard walking across the piles of videos. Handed the bat to Ted, spoke so Miskinis could hear.

"He ever comes up short, or gives you lip, use this on him. Anywhere but the head."

CHAPTER 33

"His car's here." Doc sat in the back seat of Bieniemy's sedan, 2100 block of Bedford Avenue on the Hill. A black Monte Carlo with a tag DMV identified as belonging to Darcy Charles Rosewood sat at the curb in front of a low-rise apartment building.

"You think maybe all your new-found clean living paid off and we catch him at home?" Bieniemy said to Grabek.

"I hope not. I'd hate to think the one thing goes right for me this year is in February already." Opened the door and hawked up a load of phlegm as he got out.

"Musta caught him getting cleaned up for his evening on the town," Bieniemy said.

"Is there a back way out?" Doc said.

"Gotta be a fire escape or something," Bieniemy said. "Fifty yards at least to the next street behind."

"What's back there?"

"Vacant lot. Few trees. Don't look half bad when the weather's nice."

"You really think he'll run?" Grabek said. "Us just coming to talk and all?"

"He doesn't know we're coming to talk," Doc said. "Could be up there packing if Turner tipped him."

"Turner didn't tip him." Bieniemy showed more confidence than Doc thought fitting. "Even so, if he did what we think he mighta done and sees three cops coming, he don't know it's for a chat. He rabbits and we don't catch him, he's gone."

Doc looked at the other two cops. Grabek in his early sixties, fifty pounds overweight. Bieniemy close to Doc's age, didn't look to have refused too many cheeseburgers. Plus, it was his town. "You guys go on in. I'll watch the back in case he runs."

Not yet six o'clock, heavy overcast made it seem well into dusk. Doc tripped over a tree root, cursed when he saw the layout. U-shaped in back, each prong with an exit. One in the recessed area between prongs; another exit along each side. He'd have a hard time finding a spot to see all of them in this light.

The day had been warmer, getting cold fast as darkness increased. Allegheny River less than half a mile away, northeast wind driving cold air up the hill into Doc's face. Twenty degrees, tops, and he had to pee. He hoped they didn't get to bullshitting up there before calling him in.

A clanging sound caught his ear. Could be a door opening with a panic bar. It slammed shut to confirm the guess; which one? Doc froze—and frozen—in place, not breathing. Listening and looking for motion.

Off to his right a man running, about where someone who came out the opposite side of the U would be. Doc moved that direction, tentative at first, checking for a second man to minimize the chance of having to explain why he chased the wrong guy. Moved faster as he gained confidence, the runner making noise in the underbrush. Doc took a route into the open field to gain an angle. Caught a glimpse in a pool of streetlight on Webster and pushed himself up a gear.

Both Doc's feet had been broken years ago and didn't like

to run. They'd do it as well as most feet in their late thirties, then they'd bitch all night; the weather wouldn't help. Doc didn't think he'd been seen, gambled the target would turn right and veered to cut him off. The runner went left, north on Webster. Doc made the adjustment, now thirty yards behind. Their speeds matched. The contest would be who tired first.

Rosewood—Doc ready to kick his ass if he wasn't—made a sudden right onto Elmore. Doc gained a few feet cutting the corner. Chased him between a pair of small cubic apartment buildings, the lone construction on the block. Turned left short of the intersection to cut over to Perry. Ran toward a row of three houses, two vacant, the owner of the third making a noble effort at keeping it up. Shadows calved from the larger darkness as Rosewood approached. He slowed. Word were exchanged. Then Rosewood hauled ass up the middle of Perry, back toward Webster.

Doc could cut the distance in half by not slowing and staying to the middle of the street. Stopped short on Pratt as the shadows stepped in front of him.

"Yo, homeboy," one said. Tall, funny angle to his nose, asymmetrical features. "What you doing way up here on the Hill?"

Doc stopped, put his hands on his knees. "Police officer," he said, panting. "Let me through."

"*Po*-lice?" the speaker said. "The hell you say. You best show one a them cool badges you all gots 'fore you start chasing niggas up in here."

Doc saw Rosewood running, almost to Webster now. Thought about fighting through the three before him. The one who spoke would be a tall order. The second guy even bigger. The third didn't look like he could get on all the rides at Kennywood, not that it mattered with the size of his two partners. Doc had no interest in reading his name in the morning's *Post-Gazette*. Took his time opening his coat to show the gun on his hip, badge hanging from a lanyard. "Penns River police. That man's a multiple homicide suspect."

"Maybe." The same spokesman. "I ain't never see no Penns River badge. Let me get a good look." He reached for the badge.

Doc pulled it back. "Uh-uh. No disrespect now, but you gentlemen need to get the fuck out of the way so I can get after my suspect." Who had disappeared from sight on Webster.

"Or what?" The leader smiled at his crew. "Maybe you ain't hip to the finer points of the law, Mr. Penns River cop, but that Dollar Store badge you gots only good up in that shithole bama town you from." The crew laughed. "Don't mean dick here."

"Here's the deal." Doc's anger built as he caught his breath. "There's a Pittsburgh cop going to be around in a minute or so when he wonders where I went. He has a hard-on for this guy, and I don't think he's going to appreciate you fucking me over like this."

"This invisible Pittsburgh cop got a name?"

"Bieniemy. Black guy, about my height and age."

"He talking about Killer B," the smallest of the crew said. That got a reaction from the others. Doc resolved not to hold Bieniemy's high esteem of Grabek against him.

The leader looked over his shoulder at an empty street. "Yeah, well, I guess you can go. No hard feelings, yo. Can't let just any cracker come running after our boys. This the Hill, you know."

They stepped onto the sidewalk. Doc trotted down Pratt, knowing his only chance of catching Rosewood would be if he'd broken his ankle in a pothole. Reached Webster and looked right. Nothing. Turned to his left and saw the car not thirty feet away. Rosewood leaned on his hands against the roof, feet spread while Bieniemy patted him down. Grabek sat on the hood.

Doc saw Grabek's smile, even in the gloom. "Pay me, B."

"Pay you?" Doc said.

"The over and under on you showing up was five minutes. I took the under. I had faith in you, partner."

Bieniemy leaned his forearm across Rosewood's shoulders, pushing his face into the roof. "You run into Russell Wilkins' crew back there?"

"Scotty Pippen-looking dude with Mutt and Jeff wingmen?" Doc said.

"He won't appreciate you calling him that, but yeah," Bieniemy said.

"Nothing dramatic. They held me up enough for him to get away." Doc jerked a thumb toward the car. "From me, anyway."

"Yeah, well, this an interesting neighborhood." Bieniemy pulled Rosewood's hands behind him one at a time for the cuffs. "Never know who's around the corner. Watch your head there, Darcy, honey."

CHAPTER 34

Bieniemy's interview room, so he went first.

"You know, Mr. Rosewood, when I stops by in my role as sworn officer of the law to pass the time of day, maybe ax a few questions, and the man I'm there to see run like his ass on fire, I can't help wondering why." Bieniemy stretched, shook his shoulders. "I know it's my ego talking, making me think how my extra-ordinary reputation as po-lice put such fear into you. Pride's a sin, and I'm working on it. Still, I walk up to lots a people in the course of the day. Hardly any of 'em run." Scratched his chin. "Come to think of it, been five, six weeks since I had a runner. So you'll forgive me if I wonder where the fuck you were going in such a hurry soon as you found out who I was."

Didn't matter what the rest of the building looked like, all interview rooms were the same. Little variance in size or design. Block walls and smooth paint—acoustical tile if the department had money—stale sweat and dead air. Faint overtones of booze excreted through pores and exhaled cigarette breath. And the invisible window in a corner of the ceiling, the one guests of honor looked toward like the way out.

Except Rosewood. He didn't look in the high corners. He didn't try to outstare three cops. He didn't fuss or argue or bitch. So relaxed, a passer-by might think four cops were in there bullshitting. He let Bieniemy's comment sit for thirty seconds, said, "That's a rough neighborhood. Man's got to be ready to move."

"Way I hear it, any neighborhood you live in's a rough neighborhood," Bieniemy said. "And we did mention about how we police, and all. So it's not like we come to rob you."

"Anyone can say they po-po," Rosewood said. "Don't always pay to stick around and find out."

"Let's cut the shit, Rosewood." Grabek stood, twisting his hips. Put a hand on the table to steady himself. "You were coming out as we walked up the stairs. You saw two cops and ran like hell."

"As I recall, you hadn't identified yourselves as police before I started running."

"So why'd you run?"

"Like I told you, man can't be too careful round there."

"Then why didn't you stop when we did identify ourselves?"

"Did you?" Rosewood smiled. "Guess I didn't hear, what with the blood pounding in my ears from fear." Looked from cop to cop to cop. "I don't mind you bringing in me in for some bullshit. I know you need to put on your show and I'm the flavor of the month. It's just, ain't my month about over? The slope in the 7-Eleven, didn't he—what's that word?—recant and shit?"

"Old news," Grabek said. "Too local. We have out-of-town business with you."

Rosewood snapped his fingers. "I knew it. The two cakes here from some *big* city." Turned to Doc. "Where you from, Casper? B-more? Philly? Ooh, maybe like Morgantown, maybe?"

"Penns River." Doc's voice flat.

"Penns River? You shitting me. Penns River. *Penns River?*" Turned to Bieniemy. "You chauffeuring these two ofay pigs from that shithole? Tell me they don't both sit in back, make you wear the *Driving Miss Daisy* hat, holding the door for them and shit."

Bieniemy's right arm shot out from the shoulder fast as a frog's tongue. The heel of the hand caught Rosewood on the brow above his right eye. Rosewood struggled to keep from going over. "This their case, so they have to be nice to you. You not part of any investigation I'm working on, so I can fuck you up if I want. Won't cost me a thing."

"'Cept your badge, motherfucker."

"I don't know," Doc said. "You were beat up pretty good when we brought you in. You ran right into a gang of toughs while I was chasing you, over there on—what's the name of that street?"

"Pratt," Bieniemy said.

"Right. Pratt. You caught a pretty good beating before we could get there. I'm sorry we didn't get a better look at them, but, you know, in the dark like it was…"

"I see how it is." Rosewood glared at Bieniemy. "I'm a remember this. Believe it."

"Your memory's so good, tell us where you were last Wednesday around one o'clock," Grabek said.

"Nowhere near Penns River, that's for sure."

"Who said you were in Penns River?"

"Motherfucker, you a Penns River cop. I know you didn't chase me down and drag my ass in here to ax was I in Aliquippa. No, I was not in Penns River last Wednesday at one o'clock, or two o'clock, or any goddamn o'clock. Now we got that cleared up, I guess we finished here."

Rosewood got no more than a foot out of the chair before Bieniemy hit him with the same move, this time on the right shoulder. His ass hit the chair hard.

"Bitch!"

Bieniemy hooked a chair leg with his foot before Rosewood got settled. He and the chair went down. "Stay down there a minute, you clumsy fool. Clear your head. Get your mind right. I don't want you to injure yourself on my watch."

Doc's thousand-yard stare as good as anyone's. He'd never seen looks like Bieniemy and Rosewood exchanged, Rosewood on the floor, Bieniemy looking down from his chair. More than cop and crook. Doc didn't know what. He knew criminals, Rosewood thinking Bieniemy wouldn't be so tough without two other cops with him. Doc not so sure Rosewood was right.

"You all squared away down there?" Bieniemy said. No answer. "Good. Get up."

Rosewood did his best to make it look like he'd been about to get up anyway, slowed the process to show his ass. Stood, resettled the chair, took a seat. "Do you have questions, or are we only here so you can work out your latent homosexuality?"

Bieniemy chuckled for real. "You boys have any more questions? He said he not anywhere near Penns River last Wednesday. Of course, he a lyin' motherfucker, so don't feel too terribly deterred."

"Okay, so you weren't in Penns River last Wednesday," Grabek said. "Where were you?"

Rosewood gave Bieniemy another five seconds of stink eye, said, "Aliquippa."

"Where in Aliquippa?" Grabek said.

"Here and there. You know, around."

"Around where? Any specific place will do."

"Post office."

"He didn't ax where your picture at," Bieniemy said. "He axed where *you* were."

"Anyone see you at the post office?" Grabek said.

"Whoever was there, I guess."

"Counter-person recognize you? Be willing to vouch for you?"

"Didn't go to the counter. I was browsing."

"You often, uh, browse at the post office?"

"When it ten degrees outside I do."

Grabek pinched the bridge of his nose. Tugged at his belt. Shifted in the chair like the seat was hot. Found a position he liked and took five seconds before he said, "You're going to have to do better."

Rosewood made a pout, shook his head. "Like hell. Up to you to prove I was where you want me to be. I don't gots to prove shit."

"I never said you had to prove anything," Grabek said. "You're going to have to do better than that because I have a witness who can put you there when it happened."

"Your witness a lyin' motherfucker."

"He has no reason to lie. He'll swear you were there, and all you can come up with is you were out and about in Aliquippa. No one saw you. Who's a jury going to believe?"

"It come to a trial, I expect my memory to improve."

"I'll bet." Grabek's shoulders sagged. His eyes closed, then tightened. His face pale when he reopened them. "Look. We know you were there. We know you were paid. We know it was you who was approached. The only piece we're not sure of is who made the offer. Was it Abernathy? Or Lewis?"

Rosewood smiled, laughed half to himself. "Please, nigga. Tell me this weak shit ain't the best you got."

Grabek leaned back in his chair. For the first time Doc noticed how drawn his face was. Looked like a man who'd lost his job and came home to find his wife's clothes gone. His voice so low Doc not sure he'd spoken. "You threw the pieces off the bridge. The shotguns and the nines."

"How long I got to say it?" Rosewood showed mild irritation, as if speaking to a nephew he didn't much like after one too many *Whys*? Took a deep breath as a show of patience. "I ain't been to Penns River...ever, far as I know. I got no reason to go. I only know where it at for sure 'cause it on the news all the goddamn time. Russian gangsters and niggers killed by the handful. Fucking OK Corral and shit up in there. I can't hardly throw no beer can off the bridge you talking about if I ain't never been."

Grabek mumbled something. Rosewood said, "How's I supposed to answer I can't hear the question?" and Doc sat a millimeter straighter.

Grabek said, "They're working on the bridge," so soft Doc almost stopped breathing to listen.

"So? Good for them. Keep people working."

"There's a small barge, like a flatboat, tethered to the bridge. Scaffold on it so the crew can work on the supports, rig the climbing equipment. You didn't even look, you were in such a hot hurry not to get caught with those guns. One of the shotties landed on the boat. Almost killed a guy working. Gun's not banged up too badly. They're already working on matching the firing pin with the strike marks on the ejected shells."

"So? Someone threw a shotgun off a bridge. Even if it one a those what killed them niggers, ain't me what threw it. I told you: I's in Aliquippa."

Doc sat straighter throughout Rosewood's comment until he caught himself and leaned his elbows on the table, hoping it looked like an aborted stretch. All night Rosewood sat relaxed and calm, no more concerned than a man waiting for his change at Starbucks. The fingers of his right hand started to tap a slow, regular tattoo on the table when Grabek mentioned the bridge repairs. Still doing it. On anyone else Doc might have missed it. Compared to Rosewood's previous equanimity, that small motion stuck out like fireworks at a funeral.

"No, it was you," Grabek said. "Or your partner, one." Paused for an expression of discomfort to pass. "So we have the shotgun and we have a witness and we're going to find your partner and we're going to break down the piece of shit who paid for this cluster fuck and none of you are ever going to breathe free air again. Mass murder for hire, they might even make an exception and fire up the needles. One of you...one...might—I say *might*—have a chance to stay off the gurney. It'll be the guy who goes first. Now, do you have anything else you want to tell us?"

Rosewood's face held the same level of disinterested disdain. The fingers of his right hand off on their own. Nothing dramatic. A steady tapping all through Grabek's speech. "The only thing I have to say—" tap-tap-tap, "—you find a way for a man in Aliquippa to throw something into the Penns River, then you a better cop than I give you credit for." Tap-tap-tap. "And that the only motherfucking thing I has to say."

Grabek and Rosewood eye fucked each other for almost a minute. Grabek said to Bieniemy, "We're done here. Do what you want with him."

Bieniemy opened the door, hollered for a patrolman. "Take this outside and kick him loose."

"He need a ride?" the uniform said.

Bieniemy glanced over his shoulder at Rosewood. "Nah. This one's an exercise freak. We found him running all over the Hill. He probably appreciate a chance to walk home in this bracing weather, mostly downhill the way it is. Take him out front and point the way."

The sound of the closing door still in the room when Bieniemy said, "That's your boy."

"Absolutely," Doc said. "The boat thing got him. I almost slapped you, Willie, making up that weak story. I can't believe he fell for it."

"He didn't like the shotgun on a boat story at all," Bieniemy said. "He's pretty good—I don't think a rookie would've noticed—I knew we all picked it up."

"Now all we have to do is find some real evidence," Doc said.

"One thing I don't like," Grabek said.

"What?"

"He never flinched when we threw those names at him. At first I thought he was that good. Now I've seen him react to that boat bullshit...I'm not so sure."

"I wondered about that myself," Doc said. "So far as we know, no one has stepped in to fill the vacuum those dead dealers left. I hear the junkies are hurting."

"Which means Rosewood didn't do it for himself. To take over for himself, I mean," Grabek said.

"So someone paid him to do it." Bieniemy.

"I hope to Christ we're talking about a substantial amount of money here," Doc said. "Not like a few hundred bucks."

"Not if Rosewood's involved," Bieniemy said. "Whatever he's into, he gets paid."

"Okay, then. If not Abernathy or Lewis—who?"

No one spoke while the elephant wandered the room. Grabek went first. "Get Neuschwander to dig deeper into Love's background. Tonight—right now—call your Uncle Stush and tell him we need surveillance on the bridge. They're looking for a black Monte Carlo, license number... whatever Rosewood's license number is. Someone needs to watch the bridge at least a couple of days. I wouldn't put it past him to head over there right now." To Bieniemy: "Thanks for making him walk. It buys us a little time."

"Tomorrow morning," he said to Doc, "get a canvass going on his car. Pull some generic picture off the Internet for Rosewood's year and color. Anyone saw a car looks like that, we want to know."

"I'm on it," Doc said, the official lead on this investigation. "What are you up to tomorrow?"

"What time is it?"

"After ten."

"Fuck me. I been on the run since before seven this morning. Tomorrow's Saturday. Anyone wants me, I'm dead." Grabek stood, pausing halfway to rest his hands on the table. Looked at Bieniemy. "These jigs are going to turn me into a racist, fucking up my retirement like this."

Bieniemy smiled more on one side than the other, showed his dead tooth. "Some things never change. The Black Polack rides again."

CHAPTER 35

Sean Sisler liked the four-to-twelve shift. Days were better—hell, yeah—graveyard had little to do after the first couple of hours, even on weekends. Four-to-twelve on Friday and Saturday prime time for fights at Fat Jimmy's or jacking around D and Ds near the casino. Stush gave the uniforms free rein and great latitude when deciding what constituted a disturbance in the area of the casino. How he described it: "I'm giving you free rein and great latitude to use your own judgment as to what constitutes disorderly, and probable cause for drunkenness. Personally, I'd imagine I lived in one of those houses backs up to the casino, with a bad headache and a colicky baby I'd just got to sleep. Not saying that's what you should do, though."

Most Penns River cops lived to dick with casino people. Few employees lived in town, despite promises made when negotiating the sweetheart property tax deal. Fridays the most fun, guys stopping after work for a few belts instead of waiting until later, as they would on Saturday. Howling about their wins, bitching about their losses. Making general asses of themselves so Stush's standards, such as they were, could often be invoked at will.

Sisler didn't live in Penns River, had no personal animus toward the casino. Took the job when he found out his mother had macular degeneration at fifty-five and would be blind by sixty if an experimental therapy didn't work. His father pushing seventy, passed for no less than eighty. They lived in Saxonburg, Penns River the closest town hiring when he came out of the Commonwealth's training for local police officers. The State Police offered him a job, had a policy of sending new troopers to remote locations for their initial postings. Sisler not interested. He'd disappointed his parents in a lot of ways as a kid. Wounds had mended over time and Sean Sisler had no intention of disrupting the process when time might be short.

Slow for a Friday at the casino. Heavy snow in the forecast—it should have started already—all but the most serious gamblers stayed home. Sisler on his way to Fat Jimmy's, where driving while intoxicated combined with bad conditions to create a deterrent no greater than either alone, which was none. Guys who thought themselves tough unwinding after a long week, overestimating their capacities— again—out to demonstrate flannel shirt macho on a guy who might have said something that could, under certain circumstances, have been insulting. About his ancestry. Or parentage. Sisler had a special fondness for fights that started because someone thought his masculinity had been questioned.

He pulled into his preferred spot near the body shop next door, where an overhang kept the light bar from standing out in silhouette. Settled in with a Styrofoam cup of coffee. Nine-thirty-eight. Something to do should find him any minute.

His cell phone chirped at nine-forty-nine. Stush Napier-kowski. "Where you at, Sis?"

"Fat Jimmy's."

Stush said, "I told you he'd be at Fat Jimmy's," to someone away from the phone. Then, to Sisler, "I need you to get over to the Ninth Street Bridge toot sweet, as they say. You're looking for a car." Stush read off Rosewood's plate number, the car a midnight-blue Monte Carlo.

"What his deal?"

"Get where you can see any car getting on or off the bridge on our side and see what he does. I'd prefer he didn't see you, at least not until he's done his business, but I'll live with it for you to get a good look at what he does. A decent description of the driver would be nice, not critical. Do *not* stop him. All we want to know is does the car come by and look around."

"This have something to do with Resurrection Mall?"

"Yeah. They have a suspect they like and Grabek planted one of his seeds. Let slip something unusual about the bridge this guy might want to verify. I'm not sure what. We need to know if it took."

"Will do."

"I also need you to stick around until—shit. Listen, Sis, I need a favor."

"Sure, Stush. What do you need?"

"Any chance you can pull a double? We need eyeballs on the bridge until we can get Neuschwander out there to set up a camera, and he can't do it until in the morning. I wanted you to wait for Lester to show after the shift change, but, well, I'd rather have your eyes on the bridge than his. I know yours will be open. You can leave as soon as the guy comes. If he comes."

"I'll wait for him. Heading over now." Started the car.

"Thanks. I owe you one."

Sisler found two spots with good coverage of the bridge and its approaches. Chose the one where he'd be harder to see by anyone crossing on the way out of town. Someone coming into town on the bridge had no bailout point, would have to keep coming.

Traffic nonexistent here, across the street from Resurrection Mall. Sisler parked in the shadow of an old aluminum mill, part of which had been converted into several boutique fabricating plants. The mill ran twenty-four hours a day fifty, sixty years ago, when Penns River produced almost as much aluminum as the rest of the world combined. Now the smaller businesses used less than half the space, the remainder taken as needed by squatters and fiends. The fabricators complained, the closest residents complained. Stush tried a couple of times to get the plant open so the cops could sweep through and keep everyone inside from getting too comfortable. The owner insisted on a warrant, difficult to get without evidence of a crime or a complaint from the owner of record, who was the jagov insisting on the warrant in the first place. No one knew why it became such an issue. Grabek said the owner had something there he couldn't afford to have found, maybe connected to the squatters and junkies. Dougherty looked up the official owner, saw it was a company in Florida, deduced they didn't give a shit and didn't want a sweep to turn up anything they'd have to bother about.

Snow started around two. Big, fluffy flakes swinging like leaves in the fall as they fell. So few he could count them at first. Did, for a while, to pass the time, too warm in the car to allow accumulation on the windshield.

Sister hadn't seen a car in almost half an hour by the time he needed to turn on the wipers. As he reached for the switch he saw headlights on the bridge, coming into town from

Allegheny County, moving slower than any car had good reason to. His weight shifted so little a person seated next to him would not have noticed.

The car crept down the decline coming off the bridge. Dark, hard to tell midnight blue from black in this light. Still too far away to be sure about the model. No problem. The car had to pass within fifty feet even if Sisler were seen. He waited and watched, appearing no more interested than he had when counting the snowflakes.

He made it as a Monte Carlo when it passed him coming off the bridge. Overcast, moonless night made the color less certain, prevented a good look at the rear plate. Sisler started the engine. Ninth Street ran a couple of blocks before the car would have to turn; any turn led out of town. He needed to be able to swear to that plate number.

Eased the cruiser onto Ninth Street. Get close, read the rear plate, veer off. With luck the guy would take it as a random event, a cop on night patrol happening to cross his path. Sisler wondering what to do if the other driver decided to run when the guy surprised him by making a U-turn in the middle of the intersection of Ninth Street and Fourth Avenue.

Shit. No front plates in Pennsylvania, and no guarantee of getting the numbers from the side-view mirror. Sure this was who Stush had him here to look for, Sisler couldn't prove anything. He imagined how it would play in court.

"The car drove slowly off the bridge and made a U-turn at the Fourth Avenue intersection to go back across the bridge."

Defense Attorney: "You're positive it was the defendant's car?"

"Sure looked like it."

"You get a license number?"

"No."

Judge: "Case dismissed."

Took his foot off the gas, let the car run on idle to slow without hitting the brakes. Stared into the sideview mirror and saw the license plate light wasn't lit, why he'd been unable to see it before.

Double shit. He needed to see that plate. He'd have to get right behind the SOB to use his headlights, had orders not to spook him. In thirty the Monte Carlo would be on the bridge, leaving the jurisdiction.

Sisler made a U-turn. Lit the bar, gave one whoop of the siren.

The Monte Carlo drove on.

Sisler gave another whoop.

The Monte Carlo pulled over.

Sisler veered into classic traffic stop position, a few feet behind, center of the cruiser's grill lined up with the Monte Carlo's left edge. Right headlight shining on the license plate with the numbers he'd been looking for. Unsnapped the flap on his holster, got out of the car. Shone the Maglite with his left hand along the driver's side windows as he approached, let his right hang near his hip. Rapped on the window with the flashlight.

The window slid down.

"License and registration, please."

"What I do?"

"Nothing, sir. The light that illuminates your license plate isn't working. I need to write you a work order to have it repaired."

"You give me a ticket 'cause the license plate light don't work?"

"It's not a ticket, sir. It's a notice you have thirty days to have it fixed to avoid a fine. Won't even go on your record if you get it taken care of in time."

"Then I gots to come all the way back up here to prove I got it fixed? I live way the fu—hell down the Hill District."

"No, sir. A Pittsburgh cop is fine. Go to any station, hell, even a patrol unit, show him the slip I give you and let him see the light's working, mail the form with his signature back and you're all set. I don't even have to call it in. I do need to see your license and registration. For the paperwork."

Which was bullshit, all traffic stops got called in for outstanding warrants. Sisler not ready to take the chance this mope had any and create a situation. Made a show of *not* getting into his cruiser to write it up. Finished and walked back to the Monte Carlo. Rapped with the flashlight on the window again, right hand resting on the butt of his weapon.

The window slid down. "Sign here, please."

Rosewood scribbled something on the bottom of the form. "I still can't believe you stopped me for some petty license plate light."

Sisler tore off the recipient copy, handed it to Rosewood. "Can I level with you? A guy I don't much like called in sick at the last minute and I'm working a double. That's four yesterday afternoon till eight o'clock in the morning. I was so goddamn bored—sorry, pardon my language—I was so bored I was happy for the excuse to get out of the car. Someone would've cited you for that lamp sooner or later. Might as well be me. I'm sorry if you feel like I busted your chops."

"It's all right, I guess. Just doing your job."

"Thanks. I appreciate you staying cool about it. Let's hope this is the worst thing happens to you today."

Sisler took his time getting situated in the cruiser. Watched Rosewood look like he might turn onto Second Avenue, then continue up the approach to the bridge, gaining speed halfway across. No harm done, as far as he could tell. And he had written evidence Darcy Charles Rosewood of 2105 Bedford Avenue, Pittsburgh 15219 had, in fact, gone out of his way in the middle of the night to drive twice across a bridge almost twenty miles from his home.

CHAPTER 36

Doc made it to The Edgecliff by eleven Friday night for his fish sandwich and fries with gravy. Two beers, spoke no more than he had to—if that—in bed and asleep by midnight.

Saturday morning the temperature pushed thirty, snowing hard. Three inches on the ground when he left the house at eight-fifteen. The car's roof covered again by the time he finished digging out his space and cleared a path to his condo's parking lot thoroughfare, which had not been plowed.

Almost nine by the time he reached the post office to express mail a birthday gift to his sister-in-law he could have sent first class a week ago, had he not left it to sit on the kitchen table, wrapped, addressed, and ready. The PO busier than he expected for a snowy February Saturday. Doc tucked his package under his arm, rocked back and forth and side to side. No hurry. He had no place to be. Groceries had to be bought and he needed gas. His house had a week's worth of entropy to undo. Kate had to work, so he'd watch hockey tonight, the Pens in Calgary, a late game he already doubted he'd see the end of.

His eye turned toward the motion of the opening door to see Marian Widmer come in, accompanied by a man he didn't know. Marian's hair longer than he remembered it, her face maybe even a little younger. Doc watched her enter with apparent disinterest. The second time he'd run into her since she beat two conspiracy to commit murder charges he knew she'd earned. Marian Widmer the mortar binding Doc's relationship with Kate, the reason they traveled to lounges and restaurants to show photographs of a dead woman. Last summer they'd crossed paths in a gas station and Marian spat in Doc's face.

She noticed him three steps into the post office. Turned and might have walked out had she not bumped into her companion. Positioned herself so she could speak to him and not see Doc standing six feet away, one person in line between them.

Doc mailed the parcel—his tardiness cost him almost twenty-six dollars—walked to the exit, lingering on the warm side of the door. Marian maneuvered to keep her escort between Doc and herself as they passed. Doc made no move toward her. Waited until she reached conversational distance and said, "Good morning, Mrs. Widmer. You're looking well. Younger, somehow. I don't know how you do it."

For a second he thought she might spit on him again. Had no doubt it crossed her mind. "Leave me alone, you son of a bitch. This is harassment."

"Who are you?" the man said. Almost six feet, trim, thinning blond hair. Burberry scarf, cashmere overcoat, tailored slacks, rubbers over his shoes. "You've been staring at Mrs. Widmer since we came in."

"Detective Dougherty, Penns River police. I haven't been staring. I just know better than to turn my back on Mrs. Widmer."

Marian tugged on the man's arm. "Let's go. It's not worth it."

"No, it *is* worth it. You were right. This is harassment."

"No, sir, it's not," Doc said. "I did not follow her in here, nor did I communicate any lewd, lascivious—" a pause for thought, "—threatening or obscene words, language, drawings, or caricatures. I have only seen her twice in the past two years—random meetings at public places—so 'communicates repeatedly at extremely inconvenient hours' doesn't apply, either. I'm an acquaintance, exchanging pleasantries."

"What's your badge number, officer?"

"Two-oh-three. And it's Detective."

"I want to *see* your badge, De*tec*tive."

"Then you should've said so." Doc took the badge holder from an inside pocket of his down jacket. The "Michelin Man" coat, Eve called it. The man reached and Doc pulled it back. "Uh-uh. You can look. You can't have it."

"We'll see. I'll not have my friends harassed. *Now* we can go, Marian."

"She's your friend?" Doc said. "I'm happy for you."

The man stopped short. "What do you mean by that?"

Doc kept his smile from getting too big. "It means you're welcome to her, pal."

CHAPTER 37

Wilver Faison hurried down the stairs from his family's Allegheny Estates apartment. No money to take home, all his sources of income in the Allegheny County morgue. His moms not the most pleasant person when he did bring money, so showing up without cash and her already sick, he wondered why he even bothered. David in school, which was good. The shorty didn't need to see Wilver and Imelda argue again, and Wilver didn't miss the boy pissing in his ear about Detective Doc.

Wilver not much surprised to see Deron Whatshisname fixing to rob the food court. Shooting people was something else. The other guy—the one Wilver didn't know his name—Wilver saw that face in his sleep. He'd seen cold mother-fuckers in his time—more since he started working for drug dealers—not like him. A minute away from blowing five people up, no more concerned than if he pulled on a mask to scrape ice off a windshield.

Skipped the main floor, went straight to the basement. Laundry room on one side: three washers, three dryers, no more than two of either operable on a given day. Janitor's closet and office across the hall. The furnace room at the far end opened to the outside. No one ever went there, his way in and out when he needed to avoid being seen, pretty much all the time now.

Had his hand on the doorknob and almost pissed his

pants when a larger hand came out of the shadow and kept him from turning it.

"We can talk here in private, or you can run and Officer Sisler and I can take you down outside so everyone knows we had a chat," Ben Dougherty said. "Your choice."

Imelda Faison claimed never to know where Wilver was, or when he came and went. David either didn't know, or wouldn't say. Jefferson West didn't know. Penns River lacked the manpower to stake out the Estates until someone who might be a witness came by. Doc performed his own discreet canvass, never saying who or what he might be looking for, until the janitor for the three connected buildings mentioned suspicions someone had been getting into one of the furnace rooms. Doc about to call it a day, go back to hunting sewer grates, when Wilver made the wait worthwhile.

"I been looking all over for you," he said after Wilver calmed down. Doc was happy the kid hadn't run. As far as he knew, his "backup" had the day off. His conscience bothered him less every year, lying to people who weren't straight with him. His feet's hangover from the Rosewood pursuit canceled any remaining qualms. "And you knew. What gives?"

"I ain't been around, is all," Wilver said. "I been staying down my aunt's in Pittsburgh."

"How long has that been going on?"

"Couple three weeks."

Doc gave the comment time to ripen. Said, "You haven't been up this way since then."

"'Bout a week ago. Little longer, maybe. I didn't hear you was looking for me till today when my moms told me."

"She didn't tell you any of the other times you've come to see her in the past two weeks?"

"No, man, I told you. I ain't seen her till today 'cept that one time."

"You've been avoiding me, Wilver."

"No, man, straight deal. I just heard you looking for me today."

Doc allowed that comment to ferment and develop a heady bouquet. "Tell me what you saw at Resurrection Mall."

"Aw, man, why you do me like this? I thought we's friends and shit."

"You want me to start being your friend, hold up your end of the deal," Doc said. "Today, I'm a cop. What did you see at Resurrection Mall?"

"What you mean, 'what I see?' It's a mall. All kinda shit there."

"Wilver, you're trying my patience. Pretty soon I'm going to take you to the station just for the hell of it. You were there when all those dealers got killed."

"No! I's already at my aunt's by then."

"A reliable witness identified you."

Wilver fought back tears. "You know me, Detective Doc. You know I couldn't have nothing to do with that."

"I didn't say you did. You were there, though. And you saw something."

"No, man. I didn't see nothing."

"You were there."

"Yeah. Okay. But I was nowhere near the food court where those guys got shot."

"Goddamn it, Wilver, I have two witnesses call you out by name as running hard toward the food court right before it happened. Were you meeting someone for lunch? One of the dealers?"

"Yeah, well, okay, yeah. But I didn't see nothing."

"Doesn't matter if you saw, or not. You were seen. I found you without looking all that hard, and my life's not at stake. These shooters, you bet they'll find your ass if they think you saw. Tell them you didn't see, see if it matters."

Wilver almost spoke, slumped into a squat, back flat to the wall. Eating and sleeping did not appear to have been part of his recent routine. Tired, hungry—and scared. The bad decision trifecta.

"Wilver." Doc had to say it twice to get the kid's attention. "You're not in trouble. Not with the police, anyway. That's not to say you won't be if you keep going the way you've been, but you're clear on this Res Mall business as far as we're concerned. Doesn't matter if you saw anything or not, or whether you tell us what you saw if you did. We'd rather you helped us, but we have nothing to compel you.

"The shooters won't see it that way. They killed five men in a public place in a very public manner. For money. If you can identify them, they'll serve natural life, if they're lucky. They won't think twice about doing one more. Six life without paroles is the same as five."

Wilver didn't look scared or tired or hungry or cold or angry. He looked spent. Doc couldn't tell if the kid would bawl, run, talk, or fall asleep. "Are you hungry?"

"Naw. Not really."

"When's the last time you ate? An honest to God meal, I mean."

"I don't know. Couple days. What's today? Monday? Saturday, I guess."

"So, you're hungry."

"Naw. Not really."

Wilver looked a little more with it. Thirty percent of the way back; thirty-five with luck. "How much sleep you have last night?"

"Don't know. Ain't been keeping track."

"Where did you sleep? You been keeping track of that?"

A flicker. "Around. I got friends."

"Your friends willing to catch a beating for you? Or worse? The more people you crash with, the more people know you're trying to stay on the down low. The more people who know, the better the chances are someone looking for you will run into one of them. You sure they won't give you up?"

A small smile. "Ain't none of them give me up to you."

"I didn't press a hot iron to anyone's feet. Or threaten to cut up some pretty girl's face." The smile faded, Wilver two-thirds to being all the way aware. Doc said, "Where are you staying tonight?"

"Don't know yet. Figure if I don't know, no one else will. Anyone looking for me have to get lucky."

"Good point, and not a terrible strategy. Think of this: you have to get lucky every night. They only have to get lucky once."

Wilver shifted his weight to sit with his ass flat on the floor, legs straight out. Shoulders slumped, hands supporting his weight. His face returned to tired and hungry and scared, but alert. "What you want me to do?"

"First, let's get you fed."

"Forget that. I can't get seen with no cop."

"We'll go back to my place and order a pizza. No one looking for you there."

Wilver thought about it. "That might could work. Then what?"

"Let's get that far first. Then we'll talk about it."

Doc offered a hand. Wilver hesitated, then used it to pull himself off the floor.

CHAPTER 38

"I wondered if you were coming at all tonight," Eve Stepler said when Doc came half an hour late to rehearsal. "I guess it's that Resurrection Mall thing, but I don't like to pester you about things you probably got on your mind all day, anyway."

No irony in her comment. Doc and Eve remained good friends because she never asked about his work except to break his stones. Minor, funny things she'd heard, or he'd joked about himself. She never walked away from a conversation when Doc wanted to talk, treated his work the same way she'd treat anyone else's. Most people thought discussing police work with a cop was either somehow beneath them, or the only thing to talk about. Eve took her friend the police detective as she found him.

"Tell the truth, I almost didn't come. You remember me talking about Wilver Faison? Lives down the Alleghenies, mom's a junkie?"

"Isn't he the one who saw that murder a couple of years ago?"

"Yeah, well, he has the gift. He was at Res Mall that day. Good chance he saw the shooters."

"Jesus, Doc. The kid needs to find another hobby." Eve arched her back, tried sitting cross-legged to paint the lower areas.

"Tell me about it. Anyway, he was there. If I heard about

it, others might, and depending on who those others were, it might be nice if I found him first."

"Uh-huh."

Doc loved that, Eve letting him tell it in his own time. Gave him time to think. He didn't enhance his stories—unless comic effect presented an opportunity—did sometimes look at things a different way as he phrased the description in his head. "I found him this afternoon. Convinced him moving from friend to friend was not a long-term strategy. Brought him home for a pizza and a good night's sleep, hot shower. See what he had to say when he felt human again."

"So why are you here?"

Doc stopped painting, looked down to Eve. "I put him in the shower while we waited for the pizza. Threw his clothes in the washer. Loaned him a warm-up suit while they dried and we ate. He dozed off on the couch, I went to the crapper, and he split."

"No shit?"

"No shit." Doc resumed painting. "Even grabbed his clothes out of the dryer. I don't think he stole anything except the warm-ups. I half expect to get them back, knowing him."

"What did you do?" Eve laid her brush across the can.

"Came here."

"You didn't look for him?"

"I'll give the patrols a flyer tomorrow, bring him in if they see him."

"What about Family Services?"

"He's seen that movie already. Besides, I think he's seventeen."

"Still, Doc, he's just a kid."

Doc stopped painting. Kept his eyes level, not looking at Eve. No rancor when he spoke. "Being a cop teaches you things. Like you can't help people who don't want to be helped. You know those stories where the cop or teacher won't take no for an answer and saves someone against their will? It doesn't work." Dipped his brush in the paint. "He knows how to find me. Till then, I have more work to do than I have time to do it."

They painted, the silence broken by occasional uncomfortable noises from Eve. She put her brush in the tray, laid supine on the floor. "You worried about him? This kid who ran off on you?"

"A little." Doc paused to perfect a window corner. What he fixed would not be seen by anyone farther away than the orchestra pit. "Not enough to disrupt my life, or pull other cops off work they already don't have the bodies for."

"Was it always like that here?" Eve said from the floor. "Or do I only notice now because my friend's a cop?"

"Was what always like that here?" Doc said. "And it's not just your friend who's a cop. It's your best friend."

"The cops spread too thin. Do we have fewer cops, or is it really that much worse now?"

Doc continued painting. "We're down one since Barb Smith got married and took a corporate job. All that changed was to give the floater a regular shift. We'll have a replacement by summer when vacations pick up. So, no, we're not so short you'd notice it."

"So things really are that much worse?"

Doc laid his brush across the can on the step ladder he used as a shelf. Wiped his hands with a rag. "Things were good here for a long time. Any increase from a lower starting point looks like a higher percentage."

"What about the murders? I don't think we had five murders here since I was born. Now we've had—what?" Took inventory in her head. "Fourteen in the last three years?"

"Depends on whether you call those four my dad and cousin and I did last year as murders."

"They still count as homicides, right? And they would've been murders if you and your cousin hadn't been so good."

"Don't hang it all on Nick and me. The old man got one, too."

"How is your dad? That must have shaken him up, his age."

"He's a piece of work. Swears he slept like a baby that night. Since then he's replaced everything he could with any evidence of a shotgun pellet in it. New door, new frame, even. Said the old one had rot and would've had to go, anyway, except I never heard him say anything about it before. Scrubbed the concrete in and out of the garage. Tried to patch two marks in the wall by the roll-up door three or four times, but you can still see them. Had the car repaired—new glass, new panels—then sold it. Yeah, he's fine with it."

"What about you?" Eve said it like she'd been meaning to ask for long time and knew she might not get another chance.

"I'm the one who slept like a baby. Woke up every two hours and cried." Retrieved the brush, dipped it in paint. "I'm fine now. Thought about it a lot. Got some counseling. I think my cousin had the right idea."

Eve sat up, twisted her back. "What did he do?"

"I have no idea what he's done since it happened. I mean

during. He saw the situation and took it to them. I laid back, let them come to me. Use force as the last resort. Nick sized things up, realized waiting limited his options, and decided to give them something to think about. I asked him about it before he went back to Chicago. He said it's always better to hit than to be hit."

"Is this what we can expect now, though? What happened here?"

Doc realized what he was holding before running his hands through his hair. Set the paintbrush on the tray. Rubbed his face. Hadn't noticed how tired he'd been until Eve asked the question. Not tired in the body where a good night's sleep or a few days of vegetating would help. Tired of the politics and the crime and the kids who refused to look more than an hour down the road, and the adults with the same failing. Tired of the pettiness of peoples' complaints. Tired of knowing life didn't have to be hard—wouldn't be hard—if everyone made good faith efforts to do no more than expected in a given situation, but also no less. Tired of trivialities become critical and not being able to spare the time and attention to keep from treating the critical as trivial.

He missed the bitter cold of a week ago. At least he'd been able to do something about that, pull out the Michelin Man jacket and Thinsulate gloves and knit watch cap and dare the wind to bring it on. Felt as though he'd accomplished something, working his job in miserable conditions. Tomorrow would be near forty degrees, with a forecast for wintry mix, weatherman-speak for *whatever happens, it'll be shitty*. It wouldn't matter what he wore. The cold would get inside his collar and down his back. His feet would get wet and he'd feel the bone chill even after a change of clothes and a shower. He was tired of the bullshit and everyday life had become bullshit to him.

He owed Eve at least looking at her. Sighed, said, "It's never going to be like before. The casino changes everything. Wait till they get table games."

"You think it'll be worse?"

"Absolutely. The way it is now—just slots—we still have mostly the same old problems. Leechburg Road and Wild Life Lodge can't handle the traffic. Mostly it's a few more drunks and a few more fights and a few more car wrecks. People are upset because now it happens on the Heights and doesn't keep to the Flats like it always did.

"Table games bring a different kind of gambler. They need action, like to be edgy all the time, and that means cocaine and speed, not just booze. Guy gets in over his head, needs some cash, loan sharks will find him. Gamblers aren't the most reliable pays, so enforcement comes in. Same guy wins a few hundred, wants to celebrate, and you got a market for prostitution. Rumor has it a couple are working the casino now, looking for guys who hit jackpots. Hecker would put them on the payroll if he thought he could get away with it. Get some of his money back."

"Jesus Christ, Doc," Eve said. "I hope you're not looking for part-time work with the Chamber of Commerce."

Doc chuckled. "You're the second person to tell me that this week. I'm sorry, Evie. Long day, and it looks like a long week. Didn't mean to dump on you."

"Don't be sorry. I didn't know a lot of that stuff." She folded a stick of gum into her mouth. "What are you going to do?"

"Finish painting this backdrop. What did you want me to do?"

Eve threw the wrapper at him. "I didn't mean right this minute. I mean about what you just said."

"Tonight I'm going home, pour myself a cold Bass and see if there's hockey out west. Read, maybe."

Eve waited until sure he'd finished. "And tomorrow?"

"Tomorrow I'll catch the sons of bitches who shot up Res Mall, or know the reason why."

CHAPTER 39

Rain/sleet/snow/ice pinged off the car as Doc pulled in behind Sean Sisler's cruiser on Alder Street. He should have been looking for who paid for the Res Mall hit, if not Abernathy or Lewis. He knew Rosewood and Turner were the shooters. Lacking proof, he needed to find their employer, lock the three of them in adjacent rooms, and play *L.A. Confidential*, see who talked first.

Instead he answered a domestic disturbance call, backing up Sisler at nine in the morning. Doc knew the Schatz family from his days in patrol. Stush asked him to keep things from getting out of hand, Sisler still learning the ropes.

He planned to walk up to the house, all non-confrontational and Officer Friendly-like, and observe how Sisler handled an irrational person. Two, in this case. Ed half a bubble off of level; Betty could provoke the Dalai Lama to call her a bitch. More than anything Doc wondered what prompted a fight that required police so early in the day, and who'd made the call this time.

Voices carried through the closed doors and windows. Something inside broke as he stepped on the porch. Maintained his pace, knowing Betty liked to throw things for effect, glasses and dishes and figurines she didn't like anymore. Never at anyone. Betty was a mean and intemperate shrew; she wasn't crazy.

Decided against knocking—not like anyone would answer—tried the knob and the door opened. Walked through the living room into a short hallway. Leaned on the kitchen door jamb. Drew as much attention as a dripping faucet in a hurricane.

The fight had something to do with Ed being out all night with "one of his hoors." Doc kept his eyes on the Schatzes's hands while he pondered where Ed found the money to convince even the least expensive pro to spend a whole night with him. No way anyone would do it for free.

"I told you before, I got home about twelve-thirty," Ed said.

"Twelve-thirty my ass," Betty said. "I saw you walk in the front door at a quarter after eight. *A quarter after eight!* Now you're standing there looking me in the eye and telling this cop you come in at twelve-thirty. You're a lying sonofabitch."

"If you'd shut your mouth for ten seconds and listen, you'd know I didn't say I came *in* at twelve-thirty. I said I got *home* at twelve-thirty." Doc perked up, anxious to hear the distinction. "I forgot my keys when I walked over the Legion last night. I rang the bell, knocked on the door, goddamned near got the neighbors after my ass for all the noise I made, and the whole time Betty van Winkle's upstairs leaving me outside to freeze."

"Where'd you go?" Sisler looked like he could be persuaded to smile or arrest someone, depending on how the next few minutes broke.

"I slept in the car."

"See how he lies?" Betty said to Sisler. "He just ten seconds ago said he didn't have any keys. He's too dumb to even remember his lies."

"The car wasn't locked," Ed said. "I slept in it until you come out for the paper."

"You didn't lock the car? All the break-ins around here and you didn't lock the goddamned car?" Betty engaged Sisler again. "I should get to hit the stupid bastard once just for that. It's not like a jury would do anything to me, all he's put me through." She took a breath and looked for a second as though she was done, then grabbed a mug off the table, turned, and threw it with force against the wall two feet from Doc's head.

Several seconds of stunned silence as everyone recognized the newcomer. "You know, Betty," Doc's voice flat, "if you'd hit me, you'd be on your way to jail now."

"It would've been an accident," Betty said. "No one knew you was there. Don't you cops have to say when you come in?"

"One cop's already in." Doc nodded to Sisler, who looked a little sheepish. "We don't have to announce *all* our comings and goings. As for the accident part, right now I'd say you're the only one here who'd argue the distinction."

"Now you see what I put up with every—"

"Shut up, Ed." Doc gave the world a few seconds to recognize this would not be a routine calming of the waters. "You say you slept in the car. Where?"

"What do you mean, 'Where?' It's in the driveway. You walked right past it."

"Did you curl up in the back seat or recline the front?"

"Uh, the front. I got a blanket I keep in the trunk and stretched out as best I could in the driver's seat." The blanket story rang true, Ed well-known for taking advantage of the

Hotel Chevrolet when relations became testy during more temperate weather.

"Rested your head on the window, didn't you?" Shot Sisler a quick *here's how we do this* look. "So it wouldn't loll around and wake you."

Ed's head drifted left as he thought. "Yeah. So it wouldn't slide off the headrest and wake me up. Bad enough I had to spend the night in the goddamned thing," staring at Betty. "Might as well get as much sleep as I could."

"All right," Doc said. "With your head in that position, the corner of the inside of the driver's window is going to be a lot warmer than the outside, right? From your body heat and breath."

"Yeah, I guess so." Doc had everyone's attention now. "I didn't check it or nothing."

"We'll check it now," Doc said.

"Hell, that was at least a half hour ago," Ed said. "It won't still be warm."

Doc sighed. "If it was warm, moisture condenses on the inside of the window. You know, like on the outside of a glass of iced tea. Water forms on the warm side."

"So?"

"So, cold as it is, there should still be moisture, maybe even ice, on the inside of the window, in that little corner. If there is, that's where you slept and Betty owes you an apology. If there's not, you're a lying sack of shit, just like she says. You want to take a look, Sis?"

Sisler already had his jacket zipped. "Absolutely."

"Let's not be too hasty," Doc said. "We have a domestic disturbance requiring police intervention. With violence."

"No one's hurt," Betty said with diminished venom.

"That's not your fault," Doc said. "You barely missed me with the mug. Lucky for you I'm not cut."

"Sorry."

"So we have a domestic with violence—which are always risky for everyone, including the cop—and, to tell the truth, all us cops are about sick and tired of your bullshit. Both of you." Shifted his glance between them so neither would question he meant it.

"Here's what we're going to do." Paused to make sure his audience hung on every word. "We're all going out to the car and check the window. If there's a patch of water, or ice that looks like it refroze, that's where Ed slept and Betty's going to jail. If there's no ice or water, Ed goes. You two's free passes are over."

The dynamic in the room had shifted. No longer a domestic dispute. More like a frustrated parent and two kids who'd misjudged his patience. Doc let it sink in, said, "Get your coats."

Betty lagged behind coming from the closet. "All's I got on is bedroom slippers. I'll catch my death if I go out in that mess."

"We'll wait," Doc said.

"Like hell," Ed said. "That water's melting or evaporating or whatever every minute we're in here."

"It's okay," Betty said. "You two cops go out and tell me what you see. I trust you."

Doc looked at Sisler. Ed barged between them. "Let's go."

Doc and Sisler shrugged at each other. Doc stepped back, waved for Sisler to go first. Ed walked down the three stairs from the porch and ran like hell at a forty-five-degree angle away from the driveway, toward Alder Street.

"Son of a bitch," Sisler said under his breath, took off running.

Doc stayed on the threshold out of the weather. Ed zigged once and zagged once before reaching Alder. Sisler didn't know the low spot, now filled in with three weeks' of accumulated snow and ice. Lost his balance, fell onto his chest and face like someone who'd been shot in the back.

Ed on Alder, slipping and sliding on snow packed hard as asphalt, now glazed with freezing rain. Sisler ran through the neighbor's yard, his boots gaining better traction in the crusty snow as he closed the distance.

Doc cursed to himself when he realized Ed would reach Leechburg Road before Sister caught him. Either way he turned, Doc would lose sight, which he couldn't afford to do, having started the whole thing. Pulled his collar up to keep out what rain he could and took one step on the porch when a car pulled off a salted Leechburg Road onto the skating rink Alder had become, into Ed's stumbling path. The car fishtailed. Ed moved to avoid it and guessed wrong. The impact with the sliding car rolled him over the hood.

Sisler got there in time to press Ed against the windshield as the car slid the last few feet. Doc yelled for Betty to call an ambulance and ran into the rain. Said, "Hold him," to Sisler as he passed, knocked on the driver's window showing his badge.

The late thirties woman behind the wheel looked as if Bigfoot was trying to get in. Pale, staring. Doc not sure she was breathing. The airbag hadn't deployed and she didn't appear to be hurt. Doc took off a glove and tapped three times with a knuckle he hoped would sound less threatening. Smiled and made a cranking motion.

The woman lowered the window and said in an airless voice, "Is he all right?" Still staring at Ed through the windshield.

Doc almost smiled. Never met her, had a real good idea of what she looked like when she was four years old. "I think he's okay. Do me a favor and put the car in Park for me. We may want to keep him on the hood until someone can have a look at him."

"Ohmygodyes." Almost pulled the shifter off making the change. "I never saw him. I dropped my daughter off at school and stopped at the store for a few groceries and was coming home to—I work at home and didn't want her to walk to school in this weather and I didn't have a big gap to turn left so I went a little faster than maybe I should have but I never expected to see—"

"Don't worry about it, ma'am," Doc said before she hyperventilated. "Two cops saw you do everything right." Jerked a thumb toward her windshield. "This is on him. Wait here and get ahold of yourself for a few minutes. Deep, even breaths. Be sure to breathe out." Reached across and turned off the ignition. "Get out and walk around if you want. You need to use the bathroom, let me know. It happens sometimes after a fright."

The woman nodded, started taking exaggerated breaths. Some color returned and satisfied Doc she wouldn't become the more serious casualty of the two.

He stepped back, looked to Sisler. "How is he?"

Sisler looked as though he didn't know how to feel. Part scared, part pissed, might laugh if an opportunity presented itself. "I don't see any blood."

Doc elevated his volume a notch. "Ed? You all right?"

"My back hurts. My legs hurt. Shoulder."

"Feel like anything's broken?"

"Don't think so. Sore. Stiff. Like I did too much yard work. You know."

"You okay holding him there until the ambulance comes?" Doc said to Sisler. "I don't want to move him with a possible back injury."

Sisler shifted his weight. "I'm good. Way he is right now, it's all leverage. I get tired I'll say so."

Doc about to ask him something else when the driver coughed, made a sound he didn't recognize, then vomited against the windshield and dashboard. Would have hit Ed in the face but for the glass.

"Oh, for Christ's sake." Doc reached in, tried to drag her out. Seat belt still fastened. Reached around, got her loose, eased her out of the car. Helped her lean over in case any was left and heard Sisler curse as Ed spewed on the outside of the glass.

"Get any on you?" Doc said.

Sisler checked, started to laugh. "I'm good. He got some blowback on his face."

"Good. Leave it. I'm going to get her some help."

Walked her back to the Schatz house, told Betty the woman needed to use her bathroom. Waited for Betty to come back.

"Here's the deal, Betty. You're going to wipe out the inside of her car so she can drive it. Then you're going to give her thirty bucks to take it to Prizco's or someplace and have it cleaned and smelling pretty. You understand me?"

"Why the hell'd he run for, the dumb bastard? Youns wouldn't a kept him more than overnight, would you?"

"If that. I'm making a bigger point here. You two get way too much police attention. Next time we show up here, we're not leaving empty-handed. You understand me?"

"Hey, it ain't my fault he ran. He's the one was out all night. All's I did was get the paper."

"Yeah, and make a federal case out of it. And throw a mug at me—"

"I didn't know you was there."

"We're tired of listening to your excuses. Both of you. Next time someone goes away. And you'd better hope I'm not around when it goes down, because I'll find charges. No more of this cooling off shit."

"You can't come in my house and talk to me like this," Betty said.

"I can, I did, and I don't care if you like it. Nod your head if you understand and keep your mouth shut." The woman came out of the bathroom, wan but sturdy. "Get the bucket and rags while I walk her back."

EMTs peeled Ed off the car as Doc took his time escorting the woman to her car. Explained how Officer Sisler would give her a ride home with her groceries and anything else she needed. Mrs. Schatz would clean up her car so it could be driven someplace to have it done proper, which the Schatzes would pay for. The woman tried to protest. Doc said to think of it as community service, since at least one of them had been this close to going to jail.

Sisler watched the EMTs check out Ed, rocking back and forth cop style, the leather of his belt making comforting creaking noises. Doc sent the woman—Pam Shearer—to her car to pick up the groceries and whatever else she didn't want to leave behind while Betty slopped away the vomit.

"Betty's going to clean up the car and pay for a trip to Prizco's." Doc watched Ed decide how much to pretend he was hurt. "I told her you'd give her a ride home. She lives up the block there."

"Sure," Sisler said. "Whenever she's ready."

"Hey, Ed," Doc yelled toward the ambulance. "Don't lie to those guys. You can't sue. Sisler and I will swear you ran right in front of her car. Nothing she could do. We'd be telling the truth, so I don't care who hears me tell you." Ed's recovery began and Doc turned back to Sisler.

"Why'd you chase him?"

"He ran."

"No car, in this weather, and we were already at his house. You let him go, worst that might happen is he falls. I'm not saying this was your fault." Pointed to Ed with the EMTs. "It's is an Ed Schatz production all the way. You only need to chase someone if he's a danger to others, or himself. Ed's just an asshole. No crime in that."

"He ran, Doc. He must've done something."

"Oh, I know exactly what he did."

"What?"

"He panicked. Stayed out too late last night, painted himself into a corner, and panicked."

"So he didn't sleep in the car."

Doc shrugged. "Who knows? He might have pulled in at five-thirty and took a nap there to make it look good. Doesn't matter."

"Why'd he run, then?"

"Because he'd put himself in a jackpot and didn't know how to get out." Sisler not satisfied. "A man like Ed Schatz is like...like...I don't know. A mole, maybe. Digs along, can't

213

see more than a foot in front of him in bright sunshine. Plugs away until he bumps into something. It's either good or bad. If it's good, he stays a while. If it's bad, he goes a different direction. You heard him on the car. He's not hurt bad. Now he's trying to tell those EMTs he's near death. The situation changed, so his direction did. He's a fucking mole man."

They watched the EMTs shine light in Ed's eyes, make him follow a finger, touch his nose. After a minute Sisler said: "Would you have arrested him? If the car window wasn't frosted?"

"Sis, I don't know if that window would be moist or frosty by now. I only did it to see who wanted to find out worse. Betty held back. Ed was all fired up to go. Why he ran, I have no idea. I doubt he does, either."

Doc flipped his collar up, nestled his head into the jacket as far as he could. "I hope the dumb SOB realizes how lucky he is."

"Lucky? How you figure?"

"Last time the two of us caught a runner, you shot his ass."

CHAPTER 40

Doc was soaked through, down to his boxers. Had to drive within a block of his house to get to the station, considered going home to change. If he went home he'd want to shower, drink a cup of hot chocolate to take away the chill. Ten minutes later he'd be asleep in the recliner. He kept a change of clothes at the station. He'd shower there.

Hanging his coat in the detective squad room when Neuschwander intercepted him, said he might have something on the Resurrection Mall shootings. Doc was cold and wet and miserable and wanted a shower and dry clothes. Good news on the Res Mall cluster fuck might make him less cold and wet and miserable. Neuschwander looked enthusiastic. The shower could wait.

Doc stood as close as he could to the heat vent. "What is it?"

"I've been running records checks and asking around all the contractors. Everyone put me off until I requested paperwork on the workers. Then they got in my face about how only feds can ask for I-9s and that, so I volunteered to get some feds down there. Said I was investigating a murder. I got some help there, I didn't care about any income tax or immigration crap." Neuschwander looked like a kid who'd solved the toughest problem in the math book.

Doc smiled with what he hoped was encouragement, more

due to the feeling returning to his feet. "That buy you any-thing?"

"Nothing we can take to court, but it showed me a couple of loose threads. You know, take what one guy told you to another guy—not letting him know where you got it—and it's surprising what people will tell you."

"Such as?" Doc's feet were warmer. Socks still stiff.

"I think kickbacks are being paid. Bids might be rigged, too, but I'm surer about the kickbacks. There's two problems."

Doc opened his hands, palms up. He wanted to feel better, for Neuschwander's sake, starting to put together what Doc had taught him. Bringing it to him like a dog carrying a dead squirrel to its master. So far, the story hadn't warmed Doc as much as he'd hoped, and he was too miserable to be encouraging.

"Well, to prove anything is going to take someone looking into the books on the contractors' side, and on the Res Mall side. We can't do that. Well, maybe you can. I know dick about accounting."

"Me, either. That's okay. We can call in the staties if it comes to it. What's the other problem?"

"Did I say two? Damn. I keep thinking of more."

"Lay them out one by one, but, you know, in a timely manner."

"Well, it's going to take forever. Even if the staties help us, you know how accountants are, especially if they're trying to hide something. It could take years."

"There's no statute of limitations on murder. I'd like to close this sooner rather than later, too. Whenever we get them, they'll be just as got."

Neuschwander took time digesting the idea. Penns River didn't do open-ended investigations, except for Dougherty's unofficial Marian Widmer crusade. With three detectives, cases not closed in a few weeks or months were overtaken by events.

"You think? I mean, we can probably browbeat a couple contractors into giving us stuff, but Res Mall? It's going to take warrants to see those books, and they have the juice to block us."

"Us, maybe. If we have to call in the staties to read the contractors' books—which we will, if we have to—they can handle Res Mall. The town might want to pull back so it doesn't look racist and maybe lose even more jobs. Some state cop...well, he doesn't want to look racist, either, but he doesn't have to live here. They want those books, they'll get them." Neuschwander didn't speak. "What's bothering you, Noosh?"

"Nothing, really. It's just...I don't feel like we have a good grip on this. It's...slippy. You know, like trying to open a jar when your hands are greasy. We let a piece of it go to the staties...well, you know what they're like to work with."

"Some of them aren't so bad. It's not like they're feds." Now Doc had to think a little. "You know what? Don't worry about it. Doesn't matter who works it. If we have to go down that road, someone above our pay grades will sort out the jurisdictional issues. Not our problem."

Neuschwander not at all happy now. "Damn, Doc. You ready to quit on this?"

"What makes you think I'm ready to quit?"

"Well, everything I bring up, you right away talk about giving it away. We worked everything ourselves when we had those homicides a couple years ago."

Doc's voice harsher than he meant it to be. "We didn't close them, either"

"That Widmer guy's in jail for the Cropcho woman."

"Okay, one, and he was teed up for us. Who killed the guy in the vacant? What's his name, Frantz?"

"The Polack from Youngstown did him, right? Orszulak."

"Did we take him down for it?"

"Well, no. He got clipped before we had a chance."

"Did we find the guys who clipped him?"

"Didn't we decide Mannarino had him done?"

"Did we prove it?"

This reply came slower. "Well, no."

"We figure Mannarino also did Donte Broaddus. Did we prove it?"

Momentum drained from the conversation. "No."

"That's right. Whoever did both of those walks around as free as you and me. We aren't here to make educated guesses about who killed who. We're here to lock them up, and I'd like to do a couple before I die.

"I'm not giving up on this. We have two good suspects with nothing hard to tie them to it. You're doing exactly what you should be doing: following the money. The problem here is, this money may have to be tracked from the top down, and we'll need help to get at it. I'm tired of running into people on the street I know are killers and them knowing I know, and both of us knowing there's fuck all I can do about it. If it takes the state police to bring these sons of bitches down, I'll hold the door and make sure I'm not blocking the photographers' view when they make the arrests."

Neuschwander couldn't have looked more shocked if he'd been slapped. Doc patted his upper arm. "I'm sorry, buddy. You're doing good work here. Keep pushing. I'm tired and I'm cold and I'm wet and I'm wishing it was Friday and it's barely noon on Monday. Tell you what. Let me get on some dry clothes and I'll buy you lunch at the Back Door."

"No, it's okay. I know you're not mad at me."

"Let's go, anyway. I'm entitled to have one thing go right today, and I'd rather talk about your kids than eat alone. Give me fifteen minutes."

CHAPTER 41

Doc got fifteen seconds before Stush called him into his office. "Shut the door, Benny. Have a seat." Doc shut the door and sat. "You run into Marian Widmer the other day?"

"Saturday. At the post office."

"You give her a hard time?"

Doc pulled back his first thought. "Define hard time."

"What did you say to her?"

"As I recall, I complimented her on her looks."

Stush left time for an amended statement. Said, "That's not how I heard it."

Doc loved Stush as if he were his real uncle, in no mood for dancing around. "Tell me what whoever it was said and I'll tell you how much of its bullshit."

"What makes you think any of its bullshit?"

"Because I know what I did and it doesn't rate this."

Stush took a mint from a bowl on his desk. Unwrapped it, put the whole thing in his mouth. Crumpled the wrapper and threw it in the wastebasket. "How'd it go with the Schatzes?"

"Betty threw a mug at me and Ed got hit by a car. Come on, Stush. I'm wet and I'm cold. You called me on the carpet and I'd like to get off it so I can get dry and warm again. What did Marian Widmer tell you?"

"I haven't seen her," Stush said. "Rance Doocy—you know, Dan Hecker's right-hand man—called this morning.

Said he was with her in the post office Saturday and you made a scene."

"That was Doocy?" Doc snorted. "You'd think with all Hecker's money he could afford a chin."

Stush stifled most of a smile. Turned down the intensity of his voice. "Tell me what happened."

"I went in to mail a package. Marian and this suit walked in a couple of minutes later. I think there was one person in line between me and them. When I was done I waited for her by the door, and complimented her on her looks."

"Compliments can cover a wide range with you," Stush said. "What exactly did you say?"

"I don't remember exactly. It wasn't like I scripted it out."

"Make an effort."

Doc hated having his own pet phrases used against him. "I might have implied it looked like some work had been done. Nothing vulgar or lewd."

"Doocy said she's considering a harassment claim."

Doc smiled, and meant it. "Yeah, he mentioned something about that. I told him it didn't apply. Recited some of the statute for him, so he wouldn't make himself look foolish. You can't be nice to some people."

Stush rocked back in the chair. Stifled the laugh, not the smile. "Benny…"

"Here's what happened. I made my friendly, and highly complimentary, comment when they passed by. Doocy got the red ass, said I'd been looking at Marian since she walked in. I said, yeah, I make it a point never to turn my back on Mrs. Widmer."

"Aw, shit."

"Then he got to talking about harassment and I told him

why it wouldn't fly. I think we left it with him saying he was with her and I said he was welcome to her. Not as harsh as it might sound the way I told it to you just now."

"So you know," Stush said, "I wasn't the first person Doocy called this morning."

"Chet Hensarling." The mayor.

"And Chet called right after Doocy did."

"Sorry, Stush. I know you don't need Chet up your ass right now." Doc *was* sorry. About Stush getting dragged into it.

Stush held his reading glasses by one sidepiece, tapped them into an open hand. "You really don't give a shit, do you?"

"About what?"

"About anything you don't feel like giving a shit about. This job? I'll fight anyone who says you don't care. Your friends. Your family. All those are important to you. But anything you personally don't see a use for?"

"You mean bullshit."

"Sure, it's bullshit." Stush tossed the glasses onto his desk. "It's the people who bring the bullshit make the rules. You think you can ignore the parts you don't like—make fun of them, even—and none of it will roll back down on you."

Doc got quiet. "You know me better than that."

Stush tapped his belly. "You're right. I apologize. You'll start the shit, knowing it rolls downhill and you'll be at the bottom, and you *still* don't care. You'll take it. Hell, Benny, I think you like it. Why is that?"

"I don't know," Doc said. "I really don't. It's not like I can't leave well enough alone. It's more like I don't want to."

"Benny, Benny, Benny." Stush watched a short movie only

he could see. "You would've been one hell of a beat cop sixty, seventy years ago." Eased his way back to the here and now. "Here's the thing: it don't work like that anymore. You know me, too. I'd a paid money to watch you give that Widmer broad the business. She's trash who doesn't deserve to breathe free air. Right now she's breathing it, and we have to share it. I need you to leave her alone. For your Uncle Stush. A personal favor."

"It's not like I'm out looking for her," Doc said. "Both times we ran into each other were random."

"I know, and I believe you. What I want you to do for me is to leave her alone. Don't walk away, or make it obvious you're avoiding her. We're the police here. We don't walk away from anybody. Just, you know, keep your mouth shut. Can you do that? For me?"

"Yeah," Doc said. "I can." Took his time to form the next question. "You know I'm still showing her pictures around, right? On my own time."

"With that barmaid. Kate, is it?"

Doc nodded. "Is that going to be a problem? If I keep it up?"

"Even a cop's entitled to a social life." Stush scooped a handful of jelly beans. "Besides, I want that whore in jail. She owes us."

CHAPTER 42

Rodney Simpson knew his mouth hung open. He didn't care.

"You're firing me?"

"Ain't what I said." Cassius Abernathy sat back in his chair, spread his hands. "The Rev wants me to make sure you understand we laying you off. Said 'fired' make it sound like you done something wrong. This got nothing to do with you. We can't afford to pay you, so you're laid off."

"Laid off and fired ain't no different."

"I feel you," Abernathy said. "They don't seem no different to me, neither. I axed the Rev 'bout that. He told me used to be, getting laid off a temporary thing. Bidness got bad, people let go till things picked up again. I guess construction work, some mills and mines all like that. Company had lay-offs wouldn't hire no one new when things picked up, brought back the same workers. Says he don't know when it changed, when 'laid off' come to mean 'don't come back.' He promises he'll bring you back soon as he can."

"It's bullshit, what this is. Ain't no one worked more than Rodney on this motherfucker. No one."

"Watch your mouth, boy. Fired or laid off or what, you in a church here." Rodney swallowed an answer. "No argument from me 'bout how hard you work. Life ain't always fair. My experience, life almost never fair. What make a man is how he deal with it. Get your things." Put on a show of sorting papers on his desk.

Rodney made no motion to leave. "What you want, boy?" Abernathy said. "I got work."

"That's what I want," Rodney said. "Work. Put me to work."

"I told you. There's no work here for you. Pick up your things."

"You said you can't pay me," Rodney said. "I know there's work. I'll do it free."

Abernathy stopped pretending to be busy. "You're saying you'll work for free." Not a question.

"I'm playing the long game, Mr. A. We both know there's money to be made here. We just have to keep things together till it come available."

Rodney had Abernathy's full attention. "What money you talking about? This a church, boy. What they call a non-profit organization. Anything extra go to the church."

"A lot of money pass through here before it's over. Enterprising man know how to get a little to stick to him." Abernathy gave him the look that faced down a hundred prison hard cases over the years. "Ain't no way I'm talking about stealing from the church. What Doc Love doing here a good thing. I'm all in and shit. There's other things, you know, perennial to this, where a man can stay alert and help himself. Look at them what runs these bidnesses. They good people, they all love God, but they ain't savvy, you know? They be needing help, sooner or later."

Abernathy made Rodney wait for what seemed half an hour, couldn't have been more than ten seconds. "Tell me."

"Reverend Love say he can't pay me. That means he got

no use for me worth paying for. Way I sees, it not so much a matter of how much he can afford to pay than how he can't not afford to have me around. He don't see that. I'm hoping you do." Abernathy gave away nothing. "I respect Doc Love and all. You know I do. We—you and me—we see opportunity different. He looking at Res Mall to help others. More power to him. I don't see no conflict in helping yourself at the same time, is all."

"Doing well while doing good," Abernathy said.

"Yeah. Something like that. A lot of money be passing through here. Work crews making money. Bosses making money. Doc Love making money. Pretty soon bidnesses making their own money here."

"It's the church making money," Abernathy said. "Not Dr. Love."

"His choice," Rodney said. "He could be. A lot of money come and go. A man with some talent, don't get greedy, could take a little and it never be missed. Like scooping cupfuls of water from a river." Rodney paused, tried to hold Abernathy's gaze, pulled away. "I know you know what I'm talking about."

"I do?"

Rodney took his time. A hard decision to be made before he said more. "I seen you. More than once. With the bosses. Sometimes with the workers. I wondered why Deacon Lewis ain't in on it, him the one writing the contracts. Then I finally figured out what his problem is: he don't get it." Rodney tapped his forehead. "He don't grasp the opportunity, dig?"

"Go on."

"He in the perfect position to make this work, but you the

one doing it, and I'm thinking, god*damn*—sorry—but you getting it done. Not so's it hurts what we doing here, and not so's you getting rich—least you ain't showing off like it—but you taking money out of here. I ain't fussing. You deserve it for seeing what's possible. All's I'm saying is, I see it, too."

"What do you want?"

"I want to help you. I help you, you teach me."

"Help me with what?" Abernathy's voice so soft, Rodney almost didn't hear him.

"Whatever you need. Money's tight around here. Maybe you need someone to shake the tree for you."

"You don't think I can shake it myself."

"That's not no way what I'm saying. I'm just looking to cut myself in a little. I ain't begging. I got talents. Set me to do something can help you, and let it help me. Same's as you doing with the church, but, you know, shrunk down."

"You want to do something for me?" Abernathy said. "Something to get things up and running again? Get the money spicket working?"

"Absolutely. I'm your man."

Abernathy leaned onto his elbows, kept his voice low. "Find the stupid motherfuckers offed them niggers in the food court. The problems we had were bad, but we could find a way around them. That's gone now."

"I thought the dealers *was* the problem. Keeping money away and all. I heard you tell the Rev."

"They were *a* problem. Getting their shit blown up the way they did give us a problem way worse. I mighta got them out and no one be any wiser how it got done. Now I don't know how we ever get the stink off us."

"I thought whatever bad come outta that would blow

over. I mean, this a church. People knows shooting ain't the regular way things go."

"Blow over? Boy, it can't begin to blow over till whoever done it out the game. Till then, good, clean folk who mighta thought of spending some money down here think it ain't safe, crazed shotgun killers running around in broad daylight and shit. Those motherfuckers needs to get caught, and quick.

"You want to help? You hang with some of the homeboys here." Rodney couldn't hide his surprise. "Yeah, that's right. I seen you, too. Find out something about who responsible for this cluster fuck. Give it to me and I'll find a way to show people who might want to leave some money here we got things under control. Let me see what you can do, the money start to flow, I'll find something for you even if Reverend Love don't. Till then, I don't want to have to account for why you hanging around here. You laid off. Get the fuck out."

CHAPTER 43

Doc found Delonte Bickerstaff the same place as before. Near the entrance to Resurrection Mall, not so close he'd discourage shoppers. "Mr. Bickerstaff, I wonder if I could interest you in lunch today."

"Has the humanitarian urge overtaken your sense of smell and decorum? I'm no cleaner than the last time you were here."

"I know a guy at the YMCA. You can use their showers."

"After which I'll put on the same clothes."

"I don't see why. I scrounged a couple pair of coveralls from maintenance. I took off the county badges so you won't look like you're doing community service."

"You thought of everything, didn't you?" Bickerstaff waited for Doc to agree. Doc outlasted him. "What about my stuff? I'll have nothing left if I leave it here. We watch each other's backs, but our possessions belong to whoever has them."

Doc held out a black plastic contractor's bag. "Will this do?"

"I don't know if everything will fit." Doc produced another bag. "All right, goddamnit. Let's go."

They piled the bags into the trunk of Doc's city car. Seat belts on, Doc handed Bickerstaff a worn toilet bag. Bickerstaff opened it to find soap, shampoo, a disposable razor, shaving cream, toothbrush, toothpaste, and deodorant. "Where are the clothes?"

"After you're cleaned up."

"Good idea."

An hour later Doc and Bickerstaff sat in Caroline's Family Restaurant, ahead of the lunch rush. Doc ordered a club sandwich with chips, and a Coke. Bickerstaff stared at the menu. Doc kicked his shin gently. "Whatever you want. It's on the city."

"I'll have the twelve ounce sirloin. Baked potato with sour cream and chives. House salad with French dressing on the side. Ice water."

The waitress left. Bickerstaff said, "How do I rate an expense account?"

"Official business."

"What kind?"

Doc hesitated, hoping to lend the weight of implied thought to something he'd rehearsed half a dozen times. "Mr. Bickerstaff, do you know what makes a good cop?"

"I could say training and hard work and intelligence and a conscientious attitude, but you have something in mind already."

"Sources," Doc said. "A cop is no better than his sources."

"Oh my God. You want me to snitch."

"No," Doc said. "I do not."

"You have another name for it?"

"A snitch is a lowlife degenerate common criminal who trades information to keep his ass out of jail. Half of what he tells you is bullshit and the other half has an agenda."

"How would I be different?"

"First off, you're none of the above. There's nothing you want from me, so I can trust you."

"You're right: there's nothing I want from you. Why should I do it?"

"Two reasons. One, you're not any happier than I am about how things are downtown. You see what's wrong, who's doing it, and no one pays any attention to you. You're a fly on the wall."

"For now. Once people start going away, they're going to wonder what happened, and I'm out there all alone for any-one who figures it out."

"That's another way you'll be different. I'm not coming to you for information. If you learn something that might interest me, you go to any pay phone and dial three-one-one. Give the dispatcher a code word. Then we'll talk."

"You're saying you're not going to come to me with questions?"

"I'm not saying I never will," Doc said. "If I do, it will only be to confirm something I've found elsewhere."

"I'm not tied to my current location, you know. A man like me, things come up. I have to be ready to go where life takes me."

"If I miss you, I miss you. I'm not asking you to do my job for me. Point me in the right direction once in a while, is all."

Bickerstaff worked on his salad. Didn't speak again until their meals arrived. "You said two reasons."

"The time may come when your present circumstances don't appeal to you as much as they do now. It might be nice to know someone who'll put in a good word when a city job comes available, or hook you up with a cheap, clean place to live. Only if the idea appealed to you, of course."

Bickerstaff slid a piece of steak through a puddle of A-1. "The city isn't paying for this, is it?"

"Indirectly."

"As in, the city pays your salary, and you're paying for the meal." Doc shrugged. "Why?"

"Downtown is getting away from us. We didn't know those five at Res Mall were dealing until they were dead. We still don't know who's filling the vacuum. We need a better handle on what goes on down there. I'm not asking you to talk to people, or poke around on your own. Tell me what you see. I need the help."

Bickerstaff finished his potato, skin and all. "You really are depressing, you know that? Has the mayor, city council heard your rap?"

"I try to keep it on the down low as much as possible."

"Good idea. I'm going to assume you checked me out before you made this offer, you being a cop and all."

"Nope." Doc meant it. "You want to tell me your story, I'll listen. You don't want to, that's your business."

"You're asking a lot," Bickerstaff said.

"I know. You don't need to answer now. I'll take you back and you can call me sometime with information, or not. You won't hear from me again unless you call."

"You are the most trusting cop I have ever seen." The last of the steak disappeared. "Do you know if they still make those brownie desserts?"

CHAPTER 44

Christian Love greeted Doc as he would a pierced and tattooed young man calling on his daughter. Offered him coffee and a seat, spoke before Doc got settled.

"What's your business, Detective?"

"Doctor Love, sir, I'd like to keep this visit off the record, as much as it can be. That's why I asked to see you alone, and I appreciate you doing it. I have some things to tell you you're not going to like, and I apologize in advance for that. I'm hoping I can do you a courtesy, keeping you advised of things before they're brought to you officially. So you won't get caught unaware. No one else knows I'm here."

If that impressed Love, he hid it well. "What courtesy are you about to do me?"

"Things are progressing," Doc said. "We have a couple of suspects—pretty good ones, I think—and we have a witness." Doc paused until Love stopped pretending to read papers on his desk. "We also found some financial issues with the contractors working on Resurrection Mall."

"'Financial issues' is a very...sterile way to put it." Love's full attention now on Doc. "Specifically what?"

"Bid rigging and kickbacks."

"Do you always look into the finances of a property where homicides occur, or only when there are African-Americans with you might call *histories* involved?"

"We have one witness to the actual shooting; more would

be better. The shooters had to walk right past the work area, so there's a decent chance someone saw them. A detective's been checking the work crews, looking for anyone here that day who might've seen the shooters come in. Should've been pretty straightforward, except the contractors' records aren't what you'd like to see from a professional operation."

"You're aware many of them are minority contractors."

"All we cared about was who worked that day. No one could tell us. We heard a lot of *day laborers* and *they come and go.* So our detective, bless his heart, asked about their tax records. How was withholding being taken care of, did they have peoples' socials. Stuff like that. All he wanted was a list of who might possibly have been there that day."

"I believe you're about to tell me he didn't get it."

"You're right. The thing is, they all got the red ass about it. Told him how a local cop couldn't ask to see their tax records and did they have I-9s for everyone. Said all that was federal and none of his business. The response was out of proportion to what he asked for."

Doc paused for an expected comment, didn't get one. "So our guy says he's investigating a murder. He doesn't care about tax issues or illegals or anything else. All he wants to know is who was there. If getting a fed down to look into a few peripheral things is what it takes, he's all set to make a phone call. That bought him some cooperation. You're paying prevailing wage on this job, right?"

"Of course. I'm not going to take advantage of anyone."

"I didn't think you would. Here's the thing. The contracts are written to pay prevailing wage, but the contractors are still hiring day laborers and paying them cash as much as they can get away with. They don't clear enough to break even if they don't."

"That's one contractor skimming," Love said. "Tell me who it is and he'll be gone tomorrow."

"No, sir. Our man picked up that story pretty much across the board. The contracts only go to those who play ball, and they all pay a premium to get them. For some it's a pretty hefty premium."

Love stared at a spot on the wall behind Doc. "You're telling me Deacon Lewis is extorting them?"

"No, sir, I'm not. We really don't know who it is, or how it's being handled. None of them would go on the record with names, but, the way they talked, our man had the impression it was more likely Abernathy."

"Abernathy doesn't handle the contracts," Love said. "Lewis does."

"I know. Something's not right. That's why I'm here."

"You're here because you want something from me."

"I'm not here to ask you for a thing," Doc said. "After we talk, if you learn anything of interest and want to share it, I'll be grateful. That'll be up to you."

Love sat at an angle to his desk. Right hand flat on the surface. Left on the arm of the chair. No tells. Doc assumed Love had been played by cops before, considering the kinds of people he did business with. No point saying he wasn't here to play him; that's what he'd say if he were.

Love said, "All right. You don't want anything from me. What *do* you want?"

"I want you to keep your eyes open. For your own good."

"Are you threatening me?"

"No, sir. This has attracted a lot of media. You tend to

attract media on your own. No offense; we both know it's true. Word of this kickback business—rumor or not—is going to get out. It won't come from me, and it won't come from the cop who told me. This is a small town, and people aren't used to national media hanging around. Sooner or later a familiar face is going to get a local to say something we'd all rather have left unsaid. I don't want *60 Minutes* or *Dateline* to walk in here and ask you questions you had no reason to expect."

Love raised two fingers from the desk for a second. "Appreciate it."

"And there's also our investigation. We may have to look at those numbers, see if there might be motive or mechanism to the shootings involved. If the contractors' books get looked at, there's a good chance yours will, too, if only to compare them for discrepancies. Penns River doesn't have the resources to handle an accounting investigation. The state does, and they'll come with warrants and subpoenas and take over the place."

"Let them come. It's not as if I can stop them, even if I wanted to. Which I wouldn't."

"You can be ready, though. If it comes to it, and you've already had some kind of audit run..." Doc opened his hands. "All I'm saying is, if there was anything to find and you found it, it would look better. They'll still look, but you'll have got out in front of it."

Love's posture had relaxed. Still one hand on the desk and one on the chair, no longer flat and neutral. His eyes softer, so little only a pro would notice. "Anything else?"

"Just that I was never here and we never talked about this. I won't be back in anything other than an official capacity."

"You don't want me to tell you if our internal audit finds anything? If we have an audit, I mean."

"Sure I do. I won't ask. That'll be up to you, unless circumstances force me to come back with a warrant."

Love shifted in his chair to look out the sole window, which opened along the main promenade of Resurrection Mall. Doc didn't have to look to know what Love saw. A mess. Most of what had been completed too close to the office to be seen from above. Several small groups chatted in the food court. Beyond them, half a dozen small businesses still setting up. The opposite side of the main entrance a maelstrom of plastic and canvas sheeting, scaffolding, ladders, troughs, and work lights. Even the finished areas had the shabbiness of something clean and neat and done on a shoestring, more like the last holdover of a decaying neighborhood than a new addition.

"Why are you here?" Love said. "I know a little about you. You're close to the chief. I also know enough about police work and politics to know that doesn't give you complete immunity. You took a chance coming here. Unless he sent you."

Doc took his time to answer. "I was born here. Grew up here. The economy was already bad then, and it never got better. My parents remember when this was a place worth moving to, when there were jobs and money. Not a lot of money—millhunk money—still, decent jobs. Where we are right now—" pointed to the floor, "—used to be busy all day. People coming and going, shopping. If what you want to do here can take the shithole it's become, excuse me, and turn it even part way around, I'm good with that."

Love spoke to the window. "Do you think I'm a carpetbagger, Detective Dougherty?"

Doc hadn't thought of it in those terms before. "A little. You didn't pick Penns River as an act of charity. With the casino and a few other facts of life around here, you get to expand your church and make more of a splash than if you'd bought a bigger building in Pittsburgh."

"So you see me much the same way you see Daniel Hecker. Exploiting the town for my own benefit."

"Not at all. You have your reasons for being here, but in the end, you want do well by doing good. It's the nature of your business. Hecker's a parasite. Puts on airs like he's a savior when all he cares about is how much money he can haul out of here. He picked us because we were easy. You picked us because we were hard."

Love shifted to face Doc. "You don't think much of Mr. Hecker."

"You've never spent much time in a casino, have you?"

"Literally no time at all."

"I didn't think so. I'm trying to think of how to describe it. You ever watch the TV show *Deadwood*?"

"I've heard enough of it to suspect it wouldn't be to my taste."

Doc snorted. "No argument there, though I'd love to get your opinion on parts of it. Anyway, the main bad guy is Al Swearengen. One day he's talking with his closest competitor about the problems with running their businesses, which are combination saloons, casinos, and brothels. Al turns to Cy— the other guy's name is Cy Tolliver—and Al says, 'You know, sometimes I wish we could hit them over the head, take their money, and throw their bodies in the creek.' That's what casinos are like. They dress them up all shiny and exciting, but don't kid yourself. They feel like you stole every dollar you leave with, even if you brought it in with you."

Love might have had a twinkle in his eye. "You don't think the same of me?"

"You and he appeal to different constituencies." A half smile. "You get the benefit of the doubt."

Love responded with a full smile. "For how long?"

Doc laughed. "Till you screw me."

Both men in good spirits now. "Then what will you do?"

"Beats me. Been so long since I trusted anyone, I forget what my end is."

Wood fell in the work area, hollow echoes ricocheted off walls through the food court. Love turned away from the interruption with remnants of his smile. "I appreciate you coming to see me today, Detective Dougherty. I know I said that before, but I want to make a point of it. You didn't have to, probably should not have. Our earlier meetings were not cordial, yet you accepted the risk. You have my word not to speak of this to anyone, and my invitation to come back any time you want to talk off the record, no matter the topic. I suspect I can learn a lot about Penns River from you, and I dearly want this church to be a good citizen."

He rose, hand extended. They shook and Doc left, unsure whether Love thought an attempt had been made to play him, or if Doc had been played himself.

CHAPTER 45

"You get enough to eat? There's more fish."

Doc pushed back from his second fish sandwich dinner in less than a week. His mother called before he got off work: fish sandwiches for supper. As close as she ever got to asking him to come over. Sunday dinner was assumed, though Doc missed this week to help a friend organize his garage and stayed for his payment of pizza and beer and a chance to chase small children around the house. "I'm done, Mom. Thanks. That was excellent."

Ellen made part of a face, cheered herself with, "I'll wrap the fish up for you to take home. I know you nibble on them cold." He did, too, and would before he went to bed.

Doc offered to help clean, knowing she'd have none of it. "Go watch hockey with your dad." She'd be there in a minute. Doc hated the mess she had to clean from hot oil spitting onto the countertop. The Formica had to squeak before she'd ask if anybody wanted anything and sit down to watch the game.

He thought sometimes of not accepting an invitation, save her the work. Then he remembered how their visits went, how he and Tom would talk about sports or the town or yard work while she'd sit and pretend to be interested. Getting him to sit and eat what she cooked was her triumph, and he owed her a few. That and not knowing how many more fish sandwiches were left.

Tom in his recliner. Doc near the arm of the couch, rested his water glass on an end table. Tom glanced over his shoulder at Ellen running water and scrubbing. "How's things at work?"

"Busy," Doc said.

"Good busy or bad busy?"

"I'm a cop," Doc said. "There is no good busy. Best I can say is we might be making progress on Resurrection Mall."

"You have any suspects?"

Doc swallowed water. "I think we have a couple of good ones. Maybe even a witness. Shit for evidence, except one of Grabek's shots in the dark from the hip might finally pay off."

"How so?"

"We're all guessing the killers threw their guns in the river on the way out of town, so we'll never match the murder weapons to anything or anyone. Willie told a suspect there was a construction barge under the bridge and one of the guns fell into it."

"Bridge work? In this weather?"

"That's what I thought. Except this clown drives all the way up from the Burgh the same night to check it out. Sisler even got his signature on a ticket. Stush was so happy he got Chet Hensarling to authorize paying for cold weather divers to see what they can find once the ice breaks up."

"Wow." Tom sat back, impressed. "That was stupid."

"What do I keep telling you?" Doc said. "This is why they're criminals. Stupid and lazy. Invest more time and effort getting out of honest work than it would've taken to do the damn work."

Conversation paused while Brian Williams noted who'd

hosed them today. Ellen even stopped working to stand in the doorway where she could hear. Said, "Bastards," under her breath when the commercial came on, went back to cleaning.

Tom waited until water ran in the sink. "You still trying to put that woman lives up the hill away? The one you think had those people killed a couple years ago?"

"She *did* have those people killed. Yeah, I look into it once in a while. Why do you ask?"

"I hear you and her had words the other day." Doc grunted, recapped Saturday's post office adventure. "You be careful around Doocy," Tom said. "He can have your job."

Doc shook his head. "No, he can't. He may work for a guy who thinks he owns the joint. He has no official standing."

"You know what I mean. Doocy tells the mayor to eat shit, Chet's only question is 'do you have a spoon?'"

"I'm good with Stush," Doc said. Sipped his water. "Hensarling can't fire me, even if I did piss him off. I'm in the union. He needs cause."

"It'll be him decides who'll be chief when Stan retires."

"Come on, Dad. Even Stush has this figured out by now. I don't want the job."

Tom tilted the chair forward, drank iced tea from a glass resting on a convenient speaker. "What if it came down to you or Harriger? I mean, they'd give it to you—I can see Stush getting them to at least offer—but Harriger gets it if you don't take it. There's not really anyone else here could do it."

"It won't come to that."

"It could."

"It won't. If I said no, they'd half to look outside. Half the force would quit if Harriger took over."

"Guys say that now, when it's just talk," Tom said. "When the time comes—if it comes—a lot of tough talkers will think about their car payments and bills and kids needing clothes and realize there's not much else they can do and there are no other jobs. You see where Cheswick laid off their only cop the other day? Harmar's going to cover them."

Doc knew. He also knew the odds better than fifty-fifty he'd have to make this exact decision someday. "I have faith in Stush."

Tom let out a small sigh. "Stan Napierkowski is sixty-some years old and at least that much overweight. His next heart attack will kill him. He'd never let either of us down on purpose. Just remember it might not be up to him."

The one subject Doc liked less than talking about becoming chief: the mortality of those he loved. Old enough to understand its inevitability, too young to resign himself to accept the loss of people he couldn't imagine life without.

Ellen came in from the kitchen drying her hands. "I thought you two were watching hockey. Anyone want anything?"

"What time is it?" Tom checked the clock. Seven-fourteen. "Oh, shit." Took the remote off the speaker to change channels.

"Benny," his mother said, "you want some iced tea or water?"

"I'm good, Mom. Sit down and watch the game for a while, okay?"

CHAPTER 46

Penns River's temperatures up to seasonal norms; twenty-three the forecast low. Sean Sisler didn't bother to hide his cruiser in the parking lot of a defunct tire store across the street from Allegheny Casino. Ran the engine and defroster when things got uncomfortable or windows fogged. Sipped Wendy's coffee from next door, not worried about bathroom breaks. If anyone wanted him, they'd call.

A car went past every thirty to forty seconds on average. No cars leaving the casino showed obvious driver impairments or broken windows, though the car thieves were known to be more professional than that. Rested his head against the driver door to see if there would be a difference in the moisture or ice from his body heat like Doc had told Ed Schatz. Not as cold tonight, and Sisler wondered if his frequent defroster use invalidated the experiment.

He passed the time inventing stories of where cars had come from and where they were going, or how well a driver had done in the casino. Every ten minutes or so he keyed the radio to make sure it still worked. It always did, and he still kept checking, a cop's security blanket.

The call came at eleven-forty-three. "PR Six, do you copy?"

"I'm here, Brenda. What's up?"

"The casino called with a possible DWI. He didn't see the guy get into his car, but said he doesn't think enough people

244

have left in the past few minutes to make him hard to spot."

Sisler's line of sight came up to take in the lot across the street as Brenda Schmidt spoke. A dark Nissan Altima pulled out of the exit to his left. No other movement in the lot.

"I'm on it. Out."

He let the Nissan pass the funeral home before he moved up and maintained a position where the driver couldn't miss seeing him in his mirrors. Both cars traveling at forty-five. Quarter of a mile down the road the Nissan's brake lights flashed twice. Its speed fell to thirty; limit was thirty-five. Lots of people did that when they saw a cop. Not what Sisler would call articulable suspicion.

They drove in tandem past the Y where Edgecliff fed into Leechburg Road. Any time the speed touched thirty-five the Nissan's brake lights flashed, as though the driver believed he, alone among all the drivers in the world, would be cited for driving thirty-six. Sisler imagined him flicking his eyes back and forth from the speedometer to the road. Who worries about that fine a distinction so much he's on the brakes every five or ten seconds?

Drunks.

Sisler flipped on the light bar. No siren, not this time of night. Still some residences sprinkled among the businesses on Leechburg Road, most owned by older folks who hadn't sold with their former neighbors. The last thing Sisler wanted was to hear from some old biddy how his siren woke her in the middle of the night for no good reason, what the hell was this, Pittsburgh?

The Nissan stopped in the parking lot of an auto shop less than a quarter mile from the police station, which Sisler thought was damned convenient if he had to take the driver in. He pulled behind in classic traffic stop position, checked the plate. The car registered to Rodney Simpson. It was clean, and so was he.

Sisler exited the car, slid his baton into the ring on his belt with one hand, turned on the big Maglite with the other. Shined the light inside the Nissan. Black male, twenties, both hands on the wheel. The window still up. Sisler knocked with a knuckle. "Put down the window, please, sir." Then, after it opened, "License and registration, please."

"What I do?"

"You were driving erratically. I need to see your license and registration, please."

"I ain't driving no kind of 'ratic. This some driving while black shit, what this is."

The driver smelled like the survivor of a distillery explosion. Sisler could afford to seem magnanimous. "I'll be happy to provide a number you can call to complain if you think you're being treated unfairly, sir. License and registration, please."

"What if I say no?"

The car's clock read eleven-fifty-three. Seven minutes till end of shift. Sisler didn't mind working overtime to write this asshole up, could live without the attitude. "Sir, that's a lawful and reasonable order. Failure to comply would subject you to arrest."

The driver looked straight ahead. "You gonna arrest me? By yourself?"

Sisler almost smiled. No doubt he could take this bantam alone. With a shift change in seven minutes, he could have three cops there in under ninety seconds if he wanted them. "Sir, you don't want to be arrested over something petty like that, do you?" Sisler had bigger and better things in mind for this jagov. "You don't look like someone I'd want to mess with on my own. If you make me call for help, get other people involved...Let me have the license and registration and we'll do this the easy way."

"That's a'ight. I get 'em for ya." The glove box took three tries to open. The wallet came from a hip pocket. Cards were shuffled, some dropped. "This it?"

"No, sir. It's a Sam's Club card. How about there, on the left. Behind the little window." The driver made to hand out the entire wallet. "Take it out of the wallet, please."

The driver was, in fact, Rodney Simpson. Lived in East Liberty; no outstanding warrants or previous arrests. One citation for ignoring a *No Turn on Red* sign. No evidence of being as tough as he acted.

Sisler walked back to Simpson's car. Returned the license and registration. "Everything looks good there, Mr. Simpson. Now step out of the car, please."

"Step out? What for? You just said everything in order."

"The license and registration are in order. I stopped you for driving erratically. That means I have to conduct a field sobriety test. Please step out of the car."

"What if I don't?"

Oh, for shit's sake. "That's going to fall under the same *reasonable request* business we talked about before, Mr. Simpson."

"Not for no test, it don't. I know my rights. You need a warrant or one a them supeenies."

"I only need a warrant if I want to take blood, sir. All I want to do now is see how you handle a few simple coordination tests. You pass them and you're on your way. No harm done."

"Coordination tests, you say? Like what?"

"Walk a straight line. Touch your nose. Stuff like that."

The door swung open. "Fuck, yeah, Rodney be all over that. Touch my nose with my eyes closed and shit, know what I'm saying?"

Sisler hoped Simpson couldn't see him smiling. Walked twenty feet into the parking lot. Held out his left hand, fingers extended toward Simpson. "Okay, Mr. Simpson, you see my hand? Walk straight as you can toward it."

Simpson started walking. Sisler said, "Come right a little, away from the street. You don't want to get hit." Simpson stopped in front of him, well satisfied by the journey. Sisler said, "Next I want you to extend your arms away from your sides. Like that. Good. Now close your eyes and touch your nose with your index finger."

Simpson smiled, sure he was about to get over. "Which hand?"

Sisler smiled, knowing he wasn't. "Your choice." Stepped forward to help Simpson maintain his balance when he wobbled. Put the beam of the Maglite in Simpson's eyes to disorient him. "Mr. Simpson, you have been unable to perform two simple sobriety tests. I have to ask you to come with me."

"You arresting me?"

"I will if I have to. Right now we're going to get one of those warrants you were talking about. For a blood test to see how drunk you really are."

CHAPTER 47

Eight in the morning, heavy frost on the ground. Colder than a loan shark's heart, something Stretch Dolewicz had been trying to impress on Stretcher Suskewicz for weeks. No emotion. They're not people. They are what you're owed.

They sat in Stretcher's car outside Glimko's gas station. Two pumps in front. No card reader; go inside to pay. Cash or debit card only. Glimko's name appeared nowhere. Hand-lettered signs in the windows read *Gas* and *Snacks* and *Live Bait.* Others could have read *Grass, Speed,* or *Oxy. We purchase used goods* would also not be inaccurate.

Glimko owed five hundred a week and had been pissy about it of late. Tommy Vig's hard-on was for him—not Henry Miskinis—for sharking on Tommy's turf. Miskinis had his video store busted up for no more than a lesson in etiquette. Glimko's unauthorized business expansion meant he now owed a grand a week. Vig's sloppy research gave Mannarino an excuse to keep it all. As a lesson.

Both men got out of the car. Stretch came around front and slid into the driver's seat. "I'll be back in ten minutes. You aren't out front with the money by then, I'll come in. No one wants that." Paused for effect. "You like this job, you'll have the money in ten. Now go get 'em."

Stretcher knew he might not even have ten minutes. His uncle would drive for five minutes, then turn around. If traffic held him up on the way out, he'd be back in less than five, would count it as ten. Stretcher went inside with the attitude he had eight minutes, nine with luck.

John Glimko sat on a bar-style stool behind the register, down vest hanging open over a flannel shirt not tucked into his jeans. The Petrone Glass patch on his ball cap loose on one corner. Stretcher said, "I'm here for the man's envelope."

"Where's your uncle?"

"*I'm* here," Stretcher said. "Get the envelope."

"Don't be a hardass, Junior," Glimko said. "Your uncle don't talk to me like that and he's earned the right. I been here since before you were born and I'll be here after you're gone, you keep this shit up."

"Stop right there." Stretcher lacked the experience to do the stare and voice as well as his uncle. Stood close to the counter, playing up his height advantage. "I don't care if you respect me. I don't care if you like me. You *will* respect the position. Whoever walks in here—me, my uncle, some jagov you never seen before—you have the envelope ready the same as if the man himself walked in. Now get up off your fat hunky ass and get it."

"Fuck you, kid. I was going to. Now you have to wait until my fat hunky ass is ready."

Stretcher reached across the counter, bunched Glimko's shirt and vest in his hands. Dragged him off the stool at an angle to the end of the counter, dislodged the register's connections. Swung him into the small shopping area and into a wire rack holding snacks and candy bars. Glimko struggled to keep his balance. Stretcher planted a foot on the center of his chest and pushed him and the rack over. Tore one end off a sleeve of half a dozen powdered sugar mini-doughnuts.

"You want some respect? You want to be friends? I'll buy you breakfast."

Stretcher squeezed Glimko's jaw open, forced a doughnut into his mouth. Then another. Got all six in and pushed Glimko's mouth shut. "Chew, motherfucker. Be careful when you swallow. Spit out one crumb and I'll take you outside and curb you."

Glimko's jaws worked as he struggled to sit up. Stretcher let him get his torso erect, ass on the rack. Crumbs and bits of powdered sugar crawled out of Glimko's mouth as if fleeing. He chewed—more like moving softening bits of doughnut around his mouth—and swallowed, chewed and swallowed. Started to cough, then choke. Pointed to his throat.

"A little dry? Stay there. Don't spit." Stretch took three steps to a cooler, tossed Glimko a quart of milk. "Most people dunk first."

Glimko struggled through the rest of the doughnuts, stopping for sips of milk. Finished and looked straight ahead.

Stretcher said, "You gonna live?" Glimko nodded. "All right. I got you breakfast. You didn't have to lift a finger. I proved I respect you, we can be friends. Now get off your fat ass and get my fucking money. You got one minute."

Glimko struggled to his feet. Walked stiff-legged toward the back. "Hey, Joe," Stretcher said. "How's the shylock business?"

Glimko stopped. "What are you talking about?"

"You're not going to make me bring you over here for dessert, are you?"

Glimko's shoulders sagged. "It's nothing major. I was

gonna tell Mike about it, swear to God, if it started making noticeable money."

"Well, Tommy Vig noticed."

"That cheap cocksucker knows how much change is in his couch. What I clear wouldn't cover his car payment."

"I sure as hell hope you're clearing at least five a week," Stretcher said. "That's the tax increase. There better be a grand in that envelope when you hand it to me."

Glimko turned around. "A *grand?* A *week?* Are you fucking kidding me? I don't net that much from everything we got going on here."

"Raise prices." Stretcher gestured to include the entire store. "Maybe find a way to make the legitimate business you're supposed to be running turn a fucking profit for a change. The man don't care. It's a grand. Oh, and, Joe?"

"What?"

"Don't come back with anything in your hand but the envelope. Think what you want about me, but if you do anything that disrespects the man, even by proxy, it's gonna hurt a long time."

Glimko never left Stretcher's sight. Reached around the door frame to the storage room to retrieve a manila envelope wrapped with a rubber band. Held it up so Stretcher would have no doubts. "I was just jagging you, kid." Stretcher shot him a look. "Sorry. Ted. Stretcher. No harm meant."

Stretcher counted five hundred in the envelope. Opened the register and took all the bills. "This is only seven forty-two, altogether."

"Christ, kid, I only expected to pay five." Stretcher rubbed his thumb over two fingers, then gestured toward himself. Glimko pulled a roll from his pocket, counted two hundred fifty-eight dollars.

Stretcher put all the money into the envelope, wrapped the rubber band around it, stuffed it into an inside pocket. "I come every Tuesday morning. I want to see the envelope in your hand before I walk as far as the register. You don't have to say hello. We don't have to bullshit around. I want to talk, I'll talk. Your job—all you have to do—is toss me the envelope. I'll turn around and leave before I ever stop walking. Make a mental note."

Not outside thirty seconds when his uncle pulled into the lot. "How'd it go? He give you any trouble?"

"We had some doughnuts and talked it over," Stretcher said. "I think we're good now."

CHAPTER 48

Monday had not been a good day. Doc wished for no worse than a neutral Tuesday the way a man who wakes up stiff and sore hopes he slept funny and doesn't have the flu. Got away with it until almost ten-thirty, when Daniel Rollison called from the casino and invited Doc for an audience.

Doc didn't know what he'd done to deserve Rollison. They first bumped into each other on the Marian Widmer homicide investigation. Rollison's current job as head of casino security required them to interact from time to time. Doc viewed their visits as not unlike back pain: wouldn't kill you, made the whole day shitty.

Most days Doc would have told Rollison to come by the station. Made an exception because Rollison implied information on the Resurrection Mall shootings might be available; Doc had to come to the casino to get it. Rollison not above trumping something up; he'd done it before. Doc couldn't figure an angle, so he made the trip.

Rollison had the kind of office a semi-big shot in a second-tier joint rated. Nondescript desk, pleather loveseat and visitors' seats. The chair behind the desk had Staples written all over it. Nice Staples, nothing to be confused with Steelcase. Generic prints: flowers, a Monet reproduction, a landscape. At least the walls weren't block.

They didn't shake hands. Rollison didn't invite Doc to sit.

Doc sat, gestured around the room. "Who picks the décor?"

"What?" Rollison said. "You mean the art?"

"I guess you could call it art. Looks corporate."

"Came with the office. It was on the wall when I got here."

"I figured you for better taste," Doc said. "These guys aren't even on brand. Big-time casino like this, I expected velvet. Dogs playing poker. Something classy."

Rollison had no sense of humor. Fine with Doc, who hadn't come to amuse him. "You called the meeting. Why am I here?"

"We had a customer last night who was overserved. Our doorman called the station, per a discussion I had a few weeks ago with Chief Napierkowski."

Doc flashed to the disheveled guest he'd seen in an overnight cell. His interest level ticked up a tenth of a point. "I'll be sure to tell the boss, though I expect you've done so already. No point doing the right thing if you're not going to get credit for it."

Rollison's expression didn't change. Gave the impression Doc could have said nothing, or talked for half an hour, and received the same reaction. "I wouldn't have called you in for that. The customer I'm talking about is a young black male, who apparently spent most of his evening hitting on one of our bartenders."

"Male or female?"

"Nice looking colored girl," Rollison said. "You can talk to her later if you want."

"That's decent of you. Letting me talk to someone. Do I need a note with why on it, or can I run wild?"

Rollison gave the same no reaction as before. "Among the

things this customer told our bartender is—"

"This bartender have a name?"

"Gwen. Barber." Again Rollison waited for Doc, who waved him on. "Based on what Gwen told me, this customer worked at Resurrection Mall until recently, possibly as late as yesterday. He got laid off and came here to drink away any hard feelings."

"I don't suppose it worked for him any better than it usually does," Doc said.

"Not the way I heard it. He spent the better part of an hour telling her how he'd been screwed over."

Doc began to put things together. "If this is the guy I think it is, his blood alcohol was point two one when they brought him in. He didn't get that drunk in less than an hour."

"Gwen said he came in drunk. She only served him three drinks."

In an hour, to a man who must have already shown the effects. Doc almost said something, decided it would be better to do something, and figuring out what required thought. "She didn't get this guy's name, did she?"

"Rodney. Said he's one of those third person talkers. You know, like he's someone else. *Rodney did this* or *Rodney did that*. Had a very high opinion of himself."

"That kind usually does."

"What disturbed her was how he hinted at things. He told her how Resurrection Mall made a big mistake letting him go. How he'd done more for them, put more of himself on the line than anyone, including the preacher. She asked him what kinds of things. For a while he wouldn't say and she thought it was all show, him trying to pick her up. Then he said something she said scared her."

Doc cocked an eyebrow. This might be worth hearing. Might be. Rollison had a history of feeding Penns River cops bad information if it suited the casino's purpose. Rollison in the midst of one of his patented pauses, waiting for a reaction. Doc said, "Which was..."

"He made her ask, too. When she finally did, he said he couldn't tell her. He could if he knew her better—a lot better—said if she watched the news at all she knew things about him, things he'd done. Not straight out the way I told it. Hinting around at it."

The little cop in Doc's head thought of how drunks couldn't help themselves sometime. What was the line from *Tombstone? In vino veritas?* What he said was, "Player talk."

"Probably. But worth checking out."

"Yeah." Doc took out his cell. "You mind if I make a quick call?"

Rollison turned his desk phone around. "Use mine. Cell signal is lousy in here. I'll step out if you want."

"No need." Doc made a mental note about the cell service. Wouldn't put it past a casino to have a short-range jammer set up. Illegal, but he doubted any fine would cut into the profits made from undisturbed gamblers.

"Eye Chart? Doc. The drunk Sisler brought in last night. Is his first name Rodney?...He still around?...Hang onto him for a while. At least until I get there. Lose his car in impound if you have to. I'll explain when I get back." Hung up. "I better get back before he wanders off."

Rollison waited until Doc touched the doorknob. "You're welcome."

Doc almost let it pass. Turned to Rollison, said, "You're right. Something like this rates a thank you. It crossed my mind. Then I remembered you were bent on the Widmer investigation. Sent us false leads on the Broaddus killing. People you play with almost killed my family last year. I have to assume you're working an angle, which means I don't know that I have anything to thank you for, except maybe wasting my time."

Rollison gave his standard face. Except for moving lips, he might have been on loan from Madame Tussaud's. "Get over it, Dougherty. We both have jobs to do. It's a small town. Our paths cross. You take things too personally. You do your job, and I'll do mine."

"I wouldn't mind, except your job includes obstruction of justice."

"Then charge me."

"I would if I could."

Doc imagined the faintest trickle of a smile from Rollison. "You can't?"

"Prosecutor doesn't like the case."

"She has no evidence."

"She has some, maybe even enough. Problem is, she likes her job too much. Over half the DA's campaign contributions came from your boss."

"Campaign spending is overrated."

"Not when you run unopposed."

"He didn't run unopposed."

Doc's turn for an icy smile. "He might as well have." Word around the Hall was Hecker had paid the opponent more to tank the race than he spent on the winner's campaign.

"Maybe you should run yourself," Rollison said, smiling for sure now. "It's an administrative position. No knowledge of the law required. You're more than qualified."

Rollison had never done Doc any real harm. Common knowledge he'd been appalled by the attack on the Dougherty home, not that he'd ever said anything to Doc about it. Still, Rollison was bent. There was something respectable about Mike Mannarino's inherent criminality. Everyone knew he was a criminal, and he never tried to bullshit anyone beyond what was necessary to stay out of prison. Rollison lived in the gray areas of legality, as involved as he had to be and still allow for his wits and his employer's money to arrange for someone else to take the fall.

Doc left the door ajar behind him.

CHAPTER 49

"You got lucky," Grabek said to Doc. "Simpson's hearing ended before Zywiciel and I could get to the courthouse."

"How is that lucky?"

"The way I hear it, Simpson was either still a little drunk or a lot hung over and started mouthing off to the judge. You know how much Molchan loves mouthy drunks in his court."

"What did he do?"

Grabek laughed, no humor in it. "He gave Simpson a couple of chances to calm down and do the right thing. Apparently our boy missed the hint, so Molchan gave him another day and night in the tank to get his mind right. What do you want to do with him?"

"Since we have him all day, let's get some details from the barmaid, see how he likes hearing his story from the other side, sober."

"How do you want to play it?"

"Hard. If he's edgy enough to provoke Molchan into a contempt charge, I want to find his buttons and push them."

"Perhaps he will become so cross he'll make a mistake?" Neuschwander said.

Doc smiled. "Something like that."

* * *

Rodney Simpson looked like his clothes had gone through the laundry with him in them. Young black man on the come suit wrinkled. Shirt untucked on one side, tie stuffed into the breast pocket. Suit coat tossed over the back of the chair. Grabek pulled him out of his cell where he could have rested, made him sit in the interview room. Interrupted any time Simpson's head got too close to the table. Provided all the coffee he wanted and then some, caffeinated with plenty of sugar, "To help sober you up." Simpson jitty as a shrew on a hot plate by the time Doc got back from interviewing Gwen Barber.

Doc and Grabek paused outside the room. Neuschwander already in the booth to observe and run the video. "You want good cop or bad cop?" Grabek always wanted to be bad cop. Today he owed Doc a courtesy, since Doc not only brought back the lead, he'd had to talk to Rollison to get it.

Doc pointed to himself. "Bad cop." Pointed to Grabek. "Worse cop. I got a feeling about this guy. Let's fuck with him."

Walked in together, took seats on opposite sides of the table so Simpson couldn't see both at once. Didn't say a word. Didn't stare or challenge. Checked him out.

Simpson lasted two minutes. "What? You come in here to eyeball me like we in the fucking zoo? This some bullshit you got me up in here for. I'm a get a lawyer and own this shit-hole 'fore I'm done."

"Has he been Mirandized?" Doc said to Grabek as if they were alone.

"I imagine Sisler got him last night." Both men continued their visual inspection of Simpson. "Don't know if that covers this separate charge."

Simpson looked toward Grabek, so Doc went next. "We'd better do it again, then. Save us trouble later, after he lawyers up."

Simpson had turned in Doc's direction, so Grabek said to the room in general, "Hey, Rick. Bring us some Miranda paperwork, would you?" Then, to Doc, "You work with Sisler yet?"

"Didn't you hear? We're famous." Doc told Grabek of the raccoon shooting, about to move to the saga of Ed and Betty Schatz when Simpson interrupted.

"Yo, what the fuck you talking about?"

"Shut up," Grabek said.

"Me shut up? What you two bring Rodney in here to listen to you talk about shit don't got nothing to do with him for?"

"Shut your mouth," Doc said. "We're trying to do you a favor."

"You want to do Rodney a favor, let my ass go. I admit I did some drinking last night, but this contempt bidness some bullshit."

"Cool your jets, homey," Grabek said. "We know your employment situation. It's not like you have anyplace better to be."

Simpson turned in Grabek's direction. Doc spoke first. "You're better off in here. The weather's shitty."

Simpson's comment to Doc cut short by Neuschwander with the Miranda form. He read aloud what any American who'd been in a room with a television in the past fifty years knew by heart, asked Simpson if he understood. Simpson did. Neuschwander handed him a pen, slid the form across the table. Simpson took the pen, centered the paper in front of him, looked at each cop in turn.

"What if I don't sign?"

Doc said, "Then you don't sign. Doesn't matter to us."

Simpson continued to look toward Grabek. "I don't sign, you can't talk to me, right?"

"You signing is for convenience sake," Doc said. Simpson almost turned his way, caught himself. "Saves time at trial. We can prove you were read your rights and said you understood them." Pointed to the window in the wall opposite Simpson. "We got it all on tape. Quicker to submit the form as evidence than have to run the tape. That's the prosecutor's problem. You don't want to sign, don't sign."

"I don't see why I should talk to you at all. All's I done's get a little liquored up."

"Then don't," Doc said. "You tell us you aren't talking, you want a lawyer, we'll stop until the lawyer gets here."

Simpson gave up, turned toward Doc. Grabek said, "Did you pay attention at all, dipshit? Do you understand what rights are? You have a right to remain silent. That means we can't make you talk. You have a right to a lawyer. That means we have to get one if you want one. Did anything else pass by you too quickly?"

Simpson looked from Grabek to Doc and back. Settled on talking to Neuschwander, more or less in the middle. "Okay then, good. I want a lawyer. Enough a this bullshit."

"Do you have one, or do you need us to get one for you?" Doc said.

"I guess you gonna have to get one for me." Simpson seemed pleased with himself.

Doc stood, Grabek a second behind him. "Looks like

we're done here. Noosh, take him back to his cell and call the lawyer. What time is it?"

"Two-thirty," Grabek said.

"Getting late." Doc spoke to Neuschwander. "Tell the lawyer he doesn't have to come today if he's busy. Anything we have to ask Mr. Simpson can wait until after he sees Judge Molchan in the morning. Tell him ten, ten-thirty will be fine, unless he wants to go to court for the judge's lecture."

"What?" Simpson lost the smile. "Back in the cell? Till when?"

"I don't know," Doc said. "I don't handle prisoners. When's court?"

"About nine, I think," Neuschwander said. "They'll probably come for him around eight-thirty."

"Eight-thirty?" Simpson said. "You said it's what? Two-thirty now?" Counted on his fingers. "That's—that's a long fucking time to sit in that nasty ass cell. I want to see the lawyer *now*."

"Fine," Grabek said. Then, to Neuschwander, "Tell the lawyer to get his ass over here. Put Rodney back in his cell till he shows. We'll talk to him tomorrow." Grabek and Doc made for the door.

"No, no, man. I don't want to go back there already. You smell that motherfucker? Can't I stay here for a while? You can cuff me if you want, so's I don't go nowhere."

"This look like the lounge to you?" Grabek said.

"It wasn't us puked and shit in your cell overnight." Doc continued for the door, keeping Simpson in his peripheral vision while the decision got made. Turning the knob when Simpson gave.

"All right. You want to talk for a little bit, we'll talk. I can stop whenever I want, right?"

"You sure you don't want the lawyer?" Grabek said. "We can wait."

"No, it's cool. Rodney can talk some now."

"I don't know," Grabek said. "He asked for a lawyer. You guys heard him. It's on the tape. We talk to him now...I don't know. You better take him back, Rick. Let's stay on the safe side."

Neuschwander put a hand on Simpson's upper arm. Simpson tried to shake him off. Neuschwander stronger than he looked. "All *right!* What I got to do to not go back there, least for a while?"

The detectives exchanged looks. "We got a lot of stuff going on today," Doc said. "We're not going to clear time for you if you shine us on like you been doing. I mean, you want to answer some questions, okay. We'll talk. You give us the runaround? Back you go."

"A'ight." Simpson looked at Neuschwander's hand, still on his arm. "I said a'ight, goddamnit. You can let me go now."

Neuschwander let go. Grabek said, "Sign the paper." Simpson grabbed the pen from the table, rerealigned the paper with force. Grabek said, "Don't get cute and scribble any old shit there and think you can say you didn't sign. I can't read it, back to the cell you go."

Simpson exaggerated the care with which he wrote his name. Neuschwander took the document and left. Doc and Grabek resumed their previous seats.

"So, what you want to talk to Rodney about?" Simpson said.

"Cool your jets, Junior," Grabek. "The sooner we're done, the quicker you go back to that shithouse you made for yourself."

"What time they have it cleaned?"

Both detectives laughed. "This is not the Clarion," Doc said. "Housekeeping doesn't come by every day and clean up after you."

"How often they clean them?"

"Beats me. Couple-three times a week, I guess. How'd it smell when you got there?"

"I don't know. I was—uh—a little under the weather. I don't remember stinking so bad it was memorable, or nothing."

"Probably got to it that day," Grabek said. "Not likely they'll be there again until at least tomorrow. Good chance it won't be till after you leave. So they won't inconvenience you."

"Got-*damn*," Simpson said under his breath.

"What happened at Res Mall?" Doc said. "To get you canned, I mean."

Simpson still engrossed with the unsanitary habits of white people. "Huh? What?"

"Why did Dr. Love fire you?"

"Weren't him. Not in person, anyway."

"What did you do to earn it?"

"Rodney didn't do shit, yo." Simpson sat up, indignant. "Busted my ass down there. Deacon Abernathy told me Dr. Love said they had to cut expenses some way, so I had to go."

Doc shrugged. "You got riffed without prejudice. It happens. No one's going to hold it against you."

Simpson looked confused. "I got...what? Riffed? What that?"

Grabek stepped in. "Reduction in force. What they call it when a company has to cut payroll. Nothing personal. Happens to most people around here, sooner or later."

"What did you do for Abernathy?" Doc said. "Before he riffed you?"

"I's like his assistant, you know? Make calls, answer phones, run errands. Make sure he had what he needed for meetings and such."

"Enough of that to keep you busy?"

"Mostly. I do things for the Rev once in a while. Drive him places. Take people to and from the airport. Shit like that."

"That all?"

Simpson got a look in his eye Doc couldn't place. "What you mean, *that all*? What you think Rodney do down there?"

Grabek said, "You ran your mouth pretty good to that cute barmaid at the casino last night. Acted like you were a player behind the scenes. Were you talking yourself up to get her pants off, or are you being humble now?"

Simpson sat back, smiled. "You know how it is. Rodney mighta, how you say...extrapolated a bit. For the lady."

"Isn't that what I said?" Grabek said to Doc. "It was all a come on? He was an errand boy. Hard up as they are, they'd never let someone really critical go. Couldn't afford to."

"Yeah, I guess." Doc hated playing it so broad, wouldn't under most circumstances. Simpson in over his head, trying to act the big man. "She was impressed. Here, in good light, he doesn't look like much. He's right, isn't he, Rodney? You were a gofer with a title. All that business about how you'd done things no one else would and no one appreciated? Hell, no one else would do those things because they had real work to do. You wouldn't be missed, running to the airport or driving the Rev around. You make the daily lunch runs, too? Take orders, who wants what on their sandwiches? Coke or iced tea? That kind of critical stuff?"

"It was more than that."

"Don't get defensive," Doc said. "No insult intended. Someone has to do those things. Now that you're gone, Dr. Love probably drives himself. Hard to make an entrance like that."

"Means someone else has to take time from their busy days to get lunch, too," Grabek said. "Unless they find some middle school kid who's skipping to do it for tips."

"Hey, fuck you. Both of you." Simpson getting his ass on his shoulders. "There's lots more I did. Lots. I just ain't saying because it private bidness. Res Mall and people there don't need no loose talk around. Keep it to myself out a respect."

"Funny," Doc said. "Those people you're respecting so much today were all dickless bitches last night when you talked to the barmaid."

"Yeah, well, I told you about that. Making an impression all it was."

"Hell of an impression," Grabek said. "I'm no ladies' man, but I'm thinking I want some trim from a chick, calling people dickless bitches is not the way to go. Black girls into that?"

Simpson gave a condescending smirk. "You want to see how to get pussy, fat man? Hang with Rodney."

Grabek laughed. "Kid, any pussy you could get with that

patter, I wouldn't fuck with your dick, even if I could be far away when I did it."

Doc still trying to figure out what the *even if I could be far away* comment meant when Simpson's red ass overtook his brain altogether. "Fuck you, fuck you, and fuck you. You don't know shit about me, about what I can do and already done and you can show me a little motherfucking respect."

"It always comes back to fucking your mothers with you people, don't it?" Grabek said and Simpson launched himself out of the chair.

Doc grabbed an arm, flung him back into the seat. "Sit your ass down. You want some respect? You want us to see what a big man you are? Show us something big. We're tired of you showing us your dick."

Simpson looked like he might rise again, thought better of Doc's extra four inches and thirty pounds. Resettled himself and gave as cocky a sneer as Doc had ever seen in an interview. "That's why you bring me down here. You looking for dirt at Res Mall. Figured Rodney one a them disgruntled employees you always hearing about."

"What the fuck did you think?" Grabek said. "We wanted advice on how to get the clap? What else could you possibly have to tell us?"

Simpson sat back, crossed left ankle over right knee. The younger kid who had something the big kids wanted and wouldn't give it to them. "Y'all don't know shit, do you? Keep my black ass down here like I'm the house nigger, make me tell you shit about what go on in the fields. Fuck getting me a lawyer. And fuck you, too."

"Neuschwander," Grabek said to the room in general. "Take him back to his cell."

CHAPTER 50

Neuschwander took Simpson to his cell; Grabek asked Doc what he thought. Doc said he had to pee, give him a minute. Killed time until Neuschwander came back to be included: his good work on the contractors and finances earned him a place at the strategy table. They came together into the interview room where Grabek waited with his elbows on his knees, head down. He straightened as they entered.

"What does everyone think?" Doc said when all were seated.

"He knows something," Grabek said. "He's too smug. Whatever he did down there, he's proud as hell and loves the idea it's killing us to find out."

"Noosh?"

Neuschwander surprised to be included, and pleased. "I agree with Willie. He's like a kid with a secret. I think he's dying to tell someone what a big man he is. What I'm not sure of is, was he involved in the shooting, or just the kick-backs?"

"Me, too," Doc said. "You said the contractors told you Abernathy ran the bid rigging and kickback operation. Did any of them mention Simpson shaking them down?"

"No, but I wasn't thinking of him then." Neuschwander took some memory time. "The way I phrased the questions, I might have been leading them to talk about Lewis and

270

Abernathy. I guess Simpson could've been the go-between. I should have followed up better."

"It's okay. You had no reason to at the time." Doc wished Neuschwander had, wondered if he would have thought of it himself. "You know how to get a hold of those guys now. The more you know, the easier it is to know what to ask."

"His other point's still good," Grabek said. "Is that why Simpson's holding out, or is he involved with the shooters?"

"Do any of us think he's one of the shooters?" Doc said. Negative all around. "Me, either. So Simpson's either the client, or a go-between. If he's involved at all."

"Go-between," Grabek said. "Where's he going to get the kind of cash to hire this out?"

Neuschwander agreed. "Go-between for who, though? Is Abernathy dumb enough to pull something like this?"

"Or Lewis," Grabek said.

Both turned to Doc, deep in thought. "We're getting ahead of ourselves. Let's not forget the golden rule of any investigation…" He came up short. "It's a Latin phrase. Shit. Basically, who benefits? The new drug dealers we know of are treading lightly, probably because they don't know if someone with bigger plans had this done. Can we agree this was not a drug takeover hit?"

Neuschwander nodded. Grabek said, "Yeah, but…" Doc raised an eyebrow. "I'm not ready to rule out Mannarino. He's been pushed around quite a bit the last couple of years. What if he decided to push back?"

"Come on, Willie," Doc said. "You like Mannarino for everything."

"Think about it," Grabek said. "Mike hires a coupla jigs to do his dirty work, make it look like some black-on-black thing. Gets his point across, and keeps his hands clean."

"Wouldn't it roll back on him once they got caught?" Neuschwander said.

"Be a half dozen people between him and them. If things got sticky, he'd either kill the shooters, or clip one of the cutouts to keep us from backtracking."

"What's the benefit to him?" Doc said.

"Re-establishes his personal crime-free zone. He's been slipping along those lines lately."

Doc looked to Neuschwander, who had no opinion. Played with a loose thread on his sport coat, said, "I wouldn't put it past him. I still don't like him for it."

"I'm not sure I do, either," Grabek said. "We're spitballing here. Tell me why I'm wrong."

"If, for the sake of argument, Mannarino did have it done, it would be to send a message, right?" Nods all around. "To send a message, word has to get out he did it. Look at how he's done business in the past. That Orszulak guy from Youngstown, dropped a body in that vacant a couple years ago. Mike left him on the steps of the Bachelor's Club, which is how he likes to mark his territory. We're pretty sure he had Donte Broaddus done, and where did he end up? Workman's entrance of the casino three days before opening. That's Mike showing his ass."

"What about those other two?" Neuschwander said. "Broaddus's cousin and the other black guy?"

"Shot from a distance with a rifle." Doc moved his fingers as if brushing away a fly. "And away from here, for deniability. Those hits were all nice, clean jobs, too. Two in the head for Orszulak and Broaddus. The others put down in the open, away from everyone, one rifle bullet, then one in the head each. No possibility of innocent bystanders getting hurt, or seeing anything. Say what you want about how Mannarino runs his crew, they do nice work."

"Who's that leave?" Neuschwander said.

"Resurrection Mall." Grabek's voice was flat.

Doc took a deep breath, said, "Yeah," as part of the exhalation. "Can we agree to leave Love out of it? I don't see him going to this length, desperate or not."

"He's on the bench," Grabek said. "He's not out of the game completely."

"Noosh?" Neuschwander nodded. "So we're saying it's between Abernathy, Lewis, and, I guess, Simpson."

"As a go-between," Grabek said. "We can talk about how dumb he is all we want. He still doesn't have access to the money."

"Good point," Doc said. "We're flailing here. Let's pick a path and take it. We can always change. Noosh, get back with those contractors who said they were being shaken down. See if you can match them up with Simpson."

"On it."

"Willie, we have Simpson at our disposal for a while. Do you think Bieniemy would help us round up Turner again? Put him and Simpson face-to-face, it might tell us right away if Simpson's who he did business with."

"If Turner is one of the shooters," Grabek said.

Doc made a face. "Another good point. We haven't quite nailed that down yet, have we?" Silence as the others waited for him to make a decision. Doc thought back to the phone call Bieniemy made for them, how Turner had answered. "I'm willing to roll the dice on this one. Willie?"

"I'm in."

"Noosh?"

Neuschwander couldn't have been more shocked if Doc had offered to pay for his kids' college. "Yeah, Doc. Absolutely."

Doc turned to Grabek. "You think Bieniemy will be willing to help us again?"

Grabek snorted. "He'll be pissed if we don't ask."

"Will you call and set it up?" Grabek nodded. "We have Simpson till tomorrow morning. When do you want to get Turner?"

"Let's go early. Eight, maybe even before. He's more likely to be at home, so we won't have to run all over hell looking for him. He'll be asleep, so we'll catch him off guard, maybe even get him over here without whatever he wears as a security blanket. And we'll go in with numbers to impress upon him this isn't a friendly chat."

"I like it. I'll ask Eye Chart to delay Simpson's release after the judge is through with him. Lose some paperwork on his car or something. We didn't have to do it today, so it'll still play."

"Simpson probably half expects it, the way we screwed with him," Grabek said.

"Even better." Doc smiled. "We may not have a fucking clue, but goddamn, at least now we have a plan."

CHAPTER 51

"How'd it go?" Stush handed Doc and Grabek each mugs of coffee. The high forecast to be in the low fifties, though shaded grass still shows signs of a hard frost when the detectives brought DaRon Turner into the station at eight-thirty.

"The most fun I've had since we started this case," Doc said. Grabek snorted and left for the men's. "Is Simpson back?"

Stush shook his head. "I don't know if they even took him over yet." Looked at his watch. "Pretty soon, though. I'd say you have at least an hour."

"Plenty of time." Doc sipped his coffee. Made a show of looking around the room. Turned to Stush with open hands, the mug balanced with care. "No doughnuts?"

"Wednesday's your day."

"Like I had nothing else to do. Sometimes I wonder how I can work under these conditions."

"You're in a better mood than you've been in lately."

"I have a good feeling about this. Turner said—"

"Wait." Stush gave Doc the hand. "From the beginning."

Stush's greatest strength as an interrogator, also the most overlooked: he was a great audience. The event didn't matter: daughters' piano recitals, son's Little League games, pissed off cops who needed to vent, or suspects who shouldn't talk to him at all. Stush never hurried a story, made everyone believe his day wouldn't be complete until he'd heard what they had to say. Suspects couldn't help themselves. Stush Napierkowski was a good man, so engrossed in their story—whatever it was—people wanted to tell it to him. Doc had tried for years to learn how to create this impression, until he realized why he couldn't: it was no act. Stush wanted to know.

"We get to this guy's place twenty after seven. It's Grabek, Bieniemy—his friend from Pittsburgh—two Pittsburgh uniforms, and me."

"This Don Bieniemy? Black guy with a scar like this?" Stush traced a line from his left eyebrow to the back of his jaw.

"The scar's on the other side. You know him?"

"We've met a couple of times. Got drunk once. Good cop, hell of a nice guy. Struck me as someone who'd have your back."

"That's him. He's been a huge help. Finding guys, bringing them in, and he knows things and has leverage we'd never have."

"I'll write his boss a letter. Sorry for the interruption." Gestured for Doc to go on.

"So we're at Turner's apartment door, five cops—all of us with some size—guns drawn. Bieniemy pounds on the door with the side of his fist. Not knocking, pounding. He's yelling, 'DaRon Turner. Rise and shine. Pittsburgh po-lice.' You've met him, you know what he sounds like talking regular to someone. He jacked the volume up like he was in the street calling Turner out. Woke up the whole building. People are pissing and moaning and we hear some banging around inside Turner's apartment. He's hollering something, people are sticking their heads out their doors telling us to shut the fuck up. It was real scene.

"Turner opens the door and we see right away he's not really awake. Doesn't even know what day it is, standing there in boxer shorts and a wife beater. He gets a look at us and his eyes get big and I get ready to chase him back inside if he decides to run and damn if he doesn't run *at* us. Tried to break through. I don't know where he thought he was going, seven-thirty in the morning, below freezing, dressed like he was, five cops to get past. Bieniemy and me and the uniforms each took a limb and Grabek held the door while we carried him back inside. He was squirming like a snake and screaming at what he'd do to us if we let him go even for a second." Doc chuckled, shook his head. "It was funnier'n hell."

"He didn't get marked up, did he?"

"He's fine. We threw him on the couch and Bieniemy pinned him there with his knee while Willie told him what was what. We got him dressed and brought him in." Doc gestured toward the interrogation room. "He's in there drinking coffee."

"Anyone with him?"

"No. We decided to leave him alone with his thoughts. Maybe he'll figure out why he only has on one sock."

A knock on the doorjamb. Jack Harriger in full dress uniform, even the hat. "I hear you're going to put two suspects together."

Doc stood, reached toward Harriger. "Stand still." Plucked lint from a shoulder board.

"I want in on the interrogation," Harriger said.

"Don't you have a senior center presentation today?" Stush said. "What time?"

"Ten-thirty."

"Hell, Jack, we'll never be done with these guys by then. Simpson won't even be out of court before nine-thirty, quarter to ten. Assuming Judge Molchan doesn't jerk him around."

"I'll cancel the seniors. This is more important."

"You don't cancel seniors, Jack. They're the last people in town you want pissed at you. They scheduled doctor appointments and shopping trips around this. You need to be there."

"It's a dog and pony show for a bunch of retirees. This is a homicide investigation. They can be rescheduled."

Stush waited for Harriger to come up for air. "Jack, we have limited resources. I think the best way we can show everybody involved how we use what's available to our best advantage is by sending you to the senior center in your dress uniform. I'll help out with the interrogations."

"Goddamnit, I'm tired of being shunted off to do every shit detail you can think of while real work gets done by junior officers!"

Stush cut in before the rant established a roll. "Knowing your regard for the chain of command, *Deputy*, do I have to remind you who you're speaking to? Do you have anything to do until it's time to go?"

Doc thought he saw Harriger's brush cut quiver. Could have been his imagination. "Yes."

"Then go do it. I'll call you if we need you." Stush gave Harriger a look he used no more than a couple of times a year. Harriger turned on his heel and left.

Grabek came in. "What's the plan?" Stush said.

Grabek nodded toward Doc. "The plan," Doc said, "such as it is, is wait until Ray McKillop brings Simpson back from court. Neuschwander will come a little ahead of them, and we'll time it so Simpson and Turner can't help but make eye contact. Bump them into each other if we have to."

Silence while Stush figured out Doc had finished. "That's it?"

"Uh, yeah." Doc's enthusiasm flagged, recovered. "Willie and I will be in position to watch them both. We're thinking neither has the presence of mind not to be at least shaken."

"Assuming they know each other."

"Yeah. Assuming that."

"It's not a complete shot in the dark," Grabek said. "We're pretty sure Turner is one of the trigger men." Related recent events in Pittsburgh. "Simpson's into something dirty at Resurrection Mall. Could be a contract racket, could be more. We want to see if it was Simpson Turner thought he was talking to the day Bieniemy set him up."

"Worst case, if we're wrong," Doc said, "we wasted a morning."

"We also put the fear of God into Turner," Grabek said. "He doesn't seem to be too well put together."

Stush rocked back. Sipped his coffee. "Sure wish someone had brought doughnuts." Rested the mug on his returning belly. "We're this desperate?"

Doc and Grabek exchanged looks. "I wouldn't say desperate," Doc said. "I am open to suggestions."

Stush tapped a finger against the mug, still held on his personal, portable shelf. "What the hell. I mean, you went to all this trouble. I'll hang around, help you watch them when the time comes."

Neuschwander skidded around the corner at nine-forty-eight. "Mac's thirty seconds behind me."

The four of them went into the common area separating the offices. Doc opened the interview room door. Said, "On your feet!" to Turner, went in to ensure compliance. Held back a second at the threshold until Grabek nodded for him to come out. Took Turner by the arm and steered him to the hall, in the direction McKillop would come with Simpson. A little louder than necessary, he said, "You're doing good. This is the kind of stuff we need. When you're done in the bathroom, we'll see about getting you some breakfast. Pancakes and bacon okay?"

Turner looked at Doc like he'd grown a third eye as McKillop and Simpson rounded the corner. McKillop stopped to avoid a collision. Doc brought Turner up short, forcing him to look at the oncoming traffic. Turner froze.

Simpson pissed his pants.

CHAPTER 52

"Goddamn right he gave you up. You think we take five cops around to random buildings, just to see who's there?"

Grabek had no intention of wasting the gift he'd received. He and Stush in the interrogation room with DaRon Turner. Grabek sat close to the table, not quite in Turner's face, well inside his personal space. Stush several feet back, hands folded across his belly. Looked no more interested than if Grabek were sorting out a lunch order.

Turner made a game effort to brazen it out. Hadn't asked for a lawyer. Thirty-five years a cop, Grabek still could not believe the number of people who don't lawyer up until it's too late. Believed asking for a lawyer the same as confessing, like they wouldn't be there if police weren't already pretty sure they had the right guy.

Turner stared, stone-faced, into the two-way mirror on the opposite wall. Grabek shifted his chair closer, leaned in to speak into Turner's ear. "It gets worse. The one thing you knew you could count on, your rock, was Rosewood." Turner's left eye might have twitched. "He gave you up, too."

"Now I know you a fucking liar."

"He didn't give your name," Grabek said in the same tone. "You did that—linked the two of you together—on the phone last week. Rosewood put you both in for the hits at Resurrection Mall." Turner still as a frozen lake. "See, we told him we had one of the shotties. You threw them in the river, right? Off the Ninth Street Bridge on your way out of town. That was smart, almost. No way you wanted to get caught with those pieces on you. Well, we told your boy Rosewood a barge was parked under the bridge for a work crew. Said one of the shotguns landed there instead of going in the river. That was bullshit, but damn if he didn't come all the way up from Pittsburgh to drive across the bridge that same night. That's all he did, too: crossed the bridge, looped around, and drove right back out. Now why the hell would he come all the way up here to check out that bridge in the middle of the night if he didn't think it might be true?

"The navy's sending special cold-water divers soon as the ice breaks up, with metal detectors. Did you know metal rusts slower in cold water? We get even one shotgun, and match the strike marks, or, even better, one of the nines..." Grabek made an exaggerated kissing sound.

Doc and Neuschwander got a late start with Simpson. Getting the detectives' room ready for the questioning— Penns River had the one genuine interview room—Neuschwander realized they didn't have a second set of video recording gear. Ran home to get his personal laptop while McKillop took Simpson to the men's to clean up.

Doc unimpressed with McKillop's efforts. "You couldn't get him smelling any better than this, Ray?" Neuschwander put the final touches on his impromptu video studio and took a seat.

"He's good," McKillop said. "You want some serious stink, check out his cell. You need me for anything else?"

Doc gave Simpson a good looking over. "I think between Neuschwander and me we can handle this one."

Doc deposited Simpson into a plastic chair positioned in front of Neuschwander's web cam. He'd considered giving him Grabek's seat, thought better of it.

"You are a piece of work, Rodney." Doc forced himself to look more comfortable than he felt, rocking back in the chair, government-issue artificial leather squeaking instead of the relaxed creaking of Stush's genuine leather. "We know you're not one of the shooters, and we know you don't have the kind of money to set up something like this. Yet, there you were, piss running down your leg just from the sight of DaRon Turner, who we do figure as a shooter. I'm dying to know how you fit in here."

"I don't know what you talking about." Simpson's voice not at all like yesterday's. "I never seen him before."

"Really?" Doc kept his eyebrows raised to be sure Simpson saw his amazement. "You wet your pants every time you see someone you don't know? Your dry cleaning bills must be hell."

"No, not like that. I been sick. I got a condition, you know?"

"Yeah, I know," Doc said. "You got a condition called scared shitless about going to prison for the rest of your sorry life. You'll do well there, young, good-looking man like yourself. I'm sure you'll be very popular. You'll be fighting the boys off."

Simpson tried for stone face. Couldn't manage it. His eyes wandered. Feet jiggled. Chin shook.

"Don't be any stupider than you've been already," Doc said. "We know you didn't shoot anyone. We know it wasn't your idea. We know it wasn't your money. You're what's called a cut-out. Someone paid you gofer money to take all the risks."

"Rodney weren't no gofer." Lips and chin still trembling, he sat up straighter.

"You know where Turner and I were going when we ran into you? Well, Turner was going to the bathroom. Then I was going to the Clarion to order a Traveler's breakfast to go. Two eggs, pancakes, syrup, choice of sausage or bacon, toast, and coffee. Three-ninety-nine. Hard to believe they can make money on it, but I guess they do. He'd earned the meal. Already told us how it went down. Where they parked, which entrance they used, getting rid of the guns. I never had to prompt him."

Doc lowered his voice. "I think he wanted to tell. He needed to. Rosewood's a truly evil son of a bitch. Kill you soon as look at you. Turner doesn't have the hard center for this kind of work. Thought he'd step up—he hasn't said why yet, but he will—then found out blowing chunks out of people isn't the same as playing *Grand Theft Auto*. Nothing like it at all." A beat. "You ever kill anyone?"

"Who? Me?" Simpson about five football fields into a thousand-yard stare. "No. Never."

"I did. Last year. It was him or me. Maybe him or my whole family. We talked while he died."

Simpson looked to see what kind of cold motherfucker would chat up a man he'd shot. "What you talk about?"

"He asked me a question. I answered him. Made me sick for a week, thinking about it. Him laying there, both of us knowing he'd be dead in a minute. Both of us knowing I put him down."

"What he ax you?"

"He wanted to know if I'd been in the military." Doc's voice changed in tone as the image came to him. Kneeling at the foot of his parents' stairs, watching a man bleed out in the moonlight.

"Was you?" Doc nodded. "Why he want to know?"

Doc smelled the gunpowder and how the concrete had felt when he knelt on it. "Said his boss had underestimated us, me and my cousin."

"That all?"

"All he had time for." Doc didn't speak for so long Neuschwander cleared his throat like he might. Doc raised a hand. "That was one man I killed in self-defense, after nine years in the army. Turner helped chew up five. It's too much for him. He needed to tell someone. Like you needed to tell that pretty barmaid the other night. Pretty soon he's going to talk to my partner about Rosewood, and about you. And when he does, you are well and truly fucked. This is contract murder, and the contractor is just as guilty as whoever pulls the trigger, and it's still a capital crime in Pennsylvania. No one's been executed here in...I don't know, fifteen or twenty years. It's still life without parole and there's only one deal available between the three of you."

Doc sat back in the chair. No one spoke for thirty seconds, when Neuschwander said, "Tick tock." Doc could have kissed him.

"You saw what your boy Simpson did, right?" Willie Grabek went for the close. "He saw you, in here with us, my partner making like everyone was friends, and he pissed his pants. Pissed. His. Pants. At the sight of you. You know why? Because he's afraid you're going to cut a deal before he does. You know there's only one deal to be made here, and the first one to come in gets it. Right now my partner's telling Simpson how he didn't pull the trigger; you and Rosewood did. Why should he get the death sentence when you two are the killers?"

Grabek had wrung most of the vinegar from DaRon Turner. More subtle and controlled than Rodney Simpson, he didn't make his distress too obvious. No trembling chin and jiggling feet. Turner's tell was a body posture caving in on itself like a dwarf star collapsing into a black hole. His head slipped down and his shoulders sagged as he sat slack-legged in the metal chair.

"You can think I'm bullshitting all you want, but believe one thing: Simpson *will* make that deal. He's smarter than you. He may have blood on his hands, but it's all over you. He set those mopes up to be killed and made sure he was nowhere around when it happened. You were there. You were seen. You fucked up ditching the weapons." Grabek gave what he'd said time to sink in. "You're going away forever if you don't get in front of this. What's it going to be?"

Turner looked like he might speak. Grabek backed off. Stush hadn't moved in his chair since the interview started, except to tap his thumbs against his belly once in a while. After two false starts, Turner said, "You say a witness can identify me?"

"Yeah. He got a good look."

"He say. Well, I say he a lying motherfucker."

"If he is, it's the first time," Grabek said. "We know this guy, some of us cops. He's straight up."

"Well, he lying now. Or maybe he making a mistake. I guaran-goddamn-tee you he didn't see me there."

Grabek didn't know what Dougherty's alleged witness had seen. If anything. "You say a reliable witness is wrong? Prove it. How is it he couldn't have seen you?"

"'Cause I weren't there."

"Where were you, then?" Grabek thought of the zoo story Turner tried out at The O, didn't mention it.

"I don't remember. That was what? Three weeks ago? I don't know where I was someday three weeks ago. I had no reason to remember."

"What do you usually do early Wednesday afternoons?"

"Different things. Not like I have a regular routine for every day."

"I guess not, in your line of work."

"What line a work you think I'm in?"

"Knucklehead," Grabek waited for some kind of objection. Didn't get it. Fought back a smile. "You're going to have to remember where you were and find a way to prove our witness is wrong. You have a lot of confidence you can do that?"

Another long silence. "I think maybe I do need a lawyer."

"That's your right, son," Stush said before Grabek could speak. "We stop any time you ask. You can call any lawyer you want, or we'll call the public defender's office. With luck, they can have someone here in an hour or so. We won't bother you while you wait." Gave Grabek a look, *I'll handle this.*

"Okay, then. Call the PD."

"Detective Grabek will take care of it right away." Ignored Grabek's stare. "One thing for you to think about while we wait: you can stop us from questioning you, but you can't stop the clock. If Simpson makes a deal while we're waiting, or while you're conferring with your lawyer, then there's nothing left to talk about. You have to decide before he leaves to make the call. Once he's out of the room, this interview is over, and so is our ability to negotiate."

The longest silence yet. Stush tapped his thumbs. Grabek half afraid to breathe, close as he was to Turner. A minute. Two. Turner said in a voice more air than sound, "What you want to know?"

Grabek looked to Stush, who nodded. "Who did you think you were talking to on the phone when you agreed to meet us at The O?"

"You're wasting time, Rodney," Doc said. "My partner's not nearly as patient as I am. He's going to break Turner down sooner or later. He does it before you wise up, and you'll never see a horizon again."

Doc couldn't be sure the interview hadn't gotten away from him. Simpson spent the past hour falling apart. Still no concessions. Something scared him more than an eternal prison sentence.

They had shit for evidence; needed at least one confession. Even better, get people pointing fingers at each other, give Sally Gwynn some leverage. Someone had to break first, and Simpson was the best bet. Doc dredged his memory for something useful, remembered the phone call Bieniemy placed to Turner.

"You recognized Turner in the hall just now, but it was

Darcy Rosewood you set it up with. How did you know to go to Rosewood?"

"How you know Darcy?" Simpson said, and Doc relaxed. A little.

"I've been telling you since you came in here, Turner's been talking to us. We know you went through Rosewood to set up the hit. Rosewood brought in Turner. Turner's been rolling on you all morning. For all I know, they're writing up the paperwork already. Your best chance is to give us Rosewood."

Simpson's spine stiffened. Said, "DaRon ain't say nothing about Darcy?"

Doc stifled a smile. "He hadn't by the time we came in here. I don't know what he's told Detective Grabek since then." A pause to let the fermentation process begin. "Look, Rosewood's a lost cause. He has too much of a record. You and Turner? The Commonwealth might be willing to provide room and board for you, if it felt like it owed you something. Getting Rosewood off the street is the kind of thing the prosecutor might be grateful for."

"It was DaRon." Came out so fast Doc not sure he heard it right. "He the one I talked to. I didn't know no Rosewood."

"You used his name not a minute ago. Noosh?"

"I heard him," Neuschwander said. "DaRon ain't say nothing about Darcy?"

"Don't tell me you don't know Darcy Rosewood," Doc said.

"I know him *now*, sure. DaRon introduced me. I didn't want to hang with him, so I only worked with DaRon."

"Why didn't you want to hang with Rosewood?

"You met him?"

"Yeah."

"You want to hang with him, not having your badge or gun or nothing? That man the grim fucking reaper."

"You know this for a fact?" Doc said.

"Hell, yeah—I mean, don't you? You said you met him. You tell me he don't vibe death to you?"

Doc thought about it for a second, no more. Darcy Rosewood might well be the baddest motherfucker Rodney Simpson had ever met; Simpson's breadth of field was limited. Rosewood more trouble on the hoof than the average knucklehead, but Doc had seen plenty worse, even among good guys. "That's your final word, then? You dealt with Turner, not Rosewood?"

"Swear on my mother's life."

"Let's be very clear. What you're saying is, you arranged with DaRon Turner for him and Darcy Rosewood to kill the five men in Resurrection Mall. You'll sign a statement with that in it?"

"Bring it. I'll sign."

"I'll give you paper and a pen and you'll write it out in your own words. We'll have it typed up and signed, and it will say you, Rodney Simpson, arranged with DaRon Turner for Turner and Darcy Rosewood to kill those five men."

"No, man, I'm telling you I talked with DaRon. Rodney ain't never said nothing about Darcy. He was all DaRon's idea."

"All right," Doc said. "Who did you set it up for?"

"Who? Those five motherfuckers they killed. Who the fuck you think?"

"No, dumbass. Who told you to have those five guys killed?"

"Rodney can't say nothing about that."

"Rodney." Doc rubbed his eyes. "I know you're lying to me about contacting Rosewood. I'll let you put it in your statement because it'll be fun to watch the prosecutor string you up by your balls in court over it one day. This part here, I need to know who you were working for."

"Why's you so sure I's working for anybody?"

Patience, Doc thought. Simpson torn between wanting to get off the hook as best he could and satisfying his ego. Not the time to hurry.

"How much did you pay Rosewood—sorry, Turner—for the hit?"

"I'm getting immunity, I tell you, right?"

"Immunity? Seriously? Five men are dead. There's no immunity for something like this. You tell us all you can, maybe work yourself down from death row to fifteen-to-life."

"My ass, no immunity. What about Sammy the Bull? He did, like, nineteen hits and he got immunity."

"First, that was federal. They do all kinds of weird shit. Second, he gave them information on something like a hundred gangsters. Thousands of years of jail time. You bringing anything that big to the table?"

Simpson took a minute to think, the effort plain on his face. Doc moved the discussion along. "How much?"

A rumor of a smile creased Simpson's lips. "Ten."

"Ten thousand?"

"Yeah, ten thousand. What the fuck you think, brothers be out there busting caps in niggers for two bucks apiece?"

Two, two thousand; so what? Doc felt too old for all of it. Had been for a while. He didn't know how Grabek did it after thirty-some years. "Okay. Ten grand. Who the hell would give you ten thousand dollars cash and not worry about you fucking it up?"

Simpson showed as much swagger as a man with a crotch stain could muster. "I guarantee you no one worried about Rodney holding up his end."

"No offense. Who was it?"

Simpson took his time. His posture and attitude shifted again. No more hyperactive feet or trembling chin. The word flashed through Doc's mind was "comfortable." Not a complete surprise. Criminals with heavy charges on them often fell asleep when caught or after a confession, from the relief of getting it behind them. Simpson enjoying himself, screwing with Doc's head. "It make a difference if I set it up for someone else?"

Something in the tone made Doc less sure of his footing. "Hell, yeah, it makes a difference." Paused to consider which way to go. "Why would you think it wouldn't?"

"I don't mean for y'all. What difference it make for me to give him up?"

"It hurts your leverage if you don't."

"My what?"

"The less you tell us, the harder it's going to be to cut a deal with the prosecutor. This sort of thing, information is like money. The more you have, the better life is."

Another quiet minute. Simpson much calmer now. Doc not sure if from resignation or cunning. Not sure he cared anymore.

"Naw," Simpson said. "Rodney ain't see no benefit in telling."

"Lock him up," Doc said.

Grabek not buying DaRon Turner's story.

"So you dealt only with Rosewood?"

"Darcy the one brought me in. I met Rodney and such, but I worked for Darcy."

"Rosewood ever tell you who Simpson worked for?"

"No."

"You never asked?"

"You met Darcy?" Grabek nodded. "He ain't the kind of man you ask questions like that to."

Maybe Rosewood not the kind of man *Turner* asked hard questions of; Grabek couldn't wait. "Okay, here's the sixty-four thousand dollar question: how much did Rosewood pay you?"

Turner's eyes got big. "If he says he paid me sixty-four thousand dollars, he a lying motherfucker, and I'll tell him to his face."

Grabek stifled most of his laugh; Stush smiled. "Relax. It was a figure of speech. How much did you get paid for the job?"

Turner looked at Grabek as if he thought the cop might start speaking Hungarian or Klingon or something. Took time to regain his equilibrium. Sat back, straightened his shoulders, said, "I got the going rate."

"Which is?"

"You don't know, for real? I thought cops knew all that shit."

"It's a small town. We don't get a lot of that kind of business here."

Turner might have smiled. "Grand a man."

"You killed those men for five thousand dollars?"

"Twenty-five hundred," Turner said. "I only did half the work."

Grabek felt himself deflate. Thirty-five years a cop, prided himself on nothing bothering him. It was life. It was what it was. People did things he could never have imagined, and he absorbed it all like he'd seen the same thing the day before. He'd worked cases, people killed for less than ten dollars. Not the plan. No crook is going to blow out a candle for ten bucks. Not till someone's dead does the killer find out the victim had no money. Then he either panics, or feels like killing the guy again for putting him in this jackpot over a heist that wouldn't take two people to McDonald's.

Now here was DaRon Turner, professional knucklehead, puffing his chest because he was paid twenty-five hundred dollars to help kill five men. Knew that was the price going in. Could have walked away if it wasn't enough. Maybe twenty-five hundred was a life-altering sum of money to Turner; Grabek didn't know. All he knew was, he, a man who'd prided himself on being the least sensitive cop in any squad he'd worked in, felt old and tired and dirty, having spent most of a day in a small room with a man who valued a human life at five hundred dollars.

CHAPTER 53

"Their stories don't match."

"Thanks, Sally," Doc said. "That's why we asked you over. To tell us that."

Doc liked Sally Gwynn. Part of him lusted after her, red hair and green eyes and a pulse in her throat that invited thoughts best left aside during working hours. Prided himself on being one of a handful of age-appropriate men in the City-County complex who'd never hit on her. Liked to think it was a matter of professionalism, knew deep down he didn't want to become another of the shot down stories Sally told over drinks. She always left out names and descriptions, but the people she talked to figured out things for a living. For two weeks—much longer in Jack Harriger's case—veiled comments and open laughter greeted whichever city or county employee had made his move and been augured in by the Red Baroness.

Doc's issue with Sally her conservatism as a prosecutor. For all the glamor and star power she brought to a dreary town in the Western Pennsylvania hills, Sally only tried cases she knew she'd win. Everything else either pled out or nolle prossed. Doc and Grabek had cajoled her into taking Marian Widmer to trial, where Marian's attorney beat Sally like a chain gang with a bad attitude. She'd taken no advice from either detective since.

"I was wondering why you asked me over," Sally said.

"You have no evidence and the only two people talking don't tell the same story. They sort of confessed. You want me to sort of throw them in prison? Something like after-school detention?"

"Let's all take a deep breath," Stush said. "We're still comparing notes. I know it's earlier than we usually bring you in, Sally. We thought you might be able to steer us in the most profitable direction, since you're the one who knows best how it has to play in court."

"Rosewood," Grabek said. "We find him and we lean on him."

"No argument," Doc. "They both agree he was there. Whether he was just a trigger man or also the contractor, we have two sources who'll swear he was involved."

"He'll lie," Sally said.

"Of course he'll lie," Grabek said. "Both of these two jazzbos lied to us all morning and afternoon. We'll compare his lies with theirs and start to pry."

"Rosewood for sure," Stush said. "Soon as we're done here, do what you have to do to bring him in."

"What's the motive?" Sally said.

"Money." Grabek showed Sally less deference than the others. Sally much closer to his daughter's age than his, so he never thought of nailing her. For the record. Eye Chart Zywiciel suspected he treated her like shit because it pissed him off to be past the age where he might have a shot at her. "Cash changed hands for the hit. They both admitted it."

Sally didn't like Grabek any more than he let on he liked her, and didn't mind if people knew. "It's going to take more than that in court. Such as, where did—which one is it?

Simpson?—get the money. It's sure to come up. It would be nice to have an answer."

"To get whoever paid him, sure. All we need to convict the ones we have now is to know Simpson gave them money and they accepted it. They've already admitted to it."

"They don't even agree on who the money was given *to*," Sally said. "Turner says the money came through Rosewood and Simpson says he paid Turner directly." She aborted a reply with her hand. "I know one of them is lying. We'll have to prove it in court. Two conflicting stories confuse a jury."

She looked through the paperwork too fast to read it. "Look, I'm not saying I won't prosecute these guys. You two are convinced they did it, that's good enough for me. All I'm saying is we need some evidence. Something to show in court so the jury can look at it and think, 'That's how they did it.'"

"Divers are searching the river for the guns," Doc said.

"*If* they find them and *if* they can be matched to the crime and *if* they can be matched to either suspect, that would be great."

"We have two confessions," Grabek said.

"Which will be recanted as soon as the defense lawyers find out in discovery we have no evidence. You know all this, Willie. I know you do." She waited for Grabek's answer, which didn't come. "We need the top of the pyramid. I shouldn't have to tell you to follow the money, and you both say you're sure it doesn't come from...Simpson? No one is going to pony up ten thousand for the hell of it. We have to show the jury who benefits. *Qui bono?*"

"Yeah," Doc said under his breath. "*Qui bono.*"

"Did anyone offer them deals yet?" Sally said.

"Not really." Stush. "We've been offering them the opportunity to make deals all day. We've been clear only you can make an offer, and they'd have to earn it. Benny? That how it went with you?"

Doc nodded. "I presented Simpson with options. Made sure he knew only one deal would be offered, so the clock was running."

"And neither one of them would give up a personal connection to Rosewood?"

"Nope. They're that afraid of him. Like he's the fucking black Voldemort or something. He whose name may not be spoken."

"You talked to him," Sally said. "Is he?"

Doc shook his head, pushed out his lower lip. "He's a hard case, nothing legendary."

Grabek said, "He's not as hard as he thinks he is," which was how he would have described Batman. Or the Terminator. Grabek had never met a subject he didn't think he could break down. Occasional failures over the years had not altered his opinion.

Sally tapped a pen against her teeth, propped one foot on the rung of a chair. Her skirt rode up enough for Doc to have to look away. She hadn't done it on purpose—he didn't think she did—which made the effect more pronounced. "You're going to pick up Rosewood?" she said.

"Rick Neuschwander is typing up the affidavit right now," Stush said. "Willie already called his friend in Pittsburgh. They'll be ready for us as soon as Judge Molchan signs."

Sally put both feet on the floor. Doc exhaled. "I'll talk to the two you have already while you're rounding up Rosewood. I'll let them know they haven't given us what we need for a deal. One of them has to spell out where Rosewood fits. I'll leave it the same way you did: first one to tell, wins."

"What about the money?" Grabek said.

"From what you told me, Turner is off the hook on that." Nods all around. "If Simpson gives me Rosewood, but not the money man, his deal isn't quite as good as Turner's would be. He gives me both, it's a little better. If Turner gives me Rosewood, then the money source is the only chip Simpson has left. He'll have to play it, or I'll make him eat the whole charge."

Neuschwander stuck in his head. "Judge signed the warrant."

All the cops stood. Sally spoke before they could saddle up. "Remember one thing: we need to know where the money came from. Who gave it to Simpson." Grabek made for the door. "Wait, Willie. We all know the whole *means, motive, opportunity* thing is bullshit. We don't have to prove them to win a conviction. Here's the thing: juries like it. I can't remember getting a conviction on a murder case—rape, any violent crime that carries serious time—without it."

Grabek said, "I can't remember her winning a case at all," not so soft Sally missed it.

"It doesn't matter what the judge instructs," she said. "People see it on television, they want to see it in court. It lets them feel like they made us a meet a standard before they vote to lock someone up and throw away the key." She drilled a look into Grabek. "I won't prosecute without proof of where the money came from."

"Come on, Sally," Doc said.

"She's not only incompetent, she's lazy, too," Grabek said to the person referred to as "she."

"Okay, that's enough." Stush placed himself between Sally and his cops. "This discussion can wait for another time. Get Rosewood in here. He might make the whole conversation a moot point." To Neuschwander: "Ricky, I want financials for Abernathy, Lewis, Love, anyone else you can think of connected with Resurrection Mall. Someone dropped ten grand on Simpson to contract this job out. The people we're dealing with don't have that kind of money laying around. It left a trail. Find it."

He turned to face Sally. "You negotiate solid deals, maybe you won't have to take Simpson and Turner to trial. One thing, though, Ms. Gwynn." Waited for her to make eye contact. "This isn't some smash and grab bullshit you can bargain down to a misdemeanor. We have five bodies. If these guys don't do serious time, your boss and I are going to talk."

CHAPTER 54

Doc and Grabek ran with lights, no siren, getting to Pittsburgh. Met Bieniemy and three uniforms half a mile from Rosewood's crib. A simple plan: one uniform at each building exit, three detectives at the door to the apartment, as close to a tumultuous entry as they could make without a ram and tactical team.

The three detectives crept up the stairs, guns drawn. A Neshannock County no-knock warrant in Doc's inside pocket, initialed by Bieniemy to show Allegheny County had been informed. They turned left one hundred eighty degrees off the stairwell on Rosewood's floor. A door opened behind them. All three turned, guns not pointed down as much as before. A black woman in her early fifties, wearing jeans and a Pitt basketball sweatshirt. Cordless phone in her left hand. Bieniemy put a finger to his lips, held out his badge on the lanyard around his neck.

"Where you going?" she whispered.

He made the shooshing gesture with greater emphasis, nodded toward Rosewood's door. Doc pointed at it with his gun.

"Good." The woman closed her door without a sound.

Grabek went past the door. Old and fat, he never went first. Doc stepped back and put weight on his left foot. Bieniemy tapped him on a shoulder. Pointed to himself, then the door. Mouthed, "My town, my door." Doc looked at him a second, traded places. Bieniemy kicked in the door as soon as Doc had his gun poised.

"Darcy Rosewood, Pittsburgh police! You're under arrest! Place your hands on your head and get on your knees, you murdering motherfucker!"

Bieniemy barged straight down a hallway. Doc a second behind, clearing to the right. Grabek a second behind him, clearing left, moving for a pantry off the kitchen. Bieniemy kicked open a door on his left, kept moving to the end of the hall and Doc remembered he and Grabek had been here before. A door at the end of the hall, six inches ajar. Bieniemy kicked it open so hard he had to shield his face when it rebounded off the wall. "Clear!"

Doc pushed open the door Bieniemy ignored. A bathroom. "Clear!"

"We're clear." Grabek came in from the kitchen.

The three exchanged looks in the hallway. "Well," Doc said, "so much for the element of surprise."

"We have a search warrant," Grabek said. "Let's use it."

The detectives not inclined to do an FBI-style *take pictures of everything and make sure it goes back where we found it* search. Not much point with the front door jamb splintered. They spent half an hour on a quick, thorough tossing. Turned over the mattress, looked for wall panels and loose floorboards, emptied drawers. Found three handguns—none of them nine millimeter semi-automatics—a box of .357 cartridges, a box of .38s, and forty-three hundred dollars in cash. Nothing else of immediate interest.

"He's a convicted felon, right?" Grabek said when they compared notes. Bieniemy nodded. "Worst case, Pittsburgh has him on a gun charge."

"I'm not giving up on tonight yet," Bieniemy said.

"What do you have in mind?" Doc said.

"I pulled his file while we were waiting for the warrant. Checked some known associates and cross-referenced where some of these guys hang." Tapped the breast of his suit coat. "Got a list of four places worth checking out. Me and Willie and a uniform will take two, you take two with the other uniforms. They're good men. I asked for them personal. Go in strong. They'll won't just have your six. They'll take care of everything from two to ten."

On the way out, Doc asked Bieniemy if he wanted to do anything about the broken door.

"I almost forgot." Pushed it aside and walked to the head of the stairs. "Move out sale in two-oh-two! These prices are insane! Not even unreasonable offers refused! Get here quick and the shit's free!"

CHAPTER 55

Grabek and Bieniemy left the uniform at the door of Club Cheetah on Centre Avenue. The usual dive: dim light, small tables, waitresses almost wearing uniforms. Half a dozen semi-pros worked the room, looking for drinks and whatever else could be negotiated. A handful of men sat at the bar, another twenty scattered in twos and threes at tables. A haze of smoke collected on the ceiling like fog in a swamp.

The two cops wandered among the clientele. Their reception ranged from disdain to contempt to being ignored. No Rosewood.

Bieniemy moved for the bar. "Follow me. I know this guy."

The bartender a black man with arms the size of Easter hams. A shade under six feet, upper body almost round. Gold-framed reading glasses atop a shaved head. He showed no recognition of either cop. Grabek thought he'd seen the guy before.

Bieniemy had plenty of room, made a point of nudging aside a bar patron. Held up his badge. "Detective Bieniemy. I'm looking for a guy name of Darcy Rosewood. Don't be cute. We know he hangs here. I just want to know if he's been around."

"Darcy what?" The bartender rubbed a glass over the bristles in the sink, started drying it. "This ain't one a them gay joints, Officer."

"Cute." Bieniemy showed a photograph of Rosewood.

"Mug shot, huh? Shame how many young black men have these as they primary means of identification."

"Do you know him?"

"Let me get a better look." Took the photo, dropped the glasses over his eyes. Made a show of looking for light to hold it up to. "Looks a little familiar. Not like I could tell you his name if you didn't just say. Been in a time or two, I guess."

"Recently?"

"Couldn't say. Like I told you, it's not like he a regular."

Bieniemy took back the photo, eyed the bartender hard. "Aren't you even going to ask why I'm looking for him?"

The bartender slid the glasses up on his head and smiled with teeth the creamy color of a cue ball. "Why would I?"

"Because you aren't going to say, either way." The smile widened. "I'll be back, you know."

"Officers of the law always welcome. Keeps out the undesirables."

In the car, Bieniemy said, "You recognize him?"

"The bartender? He looked familiar, but I can't place him."

"That's Otis Birdsong."

"*That* was Otis Birdsong?" Their bartender had torn up the City League as a nose tackle at Westinghouse High School. Went on to Miami of Florida and a decent career with Kansas City and Baltimore in the NFL until police had to be called to a domestic disturbance and Otis put three of them in the hospital alongside his soon to be ex-wife. "This is where he ended up?"

"Sells a little muscle to keep things together," Bieniemy

said. "He's one of my snitches. Rosewood hasn't been around." Grabek gave him a look. "You see him washing glasses in the sink when we walked up? We go through our little charade when I need something in a hurry. He pretends he don't know me, I ask him my questions, he blows me off, we busts balls. If he starts scrubbing another glass when I'm ready to go, he'll call me within half an hour. He didn't give the signal, so we on to the next stop."

Doc rode with a salt-and-pepper team named, swear to God, Calvin and Hobbs. John Calvin—yes, that's who he was named after—the white guy, six-one, one-ninety, early thirties, thinning sandy hair and blue eyes crinkled at the edges. Antonio Hobbs a little taller, heavier, and younger, with a smile that implied he'd find entertainment in whatever happened next. They struck Doc as two cops from a sitcom canceled after half a season.

Calvin drove, stopped outside a warehouse-looking building on Smallman Street. "Here we are."

"Where?" Doc said. "The warehouse?"

Hobbs pointed to street level. "Down the stairs."

Doc would have missed it. A painted black railing kept pedestrians from falling into a stairwell alongside the building. One window, no more than six inches above the sidewalk, with heavy bars. No light escaped. Either painted over, blocked off from the inside, or—as Doc noticed walking by—too dirty. "What is this dump?"

"Skels," Hobbs said.

"What's that? Short for Skelton or something?"

"It's named after the clientele." Doc gave confused. "You

know how day laborers hang at Home Depot and Lowe's in the morning? This is where crooks looking for work hang at night. I don't think anyone knows the real name. Have to look on the liquor license."

"If they have a liquor license," Calvin said.

Hobbs brought them up short at the bottom of the stairs. "Walk in like you own the joint. Identify yourself as a cop, flash the tin, don't say you're out of town. We'll scope out the customers while you play Popeye Doyle."

"You'll recognize Rosewood?"

"Oh, hell, yeah," Calvin said. "We go way back with Darcy. We're such good friends, the three of us spent New Year's Eve together a few years ago. No way we're going to forget him."

Doc pushed open the door and found himself in a narrow room forty feet deep. Bar along the right, room between the stools and the wall for two men to walk abreast, if both had waists under thirty inches. No beer signs, no television, no evidence of a kitchen or backroom. Doc saw no obvious way for the bartender to get in or out. Just a dozen or so black men and two white guys drinking.

"It's okay to be a tool," Calvin said. "We don't want to be in here any longer than we have to."

Doc stepped to the bar and made room for himself between two patrons. Calvin stayed back to block the front door. Hobbs ambled halfway along the aisle, smiling as customers turned away.

Doc showed his badge with his right hand, gestured for the bartender with the left. Bartender looked at him, tossed a towel onto his shoulder, and stared over the head of the drinker in front of him.

"*Hey!*" Hobbs yelled loud enough for people in the street to hear, the bartender not eight feet from him. "The man asked for your attention, motherfucker. Go over there and tell him what he wants to know or we'll see what's in the pockets of every limber dick here. Just being in this shithole is all the probable cause we need."

Not how Doc would have played it. The bartender made a show of how slow he moved, but did come over.

"You see this guy around lately?" Showed Rosewood's photo. "We know he hangs here."

"Don't know him."

"Hey, asshole," Doc said, getting with the flow. "You didn't even look. The faster I find out what I need to know, the quicker you can get back to your Mensa meeting."

"Never seen him."

"We know he drinks here. This must be your first day of work."

"Yeah, that's it. First day. I ain't know any a these here."

"Don't lie to him, Lightning," Hobbs said. "You know I know you."

"I said I ain't never seen him before. That ain't no lie."

"Yeah, and your mama don't buy in bulk on Father's Day, neither. All right. Fine. Okay. I guess we'll do it the hard way. Go down the line, Detective. One at a time."

Calvin shifted position as Doc turned to the man sitting where the short L of the bar joined the wall. "What's your name?"

"What for?"

"So I know in case I see you again."

"You ain't see me again, and I ain't telling you shit, so be on your way."

"*Hands!*" Calvin yelled and jerked the man at Doc's back off his stool by his collar. "Show me your hands right now or I'll break them in your pockets."

"Fuck you, motherfucker," the man said, scrambling for balance. "Here. Here! Ain't nothing in my fucking hands."

"Go stand in the corner there." Calvin pushed him, not too hard. "Make sure I can see the palms of your hands or I'll ram this baton through your belly and break your spine."

Doc less than enchanted with how things were shaking out. Calvin and Hobbs worked well together; no doubt they had his back. They were also outnumbered four to one if anything sparked. Neither Pittsburgh cop seemed fazed. Brass balls were good. Death wishes, not so much.

He sidled back to Calvin. "Maybe we should take a lower profile."

Calvin grinned through tight lips, eyes scanning. Spoke so only Doc could hear. "We elevated our profiles walking through the door. No one's going to tell us dick. We only came in to see if Rosewood was here. Now we can't look like we're leaving with our tails between our legs because we didn't get what we came for. We have to make a statement. Then we can go."

"How do you want to play it?"

"Pick one you think you can make an impression on. Take him in back by the men's room and lean on him. Hobbs and I will handle things out here. We want to leave the impression we could stay all night to busting balls, but have more important things to do."

Doc took inventory. Said, "Is there anyone here you're sure knows Rosewood?"

Calvin continued his survey. "A couple for sure. Three, maybe."

"Any of them white? I want someone who knows him, but I'd also rather not single out a black guy, all things considered."

"Third guy up from the corner here. A little overweight, hair thin on top."

Doc used his peripheral vision. "Plaid shirt-jacket kind of deal?"

"Name's Monday or Mundy or Grundy or Bundy or something. I know he knows Rosewood. How well, can't say. He's white, and—added bonus—not the toughest lock to open."

Doc nodded, stepped forward. Tapped the guy on the shoulder. "You. What's your name?"

"Who wants to know?"

Doc leaned in to speak to an audience of one. "I do. Now you're going to tell me your name and the two of us are going to walk to the end of the bar there and have a talk, or I'm going to pull you off that stool by your collar and drag your ass back there. What's it gonna be?"

"Policastro."

"What?"

"My name. It's Policastro."

Doc took a second to wonder how close Policastro was to Monday or Mundy or Grundy or Bundy. "What's your first name?"

"Everyone calls me Paulie."

"I didn't ask what everyone calls you. What's your first name?"

"What difference does it make? You wanna talk or trade Christmas cards?"

Doc reached behind Policastro, grabbed a handful of collar. "Last chance, or you're going in back on your heels and ass."

"Bonaventura."

Doc relaxed his grip. "*What?*"

"Bonaventura. My first name. You want my middle name, you can start dragging."

Doc pulled the collar to stand him up. "Let's go." Looked at Calvin, who shrugged.

They walked to the back of the room, Policastro in front. Hobbs nodded in approval as they passed. The bar ended at a hallway not visible from the front. Men's room on the left. Swinging door at the end marked "Employees only." Doc stopped Policastro halfway between the men's and the swinging door, moved him against the wall on their right and leaned in.

"Darcy Rosewood. You know him?"

"I do or I don't, I'm not telling you."

"Why not?"

That threw Policastro a little. "You're a cop. I don't talk about my friends to cops."

"So you don't just know Rosewood, you're friends with him."

"That's not what I said."

"That's exactly what you said. You said, 'I don't talk about my friends to cops.'"

"Yeah, I know him. Not like we're close or nothing."

"So you're not friends."

"Not close or nothing."

Doc moved closer. "Are you friends or aren't you?"

Policastro made a calculation, said, "No. Not really."

"Then you can talk about him."

"Huh?"

"You said you don't talk to cops about your friends. Well, Rosewood isn't your friend. You're free to tell me what I want to know."

"No, what I meant was, I don't talk to cops, period."

"You've been talking to me for a while now. I think you don't know what you mean. You need to figure it out damn quick, because I want Rosewood for five bodies. Shine me on and I'm thinking accessory after the fact, *if* you're lucky. Conspiracy, if you're not."

"Bullshit. I don't know nothing about no five bodies."

"You get harder to believe all the time," Doc said. "Do you mean to tell me you haven't heard about the five guys Rosewood aced in Penns River a couple weeks ago?"

"That was way the hell up Penns River." Policastro looked close at Doc for the first time. "You ain't even a Pittsburgh cop, are you?"

"I'm the cop can charge you in Penns River where you won't have access to the higher quality PDs here in Allegheny County. You'll get some Neshannock County appointee who flunked the bar exam four times and has to work nights at Sheetz to make ends meet. You looking forward to that?"

"What the hell you gonna charge me with?"

"Pay attention. I already mentioned accessory and conspiracy. Keep jacking me around and I'll go for obstruction of justice."

"Take it easy. I was sitting there having a quiet drink and

you come in like the Nazi cavalry. What the hell you want from me?"

"Where can I find Darcy Rosewood?" Policastro started to speak. Doc cut him off. "Uh-uh. You already lied at least once about how well you know him, which means you know him pretty well. Well enough for him to tell you what he's into. Now you can tell me."

"Like hell. I already told you—"

"I know, you don't talk about your friends to cops. Here's how this plays out: I'm going to make a big deal about taking you to Penns River with me, mouthing off about charges all the while we're leaving. You'll be back later tonight or tomorrow morning, free as a bird, because you're right: I have nothing to charge you with. Here's your problem: we're this close to catching Rosewood. How's it going to look when you beat a charge right before he goes down?"

"If that's true, and you're close, I'm fucked either way," Policastro said. "Now that you brought me back here, even if you leave without me and grab him, it looks like I talked."

"Then you might as well tell me," Doc said. "No point catching hell for something you didn't do."

Policastro's body language showed his decision whether to talk had been made. How to do it and not feel any guiltier than he had to all that remained. "He has this chick he hangs with when he's got money." No eye contact. "If he did that thing in Penns River, he might be with her."

"What's her name?"

"Ebony or Sesame or Ecstasy. Something like that."

Great. Like Policastro rhymed with Mundy or Grundy. "Sounds like a dancer."

Policastro shook his head. "Hooker, I think. High class."

"Rosewood one of her johns?"

"No. He knows her from way back. They mighta gone to school together."

"Where can I find this Ebony?" Or Sesame or Ecstasy.

"I don't know. Honest to Christ, I don't. I don't run in their circle, and it ain't like he brings her around here. He talks about her a lot, is how I know they're close."

"Anything else?"

"No. I swear. Like I said, I don't know him that good. Just to see around and shoot the shit is all."

"If I find out you lied to me, we'll be back and it won't be pretty. I'm not local, but the two came in here with me are looking to make reputations."

"I'm cool. That's the straight shit."

Doc's turn to think for a minute. "How can we make this come out right for you?

"What do you mean?"

"I want to leave here looking like I got nothing so you can still show your face. How bad's it going to have to look for you when we come out of here?"

Policastro turned it over in his mind. "Push me through the doorway ahead of you hard so I stumble. Make some noise about how I'm stupid and a waste of time. Don't make it too obvious."

"I've done this before. You hold up your end, you'll be fine." Doc stepped back to give Policastro room to change position. "You ready?"

"Yeah, just let me—"

Doc shoved him through the doorway to bounce off the wall. Said, "Asshole," half under his breath. Elbowed past as Policastro struggled with his balance. Waved to Calvin and

Hobbs. "Let's go," he said for everyone to hear, not shouting, walking with purpose toward the exit. "He's too fucking dumb to know where *he* is, let alone Rosewood."

Doc waited outside while Calvin and Hobbs made their goodbyes. When all three were in the car, he said, "Either of you know a call girl name of Ebony, tight with Rosewood? Policastro says they go way back."

Calvin shook his head. Hobbs took his time, said, "You sure it's Ebony?"

"No surer than I was Bonaventura Policastro isn't named Grundy or Bundy or Mundy."

Calvin made a face; Hobbs laughed. "Really?"

"I thought he was someone else," Calvin said.

"This whore, Ebony or whatever," Hobbs said. "You think it could be Persephone Green? You remember, we busted her at that gynecologist convention a few months ago? Tall, beautiful face, ass you could park a car on?"

Calvin gave it thought. "Can't say it's not. Does Persephone know Rosewood?"

"I think they both went to Westinghouse."

"Rosewood went to Westinghouse," Doc said.

Hobbs nodded. "She'd be about the right age, maybe a little younger."

Calvin had stared at Hobbs since Westinghouse High School came up. "How'd you remember that? She went to Westinghouse."

"Piece of strange that fine, little things stick in a man's mind."

"How about let's hit this next place on our list," Doc said. "We don't find him there, are you two game to go back to the station and see what we can find out about Persephone Green?"

"Absolutely," Hobbs said. "You're our date tonight. Last thing in the world we want to do is let word get out we didn't show you a good time."

Grabek and Bieniemy and their uniform—Holloman—walked into The End Zone on the North Side together. Holloman hung by the door. The detectives went to the bar running along the right side of the room, where a handful of drinkers had drafts or shots or both in front of them. A dozen tables filled the floor area; people ate at half of them. More an old-fashioned tavern than a bar; reminded Grabek of where Dougherty hung out—the Edgecliff—a little seedier.

"What can I get you boys?" Bartender mid-fifties, light-skinned black man, hollow cheeks, bald on top. A pencil mustache he must have considered stylish.

Bieniemy leaned back on his elbows to face the room. Grabek pushed a photo of Darcy Rosewood across the bar. "You know this guy? Word is he loafs in here."

The bartender suffered from no indecision. "That's Darcy Rosewood. Comes in when he's short, wants to drink on the cuff."

"You let him?"

"Up to a point. He's always good for it. Not always in what I would call a timely manner."

"Seen him lately?"

This took thought. "It's been a while, now that I think about it. Couple, three weeks maybe. You cops?"

"Grabek, Penns River." Jerked a thumb in Bieniemy's

direction. "Bieniemy here's local." Bieniemy held up his badge for verification, didn't turn away from the room.

"Look, Detective, I don't want any trouble. This ain't no hoodlum joint. The man comes in here once in a while when he's hard up, has a few drinks. He don't give me problems, and I don't give him any. I haven't seen him and I don't know where he is, or where he's been. You're not looking to jam me up, are you?"

Grabek's head sagged an inch. A drop of sweat fell from his nose to the bar. "No, we're not looking to jam you up. We're just looking for him. Any ideas you have where he might be, we'd listen."

"I'm sorry, I really am, but I don't know him that well."

Grabek arched an eyebrow. "You let him drink free."

"That's the boss's call. Him and Darcy go way back."

"How far?"

The bartender hunched his back, lowered his voice. "Pine Grove."

"Ex-con can't own a liquor license."

"License is in the wife's name."

Grabek looked at his right hand gripping the edge of the bar. Let go and tapped his fingers to keep them loose. "How long's your boss been out?"

"I'm not sure. I only started working here about a year ago. Eight, ten years, I think."

Willie Grabek prided himself on being a prick, almost as much as he prided himself on only being one to people who deserved it. The bartender seemed straight, the joint seemed straight, and the owner must have kept his nose clean. No rule said every bar a crook drank in had to be crooked.

Grabek took out a card, slid it across the bar. "Do me a

favor. You see him, or hear anything, give me a call. Your boss might appreciate having a cop owe him a favor if anyone ever did try to jam him up." Bieniemy held up two fingers. The bartender palmed the card.

Grabek wiped sweat from his forehead. Almost turned to leave, thought of one more question. "How's Rosewood's bar tab?"

"Paid in full last time he come in."

Grabek nodded thanks, tapped his knuckles twice on the bar. "Let's go," he said to Bieniemy.

"That Darcy Rosewood you talking about?" said a voice two stools to Grabek's right. "That his pitcher?"

"Yeah." Grabek handed the photo to a black man of average height and emaciated frame. Around sixty, too many of those years spent in places not as nice as The End Zone. An afro averaged an inch long and gave Grabek the impression the man cut his own hair. "You know him?"

The man pushed away the photo. "Fuck, yeah, I know him. Motherfucker owe me money."

"Eldon, please," the bartender said. "We got families here tonight for the spaghetti."

"Well, he paid everybody else in the got-damn world 'cept me. I got a right to call him a motherfucker."

"Sounds like you have a legitimate grievance." Grabek and Bieniemy guided Eldon to the end of the bar and took positions on either side with such efficiency the man didn't miss his drink. "Tell us about it."

"Rosewood thinks he's king shit around here. Biggest and baddest motherfucker on the North Side, Homewood, the Hill, everywhere east of Chicago and west of New York.

Well, he ain't king a shit to me, and I'll tell it to his lying deadbeat motherfuckin' face."

"He's not available right now," Bieniemy said. "Tell us."

"I *am* telling you. He a lying deadbeat motherfucker. What I just say?"

"I'm not arguing with you," Bieniemy said. "I want to know *why* you say he's a lying deadbeat motherfucker. And keep your voice down, man. No need to broadcast this where it might get back to him."

"I ain't afraid a no Darcy deadbeat motherfucker Rosewood." Eldon warmed to the task, playing to a captive audience. "Bring his lying ass in here and I'll tell him to his face. He might have a bunch of Hill District niggers pissing their pants, but this North Side black man ready for whatever he got."

"What kind of money are we talking about here?" Grabek said.

Eldon's eyes got big. "We ain't talking about no chicken scratch, I can tell you that. Man into me for a pair—two!—double sawbucks."

Grabek's head sank, cradled in a hand. Bieniemy did a quick calculation, reconsidered, said, "How much is that?"

"Forty dollars," Grabek said, almost inaudible.

"Forty dollars?" Bieniemy said. Then, to Eldon, "You're running your mouth, calling down thunder, over forty dollars?"

"Might not seem like much to you working men, wearing your fine like you are. Forty half my week's rent."

"I'm sorry," Grabek said, and he was. Sweating with purpose now, his shirt sticking to him. "Forty bucks is nothing to sneeze at. How'd you like a chance at a hundred?"

319

"What I got to do?"

"Do you know where he is?"

Elson shook his head in disappointment. "You think I waste two police's time just to bitch about my personal problems? I seen him at a place a couple hours ago, running his mouth, as usual."

"Where?"

"Place thinks it's class, over to Centre Avenue. Club Cheetah."

"Deceitful motherfucker," Bieniemy said under his breath. Then, to Eldon: "That where he is now?"

"No, that's where he at couple a hours ago. He's talking to some guy I don't know about how he come into some money and there was more where that come from."

"And he included you in this conversation why?" Bieniemy said.

"'Cause he didn't know I was taking a shit while he running his mouth in the men's room. Said he's on his way to Penns River to see some preacher, runs some kind of shopping center for churches there. Didn't make much sense to me."

Grabek pushed five twenties into Eldon's hand as he followed Bieniemy to the door. Eldon looked at the bills, spoke to their backs. "Go ahead and arrest him, whatever he done. Kill the motherfucker, you want to. All the same to me."

CHAPTER 56

"I never figured Love was involved." Doc and Grabek doing a hundred on Route 28 North, siren and lights. The call already made to surround Resurrection Mall and look for Rosewood's car. Do not approach. Engage in force with extreme caution only if he attempts to leave.

"Me, either," Grabek said. "I know I said he wasn't out of the game; I never seriously considered him for it. Not that I don't think some TV preacher stealing half-dollars from shut-ins isn't capable. I thought he'd be smarter."

Sweat beaded on Grabek's face in the low twenties night. Pale as newsprint in the reflected light, the car screaming past the Shaler Township water works. "Did either Turner or Simpson mention him?"

"Not as far as Stush knows, and I guess he talked to Sally before she left." Doc told him this not ten minutes before, after touching base with Stush.

Grabek sat looking out the window at Sharpsburg and the river flashing by, Highland Park Bridge coming up. Doc focused on driving, moving right to pass a driver more concerned with not going to Highland Park than with being rammed by a police car, then hard left to keep from catching the bridge ramp himself.

What had they missed about Love? True, he'd lied. People lie to cops all the time, so often good cops didn't take it personal. Love hadn't come across that way. Uncertain.

Nervous. Doc wrote it off as natural; everything Love had built was in danger of coming down around him. The nervousness and uncertainty had been the tell, and Doc missed it.

Blew past the Hulton Bridge into Harmar Township kicking himself. Christian Love not even his real name. He sold the miracle elixir of religion to the weak and hopeless, the meek who would not inherit the earth in this lifetime. The spiel always the same: "Dig deep, we need you now," preached to people who turned down the heat in winter and did without air conditioning in summer to meet his endless requests.

Doc's anger took on the zeal of a convert, Love's perceived betrayal distracting his thoughts away from Rosewood onto how to bring Love down with him. Passed Pittsburgh Mills and moved right, let his speed taper as he approached the Creighton exit to double back to Res Mall. Almost went off the road from shock when Grabek reached over and touched his forearm with a hand hot as sunburn.

"You'd better run me up the hill. I think I'm dying." Then Grabek vomited onto the windshield and dashboard. Doc had never smelled anything like it. Moved the car left and dropped the hammer for the hospital.

CHAPTER 57

"You a bit much to have faith in, Rev. Hiring the kinds of people you do, convicts and such, then expecting folk to believe you surprised when things go wrong. I mean, I a criminal and all, but I ain't no hypocrite."

Darcy Rosewood found Christian Love a harder nut than expected. Rosewood had the goods on Love's church; no in-depth research required. Rosewood himself did the worst thing to happen at Resurrection Mall, but it had come look-ing for him. Kickbacks, rigged bids, and occasional drug sales were established long before he'd heard of the place. Not that quintuple homicide was the next logical step. Not like one of them convent bitches ordered it done, either. The culture already in place.

"Mr. Timmins—if that is, in fact, your name, which I doubt—I'll not pay you one cent to cover up wrongs that may have been done in my name." Christian Love took care to speak each syllable as if he were afraid to break the words off in his mouth. "I believe in second chances. Not in harbor-ing criminals."

"That be a hard sell when things start coming out," Rosewood said. "I don't see too many people believing you don't know any a what's going on right under your nose. Me, I *know* you didn't know, and I have a hard time believing it." Pointed to photographs on the wall; Love with Abernathy and Lewis. "It's good you all get along so good.

You be spending a lot of time together the next ten, fifteen years when this go bad on you."

"I have dedicated my life to working God's will," Love said without irony. "If He has a prison ministry in mind for me, I'll welcome the challenge."

Rosewood sighed, ran a hand over his head. Still didn't buy Love's act, though the front showed no sign of weakening. He'd laid out the ways he could save Resurrection Mall, and, by extension, Love's ministry—all of them bullshit—no nearer to closing a deal now than when he'd come in. How to play it? Laid a forearm along the width of Love's desk, swept everything onto the floor. Threw the wooden chair against the far wall, knocking down certificates and awards from the tops of filing cabinets. "No one's pure as you act. No one that stupid, either. You think they's an angle to be played. Well, you wrong. Whatever you working on, whoever you think coming to help you, I'm here *now*. Your judgment day is to-*day*. Now forget all this am I bullshitting or not and set your mind to think how you can stop me from ruining you. You need word from on high? Well, with God as my witness everything you got is ending if I don't walk out of here with something."

"Are you threatening to kill me? Who would pay you then?"

Rosewood smiled at getting a reaction. "I know how to hurt you worse than killing you."

Love folded his hands on the now empty desk, his face blank as a window blind. "You are welcome to try."

"Motherfucker!" Rosewood tipped the desk onto its front. Lifted Love out of the chair by his lapels. "I know you afraid, just not enough. Time to give you a down payment on what to expect."

Love's expression remained. "Your threats prove the hollowness of your proposal. You have nothing to trade, even if I were willing. What's been set in motion is beyond your ability to stop it. Beat me or kill me, it's the same result: you get nothing."

Rosewood threw Love against the wall. The older man stumbled over the chair base and fell, shielding his head from an open drawer with an upraised forearm. Landed on his back. Rosewood stomped once on his chest and started opening drawers.

"The top drawer on the right of the desk," Love said when he recovered his breath. "The small cash box has a hundred and forty-two dollars in it. That's all the money there is. The key is in the pile of things you knocked onto the floor. Take it and go."

Rosewood stopped, stared at Love. A smile worked across his face from left to right. "A hundred and forty-two dollars? See? I knew you a phony. Man of God, lying like you do. I know for a fact there at least fifteen thousand here, money from collections and shit. You rainy day money."

"It rained today." Love's face remained composed. A sadness grew in his eyes not even Rosewood could miss. "The state police froze our accounts yesterday and today was the last day of the month. The contractors are out of patience. They had to be paid—in cash—or there would be no work tomorrow. I've seen what happens then. Everyone says they'll come back when we can pay them, but the trust is gone, and all business runs on trust. Other opportunities with reliable payments present themselves. It would be the

end. So I paid them—personally—with what was on hand."
He rolled his eyes upward. "Fourteen thousand six hundred
and twenty-six dollars." Gestured to the overturned desk.
"Everything we have left is there. One hundred and forty-
two dollars is the entire liquid worth of Resurrection Mall. I
can't offer you more than that."

Rosewood found the key, about to unlock the drawer
when he saw a small pry bar in a box of tools under a chair.
Used it to break the lock, threw the key at Love. Opened the
box, counted five twenties, three tens, pairs of fives and ones.
Jammed the bills into his pants pocket as anger and impo-
tence fought inside him. Beat the open desk drawer with the
pry bar, swung it like a baseball bat to crush the side of a
filing cabinet. Stood over Love as if to beat him, settled for
flipping the bar onto his chest. Took a second to enjoy the
pain in Love's eyes before his parting words. "You paid the
wrong motherfuckers."

The mall's main concourse deserted, after nine at night.
Unfinished storefronts and open construction made footfalls
echo with the exaggerated clarity of a movie's overzealous
Foley artist. Rosewood felt hollow. He'd come straight here
as soon as he learned the reason Turner hadn't returned his
calls was because he was in custody. Shake down Love for
whatever he could get, add it to the forty-two hundred
stashed in his crib, and get the fuck out of Dodge. He knew
Turner couldn't do the time. Even worse, he knew Turner
knew it. The Penns River detectives' idea of pressure made
Rosewood laugh. Much of the hollowness in him now
stemmed from the knowledge Turner wouldn't laugh; he'd
roll.

Reaching for the bar to push open one of the main entrance doors when something caught his eye. Stepped back to change the angle and confirmed what he'd seen: the silhouette of a light bar on a car parked on Fourth Avenue, blocking the exit from the parking lot. Maneuvered to stay in shadow as much as possible, saw another car on the corner of Fourth and Ninth Street, with what looked like a couple of guys standing behind it. There'd be one on the Ninth Street exit he couldn't see without exposing himself. The service doors on the opposite side that opened onto Eighth Street would be covered; so would Second Avenue, behind the mall. He'd seen or heard no police. They were waiting for him to leave.

Darcy Rosewood had no fear of prison. He'd been there before and knew how to jail. Five years, ten years, really only two days: the day you went in, and the day you got out. The difference this time, he wouldn't live to see the day he got out.

He fingered the one hundred forty-two dollars he'd taken from Love, thought of the four grand in his room. Seventy-five hundred dollars hadn't seemed too cheap a price for five lives. He'd be damned if he'd spend the rest of his in jail for it. His life was worth more. Someone would pay for it, one way or another.

CHAPTER 58

Doc skipped the bypass on his way to Penns River. Everyone in place; Stush in command on site. Took his time driving along Freeport Road, digesting what had happened and preparing for what would come.

The emergency room staff ready for him at Allegheny Valley Hospital. Two orderlies pulled Grabek onto a gurney; a third swabbed the worst of the vomit from the car. Doc went in to be sure the desk knew Willie was a Penns River cop, use the standard insurance information. Didn't know if it was duty-related; no, he hadn't been shot. Cleaned himself the best he could in a men's room, asked for a report on Willie. Not next of kin so no one would tell him anything official, though the ER doc took pity and said he suspected nothing life-threatening; wouldn't be surprised if it was gall bladder. Doc considered saying the amount of gall Willie has, it must have exploded, settled for thanking the doctor and driving back to Penns River with the windows open and heater blasting in the sub-freezing night.

No radios in unmarked Penns River cars. No need to call Stush. Doc knew the current situation as well as if he were there: cops surrounded the Resurrection Mall parking lot, waiting for Rosewood to come out. Anything happened, Stush would call.

Driving Freeport Road limited his view to the surrounding buildings in Tarentum and Creighton, past Earl's where he ate chicken wings and drank beer with Jefferson West during football season. Glimpses of the river on his left between gaps in buildings. No panorama like on the bypass, which would also have been quicker. Doc not in the mood for views and not in a hurry. Passed the chemical plant a half mile before the bridge and a dull glow caught his eye, below the horizon. Drawing closer, Doc saw fire on the Penns River side of the bridge. Hard to tell what was burning until the road made a jog to the left and Resurrection Mall came into view. Lights in the parking lot, streams of water in the air. Police kept gawkers away, fireman moving everywhere. The usual controlled pandemonium of a fire in a large building. Less a mile away, he'd be there in less than a minute.

Halfway across the bridge he saw threads of people working their way south from the Allegheny Estates to watch. Confusion, noise, a crowd, erratic light, diversions aplenty for the police to deal with. Looked toward the parking lot on his right for Stush as the car tipped down the incline from the bridge into town. With Rosewood unaccounted for, firemen were in danger. Hostages a possibility. Stush would think of this. No need to call. Get to the lot and compare notes.

Diverted by the commotion, slammed the brakes to avoid a man running northward across Ninth Street. Waited for him to pass onto Second Avenue, then looked toward the gathering crowd to navigate into the parking lot. Foot still on the brake, observing children of all ages assemble to watch a building burn with the same expressions that must have accompanied circus parades. His head turned left again, the running man about to disappear around a bend in the road.

Who runs away from a fire? Get a safe distance, sure, but

to get clear and keep running? Two possibilities came to mind: someone injured, panicking and running away out of fear and pain and confusion.

Or someone who shouldn't have been there in the first place.

Doc turned left onto Second. The car crept at idle speed to keep the fleeing figure in sight.

Stush answered on the first ring. "Where are you?"

"Second Avenue."

A pause. "Where? I'm halfway between Second and Third and don't see you."

"Moving north on Second. I was coming off the bridge and saw someone tear-assing across Ninth Street going north. Does anyone have eyeballs on Rosewood?"

"No one's seen him. We're still watching the car. I been kind of hoping you could help us keep an eye out for him while we control this goddamn crowd."

"I think I might be looking at him right now," Doc said. "Can you spare someone to help me corral whoever this is? With two cars we might be able to drive him to where we can take him easier."

"What about Grabek? Oh, shit, I forgot about him, with the fire and all. How is he?"

"He'll live. Doctor says it could be gall bladder. Can I get some help?"

"Sure, yeah, I'm sorry. Neuschwander's here. I'll send him right over."

"I'd rather have Sisler. Can you spare him?"

"Yeah, sure, I can—wait one." Stush yelled at someone nearby, waited for an answer, yelled again. "I'll plug Neuschwander into where I have Sisler now. Where should he meet you?"

"I'm rolling. Tell him to call my cell and we'll coordinate. Thanks. Oh, wait, Stush?"

"Yeah, Benny?"

"Make sure Sis knows why I asked for him." Delonte Bickerstaff flashed through Doc's mind. "Hey, one more thing. There's a bunch of bums likes to sleep in the mall. Did they get out?"

"Hang on. Eddie's right here." Eddie Donavan, fire chief. "He says the fire's in the corner where the new construction is. What's that, Eddie? Okay. Eddie says the bums sleep near the front doors. Everyone's accounted for."

Doc broke the connection and speeded up as the man turned right onto Eleventh Street. Turned the corner in time to see him duck into Spruce Alley. His mind flashed to how he had to chase this asshole every time he wanted him, convinced now he was following Rosewood.

His cell rang. Sisler. "Where do you want me?"

"Come up Fourth Avenue and turn left onto Tenth. Our guy's moving south on Spruce Alley. No siren or lights, have the spot ready. He knows I'm here. I want you to be a surprise."

"Stealth mode?"

"Too many people headed over to watch the fire. Headlights are fine. Shit."

"What?"

"He's running through the Senior Center parking lot. Try to hover on Third Avenue between Tenth and Eleventh till I see which way he goes."

Doc pulled through the parking lot, closing the distance.

Rosewood not as tough as Turner and Simpson thought; Doc sure he was better than Rosewood expected. He still had no desire to take him alone. He'd drive him like hunting a deer, keep the pressure on until Rosewood ran into Sisler. Then they'd take him together.

Rosewood broke left on Third Avenue. Doc smiled. *He* had the home field advantage tonight: Third ended at Eleventh Street. "Get over to Eleventh and turn left. He doubled back into the dead end. I'm on him. He turns right and he'll run straight into you."

"Turning now...is he there yet?"

"Not quite...there! Turning your way. You see him?"

"Not yet. Coming down Eleventh."

"Try to get the spot on him." A beam of light crossed Doc's path before he finished the sentence. "You see him?"

"Yeah. Stepping onto Eleventh now." Sisler animated as a stretching dog.

The timing was off. Doc had hoped Rosewood would already be moving in Sisler's direction when the spotlight came on. Sisler moved quicker than expected, gave away his position. Rosewood would turn left for sure now, placing both cops behind him. Still, with Rosewood on foot...

"He's running into the parking lot," Sisler said.

A medical building backed up to the Allegheny Estates, its driveway twenty yards west of Third Avenue. Rosewood angled across the street and up the driveway, running hard. "Move in," Doc said. "We need to get him before he leaves the parking lot."

Punched the gas, turned into the lot fifty feet behind Rosewood, Sisler fishtailing into line behind him. Rosewood veered left, climbed a chain link fence separating the driveway from a pair of outdoor basketball courts. Doc sped to the spot too late.

"He's in the Estates. Back out and try to head him off on Hileman. I'll follow on foot. Call for Stush to get someone to seal off the east side on Fourth Avenue." Out of the car before it stopped rocking. Stuffed his cell into his coat pocket and went over the fence, Sisler's lights reflecting off the metal roof of the building next to the courts.

Rosewood ran north, then angled east, through the court-yards of garden-style apartments with off-street parking near each unit. Security lights cast pools of not-quite-as-darkness around the buildings and parking areas. Lose sight of him here and unpleasantness could ensue.

Doc lost sight of him around back of the second building he came to.

Stopped, reached into his pocket to close the cell connection. Controlled his breathing to listen. He'd run less than fifty yards; Rosewood had been running at least since the encounter on the bridge. He had to be more tired than Doc.

No close sounds. A few stragglers walked toward the fire. Doc under a small stand of trees, saw red and blue lights and a moving spotlight come north on Fourth Avenue. With Sisler on Hileman and the new cop, two avenues of escape were sealed. Rosewood wouldn't go back the way he'd come, knowing he'd have to get past Doc and run into every re-maining cop in Penns River. West the only available direc-tion. Toward the river.

Doc started that way, turning on alternate steps to keep his back covered. Another chain fence separated the Estates from an almost empty industrial complex. Rosewood couldn't go over the fence without being seen or heard. That closed off the west. Sisler had the north. The new officer east of the last known position. If Doc could secure the south, they had Rosewood hemmed in.

He backed across the basketball courts, toward his car on the other side of the fence. He could afford to give ground, so long as he didn't let Rosewood past him. Reinforcements were handy, damn near every cop in Penns River within a quarter of a mile working crowd control at the fire.

His cell chirped. Doc cursed under his breath. "Dougherty."

"Mike Zywiciel, Doc. I'm on Fourth Avenue, north of Eleventh. Where do you want me?"

"You're good. No one gets past or behind you. Do you know what this guy looks like?"

"I know he's black. Thirties. Six-foot tall or more."

Laughter to Doc's left. He looked and saw half a dozen high school-aged boys walking toward the fire. "You have much foot traffic there?"

"Some," Zywiciel said. "Not as much as before. Most everyone who wants to watch the fire is there already."

"Keep an eye on any groups. You see someone you don't like the looks of, stop him. Be very careful."

"Copy that," Zywiciel said. "I'm not forgetting the first rule this late in the game." Make sure you go home alive.

Doc thought about calling Stush when an explosion came from the fire. Then another: the propane heaters in the construction area. Firemen might be having more trouble than expected. Set the phone to vibrate and held it in his coat pocket.

Five minutes. Ten. They'd lost the initiative. Rosewood

could wait them out. Three men couldn't contain a perimeter this size; forget trying to shrink it.

He called Stush. "Do you have anyone you can spare?"

"What's your situation?" Stush said. Doc told him. "Benny, I gotta tell you, we got a hell of a fire here. The parking lot helps us keep people away on one side, but we got cops spread out half a block away on the other three, and I'd like to keep people farther away than that. A couple of propane tanks just blew, and we got kids taking dares to see how close they can get."

"I need bodies, Stush."

"I know. I need to worry about what kind of liability we're looking at if one of these goddamn kids makes a run for the building when something else explodes." A pause. "I'll send you Ulizio. And—and—shit, and Harding. Put them and Sisler and Eye Chart each on a corner while you coordinate. It's the best I can do until things quiet down here."

Not enough, and Doc knew it. Stush knew it, too. It was what he had. "All right," Doc said. "Send them. I'll see what we can do about not letting him get too comfortable. Maybe he's as nervous as I am."

CHAPTER 59

Darcy Rosewood couldn't believe his luck. After all that had gone wrong since he first heard about Turner—Love's stonewalling, the police waiting for him, damn near walking into one of them—he'd chanced into an unlocked van in an Allegheny Estates parking lot. Didn't even have to try the door handle. Stupid bastard parked it where Rosewood could see the lock button wasn't depressed.

He realized within a couple of minutes anyone walking past would see him in the front seat. Unlocked all the doors, turned off the dome light, let himself in back. Not a full-size van, still plenty of room. No windows along the sides, one on each back door. Found a position where he would be hard to see and could keep an eye on the window, made himself comfortable as possible. A mover's pad served as a decent mattress and good blanket.

The police would come, no later than daybreak. Rosewood a little surprised they hadn't started fanning through this block already until he heard the explosions. The fire must have more of their attention than he'd planned. Good. He needed time. Getting lucky with the van didn't mean his plan hadn't gone to shit.

His knew no more of Penns River than he'd needed to do the Resurrection Mall job. The bridge, the parking lot, and the road to and from Pittsburgh. His car gone forever. No tools to break into another; couldn't afford the noise of smashing a window. Not like it mattered: he didn't know how to hotwire an engine. If the police were on him here, they'd already been to his crib, so his cash was gone, too. The one hundred forty two dollars he'd taken from Love, plus what he had in his pocket going in, were his bankroll. Rosewood settled in to rest, get warm, and think of how far he could go on foot with three hundred dollars and a gun.

Doc got his four uniforms situated on each corner of the block, spotlights covering the streets as well as they could. Made sure they knew the route he'd take and moved into the Estates.

Doc had no interest in catching Rosewood himself. After Resurrection Mall, one more body—even a cop's—would be nothing. Doc confident he could take him in a fair fight, didn't expect to get one, saw no reason to give one. He'd flush Rosewood into one of the spotlight beams and let four cops in cars run him to ground.

The trick was not to get taken by surprise himself. Not in Rosewood's best interest to shoot Doc. Announcing his position and intent with thirty cops less than a mile away would be suicide. Of course, Doc had no idea how dire Rosewood thought his position, hoped he didn't have a James Cagney/*White Heat* complex.

Entered the Estates on the Pine Court side, near two buildings used as equipment sheds and leased storage for the tenants. Flashlight out, rather give his position away than miss something and get surprised from a direction he thought safe. Look behind one building, pass in front of it, repeat for the next.

Walked through a string of shivering trees toward one of two parking lots. This one about a hundred feet by fifty, spaces on both sides, one entrance to Fourth Avenue. No one around at ten o'clock. Everyone either at the fire or inside watching television.

He crossed behind the main building, with the offices and maintenance facility and model apartment. A cluster of trees broke up what moonlight made it through scattered clouds. No streetlights in the parking lots; the security lights didn't kick any ass. Not much crime within the Estates, despite the favorable conditions. Most of the rough trade either lived here, or their mothers and grandmothers did. Mike Mannarino not the only guy who didn't like shit where he ate.

Another parking lot ran from behind the main building all the way to Hileman Drive. Narrower than its brother, parking on one side only. No trees to impede the moonlight. Nothing moved. Doc about to veer toward the trio of buildings on the northeast corner when he noticed fog on the back windows of a small white van parked in the last space on the lot.

He stepped back to stay out of sight from the van, drew his weapon. Shone his flashlight into a window, up high, then along the path of the lot, hoping to create the appearance of someone who had passed by. Turned off the light and advanced, gun pointed down, moving sideways, legs weaving as he moved to his left. The van had no side windows. Fog on the left rear porthole, no question. Doc opened his cell and placed one hand between his mouth and the van. Dialed Zywiciel.

"Yeah, Doc."

"Put Harding and Ulizio on the Fourth Avenue corners. I

want you and Sisler to roll into the parking lot off of Hileman. There's a white van all the way at the end with someone in it. Take your time and be quiet. He's not going anywhere while I'm here. We'll take him together."

Rosewood thought he had less than a fifty-fifty chance of pulling off his new plan. He'd gone to prison the last time he'd made such a low percentage move; time not on his side. The fire would go out, and the cops working crowd control would come. He had to move before more cops got on him. Wait for a small group to come by and fall in with it. Only a couple Penns River cops knew him by sight. No way could some ofay Barney Fife who'd never seen him could identify him in this light. Melt into the dispersing crowd and get some thinking distance. Unless the police stumbled onto him here first.

That much of the plan set, he knew he should think of what came next, kept putting it off. Every consideration lowered his estimate of survival chances. He didn't know where to go, where things were, and walking down Route 28 to Pittsburgh didn't interest him. Too far, and a BOLO would have cops in every shithole town looking for him. If he made it to Pittsburgh, what then? No home to go to, no ride. His way out had to be found here.

The gun would buy him a place to spend the night and a car to take him away tomorrow, after the police had time to assume they'd missed him. He had to pick the right group to fall in with, and the right person in it. Till then, the mover's pad was more comfortable than he'd expected.

* * *

Zywiciel's car left room behind the van for the police to operate, not enough for the van to move. Sisler parked broadside thirty feet up the way, blocking the route to the street. Zywiciel behind his car, Sisler and Doc at the rear of the van, guns drawn. Doc nodded. Sisler's hand extended to take the door handle. Zywiciel aimed for the center of the van, gun in one hand, flashlight in the other. Doc moved in a step, one hand poised to grab the left door. Looked over his shoulder to Zywiciel, who nodded. Made eye contact with Sisler, mouthed, "One...two...*three*," and Sisler jerked open the right door, Doc pulling open the left half a second later. Zywiciel shone the light into the van as Doc and Sisler made their presence known.

"*Freeze! Penns River police!*"

The man inside scrambled toward the front, hands near his face.

"Watch him, Doc!"

"Show me your hands!"

"No! No! Don't shoot!"

"Hands! Let me see your hands!"

"Ain't nothing in 'em. Here! I'm showing ya!" Hands pushed toward Doc and Sisler from the van.

"Stay put, goddamnit!"

"Hold them out, palms facing me!"

"Okay, okay! I'm doing it."

No more than ten seconds between the time Sisler took the door and he and Doc dragged the man from the van by his wrists. Zywiciel stepped from behind his car, flashlight beam on the man's face, gun drawn.

Doc took the man by the chin. "Who the fuck are you, and what are you doing here?"

Rosewood sensed his opportunity when he heard the commotion thirty yards away, in the other parking lot. Threw off the mover's pad and out the back door of the van while the police bitched about getting the wrong man. Surprised to see three cops there, even more so when he saw a car parked on the corner, its spotlight alternating between Fourth Avenue and Eleventh Street.

The light passed over him, moved back. Rosewood fought the urge to run. What had the cop seen? A black man in a parking lot of a ninety-percent black apartment complex. The street empty except for him, the cop, and some kid going home from the fire. Shoved his hands deep into his coat pockets, gripped the pistol. Ran through his options and walked into the light.

The cop stopped him thirty feet away. Said, "Wait right there, please, sir," and got out of the car. Hands empty, holster strap undone. Average height, twenty pounds too heavy. "What brings you out tonight?"

Rosewood tried for aggrieved citizen. "I got to have a reason to be out?"

"Tonight you kind of do. We got a bad criminal in the area. Be better for everyone if you stayed in tonight."

"That what the commotion about back there?"

"I couldn't say, sir. I just think it might be safer if you postponed your walk tonight."

Rosewood swallowed, took his right hand—empty—from his pocket. Pointed toward the fire. "My kids watching the fire. Getting late and tomorrow's school. I'm going to get them."

Damn near every cop in town over where Rosewood said he wanted to go. Had to go, now that he'd told this one. Gambling the two who knew him were doing whatever fucked up thing was going on behind him. Rubbed his hands together, put them back in his pockets. If this cop asked for ID...

The cop's posture relaxed. "Go on, then. Do me a favor, though?"

"What you need?"

"You see anything looks funny, tell one of the cops over there. Don't do anything, just get clear and tell someone. You don't want to fool with the man we're looking for."

Doc so mad he wondered if his head might explode for real. Felt the arteries and Eustachian tubes in his neck swelling, pressure in his temples. For a second he envied Grabek, made peace with the idea he was having a stroke. Closed his eyes, took a deep breath and let it out slow, through his mouth. "What's your name?"

"I told you already: Lamar Gaddis. G-A-D-D-I-S. I lives right there—" pointed to a building, "—in Apartment two-oh-three. You holding my damn license. You can't read or something?"

"Mr. Gaddis," Zywiciel said. "This might not be the best time to agitate Detective Dougherty."

"I'm sorry as all hell if I *agitates* him. Man minding his own bidness, not bothering no one, you come busting in with guns ablazing. Like to scare the living shit out of me."

"No one fired a weapon." The idea appealed to Doc more by the second. "What were you doing in the van?"

"Trying to get some sleep," Gaddis said. "That a crime now?"

"*Why* were you trying to sleep in your van if you live right there—" Doc pointed, "—in two-oh-three?"

Gaddis dropped some of the attitude. "Had words with the wife. Thought it might be good to let her rationalize a little."

"Must've been some serious words," Zywiciel said. "It's freezing out here."

"Yeah, well, you know how it is."

"Try me," Doc said.

Gaddis's eyes flicked from one cop to the other. Zywiciel must have seemed least unsympathetic. "I stopped for a pop on the way home. Ran into a few people I know. You know how it is. Couple a drinks with a guy, another guy comes in so you stay for a couple with him. Time got away from me."

"And your wife's so pissed she threw you out," Doc said.

"Ain't no one throw Lamar Gaddis out his own house. I left till she come to her senses."

"Uh-huh," Doc said. "How often's this happen, you coming home late and lubricated?"

Gaddis still looked at Zywiciel. "Not too often. Once in a while."

"How often is not too?" Doc said.

"I don't know. Maybe twice, three time a week. You know how it is."

Doc wondered if Gaddis realized paperwork and civil suit were all that kept him from kicking the man's ass back to Apartment 203. Handed back the license. "Here's the deal,

Mr. Gaddis. Get your ass home—right now—and we'll forget all about this. If I can still see you in thirty seconds, you're going to jail."

"What the fuck you arrest me for?"

"If any other cop sees you tonight, even in your van, you go to jail."

"What? *What*? The fuck you gone charge me with?"

"Public drunkenness." Gaddis gave exaggerated disbelief. "Run your mouth again and I'll add drunk and disorderly. Keep it up and I'll go for the hat trick with resisting arrest."

Gaddis glared at Doc. Zywiciel pulled his ticket book from his belt. "What's your apartment number again, sir? For the ticket."

"The ticket? The fuck a ticket for?"

"This one's for public drunkenness."

"I ain't that drunk."

"You're drunk enough," Doc said. "And you're in public. Now get your ass out of public and we'll call it even." Gaddis's stare gained intensity. "Thirty. Twenty-nine. Twenty-eight..."

"Awright, awright, I'm gone. Fuck all y'all."

Gaddis turned, walked toward his building, where everyone hoped a rationalized Mrs. Gaddis waited. Gaddis's pace reflected his anticipated reception. Doc raised his voice. "Twenty-seven. Twenty-six. Twenty-five..." Gaddis began to trot.

"Be a while before he comes home drunk again," Zywiciel said.

* * *

Wilver Faison knew Penns River not the smartest place for him to crash. The highest percentage to find a place indoors, also where someone with bad intentions most inclined to look for him. Tired of being cold all the damn time; he hadn't felt warm for real in over a week. The furnace room of his mother's building would be at least be that. Risky, but warm.

The fire a nice diversion. People coming and going, many of them around his age, made him blend in. He watched the propane tanks blow from a spot where he folded himself into the shadows like a handkerchief in a basket of bed sheets. Started toward the Estates with everyone's attention still on the fire. Keeping to darker areas not much of a challenge, given the number of working streetlights.

About to turn into the parking lot next to his mother's building when he heard the commotion from the other lot. Bunch of hollering and "Show me your hands" and "You gotta be fucking kidding me." Stashed himself behind a tree and watched three Penns River cops haul a guy out of the back of a van. No idea what all that was about. One of the cops looked like Detective Doc.

Wilver heard a sound to his right and the cold of the night was replaced by one much worse. The back door opened in a van not twenty feet away and one of the men he'd seen at Resurrection Mall with a shotgun climbed out, looked right at him, then turned to check out the cop action at the other van. The man watched for no more than ten seconds and walked in the other direction.

Guy was around the corner before Wilver found it in him to exhale. Made a beeline for his mother's building—didn't think of it as his building anymore—stopped outside the furnace room door. Knew he'd been luckier than he'd imagined possible. Seen this situation in his dreams half a dozen times since Res Mall, the guy looking right at him, and every time Wilver woke up a second before his shit got blown all over whatever he stood in front of. Tonight the killer looked right at him, and Wilver got a pass. He recognized dumb luck when he saw it.

Detective Doc had been right: Wilver had to be lucky forever; the other guy only had to get lucky once. No way for a seventeen-year-old to live the rest of his life.

What to do? Wilver thought, hand on the doorknob. Go in and get warm? Or take advantage of his luck for a change? Every cop in Penns River within a quarter mile of him right now, one of them among the few people he trusted. Never be a safer time to get out from under this.

Wilver let go of the doorknob and walked toward the van where he'd seen the cops.

Rosewood went south on Fourth Avenue and lucked into a half dozen people walking back toward Allegheny Estates. Three men, three women; one pair looked to be a couple. All in their late twenties or early thirties. Either of the women looked like potential short-term landlords. Rosewood let them pass, fell in behind. No one noticed, people coming and going all around as the firefighters gained the upper hand at Res Mall.

He needed one alone to go to the farthest building. Or one to break off from the group early. He'd have to go to what must be Plan F by now if they all walked into the same building together. The couple veered off shy of the Estates. The men went into the building closest to where Rosewood had been hiding. The two women kept walking and he went through what had to happen in his head. Come up behind the last one, gun in her kidneys, hand over her mouth. She takes him home and he ties her up for the night, takes her car tomorrow. By the time she gets loose or someone misses her he'd have another car and be miles away. Wouldn't hurt her unless he had to. Not rape her. He was a professional, not a pervert. The situation reminded him of that *Three Days of the Condor* movie, Robert Redford the spy picking out Faye Dunaway at random to help him. If the girl got some a that Stockholm Syndrome and wanted to share a piece, be okay with him.

Halfway to the corner of Fourth and Hileman the shorter woman hugged the other and turned left, into the Estates; the taller went on. Even better she lived farther out. The police would focus their search here. Rosewood about to close on her when a Penns River police car cruised into the intersection at idle speed. The spotlight sprayed the street, focused on him. The car stopped.

Rosewood took his hands from his pockets as he'd done before. Slowed his pace. If this was the same cop, he'd say he'd missed his kids.

The cop got out of the car

Wilver caught Sisler and Dougherty before they split up after the Lamar Gaddis fiasco: Rosewood was walking north on Fourth Avenue. Dougherty sent Sisler to cut him off while Zywiciel rolled in stealth mode as backup. Dougherty hurried to get behind Rosewood, told the kid to get on the other side of the van and stay there.

Sisler idled the cruiser toward the corner, not wanting to arrive too soon again. He'd be warm in the station now if he hadn't been overeager the first time. Paused in the intersection, played the spotlight down Fourth Avenue. A small knot of people approached, laughing and playing, their breath clouding the air. Another figure ten or fifteen feet behind. Head down. Hands in its pockets. Could be someone cold, or someone not wanting to be seen.

The size looked about right. Sisler had seen Darcy Rosewood once, sitting in an unlighted car on a dark street. Still, he was a cop, and a good one. Extrapolations could be made. Put the car in Park and got out. Undid the strap on his holster as he stood, the car between him and the approaching group.

He recognized Dougherty coming up behind the straggler, long strides closing the distance without running.

"Darcy Rosewood, you're under arrest." The voice fifteen feet behind Rosewood, a bit to the left. "Stand perfectly still and extend your hands to the side, palms back. Do it slowly."

Rosewood recognized the voice: the younger detective from the other day. Dockery or Doctory or something. Not too impressive, if memory served. The cop in the intersection complicated matters, but he was forty-fifty yards away. Rosewood eased his hands into his pockets and turned right forty-five degrees, angling away from the police car. Played like he thought the cop behind was talking to someone else.

"Rosewood! Stop now." A gun cocked.

Where Darcy Rosewood would go wasn't jail. Death row an aboveground grave, even when they weren't executing people. The current governor more sensitive to complaints about paying to warehouse dead-enders than to the ACLU, not that Rosewood gave two shits about the ACLU. The Commonwealth would see five notches on his gun—he doubted they knew about the sixth; no one had ever bothered him over it—and say if there was ever one person fit to end the execution moratorium, it was this remorseless motherfucker.

Shooting Rosewood would be a clean resolution, remove any doubts about the evidence or conflicting stories. There would still be issues: black man shot by a white cop who'd already killed four men. (No one ever remembered his father and cousin shot three of them.) It wouldn't help that he'd have to shoot Rosewood more or less in the back. That never played well in the media, or with civil juries.

His final conversation with the Russian gangster he'd killed came to him less often now. Down from every day to a few times a week to once a month or so. Could be any time. Asleep, eating dinner, watching television. Doc would have died had he not shot Pavel first. That allowed him to sleep, the intellectual knowing of his justification.

What kept bringing the conversation back—Pavel's dying words—was the memory of how he'd felt while kneeling in the grass beside the dying Russian. Over a year now; Doc still hadn't found the word he liked. Not elation or satisfaction. Not nothing, either, though that was closer. Something in him had turned off. He would have shot Pavel, and anyone else not identified as a friend, and relished the act. Knew it was adrenaline, the reaction beyond his control. Understood and accepted it as an intellectual exercise. He still never wanted to go there again.

"Freeze, Rosewood. I *will* shoot you."

Rosewood knew the cop wouldn't shoot as soon as he said he would. No time, if Rosewood did things right. He'd looked into gun muzzles before. Another mattered to him no more than the legal penalty for a sixth—seventh—body. The other cop too far away to shoot a moving man in uncertain light with civilians in play.

He stepped to his left as he spun, his gun hand dark in bad light in front of a dark coat.

Sisler heard Doc challenge Rosewood, stepped toward the trunk of the cruiser, where the roof wouldn't protect him, took the small group of walkers out of his line. Saw Rosewood move when Doc said he *would* shoot and knew Doc wouldn't or he wouldn't have said so. Sisler could, and did. Three times, fast as he could level the gun.

CHAPTER 60

Stush called Doc and Neuschwander into his office, asked them to shut the door.

"I just got off the phone with Sally Gwynn. Remember how Simpson and Turner recanted their confessions? Well, Rodney Simpson unrecanted. He took the deal."

"How come?"

"Sally showed him what Ricky traced from his grandma's insurance. When she told him Rosewood was dead he couldn't roll over fast enough."

Neuschwander's checks on the finances of Love and Lewis came up dry. Abernathy had more money than could be accounted for, no unusual expenditures. Not one who liked to come back empty-handed, Neuschwander expanded his search and learned ten thousand dollars of insurance money, paid on the death of Rodney Simpson's grandmother, had disappeared into thin air.

Stush chuckled. "Sally did say she was afraid for a minute she'd have to drive him to the Allegheny County morgue to show him Rosewood's body in person, though."

"Turner held out?" Doc said.

"Turner never got an offer. Sally started with Simpson and had a deal before she left the room."

"She let the mastermind take the deal?" Doc made finger quotes for mastermind.

"Simpson knew more details, and all the players. The only

people Turner knew about were Simpson and Rosewood. If anyone else was involved, it would be Simpson who knew."

"Was anyone else involved?"

"Doesn't look like." Doc raised his eyebrows and Stush said, "Make no mistake, Abernathy's dirty. He'll do state time and maybe eat a federal racketeering or mail fraud charge. If—" he raised one finger, "—Uncle can be persuaded to go after him. I doubt it. The Deputy AG says the Commonwealth accountants should be able to get him out of the game for at least a few years."

"I guess it was Turner who actually pulled a trigger," Doc said.

"It's not like Simpson walked," Stush said. "He still gets natural life. All she did was take the needle off the table. She said Simpson grabbed it like she was handing out bottles of ice water in the desert. I guess his lawyer about had a fit."

"What did he want for contracting out five hits?" Doc said. "I mean, what the hell else was he going to plead to? Once you plead to murder for hire, the best deal you get is natural life."

"He had an elaborate thing worked out where she'd drop the murder for hire and Simpson would plead to some kind of money laundering and a general conspiracy charge that could get him out in ten or less. Sally said she'd consider it. In the meantime she'd be talking to Turner. If he took her deal first—"

"And Simpson tore the paper out of her hand to sign it," Doc said. Stush nodded.

Doc dry washed his face. First morning back after three days off, the fatigue still in him. "So Penns River finally puts away some killers."

Stush looked as if he might say something, didn't. Then, "Did you see Sisler this morning? He came in around nine."

"I saw him as I was headed into the men's room," Neuschwander said. "He was gone when I came out, so I didn't get a chance to talk to him."

"I was taking statements at Novotny's about those storm sewer grates until almost eleven," Doc said. "Any word on his disposition?"

"Deputy AG called first thing this morning," Stush said. "They're good with the shooting. He's still on paid leave for counseling, but no trial board or charges. The AG's office already spoke to the ACLU and the NAACP and Christian Love. The fact two civilian witnesses saw it the same way you two described it cleared up a lot of objections."

"Man, can he shoot," Doc said. "And he says he used to be better."

"The AG said they would've cleared him yesterday if they believed anyone could put three center of mass at that distance in that light under those circumstances. They set up the same scenario at their combat range day before yesterday and did a re-enactment. None of their guys could do it, so they asked Sisler to show them and he did it twice in a row. The way they talked, I think they may come recruiting."

"Shit," Doc said. "We're not going to lose him, are we?"

"I don't think so," Stush said. "His parents live in Saxonburg. One of them's blind—mother, I think—and he wants to live close. Staties will make him move, first thing."

"Yeah, the staties will post him to Philadelphia or Allentown or someplace else on the Eastern Front." Doc shook his head. "I thought it was something when he shot that rabid coon. But this, a three-tap under combat conditions from that distance? In that light? Christ."

"I might buy a deer license to give to him so he can shoot one for me," Stush said. No mean shot in his day, he hadn't hunted deer in fifteen years.

"I shouldn't need to remind you, Chief Napierkowski, what you're proposing is illegal," Doc said.

"Not if he does it in one of those State Game Lands up Emporium or St. Mary's. I know the wardens pretty good. They're not going to deny an old fat man with a bad heart the chance at some fresh venison."

"Speaking of old fat men," Doc said, "Grabek goes home tomorrow."

"How is he?" Neuschwander said.

"Good enough to go home, I guess. They gave him a gall bladder-ectomy, or whatever the doctors call it. He should be back in six weeks or so."

"If he comes back," Stush said.

"You talk to him?"

"Yesterday." Stush offered his bowl of jelly beans to Doc and Neuschwander. Both passed. Stush foraged for three blacks and popped one into his mouth. "He only took this job to help pay for his daughter's college, and she graduates in May. I think he went looking for a retirement community and got a lot more than he bargained for."

"What's he going to do all day?" Doc said. "Drink?"

Stush ate another jelly bean. "He has a full pension from Pittsburgh and doesn't have expensive tastes. Qualifies for Social Security in four or five years. The way he was talking, he might take a school security or mall job to hold him over."

"I don't see Willie Grabek as a rent-a-cop," Doc said.

354

"He's got the lazy part mastered, but his prestige would suffer."

"I think he's looking for something more in the supervisory line," Stush said.

Doc's look implied replies under consideration. Stush smiled and ate the last jelly bean. "Detective Neuschwander," he said, shifting his attention. "I submitted paperwork today to get you a commendation for your work on this case."

"Me? What did I do?"

"You make it sound like a sentence instead of an award," Doc said, who'd known all about it.

"I don't mean to be ungrateful, but you and Willie found all these guys and Sisler shot Rosewood."

"Sally Gwynn broke Simpson down using what you found on his grandmother's life insurance money," Stush said. "You also dug up the dirt on Abernathy the staties are running with. I don't know if any of these people would be going away without your contribution."

"Yeah, but…" Neuschwander more accustomed to being taken to task by Grabek, ignored by everyone else but Doc. He looked like a third grader who got paired with the prettiest girl in class to learn to square dance. "You had Turner dead to rights when the divers found that shotgun in the river."

"They found a murder weapon." Strike marks from the firing pin matched three of the shells. No recoverable prints. "Sally still would've had to tie it to Turner."

"Don't ever think because you don't spend a lot of time with suspects that what you do isn't valuable," Doc said. "Stush is right. It wouldn't have closed without you."

Neuschwander had to gather himself to reply. "Thanks, Stush. Really. I don't know what to say."

"Good," Stush said. "You start talking, you'll get all emotional and we don't need that. Now, if you'll excuse us, I need to talk to Benny for a minute. Take an extra doughnut on the way out as a bonus. If any are left."

Stush waited until the door closed. "Christian Love wants to see you."

"Why?" Doc sounded like a kid who'd been told to do his brother's chores.

"He didn't say." Stush picked up the jelly beans again. Swished them around in the bowl, put it back without taking any. "About the other night. At the fire."

"Yeah?"

"Were you slow? With Rosewood, I mean."

"Slow? Slow how?"

"You had your gun out and cocked. Sisler still shot first."

"He could see better." Stush made a face. "I couldn't see Rosewood's hands from my angle. He spun Sisler's direction is all."

Stush took his time. "I think about what it must've been like that night, at your parents' last year. I read the reports and went out one day and walked the scene by myself, all the way across the creek to where your cousin shot the Russian. I can play it out in my head like a movie, but I can't imagine myself in anyone's place. Not even your old man's, on the floor behind his car with a shotgun. I been a cop thirty-four years." A pause. "I know the one you shot died talking to you. Are you all right?"

"I had my counseling. I'm working."

"The chief didn't ask if you were all right. Your Uncle Stush did."

Doc looked over Stush's shoulder through the window to the panorama of the parking lot and leafless trees beyond. "I'm okay. What I remember most is talking to Pavel while he was laying there, dying. You know, there we are, talking, pointless stuff about—hell, mostly he bitched about Yuri. What comes back to me most is, never, not once, did I think about calling an ambulance."

"Weren't they jamming the cells?"

"Yeah, they were. I couldn't have made a call if I wanted to. Thing is, it never crossed my mind. Never reached for it, not even a twitch. He asked me a question and I answered it while I watched him die."

"The way I heard it, he wasn't going to wait for an ambulance, anyway."

"Probably not," Doc said. "I still don't like the feeling."

"Did it make you slow the other night?"

Doc took effort to think about it for the first time. "No, it didn't. I sure am glad Sisler was there, though."

Stush spoke with Doc halfway to the door. "You still showing those pictures around? Marian Widmer and the Cropcho woman?"

"Once in a while. Not every week, or anything."

"I want you to stop. Uncle Stush wants you to stop. No, wait. Uncle Stush is asking you to stop. Let it go, Benny."

Doc hadn't expected this, took a few beats to regroup. "I'd hate to let her get away with it."

"She got away with it already. You'll never get enough evidence to get the Red Baroness to try the other case."

Smiled at Doc's reaction. "Yeah, I know you call her that. It fits."

"You're going to have to tell Kate for me," Doc said. "I may never get laid again." Stush looked confused. "Makes her hot, showing those pictures, talking to potential witnesses. Likes it when I call her Kate Beckett, busting her chops."

"Who's Kate Beckett?"

"On that TV show? *Castle?* Where the mystery writer follows the female detective around?"

"I don't watch it. The girl's too skinny. Angie Dickinson is my idea of a police woman."

CHAPTER 61

Christian Love seemed none the worse for wear after his meeting with Darcy Rosewood. He looked bigger dressed in a pastel peach sport shirt, gray slacks, and tassel loafers than in his customary suits. Stopped packing books into a box when Doc knocked on the door jamb to his office. Offered a cold drink and a seat, took one Coke and one Diet from a small refrigerator.

"Detective Dougherty, I appreciate you making time to see me today."

"You're a taxpayer, Dr. Love. I don't make time for you. I work for you."

"Not for long, I'm afraid." Love gestured around the office, sipped his drink. "We're leaving."

"Permanently?"

"I'm afraid so. I need to get back to preaching the Gospel instead of running a business. I think I forgot the importance of it in whatever plan God has for me. All of this—" another gesture, "—should have been to complement my ministry, not supplant it."

"That's a shame," Doc said. "Can you salvage anything?"

"I'll be lucky to save the ministry." Love caught Doc's expression. "The insurance company won't pay. It's an arson fire—no dispute there—and they claim things were so bad I had it burned myself."

"That's bullsh—give me a number. Rosewood had

359

nothing to do with you. We'll fill them in on our investigation."

Love smiled, more on one side than the other. "They know it was Rosewood. They have witnesses who saw him come in to see me, then leave. Right after that the fire was set."

"They think you let the contract and he did it on his way out? The man who killed five people in your building and pushed you into the financial problems they say drove you to burn the place?"

"I mentioned that. Rather, our lawyer mentioned it."

"And?"

"They said we could sue and see how it came out. It will take years, and we can't make the mortgage payments as it is, not without tenant businesses. The legal bills would eat up anything we'd get."

"Can't you get a lawyer to take it as a contingency case? Or countersue to recover your legal fees?"

"We can do either," Love said. "We might win and we might lose. Either way, by the time we're finished the bank will have foreclosed."

"What are you going to do?"

"The city might be interested in the property. Tear everything down—it's half down already—put a riverfront park in here, is what I heard."

No part of Resurrection Mall closer than two blocks from the water. Penns River so strapped it deferred payments for the winter's road salt until September. Doc wondered what Dan Hecker had planned for this plot, and how he and Chet Hensarling were setting it up.

"I'm sorry to hear that, Dr. Love," Doc said. "I mean it.

This place had potential to do some good."

"Thank you. I appreciate that. I know you didn't think too highly of us at first."

"That's not entirely true," Doc said. "I had doubts about some of the people you kept around you. I always thought the mall could bring in some jobs and might help get this part of town squared away."

"Well," Love said, "you were right about the people I kept around me. That's why I asked you to come today. I owe you an apology."

"You don't owe me a thing."

"I spoke to you harshly the day you questioned my people."

"You stuck up for people you believed in. A man should never apologize for loyalty."

"It's not the loyalty—however misguided—I'm apologizing for." Love sipped his Diet Coke. "It wasn't your questioning Cassius Abernathy that bothered me. I knew his record when I brought him on. As you said, you're a police officer. The first place a police officer looks for a criminal is among known criminals. I'd say it's excusable, but it's more. It's reasonable. That's not why I responded the way I did."

Doc knew not to interrupt a man in the process of unburdening himself. "I treated you the way I did because I saw in you a clean cut, intelligent, well-spoken front for the racism people won't express overtly these days. You were a white man who mistrusted black men. Later I understood you only mistrusted a few specific black men, and were wise to do so. I should have called you in then. I meant to. I apologize for that, too."

Doc thought of waving it off, reconsidered. "Apology

accepted. I don't think it was required, but it says something that you do. Thank you for telling me."

They sat in comfortable silence until Love said, "Will Officer Sisler be all right?"

"Sisler? He's fine. Why do you ask?"

"He shot Darcy Rosewood. That will be a burden to him."

"He has a military background as a sniper. After a shooting he gets time off and counseling. I think he'll be fine."

This silence not as comfortable. "You know a little about that yourself, I believe," Love said. "How many was it for you?"

Doc held up a finger. "One." Love looked confused. "The media hasn't been too precise about that story. My father got one and my cousin got two of the four I keep getting credit for."

"They went after your family?"

"Yes, sir."

"Then God bless you, son. I had no idea. I should have asked after you, as well."

"You're the second person today to ask if I was all right. I must look like hell."

"You look tired," Love said. "More than physically."

Doc wanted to tell Love he was right. Tired had soaked into him like cold rain on a freezing day, to the bone. He'd been off work three days and done nothing but sleep and watch television. Went to his parents' for Sunday dinner and left half an hour after. Didn't read, surf the web, or call Kate. All would have been too much effort.

Christian Love would have listened. Might even have had suggestions. Doc didn't speak up because he knew if he started in front of a sympathetic audience he might not be able to stop. Why he'd left Sunday dinner early, and why he'd not called Kate and hadn't returned her call. If he started, he'd talk until he was empty. He was empty enough already.

CHAPTER 62

"You'll never guess who come by the showroom today." Stretch Dolewicz shrugged. Mike did this all the time. "You'll never guess." "Guess who." Could be anyone from Mario Lemieux to Cher. "Jackie Glimko. Said he wanted for a car for his wife. You know, something she can run to the store and back."

"Good for him," Stretch said. "He must be doing okay, looking to buy a car."

"Your name came up. Well, mostly the kid's. Ted. Stretcher." Stretch waited for Mike to tell him. "Glim says, 'You know me, Mike, I don't like to make no waves,' and I don't know to laugh in his face or throw his ass out. That troublemaking son of a bitch been a pain in my balls since before I was boss. Whole time he's talking to me, never said a fucking word about that shylock business started all the trouble he's in. Anyway, he wants to know was I pissed or anything, so I played along and asked him why. He told me this elaborate story about how your nephew's a psycho, tried to choke Jackie to death with some of them little doughnuts last time he come to collect. Said he mouthed off a little, too. Jackie wanted me to tell the kid to show some respect, just ask for the money next time."

"What'd you tell him?"

"I asked him what the kid said. You know, ignore the doughnut thing like it don't matter to me. Glim told me the kid says he doesn't even want to have to stop walking when he comes in. Just toss the envelope so he can be on his way. Like he wants me to do something about it."

Stretch said, "You want me to have a talk with him?"

"Yeah. Tell him nice work and he should come by and see me. No hurry. When he gets a chance. Jackie Glimko's an asshole, but he's a hard case. Kid got to him like that, it's worth a mention. Word gets out, things run smoother."

Mike slipped on his overcoat. "I gotta admit, I was a little worried about the kid for a while. He did a nice job with the cars, working with guys he knew and got along with. Stepping up means dealing with all kinds. He's a good kid—people like him—but the job needs more. Hell, you know that. I needed to see if he had a hard side. Anyone who can spook Glimko over a routine collection is hard enough for me."

Mike buttoned the coat. Stretch turned out the lights and followed him out of the Aspinwall Hunter's and Fisherman's Club. Warm for March first, still above forty degrees after dark. Stretch went north on Route 8 to his house in Etna for dinner with his wife. The Pittsburgh family not like the New York crews. More of a job than a lifestyle, not much clubbing and carousing. Mike needed Stretch after eight at night, he'd catch him at home, unless he was working.

Mike drove 28 into Pittsburgh. Crossed the Veterans Bridge, got off on Seventh Avenue, then up Liberty to Seventeenth Street; parked on Smallman. Not a lot going on in the Strip District at night. A scattering of bars and restaurants still open, the wholesale markets that gave the area its cachet closed for the day. Mike walked a block to Primanti Brothers. Stopped to read the menu on the chalkboard like he always did, knowing he'd order sweet sausage and cheese, topped with fries, slaw, tomatoes, and onions.

"You read the board every time you come in here and every time you get the same thing," Ray Keaton said.

"You never know," Mike said. "They might change it someday."

"You wouldn't come in if they did. You had to drive right past the one in Harmarville to get here. You won't stop there because it's too new. Different menu."

Keaton's problem, in Mike's eyes, was he knew everything. Someone with the smarts to know everything would know he didn't know everything. Both men ordered sandwiches and Cokes. Keaton had roast beef and cheese. No small talk while they waited.

Keaton spoke first, coleslaw hanging from his lower lip as he chewed. "You got anything tonight?"

"That's it?" Mike said. "Not even a thank you for putting you onto the two jigs that shot up those five guys in Penns River?"

"Let them thank you. What happens in Penns River means dick to me." Keaton took another bite. Swigged from his Coke with a mouth half full of food. "What do you have for me?"

Mike took time chewing his sandwich, part to make Keaton wait, part to show how to eat like a human being. "There's a guy jacking trucks up and down I-79. Pistol whipped a driver last week. Name's Tedesco or something. From New Castle."

Keaton stopped eating to glare. "Why are you wasting my time with this bullshit?"

"The guy's jacking trucks. Don't you feds do interstate commerce and that?"

"In theory. In practice, I don't give a shit if this Tedesco opens his own weigh station in Cranberry Township and empties every truck that goes by. Our arrangement is for you to give us information about what's going on in New York, not finger inconveniences so we can take care of them for you. Whatever your beef is with this guy, it's your problem. So long as you don't drop bodies, you get a lot of leeway." Keaton rubbed his right thumb over the first two fingers. "Leeway costs. Pay up."

Mike made him wait again. "What are you looking for?"

"Sal Lucatorre. To start."

"Forget about Sal. He's sick."

"He has gout. It's not like he's on a respirator."

"I hear he's in a lot of pain. Takes pills, still drinks a lot. He's half out of it most of the time. People don't trust him, so Tino's pretty much running things now. Nothing obvious. Sal still gives orders, when he feels like it. Tino kind of, uh, interprets them for the crews. Makes sure nothing stupid happens. Sal thinks he still runs things, everyone else knows Tino has it going on. Everybody's happy."

"What else?"

Mike made a face. This fucking fed actually thought the boys in New York told him things. "I hear Freddy Boca's got a girlfriend likes it up the ass."

"Do you want to go to jail, Mike?"

"If you had enough to put me away, you'd of done it already."

"We have bigger fish to fry. What you got in Pittsburgh's

barely a crew. If you can help us with New York, you're worth talking to. If not..."

"Then why are you bothering with me?"

"You came to us, remember?" Keaton said. "Your feelings got hurt because the big boys in New York let the Russian kick sand in your face. Then that Penns River cop and his pain in the ass cousin took care of your problem and you don't want to talk to your uncle anymore. Well, Uncle's got feelings, too. If he thinks you toyed with his affections, he might lower himself to put you away just for spite."

Mike chewed his sandwich. Looked over Keaton's shoulder onto Eighteenth Street. He'd strung Keaton along for over a year. Gave out of date information, or things he figured the feds knew already. Settled personal scores and removed a little competition. Thought he'd earned some good will with the Penns River tip; Keaton wanted to be a hard-on.

Wise guys talked about standing up, and honor. Might have been true, once. Way before Mike's time. He doubted it. Their life was about the money. Always had been. How to get it, and using whatever means necessary to keep it. Guys didn't keep their mouths shut out of honor. They did because they'd end up in a landfill or a car trunk or getting fished out of a river with grappling hooks if they didn't. Now even bosses rolled. New York did dick for him when he needed them. Mike Mannarino swallowed a mouthful of Coke and stepped across his own personal Rubicon.

"Lucatorre, he's the main heroin connect for Baltimore. They send it down hidden in one-way rental trucks. The shit's in the truck when the guy picks it up from the rental office. The truck gets turned in down Baltimore, someone picks up the dope. They got a couple guys with access to the rental company computer records, so they know when a truck's been requested and where it gets dropped off. The guy who rents it knows nothing about it."

"Which rental company?"

Telling him a lot easier than Mike had expected, now that he'd lost his cherry.

CHAPTER 63

Small-time criminals are small time for a reason. Some are too dumb to move up. Some lack ambition. Some are stupid. Others have insufficient organizational skills. Throw in the airheads, boneheads, chuckleheads, knuckleheads, lunkheads, pinheads, birdbrains, and lamebrains and what's left are the dangerous—to themselves—subcategory who can't keep their mouths shut.

Six on a Thursday morning, Doc and two uniforms pulled into the driveway of Harley Hagenmeyer's house in the Flats. Harley drank in Fat Jimmy's no more than five days a week. Bummed drinks and cigarettes from anyone he knew still willing to float him. Worked part-time at a local supermarket where no one worked the hours needed for benefits except the owner/manager. Showed up one day two weeks ago with four new wheels on his truck and paid for his own drinks and whoever of his usual touches were available. Came in the next week with his girlfriend, Donna, showing off her new diamond earrings. The diamonds weren't big enough to make anyone rub his eye if one lodged there. Still, they were real and Harley had a receipt.

Harley didn't often get drunk at Fat Jimmy's; there were few people willing to pay for it. This time he had money and felt expansive, showing off Donna's ears and talking about buying her some tits. Not too big. Something tasteful. Got to sharing his expertise in breast enhancement—he'd been shopping on Google—and showing people how the new and improved Donna would look. Donna's natural endowment less than Ivy League, but they were hers. Shaped well and still firm and bouncy enough to draw attention in the proper weather. After downing several drinks herself, she took offense at Harley's disrespect for her gifts and remarked about his lack of physical impressiveness in some areas. Must have been her time of the month, getting snotty over nothing like she had. Harley a mean drunk, and not afraid to be so in public. The comment about Donna's period not the least of his escalating offenses, which led to her having to be pulled off him. A couple of friends led Harley to the door, where he commanded Donna to join him, as she had no other way home unless she blew someone for a ride.

Donna could hold up her end of a conversation with the best of them. "I'd blow Jimmy right here at the bar before I let you put anything of yours into me, you pencil dicked son of a bitch! Steal some rusty grates out of the road and you walk around acting like Batman couldn't catch you!"

Fat Jimmy didn't know what he'd done to get dragged into this situation. He wouldn't mind a hummer from Donna, who, despite any deficiencies below the neck, had a pair of pouty lips he'd always thought would look nice around Little Jimmy. Not in front of the whole bar, though. No one's lips were that nice.

The episode still on Jimmy's mind the next day, when he called Ben Dougherty to tell about the wheels, the diamonds, and Donna's comments. (Leaving out her blow job subplot.) That got the clock ticking on a search warrant. When Lester Goodfoot called in some missing grates overnight, the troops were rallied to intercept Harley before he could sell them.

Harley lived in a double-wide set on a foundation that extended a few feet above the ground. Ulizio went around back. Doc went up three stairs to stand on the small stoop. Lester stood in the yard where he could see the door and truck both.

Doc knocked cop style, making a fist and pounding with the side of his hand. "Harley Hagenmeyer! Rise and shine. Penns River police. We need your signature on a search warrant."

There might have been movement inside. No voices.

Doc waited thirty seconds. "Harley! Asking for your signature's a courtesy. We can go through your truck without it. Do whatever we need to get in. You can open it for us or not, up to you."

A voice now, not directed at the police. Doc about to give Harley his last chance when the door swung open. Doc stepped back, hand on his gun.

Harley wore a *Hank Jr. for President* tee shirt over his jeans. Smelled of stale beer, cigarette smoke, and dried sweat. "What time is it?"

"Six-oh-four. AM," Doc said.

"What the hell you waking me up at six o'clock in the goddamn morning for?"

"Your autograph," Doc said. "I can live without it." Held the warrant where Harley could see it.

"What's it for?" Confusion surrounded Harley like dust on a dry road. "What're you looking for?"

"You could read it yourself, but if it's too much trouble..." Doc pointed to the paragraph in question. "We have permission to search your home and vehicle for Neshannock County property, specifically, but not limited to, sewer grates. We are also authorized to seize receipts for the new truck rims and a pair of diamond earrings. We can arrange to get those by other means. It's the sewer grates we're interested in today."

One look and Doc wished he were playing poker with Harley instead of arresting him. "What? Sewer grates? Who the hell would steal sewer grates?"

"I'm pretty sure you would," Doc said. "I can't think of another reason to get up in the middle of the goddamn night to come over to this shit hole. You going to sign the warrant, or not?"

"I ain't signing shit. You can't search my truck."

"You don't have to sign. Like I said, it's a courtesy. We are searching the truck, though." Harley make no move to take the warrant. Doc stepped down, heard a grunt and a foot land on the stoop. Stopped and turned around. "Wait right there. You try to impede me, I'll add resisting arrest to whatever charge we find lying in the bed of your truck. Touch me, and it's assaulting an officer, not to mention I'll whip your ass. Now, you want to come out and watch the search, feel free. But behave yourself."

Half a dozen grates under a tarp in the bed of an F-150 that had seen better years. Doc didn't imagine Harley'd earned enough money from sewer grates to pay for new wheels and even the shitty ear buds he'd bought Donna, let alone a boob job. No matter. Sally could use what they found here to see what other criminal enterprises he had going on.

Harley pointed at the grates. "Those aren't mine."

"I know," Doc said. "They belong to the county. Put your hands behind your back."

"No, I mean I got no idea how they got in my truck."

"You and your lawyer can discuss the possibilities after we drop you off at Leechburg Road." Doc cuffed Harley's left wrist and pulled the right back while Harley continued the discussion.

"Don't you got to read me my rights? Before you cuff me and take me in, I mean?"

Doc shook his head. "Not unless we want to ask questions. These grates in your truck answer all the questions I have. You know you have the right to remain silent, right?"

"Yeah, and a lawyer, too."

"Focus on the 'remain silent' part right now. It's for your own good." Doc liked to hold back the Miranda warning. Arrested a mope once for breaking into a dry cleaner's. The guy thought he'd be clever and told everything before anyone had a chance to read his rights. Kept interrupting so they couldn't get through the recitation, under the mistaken impression anything he *volunteered* before they read him his rights couldn't be used against him.

"Let's store him in your car while we search the house," Doc said to Lester Goodfoot. "Then you can take him in and go on home while Ulizio waits for the tow truck." Lester due to come off shift at eight. Ulizio had come in early, like Doc, and would work until four. Doc could sign out at one. No detective overtime had been authorized for the sewer grates. Ulizio only collected because they needed him on patrol.

Okay by Doc. He'd made plenty of OT on the Res Mall case and had inexpensive tastes. His mother cooked half his meals, considering what she sent home with him after Sunday dinner. Kate got less expensive all the time as she found other ways to occupy herself, Doc no longer showing the pictures of Marian Widmer and Carol Cropcho around. Thought about inventing something else they could look into, as there were elements of Kate he'd be happy to continue to investigate.

No. She'd spend time with him if she wanted. If she didn't want to, Doc didn't need her around. He'd knock off at one, be home by ten after, asleep on the couch by one-thirty. Take Jefferson West, Wilver and David Faison out to eat at Smokey Bones in Pittsburgh Mills at four-thirty, if West didn't beg off and Wilver showed up; David sure to go. Back in time for rehearsal at seven-thirty, where Eve would bust his balls about…whatever; she never failed to find something. Watch the Pens game on the DVR, fast-forwarding through the commercials and intermissions until he fell asleep in the third period, roll back when an increase in the announcers' voices woke him.

Tomorrow was fish sandwich night at the Edgecliff.

ACKNOWLEDGEMENTS

There are no acknowledgements for this book that take precedence over those due The Beloved Spouse™, who is both the first and last listener. In between she fields all manner of hare-brained and half-assed ideas and never fails to help me weed out which are worth keeping, which need more thought, and which should be wrapped in brown paper, sealed in shrink wrap, duct taped, and buried in the back yard where the dirt is nice and soft.

Other notables whose contributions should not go unmentioned:

Terrence McCauley, who convinced me I'd reached a point where I could approach Down & Out Books directly and not go through the slush pile.

Michelle Turlock Isler, who, when I mentioned at the bar in Raleigh that I was looking for Eric Campbell, latched onto my forearm and marched me directly over to Eric. Michelle said, "Eric, you need to talk to him," and left us.

Eric Campbell, for seeing merit in a series that was going nowhere at the time, and for his constant support and enthusiasm.

Lance Wright, for all the behind the scenes work he puts in that makes working with Down & Out such a treat.

Wiley Saichek, for handling the aspects of marketing I loathe and allowing me to cherry-pick the parts I like.

Charlie Stella, for his conviction that I needed to stop farting around and get published.

Declan Burke, for talking me out of quitting when I'd really and truly had about enough of the publishing business.

Dana King has two Shamus Awards nominations from the Private Eye Writers of America for his Nick Forte novels *A Small Sacrifice* and *The Man in the Window*. A classically-trained musician who freelanced for ten years, he played in an army band, worked in supermarkets, tended bar, walked the floor as a retail store security guard, drove a forklift in a salvage warehouse, collected quarters from coin laundry machines, taught public school, ran a copier for a real estate business, managed a computer network training school, administered computer networks, demonstrated and installed enterprise software systems, and trained adults on computer applications around periods of "between engagements." His short story, "Green Gables," appears in the Thuglit anthology *Blood, Guts, and Whisky*.

You can follow Dana's thoughts on writing, books, and movies through his blog *One Bite at a Time*, at danaking.blogspot.com. He lives in near seclusion at an undisclosed location in Maryland with The Beloved Spouse™.

OTHER TITLES FROM DOWN AND OUT BOOKS

See www.DownAndOutBooks.com for complete list

By Jerry Kennealy
Screen Test
Polo's Long Shot (*)

By Dana King
Worst Enemies
Grind Joint
Resurrection Mall

By Ross Klavan, Tim O'Mara
and Charles Salzberg
Triple Shot

By S.W. Lauden
Crosswise
Crossed Bones

By Paul D. Marks and
Andrew McAleer (editor)
Coast to Coast vol. 1
Coast to Coast vol. 2

By Gerald O'Connor
The Origins of Benjamin Hackett

By Gary Phillips
The Perpetrators
Scoundrels (Editor)
Treacherous
3 the Hard Way

By Thomas Pluck
Bad Boy Boogie (*)

By Tom Pitts
Hustle
American Static (*)

By Robert J. Randisi
Upon My Soul
Souls of the Dead
Envy the Dead

By Charles Salzberg
Devil in the Hole
Swann's Last Song
Swann Dives In
Swann's Way Out

By Scott Loring Sanders
Shooting Creek and Other Stories

By Ryan Sayles
The Subtle Art of Brutality
Warpath
Let Me Put My Stories In You (*)

By John Shepphird
The Shill
Kill the Shill
Beware the Shill

By James R. Tuck (editor)
Mama Tried vol. 1
Mama Tried vol. 2 (*)

By Lono Waiwaiole
Wiley's Lament
Wiley's Shuffle
Wiley's Refrain
Dark Paradise
Leon's Legacy

By Nathan Walpow
The Logan Triad

(*)—Coming Soon

Made in the USA
Monee, IL
30 July 2023

40174573R00236